Tara Pammi can't rem[illegible]
wasn't lost in a book—[illegible]
was much more exciting [illegible] textbook
at school. Years later, Tara's wild imagination and love
for the written word revealed what she really wanted
to do. Now she pairs alpha males who think they know
everything with strong women who knock that theory
and them off their feet!

Lorraine Hall is a part-time hermit and full-time
writer. She was born with an old soul and her head
in the clouds—which, it turns out, is the perfect
combination for spending her days creating thunderous
alpha heroes and the fierce, determined heroines who
win their hearts. She lives in a potentially haunted
house with her soulmate and a rumbustious band of
hermits in training. When she's not writing romance,
she's reading it.

Also by Tara Pammi

Returning for His Unknown Son

Born into Bollywood miniseries

Claiming His Bollywood Cinderella
The Surprise Bollywood Baby
The Secret She Kept in Bollywood

Signed, Sealed…Seduced collection

The Playboy's 'I Do' Deal

This is **Lorraine Hall**'s debut book
for Mills & Boon Modern.

We hope that you enjoy it!

Discover more at millsandboon.co.uk.

MARRIAGE BARGAIN WITH HER BRAZILIAN BOSS

TARA PAMMI

THE PRINCE'S ROYAL WEDDING DEMAND

LORRAINE HALL

MILLS & BOON

First published in Great Britain 2023
by Mills & Boon, an imprint of HarperCollins*Publishers* Ltd,
1 London Bridge Street, London, SE1 9GF

www.harpercollins.co.uk

HarperCollins*Publishers*
Macken House, 39/40 Mayor Street Upper,
Dublin 1, D01 C9W8, Ireland

ISBN: 978-0-263-30663-7

01/23

This book is produced from independently certified FSC™ paper to ensure responsible forest management.
For more information visit: www.harpercollins.co.uk/green.

Printed and Bound in Spain using 100% Renewable Electricity at CPI Black Print, Barcelona

MARRIAGE BARGAIN WITH HER BRAZILIAN BOSS

TARA PAMMI

MILLS & BOON

PROLOGUE

ANUSHKA REDDY LOOKED around the luxurious cabin of the private jet, but it was hard, as a fourteen-year-old, to maintain interest in the aircraft or anything else for that matter when excitement filled her belly with a thousand swarming butterflies.

To stay with her grandparents and her half-sisters, for the entire summer.

Instant guilt speared through her at the thought. It wasn't that she didn't love her mom and all the adventures she had with her. As a world-renowned environmental activist and an artist, her mom traveled all over the world—sometimes to showcase her work, most times in search of inspiration—which meant Nush had, in her fourteen years, lived in the most interesting places in the world.

But her mom was also absentminded and mercurial and prone to long periods of melancholy and depression. And when that low hit, she forgot about small things. Like stocking groceries and buying clothes and books for Nush, like making sure she spent time outside and with kids her own age.

Even with an unconventional mother who'd told her at the age of eight that she'd been borne out of an affair, Nush had always longed for a permanent home base, a close-knit family. Especially the one her half-sisters had with her paternal grandparents in California, the one she'd got her first glimpse of at the same age. Their father—a has-been artist and a raging alcoholic—apparently liked variety in his lovers, and so she, Yana and her oldest sister, Mira, all had different mothers.

As allergic as Mama was to the institution of marriage, she'd never denied Anushka the knowledge of her father's family. The six summers Nush had spent with her grandparents and her two half-sisters at their sprawling estate in California had soon become the highlight of those year.

And now she would be back with them for another summer. At least that's what Mama had told Nush in between tears, all the while issuing conditions and threats and warnings about her well-being to the man who represented Nush's grandparents. All of which had been received with a patience and equanimity and even a kindness that she hadn't associated with… *Caio Oliveira*. And yet he'd been infinitely gentle with Mama's irrational outbursts.

Nush pushed her thick glasses up the bridge of her nose and studied him with as much covertness as she was capable of.

Caio was a constant in her grandparents' life. A larger-than-life former soccer player slash current coding genius from Brazil that her grandfather considered his right-hand man. She'd only ever glanced at him while hiding behind Mira because one only ever looked at the sun from a distance.

But now, at such close quarters, Nush revised her opinion of him. He wasn't the sun. He was tall, broad, a dark golden-skinned god from one of the mythical universes that populated her favorite role-playing video game. Light brown eyes with golden flecks shone with a wicked intelligence, hooded under thick dark brows that seemed to see too much with jet-black wavy hair that was cut close to his head and a jawline that was usually found on male models in fashion magazines. The man was too...*virile*, she thought, testing the word she'd heard Yana use once.

If they were animals, Caio would be the alpha at the top.

There was no other way to describe him, especially when she was a bespectacled, acne-ridden, gangly teenager who didn't know what to do with her legs or arms or her suddenly overactive hormones.

It was new to her—this sudden influx of *feelings* she had no control over. Usually, her logical brain was her best friend. The thing she could rely on to keep her strong when Mama wasn't, which had been a lot in the last two years.

But she couldn't just keep staring at him for the rest of the flight. The last thing she wanted him to think was that she was still a little weird and nerdy.

"Why didn't Thaata come to pick me up?" she said, once the flight attendant, who'd been making eyes at him, had left them alone. She wasn't as fluent in the language her father's family spoke as Mira was but she was determined to make a real effort to learn this summer.

A smile lifted one corner of his mouth, drawing a dimple on one side. "So you do talk."

An overwhelming rush of shyness hit Nush like a tidal wave. She could feel her cheeks reddening. Probably the tip of her nose too. "Of course I talk, Mr. Oliveira. But only when there's something important to be said." She cringed and sighed. Why couldn't she sound normal for once?

"Now, that's an admirable quality I find rarely, especially among adults. And no Mr. Oliveira business, Anushka. It makes me feel old."

"You *are* old," Nush blurted out, fighting the floaty sensation in her belly at how good her name sounded on his lips.

Laughter burst from him, loud and deep, drawing crinkles around his mouth and eyes. Her lungs felt like they did when she'd gone deep-sea diving—gasping for breath, unable to comprehend the magnificent beauty that surrounded her.

His smile took him from handsome to gorgeous, with a stopover at stunning.

"I mean…you're quite a lot older than me," she said, wanting to hide under the table between them.

"Twenty-seven is not that old, minx. But I'm jaded and cynical, so…" A shadow crossed his eyes, gone in an instant. "Also, the title of Mr. Oliveira belonged to my father. I'd feel like a cheap fake if I used that."

A glimmer of raw ache made those eyes flash golden at the mention of his father. "If you want me to say your name right, you better teach me it," she said, immediately wanting to distract him. "I know it doesn't rhyme with *mayo*."

"Cristo, no," he said with a mock shudder. Planting his forearms on the table, he leaned forward. "It's Caio," he said slowly.

Nush repeated his name, a few times too many even after she got it, loving the sound of it on her lips.

"Perfect, Princesa."

Mouth falling open, she bristled. "Why do you call me Princess?"

"Isn't that what your grandpa calls you? Why is that?"

"Promise you won't laugh at me."

"I wouldn't dare."

"I was always too fond of fairy tales."

"Why would I laugh at that?"

"Mama used to tell me that life's too important to bury my head in outdated tales."

He opened his mouth and then closed it. And Nush knew he'd swallowed away his own cynical opinion so that he didn't corrupt hers. That little, innate kindness instantly made her like him a little more. Now she could say she liked Caio for more than his looks.

"What do you like about them?" he asked with a genuine tone.

"That there's always a happy ending, whatever the affliction the princesses have. That there's always someone right for them. It doesn't matter if they're too quiet, or shy or even strange. I do agree that some of them feel outdated but then I just rewrite them in my head the way I want them."

"As long as you don't forget that real life doesn't work like that, Princesa. Sometimes, there's no happy ending. There's only crushing disappointment, dealt both by circumstance and people. Love is sometimes not enough."

"That's your opinion," she said, tilting her chin up.

He shrugged and the gesture pulled her attention to the breadth of his shoulders. "I never answered your question, did I? Your grandfather wanted to come, as did Mira and Yana," he said, mentioning her sisters. "But your grandmother had an asthma episode recently, and as I was making this trip anyway," he said softly, "I offered to pick you up."

"Is Nanamma okay now?"

"She is."

"Are you and Yana still dating?" Nush wanted to disappear the moment she heard her question.

Caio was her first official crush and she was already finding this whole thing painful. Not for a second could she betray her thoughts. Not especially now, when she was moving to California and would see him on a regular basis.

Not that she'd been able to stop thinking of him and Yana since she'd realized their visitor was Caio. She adored both her sisters. To see him with Yana—who was so stunningly gorgeous that, at nineteen, she was already highly sought after as a model—would've felt awkward and weird. There was that word again.

She stole a look from under her lashes, and was relieved that he didn't look irritated. "Sorry, it's none of my business," she whispered.

"It's okay, Princesa. Honest curiosity never bothers me." He drummed his fingers on the table between them. "Yana and I are not dating anymore. We realized it would hurt your grandparents and Mira and now you immensely, if we killed each other as a result of all that proximity. Which turned to be a distinct possibility."

Nush burst out laughing. It had been clear, even to her, that they really weren't suited to each other. She instantly sobered up as another worrying thought struck. "You and Yana are still friends now that you've broken up, right?"

"And why does the thought that we might not be put such a frown here, Anushka?" he said, pointing a finger at her forehead.

She pushed the glasses up the bridge of her slightly too large nose. "I don't want to have to take sides, that's all."

His thick brows drawing together, he looked thunderstruck. "Take sides? How do you come to that, Princesa?"

"I know how much Thaata values you. As high-maintenance as Yana can be—that's what Nanamma says about her—I wouldn't want to be caught between you two when I finally have a full family."

The shock in his eyes deepened until slowly, another

smile warmed them and they glowed brightly. "I see why your grandfather thinks you're precious."

Heat swarmed Nush's cheeks. Damn it, why had she opened her mouth at all? "It's not like I like you like you…that would just be ewww…because you're like really old," she added, with extra affectation she'd seen in teen movies.

His raucous laughter enveloped her. The man was really beautiful and his presence did things to her insides—specifically her lower belly and lower, where she'd never felt such things before. Intellectually, she knew what it was but still, it threw her, this feverish fascination. And it scared her a bit too.

"I appreciate your consideration, Princesa. And your generosity in considering me family." His gaze gentled. "Are you looking forward to the summer?"

She smiled. "I've always wanted to be part of a big family. Living with Mama is an adventure but it can also get very lonely." She swallowed at the sudden ache that lodged in her throat. "She was very upset today. Sometimes, she can't help herself. Please don't be angry at her for that."

He tapped at her tightly laced fingers and shook his head. "Not at all, Anushka. She was upset, yes, but I have enough sense to know that it was her grief at having to send you away." His tone was so gentle that it made the ache turn into a hard lump. "Your mother's a very strong woman to make such hard choices for your well-being. All I took from her reaction today is that she loves you very much. Not every mother could do what she did."

Tears threatened at his kind words and Nush blinked them back. "Do you think it's wrong that I'm so excited about being with Mira and Yana?"

"Not at all." His brow furrowed and his voice deepened. “Never think that. You can be sad and excited at the same time. One doesn’t invalidate the other. And families are complicated, *sim*?”

Something in his gaze made her ask, “What about you, Caio? Do you have a big family?”

“Not really. Not anymore at least”

There was a note in his voice that clearly said it wasn’t a topic he wanted to talk about. So even as curiosity pricked, she followed his lead and let it be. She didn’t want to hurt him by probing into painful matters. Running her hands over the buttery soft leather of her seat, she asked, “So this jet…it’s yours, right?”

His eyes twinkled as if he found her endlessly fascinating. “How do you know it’s not your grandfather’s?”

“My grandparents are immigrants who came to the US with nothing. They’d never waste money on such extravagant luxuries.”

“I thought I’d successfully avoided the environmentalist’s notice. But I see I didn’t escape her smart daughter.”

“Mama would have roasted you alive with at least an hour’s lecture,” Nush said with a laugh. “Is this your present to yourself for soaring stock? You’re a millionaire now, aren’t you?”

“You’re business savvy too? No wonder your grandfather is so excited to have you come live with them.”

Nush blushed. “I follow the company news. I invested the allowance Thaata gave me in your stock.”

Surprise made him chuckle. “You’re an unending delight, Anushka.”

“My friends call me Nush,” she said, even though she didn’t actually have any real-life friends. Only online ones, kids who didn’t judge her because online she could pretend that she was perfect. “Plus I’m interested in the finance software you develop. I’ve been following its development since Thaata and you were discussing it that first time I met you. I'm a coder too."

"Yeah?"

Something about the challenge in his gaze spurred Nush to reach for her backpack. It had been a gift from Mira and Yana on her last visit and it was her favorite possession. Soon, she had the program she'd written open on her laptop. Turning the screen toward him, she rested her chin on her clasped hands and waited for his assessment.

His golden eyes moved over the screen rapidly, and she took the chance to study him to her heart's content, storing away the smallest details.

After several minutes, Caio plopped the laptop closed and whistled.

"You wrote the program?"

She nodded, catching the light of curiosity in his eyes. It was a look she'd seen in her own eyes when she made forward progress.

"How long did it take?"

"A week."

Caio stared at her, his gaze calculating and shrewd. A thrill shot through her when he stuck out a hand between them. Nush let his big hand envelop hers and that swarm of butterflies took flight in her belly again. "What's… this for?"

"A partnership, Princesa. You and I are going to rule the world together."

Nush gave him her hand and promised herself she'd find a boy exactly like Caio when she grew up to fall in love with.

Maybe not as good-looking and magnetic and charming and so…out of her sphere.

But someone like him, nevertheless.

CHAPTER ONE

Nine years later

Step out of your fairy tales, Princess.
Life is to be lived, not read about.

NUSH OPENED AND folded the crisp note that had been delivered to her this morning, two days after Thaata had drawn his last breath. She'd read his handwritten message a thousand times already.

It felt like a sign. More than a sign—a wakeup call.

Had Thaata known how frustrated and unhappy she'd been of late? How stuck she felt? How she was so full of longing and resentment against one man who took up all her waking thoughts?

Her grandfather had taken a turn for the worse in the month since they'd lost their grandmother. It was a shock Nush wasn't sure she or her sisters would recover from soon. A fresh wave of grief made the back of her eyes prickle. Thaata seemed to have known all three of them needed a little more from him. More than the love and acceptance and affection he'd always given them.

Standing against the far wall, she studied the crowd that had gathered in the high-ceilinged living room of their grandparents' colonial-style house to pay their final respects to a man who'd touched so many lives through the tech giant OneTech he'd started two decades ago and that had flourished into a multibillion-dollar company with Caio at the helm in the last decade.

Among the guests were Yana's mother and her stepfather and her stepbrothers. And her older sister Mira's husband, Aristos, even though he and Mira had been separated for the last nine months. Only Mama was absent.

Nush had tried to tell her mother on her last visit to the nursing home that Thaata had taken a turn for the worse, but in the tail end of one of her bad episodes, Mama had only stared back with a glassy look.

Mira had flown in from Greece at a second's notice to look after her grandmother after her heart attack eight months ago and never returned. Not a year ago, her steady, sensible sister had shocked them all by marrying Greek business tycoon Aristos in Las Vegas. They'd never seen Mira so happy. And yet when Yana and Nush had probed Mira about not returning to Aristos, their older sister had burst into tears.

Unsurprisingly now, it was Mira and Caio who effortlessly slipped into the role of playing hosts.

Caio was the true heir to her grandfather's legacy and his vision. Her grandparents had brought up Mira since she'd been a toddler. Ever since her mother had walked out and their father had continued on with his womanizing.

Nush frowned at how good they looked together. Her brother-in-law Aristos's gaze mirrored the same irritation. Which was ridiculous because neither of her sisters were aware that her harmless crush had matured into something else even as Caio dated and discarded more women than Yana did designer handbags.

As if she'd called out his name, Caio flicked a gaze across the room.

Dressed in relentless black, he was like a dark sun among a sea of overly bright stars, all orbiting him constantly for attention. Still searching, he bent from his considerable height to kiss her sister's cheek and walked into the room.

He was looking for her. Nush knew it as surely as her heart fluttered like the mad hare racing off to the finish line. They hadn't talked since their nightlong vigil at Thaata's bedside two nights ago.

Her eyes tracked him across the large living room, caressing his features as eagerly as the sunlight slanting through the high windows did. The high forehead, the deep-set light brown eyes with their golden flecks, the arrogant nose and the thin slash of his mouth were as familiar to her as her own face.

If he'd been stunning when he'd been twenty-seven, almost a decade later now, there was a compelling quality to him that sang to her. A confidence that made clowns of twentysomething men that employed mind games and power plays in the name of dating.

Was it the mantle of responsibility that he wore so well? The well-honed instinct for success? Or the deep-seated streaks of honor and integrity that he suppressed in the boardroom as if they were a weakness but still colored his actions anyway?

It didn't matter that she'd spent the decade working for and with Caio. That they'd been business partners since her eighteenth birthday. With her grandfather's encouragement, she'd entered a partnership with Caio to build a sub-company based on the software model she'd developed. His knowledge of the market, his risk-taking meant she'd made millions before she'd turned twenty-one.

It didn't matter that her acne had cleared up, that she had filled out enough to have a semblance of curves to go with her arms and legs, or that, in the last year, she'd dated men ranging from models to CEOs to even a congressman in a desperate bid to rid herself of this strange fascination.

It didn't matter how she much she'd changed or who she became. When it came to Caio, she was still that awed fourteen-year-old who couldn't help but stare. He was still the tall, dark Brazilian god that made her skin flush, her heart flutter, her breath do wonky things with one simple look. Somehow the blasted man had imprinted on her sexuality and she needed to do something about it if she didn't want to be sixty and still salivating over him from a distance. The only saving grace was that she'd never betrayed herself or the extent of her…desire for him.

Friends and business partners and shareholders stopped Caio to offer respects, to keep themselves in his good graces. A couple of well-dressed women laid manicured fingers on his forearm. Wordlessly offering to soothe his grief, she thought bitchily.

A wave of relief flooded through her when Caio didn't even flick a look in their direction. Followed by the prickly heat of shame. At least those women had the guts to show him their interest, to make a play for him.

Not like her. Spinning fantasies around him while standing still for years.

Caio's roving gaze stopped when it found her standing under the shadow of a raised beam. The gaunt tightness of his features loosened. Even across the distance, she could see the gentling of the ruthless curve of his mouth. The warmth that deepened the golden flecks of his eyes.

The *I'm here* look that she knew, without doubt, she was the sole recipient of in the entire world. The look that had always made her feel as if there was a special bond between them. Only she got to see this softer, less ruthless version of Caio. The real man that he was under the brilliant, ruthless entrepreneur he showed the world.

But for the first time in nine years, Nush hated it. Hated how she'd boxed herself into this place with him. Hated how it had become a prison that she couldn't break out of.

"If you're going to make a move, do it soon."

Nush jerked her gaze away from Caio to find her sister Yana watching her. While Nush looked like a crow in an unrelenting, sleeveless black T-shirt and black leggings, Yana looked just as inappropriate in neon-pink pants with matching spaghetti top and an oversized jacket with bright white sequins all over it.

Neither of them had wanted to be here. Had protested about putting on a show of their grief for a loss they wouldn't be over for a long time. But Mira, ever the responsible one, had reminded them that their grandparents would want them there. Would want them to give people who'd loved them just as much a chance to show their respect.

Heat prickled her cheeks as Nush pushed her glasses up her nose. "What…do you mean?"

"It's a wonder he hasn't caught on with how you look at him, Nushie… I mean Caio's not stupid when it comes to women." Yana frowned, her voice pitched thankfully low. "But I guess you both do spend hours attached at the hip and he knows what an introvert you are and that you don't have any real-life friends so maybe he thinks it's normal for you to be fascinated by him."

Nush glared at her sister. "Not everyone is as confident when it comes to sex and romance and affairs as you are."

"I'd never make fun of you." Yana laced her fingers around Nush's stiff ones and squeezed. "I mean, everyone thinks I'm just beauty and no brains and I drove Thaata and Nanamma wild with my antics, and it's kinda true but I'm not completely without substance, Nush."

"Mira and I've never thought that of you," Nush said, feeling angry on her sister's behalf. Angry at a world that always found fault with women.

Yana was beautiful. Like world-class beautiful, with cheekbones one could sharpen their knives on, a wide, plump mouth that regularly spawned poems and dirty lyrics in homage from fans, a naturally voluptuous figure that had designers and photographers clamoring to showcase their designs. And yet Yana was routinely called a shallow diva by the press, her worth frequently reduced to her looks by her mother. Not that Yana didn't give them all enough fodder by forever getting into one mess or the other.

Beneath it all, Yana hid a heart of gold. It just needed a lot of excavation first. Both her sisters had welcomed her into their lives with open arms, and unconditional love. Nush couldn't imagine getting through the last few years of dealing with her mother's worsening mental health issues without her sisters and Caio.

And just like that, every road in her life wound back to him.

Folding and refolding a note in her hands, Yana gave a tremulous smile. "Thanks, Nushie."

What message had Thaata left for Yana? And Mira, for that matter? Were they feeling as raw and stuck in their lives as she did in her own?

"I wasn't teasing about making your move fast," Yana said softly.

Nush tried for denial but gave up as something in Yana's tone tugged at her. "Why do you say that?"

"You know how Thaata thought you and Peter Huntington Jr. would be a good match and it went to hell because he called you a giraffe with an oversized brain?"

Nush sighed. "I don't need a reminder."

Yana giggled. "It's funny because I think he's an overgrown dinosaur with a pea-sized brain. It's common knowledge Thaata and Peter Sr. have been increasingly at odds since Thaata brought in Caio."

"That was fourteen years ago and without Caio, the company would've never grown as it has."

"I agree. And then Caio roped you in and OneTech grew beyond everyone's expectations. That's one reason Peter Sr. was pushing his son at you. You're the golden goose for OneTech and he wanted to break up you and Caio."

"I'd never work for someone who thinks Caio's the enemy."

"But Peter Sr. doesn't know that and he's a master strategist. Since you and his son went nowhere, talk now is that Laura Huntington and Caio could be the new partnership that could balance out the power struggle."

Nush's heart gave a painful thud. Laura Huntington was everything Nush wasn't. Sophisticated, beautiful, curvy, witty and not at all socially awkward—a perfect counterpart to smooth out Caio's brittle edges. She cleared her throat, trying to budge her heart, which seemed to have lodged itself in her throat. "I thought the Huntingtons hated Caio."

"Not if they get him for a son-in-law. I hate to give her credit but Laura's the total package."

Despite the ever-tightening knot in her belly, Nush laughed. "Why do you hate to give her credit?"

"Huh? How are you so smart in some things and so naive in others, Nushie-kins?" Yana laced her arm through Nush's. "Because she's direct competition for my little sister. On that principle alone, I have to hate her. Also the fact that Laura's an intellectual snob who's always looked down on me might have something to do with it."

On a sudden impulse, Nush wrapped her arms around Yana's waist and planted a hard kiss on her cheek. Her sister stayed stiff at first but slowly relented. Nush bit back tears that felt like they were never far these days.

"We have each other. Always," Yana said, tone full of emotion that she rarely let even her sisters see.

Her grandparents were gone, Mama didn't want to talk to her most weeks, and now Caio might be making new alliances that would only make her an outsider in his life…it felt like her world would never stop rocking. But she'd always have Mira and Yana, Nush reminded herself, breathing the floral scent of Yana's perfume deep into her lungs. For all that her father had never actually parented her for a single day in her life, he'd given her two wonderful sisters. Nush could forgive him a lot for that.

Yana dabbed at her cheek with a grimace. "I don't see a good reason for Caio to say no to this partnership, Nushie. Laura's brains and beauty and a steadying influence over her father. And we all know Caio will do anything to keep control of OneTech."

Nush couldn't contest the point.

Caio's loyalty to her grandparents was only rivaled by his ambition. More acquisitions, more mergers, more innovation…he'd been on a warpath the last year. While she mostly tuned out those meetings, Nush remembered even her grandfather asking Caio what would be enough and Caio laughing that not until he had something in his hand.

Over the years, Nush had tried to understand where his ambition stemmed from, why no amount of success or wealth was enough for him, but she'd got nowhere.

Which had made her realize now how ruthless his personal boundaries were. Yes, she had a familiarity with Caio, more than others had, but she couldn't delude herself that she knew all of him either.

And maybe that's where your fascination comes from, a voice whispered inside her head. For all that he knew every inch of her life, Caio was still a mystery to her. And as a woman who built complex systems that ran some of the biggest infrastructures in the world, it was no wonder she was obsessed with peeling back the layers of what made him want a woman.

As if to prove Yana's point, Laura Huntington ended up being the woman who did halt Caio's purposeful stride toward Nush. Her fingers clutching his, Laura said something to him. Bending down to accommodate Laura's petite frame, long fingers on her shoulder, Caio listened, rapt. The ease with which their bodies leaned toward each other—there was a certain familiarity between them.

Nush's belly crashed down like an elevator car whose strings had been cut. She couldn't help rolling the hem of her threadbare T-shirt up and down, couldn't help contrasting her "weird" outfit, her thick glasses, her uncontrollable hair, and—the worst—her tendency to hide in corners during meetings and parties and gatherings… against the polished and entirely social Laura.

"Are they…together?" she asked, hating the crack in her voice.

"Not yet, as far as I know," Yana said with the authority of a woman who always had her finger on the pulse of all the gossip. "But even you must agree that they could be the force that would appeal to the different factions at OneTech. So if you want him, now's the time to—"

"I can't just…come on to him, Yana," Nush said, even her words faltering. The few times she'd tried to have sex—to get Caio out of her mind—had been utter disasters. She was beginning to wonder if she had some kind of mental block. If she tried it with Caio, she'd probably melt into a puddle of insecurities before she even touched him and further humiliate herself.

"Why not?" Her sister sounded genuinely confused.

"What if it destroys our relationship as it is?" she said, giving voice to her biggest fear. "I can't lose him."

Sympathy flared in Yana's eyes. "Then move on, Nush. Start living your own life instead of being a spectator in the margins of his."

"Why do you think I've been dating every Tom, Dick and Harry this past year? Why do you think I lasted weeks with Peter Jr. even though he makes me want to pluck my own eyeballs out?" That she'd hoped it would incense Caio, who hated Peter Sr. and Jr. with the same loathing as they did him, Nush kept to herself. It felt more than a little twisted to let him direct who she dated but she'd done it anyway.

"Then be prepared to see them ride off into the sunset together, Nush. Who knows? You might get to be the flower girl at their wedding."

"I'm not a kid, Yana," Nush retorted, but she knew that Yana was right.

If nothing changed, she'd have to see him marry Laura or someone else equally perfect, drunk dance at his wedding because that was the only time she danced, buy his wife and him pretty crockery for a wedding gift, probably babysit his perfect kids and be their weird aunt who taught them coding in the summer and…

Nush shuddered. "Tell me what to do. Please."

"Seduce him."

The thought of his rejection—or worse, the thought of him laughing at her attraction to him—made hot acid gurgle up her throat. Her shoulders slumped as she realized her stupid fantasies would have to remain just that. She might be a genius when it came to computers and numbers but with Caio… "I can't, Yana. I don't think I can even put it in words."

Yana sighed and pulled her closer. "Nushie-kins, you're beautiful and smart and kind and funny… Any man would be fortunate to have you in his life."

"You're my sister. You have to say that." Tears prickled and Nush blinked to keep them at bay. Maybe this was not only the year of loss but also of letting go. Of moving on. "What do I do, Yana?"

"If you can't face trying to seduce him, then break this hold he has on you. Decouple yourself from him and OneTech. Start a new branch in New York, or better yet, Switzerland. Go on a tour of the world. Have a scandalous fling or five. Step out of your lab and live your life, Nush."

By the time Caio reached her, Nush was trembling with the need for action. Marveling at how death and grief could fill one with a raw, painful urgency to live life. To move on.

Yana was right. She couldn't spend another minute much less a decade mooning over him. Couldn't stand still and be a spectator as he lived his life. Even now, she couldn't turn away as he finished his conversation with Laura and made his way to her.

As his tall form drew near, Nush noted the dark shadows under his eyes. He'd forgone a shave this morning. There was a tension to his shoulders that she recognized. Her heart ached as she remembered he'd been a part of her grandparents' life longer than she'd been.

She wanted to hold him through this aching emptiness

Thaata had left in both their lives. She wanted to lean into him and help him through the grief she saw in his eyes.

But he wouldn't lean on her. Because he was the one who was supposed to be the protector. The one who looked after every legal headache that she and her sisters would have to handle. The one who'd arranged every single detail with the funeral. The one who'd made sure their alcoholic father had showed up to the funeral in respectable clothes and mostly sober.

Because Caio Oliveira didn't need anyone in any way. Least of all her. Even as he'd entrenched himself into the very fabric of her life. And it was time to rip him out of it.

He handed her a glass of water wordlessly and leaned against the wall beside her, their shoulders just touching. Resentment built in her chest even as she took the glass from him. How did he know there was a boulder-sized lump in her throat?

She didn't have to look at him to know he'd have pulled one foot up against the wall, that the other hand would be tucked into his pocket. That his gaze would sweep over the room, assessing the situation, wondering if there was a fire he'd have to put out.

His intense physicality, his indefatigable energy had always awed her. But now it felt exhausting to be so in tune with his every word, gesture and nuance, his very breath. More than disenchanting to admit that he'd never know her or want her on that level.

Holding that feeling close, Nush drank the water. As hard as it was to bear, it was the thing that would help her move on.

His shoulder nudged hers, his profile sharp and stark. "You're upset, Princesa."

Are you and Laura Huntington dating?

Have you had sex with her?

What do I do to make you see me like that?

Do you feel this too or is it just me?

Nush looked at the empty glass in her hand, following the trails of condensation, willing her body to ignore the warmth emanating from his. To not draw the scent of him into her lungs. To not chase this shaky desire she felt at his nearness like an addict. "Is there a reason you're stating the obvious?"

If he noted her bitchy tone, he ignored it. "What did Yana say to upset you?"

"Just bringing me up to speed on some politics at OneTech."

He tapped at her knuckles. "Don't worry about it, Nush. I'll handle it."

"Is Ms. Huntington joining the executive team?" The question escaped her before she'd decided to ask it.

He sent her a long, leisurely sideways look and Nush tried to not fidget. His surprise wasn't unwarranted. Usually, she stayed miles away from the politics of OneTech, happy to be in her lab. Thaata had tried numerous times to get her involved in the running of the company but she'd hidden. Usually behind Caio's broad shoulders. Had used him as a shield again and again.

"Probably. Laura, unlike her useless brother, would be a great addition to the team. For a Huntington, I like her immensely," he said with a grin.

He liked Laura. Immensely.

She couldn't remember a time when he'd actually said he liked a woman or a man. Outside of her sisters and her and their grandparents, he had no close friends. Not in any context. The long hours he worked made him just as much a loner as she was. And his family, she'd learned long ago, was a forbidden topic for all of them.

Her chest ached as if someone was pushing a tremendous weight down on her. Even with her eyes closed, she sensed him turn fully toward her. Felt his gaze sweep over her features. His fingers were firm as he lifted her fisted hand from her side. "What did your grandfather's note say?"

She jerked her hand away, giving him her shoulder. "It's private."

"Even to share with me?"

"Despite what you think, I have a life that doesn't revolve around you, Caio. Beyond being your good little worker droid, making you millions, I mean."

She sensed his shock in his sudden stillness. "Worker droid?" Cool, smooth tone still. "Jesus, you're more than upset if you think that's what I think of you. What's going on with you, Nush?"

"Leave me alone. Don't manage me. Don't—"

"Leaving you alone during this time is the last thing your grandfather would expect of me. Whatever's…bothering you, we can find a solution."

Was that all he saw her as? As a duty he owed to the man who'd loved him? As an obligation? "Did you make the same offer to Yana and Mira?"

"Look at me, Anushka."

She hated it when he said her name in that tone. As if she needed to be reprimanded. "Answer my question, Caio."

"No, I didn't."

"Why not?" she asked, genuinely curious. What was the difference in how he saw her and her sisters? Where did that stem from?

More silence greeted her question.

"Because they're strong enough that they don't need your condescending advice and protection? Because they don't need you to look after them?"

"Cristo, Nush..."

Nush rubbed her hand over her face. God, she was just making a fool of herself. "I'm not myself..."

She felt his fingers on her shoulder, pressing gently. "You're not alone, Anushka. Not today, not in the future."

He didn't say more but she sensed his confusion. She never threw tantrums, or insisted on having things her way all the time like Yana did. Neither did she retreat behind a calm, indestructible facade like Mira so that no one could reach her behind it.

Maybe it was the fact that living with her volatile mother had taught her not makes waves, to be content with whatever life dealt, to curl herself into the smallest corner and be still. Maybe it was the fact that she'd learned to be self-sufficient, to find her happiness in books and computers from a young age. Most importantly, she never fought with anyone. Least of all Caio.

And yet now, it felt as if she'd been sleeping like one of those princesses in the fairy tales. Hiding behind computer fandoms. Letting life pass her by.

"Princesa...look at me."

She looked up, every cell in her immediately responding to his tone. The impact of those thickly lashed deep-set eyes hit her hard. A sharp nose, rugged mouth...there was a sensuousness to him that drew her like no other man could.

Could he see he was the reason she was miserable? Could he hear the thundering of her heart when he stood so close? Could he feel the prickle of heat across her skin when he focused all that energy on her?

Standing this close to him, she could see the imperfections in his face too. She catalogued them, as if they'd help puncture her awareness of him.

The three-inch-long scar that cut across his upper lip

that he'd told her he'd acquired in a fight with his older brother as unruly teenagers. The crooked tilt of his lips to one side when he smiled. The small nick under his jaw, which told her he must have cut himself recently.

"I think you should stop calling me that," she said, swallowing away the longing that rose through her.

His chin drew down, his expression taking on that hard quality that he used in the boardrooms. "That's the most ridiculous thing you've ever said to me."

A steeliness had crept into his voice that made a knot tighten in her chest. He was a master of his emotions but she heard the crack in his temper. Well, that's what she'd wanted, wasn't it? For him to treat her like he did everyone else.

"You don't think I should have a choice in what you call me?"

His eyes swept over her, as if she was someone new. As if, if he looked hard enough, he should be able to see through her sudden resentment. "Why is what I call you a problem when it was never before?" His tone gentled immediately. "Is it because Rao called you that?"

"No. Because it's condescending and infantilizing and—"

"I have never condescended to you." There was anger in his tone now, and that it excited her was a sorry truth of her life. "And the second word…" he thrust a hand through his hair, "I don't think I even know what it means."

"You're right. It doesn't matter what you call me anyway because… I'm quitting."

He stilled and Nush could no more stop taking him in than she could stop breathing. It was like when she watched one of his old soccer games and then pressed play when he was midleap. The economy, the pure animal grace of his movements, the sudden explosion from a deceiving stillness…it had always captivated her. And it happened now, live.

All of that simmering physical energy focused on her like a laser beam. Digging. Probing. Searching. "Quitting what, Princesa?" The silky smoothness of his voice only served to betray his cold fury.

Nush swallowed but forced the words out. "The job. The company. The city even." *You.* "I can't do this anymore."

Yana was right. She had to quit him like an addiction—cold turkey. Now. Before it was too late. Nothing else had worked.

He was fully turned toward her now, shielding her from the room and curious eyes. Even now, even when she was fighting with him for no good reason as far as he knew, he sought to make sure she wasn't exposed. One hand on his hip, he rubbed at his forehead with another, a vertical ridge between his brows. "You're not making sense."

Nush's gaze drifted to his mouth set in an uncompromising flat line, to his chin with the perfect little dimple, to the corded column of his neck. To the tattoo peeking out from under the undone collar of his shirt. The tattoo she wanted to see and touch and…lick.

"I don't have to make sense to you, Caio, or do anything in my life with your permission… I don't owe you an explanation."

His fingers wrapped around her wrist as Nush attempted to move past him and she stumbled into his body. She gasped at the contact but when she looked into his eyes, pure frost looked down at her. His grip on her bare arm was firm but not tight. "That's where you're wrong, *querida.* You can rant and rave at me, you can use me as a punching bag to vent your grief if you wish, you can hide from your sisters and the entire world but at the end of day, at the end of the year...at the end of all this, you and I are in it together, Nush. You and I will make or break OneTech. That's what Rao meant for this to be even when he's gone—a partnership for the ages."

"A partnership for the ages—that sounds like a curse to me. A punishment."

His chin reared down, his mouth flattening. Nush regretted the words instantly.

Eyes searching his, she wondered at the taut mask he wore, at the unflinching sacrifices he made for his ambition. She'd never seen him with a steady girlfriend. Never heard him talk about marriage or a future. And yet he was ready to settle down with Laura. Another merger in his goal of...what?

What did Caio truly want?

"You don't need me around anymore. You've never really needed me, Caio. As for my brain, OneTech owns the patent on all my work anyway. I signed a noncompete clause years ago."

"Is that what you think, Nush? That I only value your brain and what it can make for me next?"

"I don't know what to think," Nush said, cutting her gaze away from him. "Thaata's gone and it's a good time as any for me to evaluate my life. See where I want to be in five years. I have to move on before you..."

His fingers tightened on her arm as he zoomed in on that like a predator pouncing. "Before I what?"

"Before you..." Her throat was dry and her heart was beating away and it felt like every raw, uncertain, inch of her was exposed to his bright golden eyes. "Before things change even more. Before I..." She pressed her forehead to his bicep, trembling at his nearness.

"Before you what, Nush?" he repeated softly, a muscle jumping in his jaw, his gaze pinning her to the spot.

She looked up and he was looking down at her and Nush thought her heart might jump out of her chest and shout out her last secret if he didn't let her go. And so she said the one thing that she knew would fracture that impenetrable armor of his. "Before I hate you, Caio. I want to leave before everything that's good and right between us rots and dies."

He released her so fast that she stumbled back. But in the next breath, his arm was around her waist, steadying her, letting her find her balance. Watching over her even as she made a fool of herself.

Weak and spineless as she was, Nush sought his gaze but he wasn't looking at her. His dismissal of her was as complete as she'd wanted it to be. And something between them broke and she wondered if that was the beginning of the end of the bond they'd always shared.

Tucking her arms tight around her midriff, she ran from the room. Heads turned, conversations stopped, whispers abounded but it didn't matter what anyone thought of her. Not when she knew in her heart of hearts that she was a coward.

Shaking her head at Mira, who'd only make her talk about it, Nush left the house.

Quitting…was the only course of action left to her.

Quitting working with him.

Quitting this first-row seat to his life.

Quitting Caio completely might be the only way she could break out of it.

CHAPTER TWO

CAIO OLIVEIRA WAS a man who was rarely ever shocked by life. Because he arranged for it to be exactly how he liked it. From the people he surrounded himself with—there were maybe four people in the world he allowed to speak their minds with him, one whose loss was eating through him—to how many more moves he needed to make to achieve his goal, to what kind of distractions he allowed in his life in the name of fun and play: everything was thought out, everything was calculated.

For more than a decade, he'd worked hundreds of hours a week to turn OneTech into the tech giant it was today. He'd taken risk upon risk, alienated most of the board members, fought and won countless battles with Rao to achieve the level of success he had. He'd never lost sight of his why though.

He could have stopped at any moment in the last few years. He'd never have to work in his life again if he stopped tomorrow and could still live a life of unprecedented luxury. But luxury and yachts and penthouses or acquisition of any other kind of material wealth had never driven him.

Only the need to prove himself after he'd been robbed of everything that had mattered to him, the need to exact revenge on the man who'd cast him out of his own home and his father's company, who'd destroyed his relationship with his mother.

And now, after years, he had what he'd wanted all these years within grasp. Almost. Another week and he'd have been able to acquire the software giant his stepfather operated out of Brazil.

Only Rao had passed away unexpectedly—before he could sell his stock to Caio—and while Caio had enough independent wealth to not need OneTech, he did need the clout he'd have as CEO of OneTech to acquire such a big company. To force his stepfather to sell it without knowing that Caio was pulling the strings meant using one of the subsidiaries that he and Rao had set up in Nush's name.

Right now, he needed to focus all his energies on retaining the CEO position on the board of OneTech. He needed to see Peter Huntingon Sr.'s cunning strategies and counteract them. And for that, if he needed to tie himself to the man's daughter—whom he'd been dangling in front of Caio—then so be it. He would let himself be chained to a woman even if he'd never had any intentions of marrying. At least he could tolerate Laura.

Except…for the bomb Anushka had dropped in his lap earlier. For now, he could go ahead with his plans without her standing by his side, absolutely. But…he wanted Nush on his side. By his side for this next leg of OneTech's journey.

And the fact that he did jarred him on levels he didn't want to examine right then.

The only thing that existed outside of this driving need to send his stepfather and his stepbrother to their knees was his relationship with Nush. The only person he'd allowed close—which was delusional in itself because it had happened without his knowledge or permission—the only person he could be someone else with other than a man driven by the need for revenge was Anushka.

Years ago, he'd stopped trying to control how their relationship evolved. Had admitted that somehow Nush had lodged herself under his skin, never to be pulled out.

From the moment he'd picked her up on that flight years ago to this evening when she'd suddenly turned on him…she'd been the one thing Caio had never been able to box into a grid in his life. Not even Rao had stitched himself up into the fabric of his life as Nush had.

A creature of habit, he was used to having her as a part of his life. Part of his inner circle—a circle of two, as Rao once had joked, when he'd found Nush and Caio laughing at something in the early hours of dawn at their respective workstations in her lab.

How dare she now change the rules on him?

He wanted to write off her sudden anger at him as her grief and loss taking over, but he hadn't been able to let it go. Hours had passed and it stung and poked like a rusted nail scratching under his skin. It infuriated him that she had such a hold on him and yet he hadn't been able to stop himself from seeking her out. From wanting to provide some kind of reassurance—like a codependent friend or worse a spurned lover—and demand it return that things between them would go back to as they'd been.

For months now, he'd sat back and watched as she'd distanced herself from him little by little. Had watched with more than a mild irritation and at times confused and misdirected fury, as she'd forced herself into a social life he knew she didn't want, as she'd dated and partied and entertained men like Peter Huntington Jr. Even though he knew she despised the kind of crowd that trust fund brat represented. Had suppressed the urge to ask her what the hell she thought she was doing with her life. Had reassured himself that the burn he felt in his gut when he saw her with a man was nothing but his overtly possessive, protective nature rearing its head.

When he'd brought up her sudden party animal behavior with her grandfather, Rao had smiled an infuriatingly cryptic smile and said his little Princess was testing her wings, whatever the hell that meant.

Caio remembered being baffled as to why sensible, smart Nush would indulge in things that didn't appeal to her in the first place. And the worst part, he'd felt a sense of disappointment in her, a strange, stinging sense of betrayal at how she'd started pulling away from him.

But enough was enough. To think of her new interests and distractions in life as a phase was one thing. But learning that she was unhappy to the point that she felt she had to walk away, that she'd even begun to hate him…that was intolerable. On some level, it felt like a personal failure.

He stilled outside Rao's study, hand raised for a knock, a new realization twisting through him with a crystal-clear clarity.

Anushka was his Achilles' heel.

The one person that made him act out of character. The one person with whom his relationship defied any sort of definition. And that should have sent him away, should have been warning enough.

But he didn't heed it.

Past midnight, Nush found herself walking through her grandfather's study like some night wraith. She'd been unable to sleep, the thought of leaving sending her mind in a thousand directions.

One hand wrapped around a warm mug of milk, she

inhaled the scent of Thaata's hand-rolled cigars and something else.

It took her two breaths to figure it out.

Caio's scent. Of course, he'd been working out of here for a few months now. Jesus, wherever she went in this house, he was present to tease and taunt her.

His anger earlier in the evening had shocked her. Maybe because she'd never seen that cold will targeted at her. Maybe because she'd never really gone toe-to-toe with him. For a second, she'd even wondered if he could sense her frustration. If he could feel…

No.

God, she was just going in circles again and again. Driving herself out of her mind imagining things that weren't real.

Putting the mug away, she pulled her feet up and settled into the leather chair. The soft, worn leather enveloped her like an embrace she desperately needed. Closing her eyes, it was easy to imagine it was Caio's arms around her. With a choked cry, she bent her cheek to the desk.

And that was how Caio found her—rubbing her face against the rough grain of the dark oak desk he'd built with his own hands three years ago. Imagining it was those calloused fingers that stroked her.

The study door closed with a thud that made her heart follow with its own beat.

Heat and awareness charged each other across her skin as she felt his gaze take in the picture she made. Of her spaghetti top and skimpy shorts she hadn't covered up in her urgent need to escape her bed.

Arms hugging the cool wood, she stayed like that—trying to calm the ache in her breasts, the fire simmering in her belly, wondering if he'd leave. But he had every right to linger here, to mourn her grandfather and she wasn't going to push her company on him.

Straightening away from the desk, Nush got to her feet and walked around the desk on the opposite side.

"Don't leave on my account," he said, his tone smooth. His control firmly back in place. "Are you having trouble sleeping again?"

Her eyes got acclimated to the darkness as she searched for him. Moonlight outlined his broad shoulders and tapered waist. "Yes. But I'll go back now."

When his hands moved to the light switch, she said, "No, don't. I'm not…dressed properly."

His surprise was a taut thread in the room, reaching for her, pulling at her.

Nush closed her eyes, wishing she hadn't said anything at all. It revealed too much of the thrumming awareness that touched her when he was near. Telling him it was hard to be around him right now was the grown-up thing to do. Instead, she was doing everything but. Playing a stupid game.

"Nush…"

"Please, Caio. I don't want to fight."

"As you wish, Princesa."

"Why are you so easygoing with me?" she asked, breaking her own rule. "I was the one who behaved illogically earlier. The one who came at you out of nowhere."

She could see that vertical ridge between his brows again. "What?"

"You are different with everyone else. Even with Thaata, I think. You never give an inch, Caio. You're arrogant, demanding, ruthless even. Yana, I know, is definitely a little scared of you. But with me…a different side of you comes out. You're gentle, understanding, far too accommodating. Even when I'm behaving like a brat."

He laughed and she let it envelop her like a lover's embrace. His embrace. "My father would have enjoyed to hear me being called accommodating."

The clear affection in his tone was a pleasant surprise. Nush hugged the piece of information to herself, hoarding pieces of the puzzle she'd long wanted to solve. "Exactly," she said, a glimmer of her smile coating her words. "So why?"

"You resent me for treating you differently." He stated it baldly, as if he'd only now arrived at that irrevocable conclusion. "Here I thought you were the most uncomplicated woman I've ever known, Nush."

"At least you think me a woman," she mumbled to herself and then prayed to the laws of physics that he hadn't heard her. Clearly, her filter was completely off today.

His head cocked to the side and all Nush wanted to do was to run her fingers over the corded column of his throat. "Do you remember the first time I came to pick you up?"

Nush nodded. That summer had been one of the best of her life. Not only had she spent every minute with Mira and Yana but she'd also started working with Caio. Her grandparents had spent hours with her. Even their dad had dropped in for a few visits. For the first time in her life, Nush had found total acceptance, even when she was at her weirdest.

"You were terrified of leaving your mom behind. You were desperate to see Yana and Mira and your grandparents. You said you couldn't wait to spend every day making memories to take back with you for when you needed them. You…tried to be strong and brave even when you didn't have control of anything around you. You…reminded me of myself. Of who I'd been before

I lost all semblance of innocence and good. Of who I'd been a long, long time ago. Sometimes, I wonder if…"

Nush didn't say anything, so afraid that if she interrupted him, he might stop talking. He might stop sharing. He might stop giving her this little glimpse into his head.

"There's an untouched innocence to you that none of us have been able to hold on to. I know Rao and Mira, and even Yana, feel as if they could do anything to keep that part of you safe. It's the same thing that makes me feel protective of you. Maybe because no one looked out for me. I lost so much…that I can never get back. Even if I wanted it back."

A dark thread of anger vibrated in the last sentence. As if he hadn't quite let go of it, even as he acknowledged that it had changed him for the worse.

Nush wrapped her arms around her knees on the chair and studied him with her chin tucked into them. It was the most he had ever shared about his background. "I'm sorry that you were alone when you needed someone. I know how terrifying that feels."

"I know you do, Princesa." He sighed then, and it rattled in the quiet between them. "Just because I feel protective of you doesn't mean I think any less of you, Anushka."

A sudden, strange warmth came over her, leaving her trembling in its wake. Their eyes met in the darkness and Nush nodded, not trusting her voice. The silence that followed had an unusual thrumming quality to it for two people who were used to spending hours together in companionable silence. Like there were things being said without either of them saying it. And she wondered if it was her betraying herself. Wondered if the truth of her desire for him could be worse than this…strange game she was playing.

She watched as he moved around the room, touching Thaata's things just as she'd done before he'd arrived. Only now, when that shamefully needy part of her had been assuaged with his words, did she note how on edge his movements were. How unsettled the energy around him felt when he usually didn't let anything fracture his determination toward his end goal.

When he reached the other side of the desk and picked up the framed picture of her and Caio standing on either side of her grandfather—one that had been taken last year—she let out a shuddering breath. His fingers moved over her grandfather's face in the picture, his gaze far away.

"Tell me how you came to know Thaata," she said, wanting to give him something for once, wanting to take away the far-off look in his eyes.

A sudden smile simmered into existence, a pocket of light in the darkness around them. "It was Rao who came to my rescue when I didn't have anything or anyone. When I hated the world and wanted to burn it down. And I didn't make it easy for him either."

"He never told me that. Don't tell me you and Thaata used to fight?"

"All the time, especially when he brought me here in the beginning. I was like an out-of-control, festering wound. I didn't want to trust him. It was only after I'd spent several days with Yana and Mira that I believed that he meant well. That he did care about me."

"Why did he come to your…rescue?" She searched his face, desperate to see every nuance in those eyes. "I can't imagine you needing rescue in any way."

He rubbed a hand over his face. Exhaustion she'd never seen before was etched into the gesture. "I can't imagine how bad my life could've gotten if he hadn't."

Her heart ached to see him like that. "You mean you weren't born arrogant and confident and ruthlessly perfect?"

"Perfect, *querida*? Far from it." She heard his laughter and his shock in his response. "Rao and my dad worked together as entry-level engineers a long time ago when they'd both been trying to make it here. They even started their companies at the same time, Papa back in Brazil and Rao here. They kept in touch until Papa passed away when I was nine. Rao checked on me and Mama regularly. He never forgot about us." Caio sounded faraway and tense, as if the memories weren't good ones. "When I had nowhere to go, Rao invited me to come work for him. All based on a relationship with a man who was long gone."

Nush smiled. "I hope you know he wasn't being altruistic. Thaata must have known what a fantastic investment you'd turn out to be. He once told me that he hadn't imagined a tenth of the success you've made of OneTech."

Fingers tracing the edge of the desk, Caio walked around until he was leaning against it, within her reach. "Oh, I've no doubt of that. Rao was a long-term strategist. His trust in me… I can't tell you what it meant to me. But Rao believed in second chances and that's what landed us in this mess with Peter Sr. too."

"Is that why no amount of success is enough, Caio? Because you have to pay it back in spades? Why you'll go to any lengths to keep your control of OneTech intact?"

"Now you even sound like your grandfather," he said, easily sidestepping her question. Shock swept through her as she realized that each word of his was measured, everything he'd shared had been calculated to get something back. "I find it amazing how much of him there is in you. He was a pioneer and didn't let anything bother him when he was in that lab and was unrelentingly stubborn when he got a notion into his head."

And just like that, he reminded Nush of what she had to do. For her own sake. "Then you also know that I don't make decisions easily, Caio. I have to leave. Though..." she stared at her fingers bathed in moonlight, careful with her own words now, "I'm sorry for how I spoke to you earlier. It was unfair. You made a convenient target for something that wasn't your fault."

"You're sorry for the how, but not for what you said," he observed drily, almost in a matter-of-fact voice. As if he was sifting and separating her intent from her words. "You meant it when you said you'd begin to hate me if you stayed. Or do you hate me already, Princesa?"

And suddenly, Nush realized that he'd come in search of her—not just found her—that their conversation—one she'd foolishly instigated—was far from over. That he wouldn't rest until he knew all about her secret fascination with him.

This was the Caio she knew—a man who never left a stone unturned if it caught his interest. Except it was all directed at her now.

"I don't hate you." She turned her gaze to the desk, afraid of what he'd see in her expression. "I didn't know what I was saying."

"Wrong, Nush. For the first time in months, I think you were being truthful with me."

Of course, he'd noticed that she'd been avoiding him little by little for months now. The only time she hadn't been successful in completely avoiding him was when they worked together on the software solution for a ten-billion-dollar contract her design had won.

Nush tilted her chin up. "I'm twenty-three, Caio. I've been working in one form or the other for a decade now.

Between Mama and OneTech and evening classes, I've barely had a life of my own. Wanting to change it up is not so…unreasonable."

"But you fixed that with a very busy social life this past year, no?"

Heat claimed Nush's cheeks at his wry comment that he'd taken note. She had gone on date after date, plastered herself at parties Yana had dragged her to, danced at clubs even though she hated that kind of mindless chitchat and search for familiarity with strangers, given out her number to anyone who'd asked, determined to get over this stupid crush. "It wasn't enough. It didn't fix what I wanted to fix."

"I need more, Nush."

Her head jerked up, something in his tone making every sense come alert and alive. "What do you mean?"

"If you're going to hate me and clearly, you're halfway there, I think it's more than fair that I know the reason. I'd like to know why you think our relationship is…*rotting*."

Cold fury thrummed along each word out of his mouth and yet, Nush had a feeling it was directed at himself rather than her. For the hundredth time that day, she wondered if she knew Caio at all.

"What have I done to upset you so, Princesa?" The words seemed to be wrenched out of him against his will.

She swallowed helplessly, wondering what she'd set into motion. "You didn't do anything wrong, Caio. Please…believe me, it's all me. Me and my stupid…"

Suddenly, the lamp on the desk was turned on and golden light warmed her face and he was standing too close and…there was no way to avoid looking at him. Or to stop him from seeing her. Everything she felt and wanted and craved would be written in her face.

But she remained rooted to the spot, studying him in turn.

Dressed in dark gray sweats and an anime print T-shirt she'd printed for him, he looked like a dark angel demanding answers she didn't want to give. Of cheap quality, the tee had long faded, leaving the short sleeves and chest pulling tight against his defined body.

Her breaths turned shallow when he turned the leather chair.

"The truth, Anushka."

Her name, this time, was a warning and she realized with a surge of disbelief that she'd wounded him that evening. Her words of hate and resentment had found a weak spot in the mighty and ruthless Caio Oliveira's armor and drawn blood. She didn't know why, didn't know how she knew, didn't care if he was aware of it.

And even as an irrational, selfish part of her gloried in the fact that she'd at last reached him in that twisted way, a big part of her disliked herself for her willful words. She wasn't the kind of woman who took out her frustration on others. She didn't want to be full of bitterness like her mother. She didn't want to hurt the man who'd always stood by her side for more than a decade—through hardships and successes—a man who'd been kind to her, again and again, because he thought she held some indefinable quality he himself had lost.

She looked up to find him staring at her, the gold of his eyes darkening, his nostrils flaring. "I've already lost Thaata and the thought of losing you too makes me—" Tears filled her eyes and the sob she'd been fighting since Thaata's stroke, since her grandmother's death, and Mama's deteriorating health, broke through her paltry defenses.

She closed her eyes and tried to fight it, but her throat

burned and Caio was there pulling her into in his arms and there was no stopping the dam from bursting. They came in hot rivulets, of grief and loss, of bone-deep fear that everyone she loved would leave her. That she'd always be lonely and unwanted and that years would pass by and she'd never even act on…

"Shh… Princesa," Caio kept whispering, his arms a loose but comfortable weight around her shoulders. "You're not losing me, Nush."

His body was a hard shield around her that could keep all her troubles at bay. It was the kind of thinking that had got her into this mess, but right now, she couldn't care.

For a long while, Nush stayed in his embrace, letting the solid weight of him soothe her. She knew she'd left splotchy wetness on his tee, but she didn't want to move. Not yet. Not when she might not have a right to hold him like this ever again. Not when he was busy spinning strategies, making new alliances that would push her out of his life.

Her fingers gripping his biceps, her cheek pressed to his chest, she inhaled deep, willing some of that impenetrable strength into her.

A pure, untarnished moment of comfort and security and peace that she'd rarely known in her life. And she wondered if that was the reason for her attraction to him—that Caio presented an indefatigable promise of constancy, an indomitable presence in her life that she'd never had with anyone else.

Eventually, her tears dried up, and something else simmered in her veins. Like the flickering light of a candle, desire she'd tried to hide so hard for months roared to life. It was impossible to fight it when she'd programmed her brain to find the very scent of him arousing, intoxicating.

And now all she could smell and touch and feel were the hard contours of him reshaping her softness to fit him.

Nush tightened her arms around him and moved her face up into his neck, into the hollow at his throat. Moved her lips against the corded column of his neck, let the taste of his skin and sweat and *him* seep into her. For no longer than a breath's span, she lingered over that hard line between them, an airy lightness fizzing through her.

She heard the indrawn hiss of Caio's breath, the hard clench and release of his body around her. His hands gripped her hips, tight and arresting.

"Nush?" His eyes searched hers in the darkness, his features woven tight into a forbidding mask that locked up every emotion.

Even now, fear and cowardice urged her to laugh it off. To act like it was unintentional, that she was mindless in her grief. Sweat dampened the nape of her neck and her forehead.

No, she batted away at her fears.

There was nothing wrong with her desire for him. Nothing wrong that she wanted him. And God, she was tired of fulfilling that desire with men she wasn't even interested in. Of hiding what she felt. Of telling herself that it wouldn't work. Of running away from life.

CHAPTER THREE

STILL, NUSH'S SENSE of right and wrong would let her go only so far when all he offered was comfort. Words were needed and even though she hated forming them, releasing them, she knew it was time.

"I…want this, Caio, with you." Slowly, bracing herself to be pushed away, feeling as if her very existence was contingent upon touching him, she pressed her forehead to his chin.

He didn't blink or sigh or push her away and she let it all out. "I've spent months telling myself that it can't happen, that you don't see me like that, that it's madness to want you." A laugh escaped her mouth and still he didn't move or say anything and some spark of hope lit up inside her and she kept running toward the edge, rearing to jump off the cliff. "This is why I want to leave, why I find it unbearable to be near you." Another wretched sound escaped her and she bunched her hands in his shirt. "And now to know that you might be making… Do you see why I have to leave? Why I can't be here while you make new…alliances? It would be easier on me to hate you, Caio, than to—"

"Cristo," Caio said in a low, guttural growl and his head jerked down and she jerked her head up and his chin bumped her cheekbone and pain jarred through her and his fingers were over her cheek and she was breathing hard, trying to untangle herself and his hands were over her shoulders and then her mouth went flush against his.

She might have stopped breathing altogether, her heart stopping its frenzied beating. Everything in her stilled to better drink in the sensation of his mouth against hers.

And for the first time in months, she felt as if she'd reclaimed a part of her she hadn't even realized she'd lost. She wanted to own this desire. Own her choices, right or wrong, successful or full of defeat. "I don't want this to be some accident. Don't want you to say this was some kind of overflow from all the grief and loss of the last few months. It's not. This is what I've wanted for… months now, Caio. I want to kiss you. Now. I want to see if you…feel this thing too. I want to test this pull I feel. Or I'll regret not taking the risk forever."

Waiting for him to push her away or walk away was the hardest thing Nush had ever done in her life. But he didn't. Only stared at her, those golden flecks in his eyes darkening, his nostrils flaring, his entire frame tense and tight.

Letting him see the want in her eyes was the biggest, headiest rush. More than a rough, hungry kiss with another man. More than half-naked groping in the dark with a stranger.

One breath turned into the next and the next, and Nush sank her fingers into his thick hair, pulled his head down and pressed her mouth to his.

Still, he watched her, an inherent challenge in that taut jaw line, the gold of his eyes darkening. And that was its own aphrodisiac, winding her up, taunting her to rise to the occasion. Heat burned through her, leaving every doubt and insecurity in piles of ashes. She glided her mouth from one end of his to the other, rubbed up and down, sucked his lower lip between hers and then his upper. Their noses bumped, their breaths a loud whistle in the room.

Textures and sensations assaulted her, all at once. The contrast of his rough stubble and the softness of his lips made a soft moan escape her. Needing more, she explored every inch of his mouth, every slope and rise and dip and curl, the rigid contour of his upper lip and the lush give of his lower lip.

Desire trickled through her limbs like warm honey, dripping and pooling in her lower belly. Hotter and needier and hungrier and…he was kissing her back. He had been kissing her back from the first contact.

Only now, in true Caio fashion, he was taking control of the kiss.

Her pulse drummed in her ears as Nush took a hasty catalog of the new sensations vying for attention.

His fingers in her hair, gripping firmly, holding her for his onslaught, his other hand cupped her hip nudging her closer, her small breasts crushed against his hard chest and his mouth… God, his mouth. It was everything she'd ever dreamed of, his kiss hotter and filthier than her wildest fantasy.

She was panting, every muscle trembling, her skin burning up as he chased and hunted and devoured her lips, not letting her settle into or savor any one sensation. He nipped at her lower lip and he licked the hurt when she mewled and he growled against her mouth until the sheer vibrating pulse of it made her open her mouth with an answering groan. And then his tongue was swooping into her mouth. Cajoling, teasing, taunting, licking, his hands moved all over her back and the more he took and demanded and wanted, the more Nush wanted to give.

Desire made her dizzy, and she clung to him, digging her fingers into his shoulders, scratching her nails into his scalp. Throwing all her weight onto him, she nudged her hips forward and the heated press of his erection against her lower belly created the most delicious burn between her thighs.

"Caio," she whispered, sobbing and panting his name, begging for release.

It was the wrong thing to say, the wrong thing to invoke. The spell broke, as suddenly and violently as the kiss had taken off.

Caio's sudden stillness was like a cold splash of water over her heated skin. *"Merda!"*

The word reverberated between them before he set her back from him in such a sudden movement that Nush crashed into the hard, sharp edge of the desk behind her.

With another rough sounding curse, Caio reached out to steady her. But his fingers landed her hip and Nush jumped away with a gasp of pain.

"Wait, Princesa. Don't move." Going to his knees in a sinuous movement, he lifted the edge of her spaghetti top and tugged the hem of her shorts down gingerly. Even in the dark, Nush could see the blue-green bruise already taking shape.

"Cristo!" Caio stared at the flare of her hip where the bruise was. One long finger traced the edges of it before he muttered, "I didn't mean to…hurt you." Deep and hoarse and guttural, his voice pinged over her.

Nush bit her lip, trying to ignore the sensation of his fingers on her bare skin. Or how her sex clenched greedily at the sight of him on his knees in front of her, his mouth inches from flesh she'd caressed while thinking of him. "It's okay," she murmured, wanting to sink her fingers into his hair again but not daring. To touch him—even after their explosive kiss—was an intimacy she hadn't been granted yet. Her skin tingled as he stayed like that, head dipped, the remnant warmth of their kiss burning like embers within her limbs. "It just hurt a little when you grabbed me." She couldn't help pushing back a lock of hair that had fallen onto his forehead. "I'm fine."

His fingers arrested her wrist. "This is what will happen if we do this, *querida*."

"What?"

"I'll hurt you."

"You're being ridiculous," Nush said, striving for a levity she didn't feel. "It was an accident."

He sprang to his feet and away from her with that grace that, for once, couldn't hide the fact that he didn't want her to touch him anymore.

Nush stayed still, hope deflating inside her chest as fast as it had grown. Dread chased away every spark of pleasure. She'd thought to let him know of her desire, to let him see it, to find out that he didn't return her interest, or that he didn't feel the same attraction would be the hardest part of this.

But it wasn't. It was this waiting.

That Caio had kissed her back, that even now his broad frame shook with tension was easy to see. That she'd only felt a part of something that had already existed between them was clear.

But waiting for his reaction to what they'd done, waiting to see what he'd say to her in the wake of the best kiss of her life…this was the hardest part. She felt as if her vulnerability was written all over her face, a giant neon sign waiting for his decision.

For long seconds, he looked at that framed photo of the three of them again.

"Caio?"

A rough thrust of his fingers through his hair. When he spoke, he sounded cool, distant. As if the kiss hadn't affected him at all. "I should've stopped you. I will regret it for the rest of my life that I didn't."

Nush flinched as if he'd dealt her a body blow.

Caio wished he could take back the words instantly.

Cristo, he was full of a contrariness that he couldn't fathom. He didn't want to hurt her. Ever. And yet, that meant hurting her now. Killing the hope he saw in her eyes now before it was too late.

"That can't happen again, Nush," he said softly.

"And yet, it just did." Her chin tilted up in a stubborn streak he knew so well. "You kissed me back. And you enjoyed the hell out of it. I've kissed enough men to know the difference."

"I don't need a reminder of your colorful love life of the past year," he said, the taste of her on his lips a teasing promise he wanted to explore further.

Something glinted in her eyes, a flash of such pure satisfaction, that it was only then Caio realized how...judgmental and even a little jealous he sounded.

The situation was unraveling, getting away from him faster than he could fix it. And it made him lash out in a way that he'd never been with her. He did it even though he hated himself for the cruelty in his words. "I was taken by surprise. You were crying and I didn't want to upset you further by pulling away."

"You're a bastard," she said, her chin rearing down. "How dare you twist something so real up like that?"

"You have no idea how close to truth you are in your assessment, Princesa. I'm a bastard when things don't go my way. Let's do each other a favor and forget it ever happened."

Shoulders straightened, stretching the tee tight across her chest until he could see the sharp points of her nipples. Eyes swollen from having cried, mouth pink from his kisses, hair a haphazard halo around her face, she looked like one of those mythical warrior women she became in her role-playing games. The stubborn streak that made her survive without breaking would never take his suggestion sitting down. He couldn't stop admiring the quality even as he needed to push her away.

"Admit that you lost yourself to the kiss as much as I did, that you want this as much as I do. If I hadn't moaned out your name and broken the spell, you'd have been f—"

"There is no this, Nush," he bit out, his voice low and urgent. "You and I can't…happen."

She blinked. Studied him thoughtfully. He could almost see her consider this from all points, gather her arsenal, make logical leaps. Damn it, that she approached this with the weight and logic and thought she gave everything made him want to kiss and rumple her all over. "I'm not asking you to marry me, Caio."

"What are you asking me then?" The question left his mouth against his wishes. An arrow shooting out of the dark, slumbering place that was remembering how she'd felt in his arms. How she'd responded to every caress. How she'd melted against him. How, even now, he wanted to hear from her own lips what she wanted of him, what she'd wanted of him. "What is it that you think I'm denying you?"

She licked her lips, her gaze zeroing on his own. Lust was a sizzling burn in his limbs as his libido made leaps he'd never before made. "I…"

Hesitation danced in her eyes and he gobbled it up like the big bad wolf he was. Who did she think he was? A hero straight out of those fairy tales who'd give her a happily-ever-after? One of those honorable knights she was so fond of reading about? Maybe that was the problem. “A red-hot affair? A fling that would cheapen everything we mean to each other? A quick fuck against the wall in this room that belonged to the man we both lost?”

“Don’t bring Thaata into this.”

“You’re his precious granddaughter. He’s in the middle of everything you and I do.” He let out a long sigh, willing himself to appeal to her rationality. “I can’t dishonor Rao’s memory like that. I can’t…dishonor you like that.”

She stared at him, aghast. “My honor’s not tied to my having sex. With you or anyone.”

“I wholeheartedly agree, *querida*. But mine is tied to not taking advantage of the generosity and trust Rao gave me. In not taking advantage of your…affection for me.”

“You really think I can’t separate lust and affection? Grief and loss from want? Is that what you’re afraid of? That if we have sex, I’ll somehow confuse my poor unsuspecting mind and cling to you and make all sorts of demands on you? And for Thaata’s sake and your poor honor’s sake, you’ll have to agree and be tied down to me for the rest of our lives?”

That the idea of being tied down to Nush for the rest of their lives didn’t alarm him much alarmed him. He was really due for some mindless entertainment if his mind was making outrageous leaps like that out of thin air.

“What if we do have sex? Then what, Anushka? Do we greet each other as friends when it’s over? Do we continue working and collaborating as if we don’t know each other intimately? What happens when I have my fun with you, discard you and move on to the next woman that catches my fancy? Do you expect me to hold you together? Do you know if you can bear it when I lose interest in you and dump you?” He forced himself to be as crude as possible. “Because you know very well, that’s what I do. Are you telling me you’d be okay with fracturing everything good between us…all for what? For a few minutes of mindless sex?"

"Yes, I want it as long as both of us want it. I want it because…" Some sort of self-preservation seemed to have caught her there. Swallowing, she looked down at her hands, and then back up at him. "Don't use Thaata or our relationship or your bloody integrity as excuses, Caio, because that's all they all are. If you don't want to pursue this, just say that. I'm mature enough to accept that."

So be it then. "Kissing you back was the biggest mistake of my life. I have plans for it that don't involve messing up what you and I might have in pursuit of questionable pleasure. I'm not some errant knight that will hold you together when an affair ruins things between us, Princesa. Your little experience with men doesn't mean you're ready for me. The fact that you hold one kiss so high in your estimation is proof enough of how naive and unworldly you are."

Even in the meager light of the table lamp, Caio could see how she paled. How that final barb had landed hard. Now that he was so in tune with her very breath, he could see the soft gasp that escaped her lush mouth.

Fat tears pooled in her eyes, magnified by the thick glasses. She blinked and one rolled down the very cheek he wanted to touch and clasp and hold. He'd always been the one who'd offered her a shoulder when she cried, who stood by her until she found that strength again. Never the one who made her cry and it left the foulest taste in his mouth.

"I have no use for you as a lover, Nush."

"No. Only for my brain in your campaign for world supremacy," she said with a scornful laugh.

It cut through him easily, her self-deprecation, her hot anger, her bitterness, like a knife through butter. And that he'd let her get so close to wound him shocked him in itself. "Princesa—"

"Stop." Finally, she blinked, pulled in a shuddering breath, straightened her shoulders and faced him. Always fighting, even in defeat, full of that steely strength that he'd always admired. "Get out, Caio."

He regarded the picture she made for several seconds, desperate to kiss away the hurt from her mouth. Cristo, he was screwed up in every way when it came to Nush.

He walked out, closing the door behind him. He'd spent a lot of time in the last fifteen years disliking who he'd become, but he'd never actively hated himself as much as he did then.

And while he knew he'd acted for the best, for both of them, Caio had a feeling he'd destroyed whatever they'd had and whatever they might have had. But the second was only possible if he'd been a better man.

CHAPTER FOUR

THE KISS STAYED with Caio for hours, days, taunting him, haunting him, mocking his so-called steely will, now lying in shredded ribbons at Nush's feet. Or was it at that luscious mouth and eager response that it was snagged on…

His week had been busy with media interviews, board meetings, figuring out which board members still respected Rao's vision for the company *and* supported Caio's position as CEO, versus which men were ready to jump ship.

He shouldn't have had a moment's quiet to dwell on the kiss. *Or her.* And yet it came to him, at the most unsuspecting of times, halting his thoughts, making him sprawl back and live it all over again.

Her bold declaration that she'd not let him call it something else, the perfect fit of her lithe body against his, the way she'd responded to his caresses, her moans, her fierce demands—he was never going to forget how she'd melted into him. Every time he saw her, he'd see her as she'd been in that darkness.

Eyes big and wide behind those glasses, mouth trembling, nipples grazing his chest in pleasurable torment, the lush flare of her hips in his hands, the toned length of her thighs molding against his…

He pushed a hand through his hair. God, he was obsessing over a kiss.

Cursing his fractured discipline, Caio forced himself to think of the upcoming reading of Rao's will tomorrow. Once that was out of the way and Caio had the majority he needed, he needn't look back. Putting the purchase of his stepfather's company through to his CFO would be his first order.

And it wasn't just that he needed OneTech.

OneTech needed him too. Especially if he wanted to stop Peter Sr. from turning it into a cash cow with no principles or integrity.

Caio had lost not just a mentor and an investor and a professional colleague he respected, but a man who'd given Caio a purpose when he'd been sorely lacking one.

Being a part of Rao's family had given him a balance, a hope that he could build something after he achieved his goal. That he wasn't completely lost.

I've wanted this...for months, Caio.

Anushka's whispered declaration tugged at him. A vague shape of a wish teased at the edge of his consciousness and he batted it away.

Had she wanted him even as she'd dated other men?

And what do you feel about her? an insidious voice whispered much as he tried to bury it.

He let out a filthy curse that would have scandalized his mother. As rowdy as he and his brothers had been, Mama had been proud of the fact that she'd taught them manners. She'd also taught him what honor meant though only a frayed thread remained. Which said he couldn't use Nush like that.

And if that meant she hated him, so be it. If that meant they had to delete ten years of a fond, fulfilling relationship and start over as strangers, then so be it. With a ruthless will that had seen him through dark times, Caio pushed the thought of her out of his head.

It was early morning the day Rao's will was to be read while Caio was breakfasting on the veranda that looked out onto the beautiful blue of the ocean when he saw Nush.

Gritting his teeth, he tried to stop his gaze from sweeping all over her. It was a losing fight. Cristo, he'd never be ready for the sudden punch of desire that knocked him for sixes when he laid eyes on her now.

He let out a filthy curse under his breath, only realizing now how much damage the damned kiss had done. There was no going back from it. No unseeing Nush as the woman who'd so boldly declared she wanted him, who'd let him see the yearning in her eyes, who'd responded like dry tinder to fire to his every caress.

Who'd once again claimed him—whether he'd wanted to be or not—like no one else ever had.

She'd just returned from a morning run and was stretching on the lawn, chest heaving, long thigh muscles shaking. Unaware of what a delectable reward she provided him after three days of searching for her face wherever he went like some rejected loser.

He shouldn't want to look and even if he did, the decent thing would've been to look away. To not let one moment's bad decision compound into setting into motion things he couldn't take back as easily. Caio didn't even try.

She was wearing a burnt-orange sports bra and loose black shorts—an outfit he'd seen her in countless times. But this morning, he noted the swell of her small breasts pushing up and out of the bra as her chest heaved, the tight nip of her waist and the voluptuous flare of her hips, the sweet curve of her ass and those legs…she had the longest legs with toned muscles where her shorts rested. The silky sheen of miles of brown skin, begging to be touched and kissed and marred at his fingers…he swallowed.

Her thick, wavy hair pulled away from her face in a braid made that innocent sensuality she possessed shine brighter, hotter. Curly tendrils escaping it kissed the nape of her neck and she angrily pushed them into the braid in stabbing motions that made him smile.

All Caio wanted was to walk toward her and enfold her in his arms from behind. Wrap that thick braid in his hand and twist it up and away until he could see into those beautiful brown eyes. Kiss the sweaty curve of that elegant neck and taste the salt on her skin until she melted into him again. Run his hands down her body, stroke every dip and flare and inch of bare skin, learn where she was most sensitive.

He was semi-hard already, just from watching her. Just from knowing that she wouldn't stop him if he gave in to the madness and did any of those things.

And as arousing as that was, it was also the thought that cut through the haze.

There was nothing in the world that Nush did without giving it her all, without feeling it to the core of that steely sweetness. There was nothing he could give her but pain and hurt and…misery in the end. No promise he wouldn't break. No guarantee that he wouldn't ruin that sweet innocence of hers.

He was cynical to his core, and was even now making plans to ruin his stepfather. She'd be horrified when she learned he'd been planning such destruction for years, when she saw him for who he was truly then.

As if aware of his eyes on her, she turned mid-stretch. Across the few feet that separated them, their gazes met and held. Electricity arced between them, fueled by desire and something more, something he preferred to leave unsaid. Forever, if possible.

He cut his gaze away but it didn't go that far. Nothing, it seemed, when it came to Anushka, was in his control anymore.

Her face was pink and sweaty from the run. Without the glasses, her eyes looked enormous in her face. Suddenly he wondered why she didn't wear contacts or get it corrected by laser surgery. Suddenly there were too many things he didn't know about her.

Her throat moved on a hard swallow, calling his attention to the thin golden chain she wore with a pendant that said *Princesa* in gold. It was the only jewelry he'd ever seen her wear on a constant basis. A paltry gift he'd bought her for her sixteenth birthday that she'd always cherished. The weight of that was as terrifying as it was exciting.

Only your gift that she cherishes so much, a sneaky voice said in his head.

He wondered at how protective, even possessive he felt about her when he was determined to nip this thing between them.

"Good run?" he asked, determined to bring things back to some kind of even keel. Maybe it was a fool's wish but a part of him wanted that easy camaraderie they'd shared for almost a decade. He craved to be the Caio he'd been with her—fun, easygoing, free of the bitterness that had long tainted him.

Without answering, she lifted the navy-blue bottle of water and took a long chug.

Caio followed the trail of a water drop down her chin, down her long, elegant neck down to her cleavage where it disappeared. He should feel shame for watching her like that, and yet he didn't. There was no turning off the desire her kiss had unleashed.

When she finally joined him at the table, something in him calmed. Pulling a plate toward her, she applied a liberal amount of butter to her toast and then scooped three spoons of strawberry jam on top. Her sweet tooth and her utter enjoyment of food had always been something to watch. But now, there was a sensual element to it that made every muscle in him tight.

He closed his laptop with a loud thunk, giving up even the pretense of working.

Licking a clump of jam from her lower lip, she said, "If I'm disturbing you, I can leave."

If it had been anyone but her, Caio would've known that the gesture and the question were designed to go together. That she didn't realize how tempting and taunting she sounded only made him want her more. As if her innocent sensuality had been shaped to perfectly counteract his cynical disillusion of life. Even sex had at some point become boring, nothing but an exercise to relieve stress.

With Nush though, it would be hot and real and…raw.

He had the sudden, overwhelming urge to pull her into his lap and lick at that lower lip. To inhale the sweet taste of her mouth into him until he never forgot. To unravel her all over again.

"Caio?"

"Of course you're not disturbing me," he said, wondering if this was the hell his mother had warned him about ending up at when he'd get into nasty fights with his stepbrother Enzo The ones Enzo had always started, provoked Caio into, by spewing obscenities about Papa. "I'm never unavailable to you, Princesa."

She arched her brows and he realized he'd suggested something he hadn't meant to. Another bite of the toast followed before she said, "Did you need me to sign anything else? I asked your PA to check with you."

Irritation enveloped him instantly, a dark cloud. "You're still determined to leave?"

"Yes."

That's it. No qualification. No explanation.

Anger burned through Caio in fierce rivulets. But it was different from the bitterness he'd nursed for so many years. This was...pure, even selfish, a challenging burn he welcomed. "On that ridiculous yacht party with Peter Jr. and his deadbeat friends?"

"Do you want me to run my itinerary by you?" she said with exaggerated sweetness.

The minx was baiting him. Fine, if she wanted to play games, he would.

"You won't even stay for the reading of the will?"

She shrugged. "There's no real need for me to be there, right? Thaata's stock in OneTech would go to you. Mira, Yana and I will inherit various other assets. Just as he and you planned."

"You know, the more you hang out with that crowd, the more you're beginning to sound like a trust fund brat. Full of privilege and disregard for anything that doesn't touch you directly."

"That's unfair."

Some devil in him wanted to goad her, wanted to punish her for making him want something he couldn't have. "Is it? You know OneTech is in the middle of a hostile takeover that Peter Sr. has been planning from the moment he heard Rao's sick. Do you give a damn about Rao's vision? About the hundreds of employees whose fate hangs in the balance? About all the programs that Rao and I implemented that will eat dust if Peter wins the takeover and kicks me out?"

"I'm sure you have a plan to stop him from all of it. Important, life-altering plans," she bit out, throwing his words back at him. "I wasn't begging for reassurance when I said you never needed me. As to me being privileged…if that's how you truly see me, then screw you. I've never taken anything Thaata gave us for granted. I've even fought with him over who pays Mama's astronomical clinic bills and won. I've worked, just as hard as you have, over the last decade. In fact, that's all I have done." The metal legs of her chair scraped along the floor as her eyes flashed fury at him. "You know, I'm beginning to see you were right. You *are* a heartless bastard when things don't go your way. Maybe I've had a narrow escape from—"

He grabbed her wrist when she pushed off from her chair. The idea of her going off with a man he loathed was twisting him up inside out. But it was no reason to take it out on her. "I'm sorry, Nush. I have no excuse."

She stared down at him, her chest rising and falling, her usually mobile mouth pinched. Slowly, she nodded.

He should've let go of her then. Instead, he ran his fingers over her wrist, loving the wild thrum of her pulse underneath. He wanted her, he admitted to himself then, for himself. He wanted to act on it. He wanted to finish what she'd started that night and all the different filthy ways he wanted to finish it…if he told her, would she blush? Or would she, with her usual enthusiasm, tell him to get on with it?

Every muscle in him jumped at the acknowledgment. But he could find no way to rationalize acting on it. No way he couldn't hurt her in doing so. No way he could let her become such a big distraction—and that was what she would be—when he was so close to achieving his goal.

She pulled her hand away from his and stared down at her plate. "If not for the fact that Mira asked Yana and me to stay back for a few days to be with her—the first time she's asked anything for me and Yana ever," she added, "I'd have left three nights ago."

Shock pummeled him, punching his breath out of his chest. "Without even saying goodbye?"

Another shrug.

Caio decided to stop playing nice. To stop wondering the whys and whats of the inner workings of his twisted mind. Right now, all he knew was that he couldn't let Nush go off on some months-long holiday. Not until he could figure out a way to smooth this thing between them. No way was he simply giving her up just yet. "You and I signed a contract to deliver a model worth ten billion dollars in eight months. You also know that Rao's sudden death has set us back by weeks."

He paused, gathering every ounce of steely resolve he could muster. "If you leave now, I'll have the lawyers sue you."

Head jerking up, Nush glared at him. "You're bluffing. You wouldn't—"

"Try me, Princesa."

Frustration made her bang the glass against the table, spilling the orange juice all over. "Why are you doing this?"

"Why are you so determined to run away with a bunch of no-good jerks you couldn't stand to be around even as an impressionable teenager? You can't convince me that it's truly what you want."

Grabbing a napkin and wiping her fingers, she sat back in her seat and studied the man in front of her.

Anger and something else made her itch for a fight. Outrage that he was playing dirty? A strange satisfaction that finally, finally, she was seeing the true Caio? A cocktail of emotions thrummed through her and she wanted to keep drinking it. Just when she'd finally accepted that the kiss was how far he would allow it to go.

She'd stayed in her grandfather's leather chair long after he'd left that night, arms tucked around her knees, fighting the urge to chase after him. Fighting the urge to get in his face and make him acknowledge that while she'd started a tender exploration, he was the one who'd turned it into a carnal caress. Telling herself that she didn't regret kissing him. Not for a moment. Not ever.

Even now, if she closed her eyes, she could remember the bite of his teeth on her lower lip, the tight grip of his fingers as he'd tilted her head back for better access, feel the echo of his growl reverberate through her limbs.

She'd kissed other men in search of that spark, to prove to her body and mind that it was habit, or comfort or some undefinable quality that pulled her toward Caio.

But even with his golden gaze burning holes through her composure and determination, steely arrogance etched onto his every feature about how this was going to play out, Nush knew things had changed between them and it sent a thrilling shiver through her.

She'd spent years studying every nuance in his face and she knew his tics. Her heart rabbited in her chest.

It was in the way his gaze had swept over her bare shoulders and legs when she'd walked toward him. In the way it lingered just a fraction of a second longer over her lips when she'd licked the jam. In the way he even sat now, stiff and tense, as if he was consciously containing his movements.

Whether he'd act on those baser instincts driving him…she couldn't take a bet.

She lifted her coffee cup and took a sip of the smooth

brew, wanting to poke at his control. "Do you know that what you're doing is called cockblocking?"

His eyes came alive with a wicked, devilish intent that said he was ready to play. He kicked one leg out and leaned the other foot on top of the first knee in a move that spoke of pure dominance. "Is that why you're going on this trip with a bunch of brats? To chase cock?"

Her cheeks burned fiercely at hearing that word on his lips but she couldn't retreat. Not now, when it was finally on. "Did you think I'd bury myself in the lab and cry over your rejection? It's lust. And who knows? Maybe it's just a product of exposure and proximity and convenience. I have spent hours locked up with you in that lab. I'll just have to find a new channel for it."

Caio flicked at an imaginary speck of dust from his collar. "I have to tell you, *querida*, Peter doesn't have the greatest reputation in that department."

"Peter and you are not the only fish in the sea."

Anger tightened the rugged planes of his face. "So you just want to make a host of bad decisions, that you won't even truly enjoy, in the name of living it up? Run away from your commitments?"

Ire shot through her. "I'd never turn my back on contractual obligations. And it's not due for another year. I'll start work on it in six months. Get your piece ready, then we'll put it together on time."

"That borders on arrogance given that it's the most complex project you and I have ever taken on."

"Then it's your fault, isn't it? You taught me too well."

A glimmer of a smile appeared on his grave face. And for a second, he was the man she trusted the most in the entire world. "And you're the one who insisted that project planning team provide sufficient buffer period, Nush." Something glittered in those golden eyes. "You're intent on running away at the most critical juncture of One-Tech's existence. You leave me no choice but to think it's because you've been denied what you think you want."

"That's where you're wrong. I know what I want."

"Throwing a tantrum when you can't have your way, I'd expect something like that of Yana. At least she doesn't pretend to be anything but who she is."

And just like that, he delivered a truth that Nush didn't want to face. She couldn't even say he was manipulating her because he was telling her nothing but the truth. "Don't, Caio."

"Don't what? Make you face reality? Tell you that I can't afford to walk away like you, Princesa? Or to act out like Yana. Or to hide from it all like Mira. I can't do whatever I please."

"You're as ruthless as people claim you are."

It was almost as if he was glad for the aggression between them. Glad that he didn't have to pussyfoot around her now that she'd openly attacked him. "You've seen nothing yet, Nush."

Then he pushed off from the table, dismissing her as he did any other employee who didn't please him. Showing her that opaque hardness, the ruthless will that could reduce someone to a quivering mess.

"I'll hate you if you force me to stay, Caio."

He stilled, his shoulders tense. Every line of his body radiating displeasure. "Then you prove my point, Nush. You're no more grown up now than you were when you fought Rao and me about your Mom being sent to a care home permanently, even knowing that you couldn't look after her daily. Than when you used me to fight your battles with Rao."

His words made shame burn through her, rooting her to the spot. Even the warmth of the sun felt harsh and judging on her face. He tucked a lock of hair behind her ear, drawing a response automatically and mocking it. "Run away if you must, Princesa. But let's at least agree that you're definitely not ready for anything with me."

CHAPTER FIVE

IT TOOK EVERYTHING Nush had in her to walk into Caio's office at OneTech towers a week later. More than she had in her, in fact, to not turn tail and run away when she saw not only both her sisters present but also the last person she wanted to see—Laura Huntington.

Out of the periphery of her vision, she saw Caio straighten in his leather chair. With the floor-to-ceiling glass walls behind him, sunlight bathed his broad frame in an outline she knew well, keeping his expression in the dark.

That's for the best, she told herself, moving across the vast office toward her sisters. She and Caio hadn't spoken or even looked at each other in the week since their confrontation. Mostly because she'd been licking her wounds in private, letting Mira and Yana take her out for shopping and lunch and a much-needed spa day.

In hindsight, it had been exactly what she'd needed to gain perspective. Especially after learning that, in a shocking turn of events, Thaata had left all of his stock in OneTech to her. Not Caio, even though he'd promised to facilitate the transfer.

That and her mom's sudden and fiercely lucid reminder that she hadn't raised a coward who tucked tail and ran away when things didn't go her way had finally made her face up to the truth. But knowing what she needed to do didn't make it exactly easy to…do.

Caio saw her as a girl to be protected, as a naive, unworldly innocent because that was how she'd chosen to act, how she'd chosen to conduct her life.

No more.

Thaata had intended for her to head OneTech alongside Caio. That much had become clear from the fact that she'd inherited all of his stock in OneTech and not Mira or Yana.

She wasn't going to let Laura or her family railroad Caio into a partnership he didn't want, just for OneTech's sake. He'd done enough for them. Enough of him thinking OneTech's legacy and even Nush herself were his responsibilities to be protected at any cost.

It was time to grow up.

Yes, because your proposal is completely without any selfish motives, a voice whispered.

"I want to talk to Caio. Alone," she announced loudly before her determination deserted her and she retreated into sterile safety.

Both Mira and Yana looked shocked enough that Nush knew this was the right thing to do. She'd been passive and inert and living her life in her own head for too long. Her sisters' expressions were full of a confidence that Nush embraced like a childhood blanket as they left.

"If it's about saving OneTech from the hostile takeover my father's planning," Laura offered, "I should stay."

"Actually it's up to me now," Nush managed through a dry throat.

She didn't miss how Caio straightened from his chair, how his gaze focused on her face with that laser-like intense focus. Arms folded, Laura looked to Caio for direction.

Nush exhaled, fighting the thread of anger weaving through her. It wasn't Laura's fault that she dismissed

Nush, was it? She'd always preferred to leave the boardroom politics to Caio and her grandfather. But enough was enough. "Leave us, Laura. Now."

Whatever she heard in her tone, Laura complied this time. Only when the double doors closed behind her did Nush face Caio.

He'd walked around his massive desk and leaned against it, legs crossed. Through sheer willpower, Nush stopped her gaze from drifting up and down his body.

Still, there was so much of him to see, to absorb. He'd always been an energy source she'd gravitated to. From the custom-made white dress shirt that lovingly spanned the breadth of his shoulders to the column of his corded neck visible with the buttons undone to his chest, to the edges of the tattoo peeking out. He'd long ago discarded the suit jacket and the tie, had clearly run his hand through his wavy hair a few times—in anger or frustration or both.

The impact of their gazes meeting was like a thump of a fist against her chest. A flicker of heat flashed in those golden-brown eyes as they swept over her and left just as soon. Like a shooting star. Leaving Nush to wonder if she'd imagined it because she wanted to see it.

She patted a hand over her midriff, searching for the right words, nervous and way too aware of her own skin. But she had to get used to this level of awareness constantly.

"I'm surprised to see you're still here."

Nush bristled even as she welcomed the taunt. She'd take his animosity, his anger, his challenges, even deal with his monstrous ego—*Hello, Caio's ego*—if it meant he wasn't coddling her. This was progress.

"Come to say a final goodbye?"

"That would make you happy, wouldn't it? Then you can just dismiss me as..." Nush closed her eyes and fought to take a deep breath.

When she looked back at him, those golden eyes regarded her thoughtfully.

"I've decided to put off my...break for the time being. A few weeks probably. Until my new plan takes care of every problem."

Fury raced across his features before he schooled his features back into that impenetrable mask he showed everyone. "And may I ask why the sudden change of heart?" Something sinuous trickled through the air between them. "Please don't tell me there's truth to the rumors of alliance..." he spat it like the word was distasteful on his tongue, "between you and him?"

"You're the one who's obsessed with the idea of him and me, Caio. You and his father."

"So you aren't marrying that idiot then?" Caio asked, his face still set in taut lines, no glimmer of humor in his eyes.

Nush walked to the sitting area and poured herself a glass of water, her heart thundering at how close he came to the heart of the matter. "God, no," she said over her shoulder before drinking it all in one go.

She'd barely put the glass down when he stood before her, taking up personal space, sending her pulse flying.

"Then why have you been spending the last few days at his penthouse with his gang of useless deadbeats? Did you know that Peter Huntington Sr. has been going around insinuating that an engagement announcement is imminent? That your..." his upper lip lifted in obvious disgust, "union is the new direction that OneTech needs desperately."

It took some serious facial gymnastics to keep the satisfied smile that wanted to bloom off her face.

Maybe she was going about this the wrong way. Maybe putting her feelings out there every time Caio demanded wasn't the way to go. And maybe...just maybe a little petty revenge wasn't quite out of her reach.

"What I was doing with Peter is none of your business now, is it? As to his father, I'd think you'd know better than to believe anything the man says. He's always tried to cause a rift between you and Thaata. Now he's playing the same games with you and me."

Caio flicked at his cuffs and Nush knew it was to hide his relief. "For a woman who keeps changing her mind every two hours, you seem to be very aware of everyone else's motivations."

"Don't get used to it," she said on a sigh. "I'm only playing along until things settle down. Until I get what I want."

"Which is what exactly, Anushka? A week ago, you couldn't wait to get far away from…here," he said, using her own words.

"I'm allowed to change my mind, aren't I?"

"Why though?"

"Because you were right. I was running away from… a lot of things. And that's not the kind of person Thaata hoped I'd be. And you, your actions, your rejection… I can't let it define me either."

A low, soft curse escaped him. "I didn't reject you. I—"

"Let's not get into semantics, shall we?" She added a casual shrug. Maybe this was the way to get over this ridiculous attraction—to pretend that she was over it. If she did it long enough, she'd start to believe it too. "The fact is I'm not going anywhere right now. And I have a solution to keep OneTech in your hands."

A muscle jumped in Caio's cheek. Tension radiated from him as he ran a hand over his jaw. And for the first time in days, Nush felt like she was finally standing on hard ground.

"Unless…" She couldn't help adding, "You're the one with the problem now?"

"What the hell does that mean?"

"You don't look happy to see me, Caio. If it's going to be this hard for you to be around me, then I'm not sure my plan has a chance of—"

He pushed off the desk with such lethal elegance that Nush had to force herself to stay still and not step back. Stopping just close enough for her to breathe in the scent of him, to feel the heat of his body, now familiar in a different way, hit hers, unspooling that wanton need in her lower belly. Those enigmatic eyes studied her, flicking from her eyes to her nose to her mouth and then back up. "I didn't realize you were capable of playing games, Princesa." Pure challenge dripped in every single word. "Especially with me."

Two more steps and she could press her chest against his. Two more steps and she could learn if he was affected by her proximity at all. Two more steps and…

She shrugged again, and wondered if it would become a tic she couldn't control soon. "I'm just making sure you're okay with my presence, Caio. It's imperative that we get along, despite our…*differences*, if you want me to save OneTech."

"Save OneTech? Then why didn't you attend the board meeting this morning?" His mouth flattened. "I could've used your support there—seeing as you now own all of Rao's stock."

The bitter twist of his lips made her forget all her anger with him. "Are you angry with Thaata?"

He took in a deep breath. "I don't know if I should admit it to you, Nush."

Nush gripped his wrist, realizing how close they stood until he stilled. "Whatever else has occurred between us, or not occurred," she said, "I'd never turn against you, Caio. Do you think he just forgot after Nanamma's loss?"

"No," Caio said, surprising her. "Rao had a mind like a steel trap. He didn't forget anything. He left you everything knowing full well what he was doing. Knowing I'd resent him for it."

Surprised, Nush stared at him. "But why?"

Caio shrugged. And Nush had a feeling he knew. But he would never tell her. And really, she had no interest in knowing what the ongoing battle between him and Thaata had been about. She didn't need any more headaches.

"Whatever Thaata's reason, he must have underestimated my intense dislike for boardroom backstabbing *and* my loyalty toward you."

It was Caio's turn to look shocked. But he didn't let her linger on it by moving toward her, his gaze as impenetrable as ever. "You're still loyal to me after everything that happened, Princesa?"

"Of course I am," Nush said, trying to make light of the matter. "That's what being an adult is actually about, isn't it? Putting aside personal differences and doing the right thing for everyone? I've never doubted that OneTech belongs in your hands. And thankfully, I've figured out a way to make that happen."

His gaze searched hers, a vertical line appearing between his thick brows. Her fingers tingled at her side, itching to press at that ridge he got when he was thinking, wanting to smooth it away. "How?"

"We'll marry. I can sign over my stock to you, you'll be the majority stakeholder, even more than before, and I can go back to my lab."

"No. Absolutely not," Caio said in a soft voice even as the idea took wings in his head and began fluttering at a speed that he couldn't contain.

Nush would be his wife. He wouldn't have to worry

about her or how to protect her from fortune hunters and their clutches now that she was even wealthier.

Rao's vision for OneTech would be preserved.

Peter Huntington Sr.'s grubby, greedy hands could be kept off the company.

Nush was ready finally, clearly, to step in and take a bigger role at the helm of OneTech, as Rao had always wanted.

Whatever Rao had thought to thwart Caio from would again become a distinct possibility as the CEO of OneTech.

Her idea was perfect in every which way, took care of every eventuality. In theory, it was the best solution.

He would pay millions more than the stock was actually worth—he wouldn't undercut her in any way. All he'd need to do was sign a piece of paper that legally bound her to him.

The reality was a leap of a universe away. She'd be his wife. In every way that could mean. The woman he hadn't been able to stop thinking of kissing would be his wife. Would have his deepest commitment. Because for all that Rao had called him cynical, Caio had always believed that marriage was a beautiful bond between people who gave it trust and love. Papa and Mama had shared a marriage like that.

Rao and his wife had shared a commitment like that.

And while he'd never seen it in his future after the mistakes he'd made by falling for his stepbrother's intended, a commitment to Nush would be different.

And his imagination and his libido ran little circles in his head, already breaking any rules he might want to put in place.

"No."

With a long exhale, as if he was nothing but an irritable child throwing a tantrum, Nush simply ignored his outburst, picked up the watering can, filled it at the attached en suite and began watering the plants on the ledge.

Plants she'd added to his office almost two years ago after calling it "a sterile, ugly box made of glass and chrome and leather" that might permanently damage his mental balance. As he'd discovered in the last few days, while stewing in jealousy and protectiveness and something else that he didn't want to think of, there was no erasing Nush from his life.

Wherever he turned, every nook and corner of his personal life he examined over the last decade, she was present. With her laughter, with her genius, with her awkwardness, with her grief, she'd etched herself into the fabric of his life.

And if she were to become his wife too…he'd end up hurting her. Shattering her.

But Caio also knew that he had no good reason to say no to her proposal. Not unless he was also ready to admit that he hadn't been able to stop thinking of their kiss.

It had taken him every ounce of willpower he had to not check on her in the last week. To not go rushing in like some possessive, protective male on steroids and drag her far away from Peter's influence. To not demand that she should know her worth better.

Instead, he'd acknowledged—how mature and self-aware of him—that it was time to let go. Both for his sake and hers. Time for her to make her own decisions—even bad ones—even though she'd clung to him when he'd kissed her, even though she'd declared that she'd wanted him for months. He'd even told himself that he'd been right to think it nothing but an infatuation borne out of grief and loss.

The last thing he'd expected was that she'd be back, full of that verve, those big eyes staring him down, armed with an idea that could change things for the better. Or worse.

Sunlight streaming through the glass walls outlined her body, as if just for his pleasure. For the first time since she'd walked in, Caio allowed himself to take her in completely, take in the differences in her that he hadn't been able to stop cataloguing. It was a losing battle anyway.

The white dress shirt stretched tight across her chest and shoulders, and the dark skinny jeans she'd tucked into only reminded him of those legs bare, long muscles glinting. Her hair had been subdued into two braids and the glasses were back on. She looked chic and sexy and stylish in a way that didn't conform to any standards set by others.

It was all Anushka Reddy—genius coder, socially awkward with a dirty mouth and a sensuous appeal that hit one like a punch to the solar plexus.

And the thin tie, multicolored and with lines of code all over, dangling innocently between her breasts… Cristo, one look at her and all he'd wanted to do was undo that tie, wrap his fingers around it to pull her closer, to slip his fingers under that shirt and…

"Caio, you're staring." She cleared her throat, ridding herself of that huskiness he wanted to hear again and again. "In a way that tells me you're imagining—"

"Jesus, Nush. Stop."

She ran a hand over the damned tie and then played with the edges of it. Her nails, painted a dark rust color, shone bright. Like her presence suddenly brightened his office. "Look, if we're going to be married, it's better to set things straight from the beginning, don't you think?

I really don't want to pretend like we don't want to rip each other's clothes off and—"

His hand on her shoulder shut her up. Pink crested her cheeks but the daring minx held his gaze steadily. "If this is some kind of twisted game of petty revenge—"

"I wouldn't sink so low." Her chin dipped to her chest. "After Mira told me about the will and how…shocked you were, I realized what a god-awful mess I'd be leaving OneTech in if I left. Drunk Peter let me know of his father's plans for the hostile takeover. I…couldn't sleep that night. To let Thaata's hard work and vision go to waste like that, to see the culture of the company change from what you and he built, the thought of all of those community programs canceled…all so the board members could pad their already fat pockets. It would be nothing but sheer cowardice. So I scheduled a call with Aristos and we went over everything—"

"You went to your sister's estranged husband?" That she had gone to Aristos instead of him incensed Caio.

"Yes. With Aristos, there are no preconceptions. He hears me, sees me."

"And I don't?"

A short laugh, full of scorn, escaped her lovely mouth. "We both know you don't. Or rather you have an outdated version of me in your head that you won't update. And it crashes the entire system."

Caio knew she was right, at least to an extent. He had a lot of preconceptions about her. About the role he wanted her to play in his life. About keeping her separate from the dirty politics of his everyday life. About not letting anything in the world hurt her…and yet, it was becoming clear that those very notions were hurting her. That his refusal to accept her as she was now was hurting her.

"Does Mira know that you talked to him?" Caio asked, just to poke holes in her plan.

"No," Nush said with a roll of her eyes that said she saw through his cheap tricks. "It's got nothing to do with her, or you."

"Why him?" Caio couldn't help but admire her. She had covered all her bases, had thought of every possibility.

"Aristos has always been kind to me and he's an internationally renowned corporate lawyer and someone I could trust and—"

"I have a hard time believing he told you to marry me."

"No. He helped me understand how things stand. After this, I can go back to being—"

"Being my worker droid, you mean," he said, feeling the sting afresh all over again. At least, Nush had the grace to look ashamed.

"Something like that."

"You know, the number of times that comes up, I'm beginning to believe you truly think that I exploit your brain for personal gain. For the record, I resent that."

"I was angry when I said that. I'm over it now. For you to use me would mean that you have to first see me as your equal, right? It would be an actual development in our stilted relationship. I'm realizing you've a very twisted set of values."

"Nush..."

"Please, I can't spend another minute explaining to you that it's not abnormal or wrong or dirty somehow for me to want you. I'm twenty-three years old and yes, you're fourteen years older than me, but it's not like you're my father or cousin or...anything even remotely bordering on *ewww*." Her chest rose and fell with her agitation. "Although now that it's become clear how you see me, I'm half over it already. There's nothing more pathetic than lusting after a man who thinks you're a little girl who needs his protection."

She was more woman than any he'd ever met, Caio wanted to say. There was anger and determination in her, but there was also fear and something else he couldn't put his finger on. And yet, she was here. She'd taken the risk of approaching him with an idea despite the risk of his rejection again.

He held off all the words that rose to his lips, refusing to let his emotions drive him. He'd already done that once. He hadn't been cruel on purpose, but he'd been hard on her.

Arms folded at his chest, he watched her—her fire, her mobile mouth, her disillusion with him. A part of him wanted to believe that her infatuation with him had truly passed. A part of him wanted to prove the opposite—with his mouth and hands and body—that she wasn't over him. For the first time in almost two decades, his mind and his heart seemed to be going in opposite directions. Leaving him irritable and tense, distracting him from his goal.

And now her outrageous idea that they should marry... the greedy, grabby part of him said she was the most valuable possession he'd ever possessed, urged him to accept the proposition. For now, at least.

He hadn't asked her for her help.

And yet, what if he hurt her tender feelings for him? Would he be able to face himself if he took advantage of her?

"I can see that you've put a lot of thought into this," he said slowly, fighting for reason amidst two conflicting parts of himself, "but—"

"A lot of thought?" Nush snorted. "I've spent a week talking to people I don't like, hanging out with Peter and his deadbeat friends listening to them talk about women as if they were dogs or horses, a day listening to my father bitch about Thaata and Nanamma and how they cheated him out of his rights and then I went to see Mama and she was in a *mood.* You can't believe I did any of it on a sudden whim."

She settled onto the couch, and stretched her long legs out in front of her, her chin dropping to her chest. "I'm all peopled out, Caio. Probably for the next decade." A long exhale shuddered out of her. "I don't know what Thaata was thinking leaving me all that stock. They're all piranhas and sharks and vultures and... I can even see why you have to be so ruthless day in, day out."

She'd sat in that very couch so many times over the years, come to him with some problem and asked for his help. And she'd always looked at him with such trust that Caio had felt like a hero. As if she was a conduit for him to make himself feel better.

Which was problematic in itself.

"Your idea, I'll admit, has merit," he said carefully, testing out the words on his tongue. "It solves our problems in a very comprehensive way."

Fingers laced at her neck pulled her shirt tightly across her torso as Nush studied him from under her lashes. "You wouldn't have sounded like it was a death sentence if it was Mira or even Yana proposing this...arrangement. I mean, you even dated Yana at Nanamma's urging. Why is it such a leap for you when all along Thaata wanted you to marry into the family? We both know that if Mira hadn't eloped with Aristos over a weekend, she'd have been suggested to you next."

A sliver of hurt in her words made him cautious with

his own. "It's not a death sentence, Nush," he said looking down at her. "I already admitted that it's a good idea."

"But? You're not already married, are you? Because, Jesus, that could be horrible on so many—"

"Of course I'm not married."

Color high in her cheeks, she shrugged. "Well, it's not that much of a leap seeing none of us know much about you."

"I want to make sure you're not walking into this with any sort of…expectations."

"The fact that I'm here, further entangling our lives when I want to be nowhere near you, is only because I decided it's time to take responsibility for OneTech. For Thaata's legacy. Now, please, let's talk logistics. Then we can go back to avoiding each other."

"Is that what you were doing?"

"Prenup," she said, ignoring his question, counting out on her fingers. "How long we have to put up this charade for. What our statement to the media looks like. And, oh, yeah…"

"Prenup?" he said, more than surprised that she'd truly thought of everything.

"Yes. I went back to Aristos with my idea and he stressed that I get one."

"Because you can't trust me?"

"Oh, his first piece of advice was that my idea was a garbage fire. That I should stay far away from you. But then he also said that in a professional capability, you'd be the only man he'd trust, even before his own family."

"You have to know that I'd never—"

"That you'd never…ruin me financially. Yes, I know that. We're all very mature people here, with honor and integrity coming out of our asses. Honestly, all I want on the prenup is that if you cheat on me, I can sue your ass for everything you have."

"Cheat on you, Nush?" he said, her bloodthirstiness knotting his stomach tight with a hunger like he'd never known before. "That implies a prior commitment. Is this more than a simple marriage bargain on paper?"

"Yes. No." Her cheeks reddened. "I don't care if you think I'm not sophisticated enough for you to screw, Caio. But I draw the line at the world seeing you parade your long lineup of girlfriends while you're married to me. So yes, I want your commitment to not making me look like a fool in front of the world. Apparently, there's only so much my pride can take."

"And you, Nush? Will you promise the same? Will you stop chasing—"

"Yes, of course," she said, blowing at her bangs. "That's why we need to put a time limit on this. The celibate life is *not* for me."

"I wouldn't think so, given the number of dates you've been on in just the past year," he added drily.

"I hope you appreciate the sacrifice I'm making for the good of the company…blah, blah, Caio. All this adulting is exhausting." A glint in her eye caught his attention as she studied her nails. "I've completely accepted the possibility that the only two candidates that might bring me pleasure are this pink vibrator Yana gave me last year for my birthday or you."

Instant heat gripped him, a fist around his cock, making his skin hum. She was taunting him. He knew that. She was going to continue taunting him for however long they stayed married. Still, he couldn't beat away all the images her words conjured. Couldn't think of a better torment.

"Which reminds me," she said, and texted rapidly on

her cell phone. “Yana promised to get me the latest model. Might as well stock up.”

“Is that your plan then? To seduce me?”

“I guess that means you don’t assume I hatched this whole plan to have you?”

He laughed at the idea and then sobered when he saw the very real apprehension in her eyes. Grabbing her hand, which he’d done a thousand times before, Caio squeezed it. “If it were Yana, maybe yes. But you’re far too straightforward for such a conniving plan.”

“Thank the universe for small mercies.” Her throat moved on a swallow, and she plucked her hand from his. “I won’t let everything Thaata worked for get destroyed because of my insecurities.” Grabbing the oversized jacket she’d discarded, she slipped it on. “As for seducing you, I wouldn’t know where to begin. But let’s say that I do have high hopes for this fake marriage.”

“Ahh.” Suddenly, the idea of Nush trying to seduce him sounded like a fantasy he hadn’t known he’d want. “What are those hopes?”

“Either we’ll have sex and I can work you out of my system—because all the fantasies I’ve spun about how good it will be can’t be real.” Her throat moved down on a hard swallow. “Or we don’t have sex but I realize what a controlling, arrogant, emotionally cold man you are and, hello…sweet liberation from two years of unrequited lust.”

Two years? She’d wanted him for two years? Not just months. Which meant she’d dated all those men for what?

Caio rubbed a hand over his face. If he’d needed any more proof that he didn’t really know Nush, here it was. Not once, by gesture or look, had she let on that she was attracted to him. Not once had she acted differently with him.

"Why didn't you tell me?" The question escaped his lips despite his resolution to not dwell on this giant elephant that populated their relationship now.

"It's attraction, Caio. Desire. Lust. And this marriage… it's just an amendment to our partnership, isn't it? Like the one you suggested all those years ago. And when it's over, I can move on with my life. Without you in it."

She left without waiting for his assent. Because it was a given. They had no other choice.

He had no other choice. Not if he wanted to buy his stepfather's company and break it off for parts. Not if he wanted to look him in the eyes and let the abusive bully see his destruction in Caio's eyes.

Running a hand through his hair, he paced the length of his office, feeling like a caged tiger. For the first time in almost two decades, he felt like he'd been sucker punched.

He'd been angry with Rao for leaving all of his stock to Nush, for making her a target for both fortune hunters and the likes of Peter Huntington Sr., sharks already circling fresh blood. For leaving Caio with a god-awful mess instead of signing the papers that transferred his stock to Caio.

And yet, was this what his mentor had intended? For all he'd been a man of integrity, he'd played games like a maestro. Had Rao foreseen all along that Caio would be pushed to such lengths to protect both OneTech and even more importantly Nush? Or had he thought only to thwart what he'd called Caio's corrosive, self-destructive need for revenge, even from beyond the grave?

And yet, Nush had delivered everything Caio needed straight into his hands. Along with herself.

In his wildest dreams, he hadn't imagined that he'd be left with no other choice but to marry Nush. Or that every muscle in him would curl with anticipation.

Or most unthinkable of all—that the idea of marriage to the one woman who'd always brought out the best in him would fill him with a desperate need to make their arrangement permanent *and* real.

CHAPTER SIX

NUSH STARED AT the beautiful diamond ring set in a princess setting and a simple platinum band, a boulder a hundred times the size of the twinkling diamond lodging in her throat.

If only the ring had been big and garish…

If only she hadn't described the exact same style to Yana once at a jewelry store, which meant Caio had asked Yana what she'd like…

If only she hadn't wished, with all the fervent hope of a fourteen-year-old, that she'd find a man exactly like Caio to marry one day…

If only she hadn't let Yana persuade her to dress in a knee-length, ivory-colored sheath dress that made her look too much like a blushing, hopeful bride…

If only she hadn't let Mira convince her to have the ceremony in the backyard of her grandparents' house, just in case her mama wanted to attend.

If only Mama had stuck to her obstinate, hardheaded will and refused to attend.

If only all of them hadn't been convinced that they had to at least make it look real and romantic with Peter Huntington Sr. spreading vile rumors about Caio's supposed dark, wicked seduction of poor, innocent lamb that was her—because God forbid she could think for herself…

If only Caio hadn't worn a black suit that made him look like her every fantasy come true…

If only she wasn't a naive, impressionable, sorry idiot whose heart took dangerous flight when he stared at her with a thoughtful glint in his eyes when she arrived to stand by him…

If only her skin didn't tingle every time he touched her even innocently…

If only she'd realized that sneaky universe granted your wishes if you weren't careful—but not in the way you'd hoped for…

If only she hadn't acted on her desire and kissed him and didn't have to live with knowing how he tasted against her lips…

So many *if onlys* that should've stopped the fake ceremony from becoming all too real.

Until the moment when Caio had slid the ring onto her finger, she hadn't pondered too much on how the moment would land. How many real dreams she'd woven around finding that special someone who'd always want her, love her, need her in return. How much she didn't want to end up like her mom—angry and distant with a brittle self-sufficiency that had never served her or Nush well. How much shifting Caio into this new role in her mind and in her life made her feel anchorless, all of a sudden. How much of a raw, vulnerable and tangled mess a simple kiss could make of everything.

Was that her fate? To always want people in her life who in turn wanted to never let her in? To be abandoned by anyone she got attached to?

God, now she was feeling sorry for herself, and that was something she truly hated.

No, she couldn't let it go to her head or her heart. She had to stop giving away pieces of herself to Caio.

This arrangement of theirs had a shelf life.

After an hour of a placid, vacant smile, her cheeks hurt. Her scalp hurt from the complicated knot Yana had twisted her hair into and her feet hurt in the four-inch stilettos that she wasn't used to. And more than anything, her heart hurt—raged at the understanding grimace/smile Laura Huntington had cast Caio.

Commiserating with him over the big sacrifice he'd made by saddling himself with an unwanted bride, all for the good of OneTech.

It didn't matter that it had been Nush's own plan. That she'd seen the satisfaction in Caio's eyes when everything had been signed and transferred, that she needn't worry about the vision Thaata had held for the company.

With one pitying look, Laura reminded Nush that for Caio this was an unwanted wedding. An arrangement he'd been cornered into by circumstances. And it was the hard reminder Nush very much needed.

By seven in the evening, Caio had been locked up in his study with a team of lawyers and the executive team of OneTech—Laura included. Yana had kissed her on the cheek before she'd disappeared. Nush ended up dancing and chatting endlessly with Peter Jr. of all people, who seemed to have decided she needed looking after while her new husband ignored her.

After seeing her mom safely into the chauffeured car, she'd had enough.

The changes she'd wanted to make in her life didn't have to stop at owning her responsibilities with OneTech. Fake marriage or not, her life was still hers to live. Clinging to Caio for the few crumbs of his attention would only bring her back to square one.

Caio was knocking on Anushka's closed bedroom door when Mira found him. Her calm, placid gaze flicked to the dark violet velvet box in his hands and then back to his face.

"Where is she?" he said softly. Agitation thrummed through him after he'd spent three quarters of an hour looking for Nush.

Mira shook her head.

When he glared, she sighed. "I only know she wanted to get out of here."

Caio waited, knowing that Mira had more to say. Out of the three sisters, Mira was the one he understood best, the one who was the most like him. She'd gone through a lot as a child, with a mother who'd abandoned her and an alcoholic father who left her to his parents to be raised.

Mira understood responsibility, duty and that some wounds would never heal. All you could do was to make sure the poison didn't seep out and ruin the people around. It was guiding his behavior with Nush.

But the damned woman challenged every one of his good intentions. He'd planned for them to have dinner with some of his closest associates, to show her his appreciation for helping him achieve his life's goal, though she was unaware of it. He'd planned to spend the evening with her. Only when he'd emerged from his meeting, Nush had disappeared.

Did she think her responsibilities to OneTech, to him, ended with her signature? He hadn't missed the smirk on Peter Sr.'s face when he'd failed to locate his "wayward bride," in the older man's words. The older man was already spreading the vile rumor that Caio had taken advantage of the poor, clueless Reddy heiress. And that it was far too close to the truth grated on him like nothing else had ever done.

"Mira?" he prompted with little patience.

"I'm betraying my sister's confidence by discussing her with you."

"Anushka has no secrets from me," he said, wanting it to be true more than it really was.

"Yana said something happened between you. Did she tell you then?"

Now it was Caio who felt as if he was betraying the woman he'd spoken vows to this morning.

They should have been simply words. Meaningless. Trite. Even taunting. Instead he'd found a strange solemnity to them as he looked at the woman who had always given him her trust, whether he'd deserved it or not. Who'd always looked at him as if he were a sunbeam that had brightened her day. Who reminded him of the man Papa had hoped Caio would be one day. That look in her eyes was an addiction he couldn't shake.

She'd looked achingly beautiful, and yet out of place in a dress and makeup she never wore. And when he'd seen her distress, her eyes widening at the profound gravity of the ceremony, he'd felt that conflicting war within himself.

He wanted to give Nush the world—answer the desire he'd felt in her trembling form when he'd kissed her cheek—and he also wanted to protect her from himself.

Damn it, what the hell did he want? Why was he so upset that she'd abandoned him an hour after their wedding?

"I think the whole ceremony…the way it went down… freaked her out. Then there was Laura Huntington."

Caio frowned. "What didn't she like? And what about Laura?"

"You have such a razor-sharp brain when it comes to business and politics, but you are just as dense as any other man when it comes to women. I thought you knew Nush better."

She was upset that Laura was there. Caio repeated the words to himself. Because she thought Laura and he were together? Because she'd assumed he couldn't do without Laura even for an evening? Because they'd been buried in his study for hours straight after the short ceremony?

"I needed Laura there. There was something I needed to push through the board before I…" He stopped, knowing that he was explaining himself to the wrong woman. "So she disappears instead of asking me about it? And she says the way I see her is outdated."

"Did you expect her to make a scene?" An uncharacteristic hardness twisted Mira's mouth. "Nush never pushes, never demands anything of others, is too happy to push herself into a corner in someone's life, content to be there. She spends hours waiting outside of her mom's room at that home every weekend hoping she'll see her, wanting her to know she's there. She keeps bringing Dad home after one of his episodes, begs him to shower, eat, looks after him as if he were a child for days after. She dropped the idea of going to college in New York in some stupid bargain with Thaata so that he wouldn't throw Yana out of the house after she pulled another of her stunts."

"Of course Rao had manipulated her."

Mira let out a laugh. "She'll fight you if you even say that. That's how unconditional her loyalty is. Thaata loved us but yes, you and I know he was also a master manipulator."

And yet, Nush had told him that she was attracted to him. She'd taken the risk of kissing him. She'd come back after he'd told her she wasn't grown up enough for him, to save the company.

He hadn't appreciated how far out of her comfort zone

she'd gone. How much courage it must have taken to walk back into his office. For all of five seconds, he felt utterly inadequate to be the recipient of such…pure emotion, whatever it was.

A part of him flinched, wanted to run far from it.

He pushed a hand through his hair as another piece fell into place. "So Rao knew that she…" He couldn't put it into words. Suddenly, everything Nush had given him felt like a gift he didn't deserve.

"I think so. He probably also guessed that she'd come to your rescue." Mira rolled her eyes. "If he hadn't taken such a bad turn, I think he'd have had it stipulated in writing. Sort of purchased you for his precious princess."

He raised a brow, knowing that Mira was trying to get her own shots in. "And here I thought you were the sweetest Reddy sister, Mira."

She shrugged. "You know better now."

"I didn't know what conditions you agreed on for this… fake marriage, but I hope you remember Nush gives of herself unconditionally. Doesn't mean we all deserve it."

"Is that a warning, Mira?"

"I'm trying to appeal to the better part of you. Or maybe I know that I'm talking to a kindred soul. You and I don't know the weight of such…open trust and affection. Nor do we know how not to shatter it, Caio." Shadows swirled in her eyes. "If you care about her, at all, get this thing annulled as soon as possible."

"That's," he said with a smile trying to take the bite out of his words, every instinct and rational thought revolting against the idea of annulment, "between Nush and me. No one else."

Mira blinked. "She's the best of us all, Caio. Don't hurt her."

"Where did she go, Mira?"

"Yana mentioned something about a new nightclub."

And Caio knew who the nightclub belonged to. He bit back a curse as fierce jealousy stormed through him. Even as he knew Nush wouldn't do anything to break their… what was it between them? An arrangement? A deal? A bargain? And what did she get out of it? All the benefits in this marriage were his. And he didn't like the imbalance of that. Didn't like being in her debt one bit.

"How long are you planning for this fake marriage to last?" Mira asked, interrupting his thoughts.

"When are you going back to that husband of yours?" he taunted. "I hear he's been like a wounded beast ever since you left him. And Aristos's veneer of civility was thin enough to begin with."

"Touché," Mira said, as something like panic touched her eyes. "I… I'm going back tomorrow. To Athens. Wish me luck, won't you?"

On a sudden impulse, Caio gathered Mira to himself and hugged her petite frame. She was stiff in his arms for a few seconds before she sank into his embrace. "You'll be glad to know your estranged husband and you are on the same wavelength."

"What?" she asked, eyes wide and bright at the mere mention of Aristos. The stubborn Greek, who was as close a friend as Caio had had in the last decade, had won a point in his eyes when he'd arrived as soon as he'd heard of Rao's death and supported Mira through the grief. Granted, he'd only stayed for two days, but after nine months of his wife leaving him with no reason or note, as Aristos had shared after a couple of drinks, Caio had thought it showed what the man was made of.

"Apparently, he vehemently warned Nush against this marriage too."

She laughed then, and Caio thought there was both joy

and grief in the sound. He squeezed her slender shoulders, realizing only in that moment how she and Yana had carved themselves a place in his cold, cold heart. They'd fought with him, challenged him, forced him to earn a place in their family and then steadied him with the kind of trust and affection that he'd been parched for, ever since Papa had passed away and his loss had changed Mama into a shadow of herself. But they'd never resented him for earning such a prominent place by Rao's side in OneTech and that was generosity Rao and his wife had taught all three of their granddaughters.

Caio sent another heartfelt thanks to the man who'd saved him all those years ago.

Maybe Rao had succeeded at his mission to chip away at his bitterness to a small extent, he thought. Or stopped the poison from spreading further and turning Caio into a toxic man in the very shape and shadow of the man he loathed.

Maybe there was a future ahead of him outside of the revenge he'd planned for so long. Or maybe he was buying into the romantic nonsense of today's ceremony. There was no way he could build ridiculous, far-fetched dreams around a woman who deserved better than him. All he knew, all he planned for his future was destroying someone else.

"Will you tell Nush I said goodbye?" Mira said into the comfortable silence. "I'm leaving first thing in the morning. I don't want her to think I abandoned her."

Caio nodded. "I hope you know that you're not alone, Mira, even if Rao's gone. If you need anything—"

"Ahh…but you and I both know that in some aspects of life, we are alone, Caio. It's written into our DNA."

"What's the point then?" he asked, feeling an intense vulnerability he hadn't known still lingered.

"The point is that there's always choices, Caio. I'm making a choice to return to Aristos, even though…" She sighed. With a familiarity that made him smile, she tapped his cheek with her fingers and smiled. "Let's hope we don't mess this up."

Caio pressed a kiss to her head and left to find Nush.

CHAPTER SEVEN

It took him two and a half hours to find Nush.

She hadn't been at Peter Jr.'s nightclub. Or rather it had been a short stop in apparently a long night of chasing entertainment like some college kid off on a night's rampage.

She's no older than a college kid, a voice whispered and he cursed. Neither had she been exaggerating when she'd argued that she'd buried herself in that lab for more than a decade. Just as he'd buried himself in acquisitions and mergers that would bring him closer to his goal. Their innate nature as loners had become the foundation of their relationship.

He'd had to track down Yana and threaten her—which wasn't an easy feat since nothing and no one could really control the volatile middle Reddy sister—and get Nush's location out of her. Even that was only after she'd received a text from Nush that she'd needed help.

So here he was, outside of a luxury hotel, still chasing her. Solar lights placed along the huge courtyard punctured the bitter darkness of predawn. He'd taken no more than two steps when he saw her and stilled.

Patchy moonlight glinted along her neck and her chest as she walked through the double doors, her gait slow. She came to a halt below the entrance archway. Her hair was still in that complicated knot, but she'd changed out of the wedding dress into a black leather skirt that skimmed her knees and a ribbed white skintight top that hugged every inch of her small breasts. A white dress shirt—her signature item—flapped over her shoulders. He followed the line of her long, long legs to find her feet encased in glittery pink high-top sneakers that brought an unexpected smile to his lips.

His chest loosened, relief spreading through him. This was the Nush he knew, the girl who'd always made him laugh, the girl who'd been a bright spot in his dark, revenge-obsessed thoughts.

And yet, she wasn't just that girl anymore either.

This was a woman who'd boldly told him how much she wanted him, who'd marched into his office with a solution. This was a Nush he wanted to know more of, a woman he could see himself… With a sigh, he cut off the direction his thoughts were going in too often.

Drawing closer, Caio noted that she held her bent arm close to her chest. Then the sling wound around her neck. "What happened, Princesa?"

She stiffened, her eyes huge and wide behind the thick glasses. "Caio…" She looked at her watch and then around herself. "What are you doing here?"

He touched his fingers to hers, and nodded at the cast around her wrist. "You're hurt. How?"

"Oh, there was a scuffle at the club. I slipped and broke my fall with my wrist. The X-ray showed a hairline fracture." She sighed. "It's been quite the eventful night."

"And day," he added.

"Hmm?"

"It was our wedding day, *querida*." He'd no idea why he felt the need to remind her of that. He was beginning to wonder if he knew right or wrong when it came to her.

She plucked her hand from his looking like a deer caught in headlights. “Did Yana send you? I’m sorry that you had to drive here at this time—”

“Yana didn’t send me anywhere. I spent most of the night already looking for you. I don’t like not knowing where you are.”

She raised a brow, all outrage and bite. “Since when did I have to report to you?”

“Since always, Nush,” he said, her temper egging his on. “Why didn’t you call me?”

“I lost my phone.”

“And yet, you called Yana.”

“I don’t remember your number.”

His mouth twitched. “You’re a horrible liar.”

The bank of elevators behind them pinged. A familiar figure exited the glass car and every muscle in Caio’s body tightened with such ferocious anger that he covered the little gap between him and Nush as if she were prey.

His new, albeit unplanned acquisition.

His wife.

His. In every way that mattered.

Cristo, he couldn’t remember one good reason why he shouldn’t think of her as his, why he shouldn’t welcome this fortune that had directly fallen into his lap.

Peter Jr. took one look at him and his steps faltered.

A palm landed on Caio’s chest and his muscles clenched at the innocent contact. “Stop posturing around and intimidating Peter.”

“It’s not my fault if he’s scared of me. He knows he shouldn’t be sniffing around you.”

“Jesus, he’s not sniffing around me. And believe it or not, he was the only one who paid attention to me today.” When Caio stared at her, she pointed to the cast.

"Apparently, away from his bullying father and his band of toxic peers, he isn't half-bad. He even apologized for… Anyway, we actually talked and laughed and danced… I enjoyed his company."

Mira's words came back to haunt Caio. God, Anushka *was* too soft for her own good. Too forgiving. "Your discovery is a little too late, Princesa. He can't have you."

"What?"

He tucked a wavy lock of hair that fluttered at her jaw, taunting him. "I said he can't have you." Caio softened his own voice. "You're mine, Nush."

"Either you're continuing with the theme of mocking something that I consider sacred or you're an arrogant ass who doesn't want me but doesn't want anyone else to have me," she said, swaying on her feet, "and I—"

Caio steadied her. "You said we weren't even allowed to indulge in mild flirtations. I'm just reminding you of your own conditions."

Big, wide eyes considered him, exhaustion written into her features. "You could have just said that instead of issuing…possessive statements."

With Mira gone and Yana's unreliable and chaotic schedule, he didn't want to leave Nush alone at that big house. Which meant she was coming with him to Brazil tonight.

A huge part of him protested. He wanted to keep her separate from the poison in his life. Wanted to keep her away from all his bitterness. Wanted to keep his own image untarnished in her mind. But it wasn't an available choice anymore.

Anticipation coiled through him even as he acknowledged he had quite a fight on his hands. "Are you in pain?"

She pushed the bridge of her glasses up her nose and

nodded. "I don't think the pills have taken yet. Especially not enough to make me tolerate your territorial, jealous husband act."

When she stepped to his left, he got in her way, blocking her with his body. It was confrontational in a way he'd never addressed her before. But it didn't feel wrong either. Nothing felt wrong anymore. In fact, every filthy thought, every overwhelming urge, every spike of hot need pulsing through him felt deliciously, irrevocably right.

What the hell had those vows done to him?

When she signaled to Peter Jr, he appeared with an umbrella in hand, a small smile twisting his mouth.

Caio addressed the younger man. "Leave, Huntington."

Peter glanced in Nush's direction, mumbled something to himself, pretended as if he was considering standing up to Caio and then ran down the steps without a backward glance.

Mouth falling open, Nush stared at the fast-receding man. She slapped at Caio's abdomen with the back of her hand, her eyes round with anger. "He was my ride."

"You have me."

"Stop reminding me of those ridiculous rules. It's not like I was going to elope with him."

"I don't want you around him."

"You're a thug, Caio Oliveira," Nush said, turning to him, gaze pinning him. "A bully. An arrogant ass. And I don't need your pity. It's bad enough..."

"Bad enough what, Nush? What was so bad that you've been running from me all night?"

"I'm not running from anything. I smiled at that mockery of a ceremony. I ate cake and laughed about the silly jokes everyone made about how you've had to jump in and save the poor, plain, weird Reddy sister again. I signed every piece of paper you put in front of me. And when you told me to leave, I followed your order, without looking back, like a good little solider."

Her voice was full of an ache that he knew he was the cause of. It terrified him like nothing else had ever done. Her lower lip wobbled before she bit down on it.

"You're acting like this was a real wedding day…"

"What would make it real then?"

His question vibrated in the air around them with all the intensity of a lightning strike. And suddenly, Caio wondered if it could be that simple. If that was what he'd been fighting against since she'd walked into his office and declared her outrageous proposal.

The idea of simply keeping Nush was a dangerous thought on so many levels and yet so alluringly appealing to the deepest core of desires and wants he'd buried under need for vengeance. Suddenly the sweet forbidden temptation that she was, was very much within reach. And he knew he wasn't going to be able to let go of her.

Not now.

Not ever.

"What are you saying?" Nush said in a whisper.

"What would it take from me to make it real? A promise of fidelity? My commitment to make this work? My word that I don't want anyone else? Only you." Lightning flashed across the sky as if to underscore the fierce resolve in his words. A tremor skittered across her shoulders. "Ever since that kiss, all I've done is think of what else I'd do with you." She didn't say anything for so long that Caio felt a flicker of unfamiliar fear twist through his gut. "Come, Princess. You're in pain. We can discuss this later when—"

"You want this to be real? Our…" she stumbled over the word, "marriage? When did you decide that?"

Shedding his jacket, he draped it around her shoulders,

careful to not jostle her wrist. "I see no reason why it can't be the real thing. Not when we both want each other, not when we're already tied to each other. Not when I know no other woman would give me the kind of…loyalty that you do. The ceremony we had, the dress, the cake, the guests, the ring…it spooked you because it felt too real, didn't it?"

Even in the little illumination, he could see the shock in her eyes. "Why did you go to such trouble?"

"I only plan to get married once, *querida*, and I thought it a fitting tribute to your grandparents' memory to have it at their house."

She pushed at him with an angry growl. "Don't play games with me, Caio. Please. This…what you're proposing, it can't have anything to do with Thaata or OneTech or anything else. It has to be about you and me. If not, if you're playing with my feelings for any other reason, then you're…you're a monster and I'd never forgive you."

Her gaze held his in a silent, soft challenge and yet her words struck him hard at his core. Mira's words came to him and he marveled at how well she knew Nush. If he got this wrong, if he ruined this between him and Nush, if he fractured her faith in him, it would shatter her and that in return would destroy him. At a level from which he'd never recover.

It was a risk with odds set high for failure because he could never give Nush all of himself. Parts of him had been lost long ago, to even himself.

And yet, the want in his gut persisted. The idea of leaving Nush behind as he watched the destruction he'd set in motion alone, thousands of miles away from her, felt empty. All his hard work and persistence and sacrifices, everything he'd denied himself in the pursuit of revenge…

couldn't she be the respite he allowed himself? Wasn't he allowed to be selfish for once?

He knew her more than he did any other woman. He liked her company, he trusted her and damn it to hell, but he wanted to finish what she'd started in that study. He wanted to take her to his bed and keep her there until all she knew was him.

It was just a matter of making sure she knew what he could give and what he couldn't. And he'd begin with the truth. At least in this. "When I made the arrangements, it was to ward off filthy rumors that I was taking advantage of you. I wanted the board and the world to see that it was more than a convenient paper arrangement. That you and I share more."

"But we don't share anything more and it *is* nothing but a filthy, monetary transaction—that you kicked me out of that room before my signature dried is proof enough."

"I've been working toward a…time-sensitive acquisition for a long time," he said, hating that he'd already hurt her. "That paperwork needed to be signed and sealed before I left town."

"You turned the wedding into an empty mockery of the real thing when you know how much I… Maybe you were right that I don't really know the real you," she said in a defeated tone that sounded like a death knell. "Not two weeks ago, you told me we can't have that sort of relationship. You said it was the biggest mistake of your life to kiss me. So what's changed?"

Caio picked his words carefully. "Marriage is not some cheap, dirty affair, Nush. It's a commitment, bigger than anything I've ever made to anyone. Doesn't that say something?"

She searched his eyes. "You're not letting me have you

as some sort of medieval honor payment because I signed over my stock to you without a peep, are you?"

Hand under her chin, he tilted her face up, letting her see the desire he'd been fighting from the moment she'd touched her lips to his. "There's nothing honorable about what I want to do to you. Is that answer enough?" He didn't have to bend too much to speak at her ear and he loved that too. He loved that she fit so well against him, that she fit so well into his life. The shiver that wrecked her when their bodies grazed found an answering thrum in him. "As for who's going to have whom…we'll see about that, *querida*."

She licked her lips and he groaned. "And if it's horrible and boring and clunky…then what? You'll return me with a patched-up label and the deal's off?"

"Maybe," he said with a laugh.

She growled and punched him and called him names and he gathered her closer. Just one arm around her shoulders, without betraying the demanding tightness of his own body.

Only then did he realize that she was shaking. That she was nervous around him, that this bridge they were crossing to a new place in their relationship wasn't easy or simple or uncomplicated for her and that she'd still made the first move. That she'd thought this was worth exploring, worth being so honest about.

It was just his male ego that was flattered at her interest, he told himself and yet, the lie didn't stick. It was more. The dark, empty corner of his psyche being soothed.

"I consider marriage sacred. Not a game, not a bargain, not a show we put on for others. Not an experiment we try until we get bored."

"It's not any of those things for me either." He pressed his mouth to her temple, unwilling to wait another second for the taste of her skin. With his finger, he traced the arch of her neck and the pulse fluttering violently there. A soft gasp escaped her, turning him rock hard, but she still held herself stiff. "If it gets that bad, Nush, I'll let you dump me."

"You're an arrogant, conceited bastard," she said, looking up at him, "and I'm not—"

Suddenly, the sky opened in dense sheets of rain. In the breadth of a few seconds, they were both completely drenched.

Caio could no more stop looking than he could stop breathing as he gathered his jacket around her shoulders. The flimsy excuse for a top stuck to her skin, revealing the stiff points of her nipples.

Desire punched him, the pouring rain no match for the heat of his body. Caio bent and lifted Nush until she was safely tucked against his chest.

For all of thirty seconds, she was quiet, overtaken by shock, one arm clutched close to her chest. Then she was demanding to be put down, yelling that he was a caveman and that she wasn't fragile and how dare he…

Hefting her up in his arms, Caio pressed a rough, sudden kiss to her lips. Like a fierce summer storm that didn't last too long, her ferocity died and she clung to him, moaning, licking, kissing him back.

She tasted like cold rain and liquid desire, the tips of her fingers digging into his shoulder. He swallowed her moan of complaint as she tried to get deeper, delve closer. The depth of her desire for him, the explosiveness of her response left him shaking and his steps faltered as he wondered if he could keep her for a lifetime without letting her see all of him.

But he'd try, because the alternative of an empty future after he achieved his goal didn't bear thinking about.

CHAPTER EIGHT

NUSH LOOKED AROUND the luxury rear cabin of the private jet she'd been deposited into by a wet, thoroughly rumpled Caio.

She had no memory of the car ride except for snuggling up against the damp warmth of his body and the misery of being stuck in a bodysuit that clung to her skin like a wet rash and the constant pulse of pain radiating from her wrist.

She looked around the spacious cabin with its gleaming wood paneling and ultra-modern shower in the corner. The dark navy-colored duvet was soft against her fingers. She grimaced at the wet patch her rain-soaked clothes had immediately left on the bed and hopped away to sit on the single chair.

With her left arm tucked against her chest and the shoes wet and tight, trying to pull them off was a losing prospect. Except for a few unintended crunches for her ab muscles, she got no further. With a frustrated cry, she gave up. Instantly, thoughts rushed in like a tsunami.

A real marriage...to Caio.

A shiver ran down her spine and it had nothing to do with the dampness of her clothes. A lifelong commitment, a partnership and he would be hers...forever, in a way no one had ever been. She didn't miss how high-handed he was being, bringing her aboard his jet, assuming she'd happily go wherever he brought her. His sudden decision that it would be a permanent partnership.

The sheer arrogance of the man took her breath away. It was also the same decisiveness that made her feel all warm and gooey inside. Because Caio moved through life with a conviction, a commitment that never wavered once he gave it. And that he was promising it to her was a breath-stealing temptation, a fantasy coming true. Beneath all her affront and outrage at his executive decision, the woman in her, the romantic fool in her wanted to grasp it with everything she had.

But the little girl in her—the one who'd survived a chaotic childhood, the one who faced abandonment at every turn—was terrified that she'd lose him if they did this, that he'd abandon her too if she let herself have this.

You're mine, he'd declared with such raw, possessive intent that reminded her that there were facets of Caio she didn't know. That he carefully controlled what he did share.

How would a relationship ever work if he didn't even let her know him? If everything was based on logic and compatibility, or on the minimal facts that she was loyal and attracted to him? If he always controlled the reins of it?

Nushie, it doesn't have to be any different from the affair you proposed, that same voice whispered again and Nush grabbed it with both hands. A quiet determination stole through her.

If he truly wanted this to be a real thing, then he'd have to give her all of him. He'd have to prove it to her. Until then, she'd treat this as a temporary madness they were giving in to. That way, at least she wasn't leaving herself even more vulnerable to him.

"Are you kidnapping me?" she asked when Caio walked into the cabin a few minutes later. The question was nothing but token since they'd been airborne for a little while now. She also had no doubt that he'd changed his plan to accommodate her because of her broken wrist. Ugh, so much for starting off on an even footing.

"I'm taking you with me on a trip that's been on the schedule for a while," he said, without meeting her eyes.

What she'd thought a luxuriously expansive space just minutes ago shrunk with his broad frame in it. There was a strange tension to his frame as he moved around the cabin, grabbing things.

Was it because of their particular destination? Or because he was already finding her presence intrusive?

They'd share spaces like this on a daily basis—the bedroom, the kitchen, the bathroom, even a tub maybe. For days and months and years…*if* it worked out. They'd create their own traditions, make holiday memories, maybe even have kids. He'd be hers forever—unapologetically hers, irrevocably hers.

He wouldn't leave her for anything, wouldn't make her wonder if he'd break his word or send her off. As a mentor, friend and colleague, he'd been steadfast. As a husband, he'd be…

Jesus, Nushie, why don't you just prostrate yourself at his feet then? The caustic words sounding very much like Yana put a break on her spiral. It was wishful thinking, a fantasy she'd weaved.

He was secretive and arrogant and controlling, she reminded herself. And he thought her some kind of unicorn he had to protect.

God, she was going to lose it with such constant, conflicting thoughts.

"Because I can't be trusted to look after myself?" Her words came out full of distrust and fear.

"Because you're hurt and I don't want you fending for

yourself alone in that big, empty house." He sighed, added as an afterthought, "And because I want you with me."

"Where are we going?"

"To an island I own off the Brazilian coast."

"Is that where your family lives?"

"They used to. Before..." his jaw clenched and released, "a long time ago."

Nush frowned. "Wait, this acquisition...does it have something to do with your family?" Because that would explain the lengths he'd gone to, wouldn't it?

Marrying her.

His barely hidden agitation as she'd signed the stock over.

The hours and hours of strategy planning with his executive team.

His furious determination to acquire the company despite Peter Sr.'s vicious protest that it was nothing but a liability unsuitable for OneTech.

"It's a long story to get into now, Princesa."

"We have a long flight ahead of us," she said, before leaning her head back and closing her eyes. "I'd like nothing but—"

"Here, let me."

Nush sighed as long fingers cleverly massaged her temples and relieved the tension that had been building all day. She tucked away the fact that he hadn't answered her question, for now.

With a groan she couldn't suppress, she leaned her head forward until it hit his abdomen, begging for his fingers to go deeper and farther. He granted her unspoken request, his fingers kneading gently at her scalp and then back around. With her arm between them, Nush steadied herself with a hand on his stomach.

Tight, hard muscles clenched under her touch. She

spread her hand around innocently enough, needing to touch more of him. A ripple of movement was her reward. Then she played with his belt buckle, the cold metal a nice break from the warmth suffusing her. A different kind of tension thrummed into life as she imagined sending her fingers on a southward quest. Her mouth dried at the thought of tracing his shape and length, of raking her fingernails over rock-hard thighs…

"I've asked the staff to bring you something to eat," he said, stepping back. Cutting the contact without pushing her away. "A shower, food and sleep."

She nodded without looking at him and fisted her hand that felt suddenly bereft. Damn, why had she hesitated?

"So docile, Princesa? You must be in a lot more pain that you're letting on."

She looked up to find him regarding her with a frown. "It's been a long day and I'm just gathering my thoughts. But I can't pin one down."

"Anything you want to share?"

Nush stared at him, wondering at how easily he turned it back to her. How he deflected her delving into his mind, his heart. Neither had he missed that her suddenly subdued temper meant something deeper was needling her. "It's not an easy jump to think of you as my…husband," she said, testing the shape and weight of the word on her tongue. "I've never even thought of marriage in my future." She didn't say it might have been because her present had been mostly obsessed with him.

"Which is why I'm not going to rush you into anything."

Anything like what? Sex? Was the damned man going to leave her hanging again? "You know that I grew up with Mama hating anything related to marriage. She thought it was nothing but an institution held up by men to control women."

"It does become that in certain circumstances, full of poison and control," he added in such a savage tone that she was shocked by it.

When he didn't elaborate, she said the first thing that came to her mind. "I always wondered if she sometimes regretted not accepting when my dad proposed. Although seeing that he's incapable of anything but his commitment to alcohol, she made the right choice."

"He proposed to your mother?"

Nush nodded.

"Does it bother you that you…are illegitimate?" There was a fierce quality to the question as if the injustice of it bothered him.

"Not really. Being Mama's daughter meant understanding real-life matters at a very young age. And that I got to meet Thaata and everyone when I was four made me realize it didn't make a difference. Mira and Yana had nothing I didn't have. In fact, I was the one who had a mother that loved her. Even if sometimes, her mental health didn't make for the warmest, greatest upbringing."

"Your devotion to her is admirable."

Nush frowned at his question. But one look in his eyes told her he wasn't being contentious or dismissive, that he was even angry on her behalf.

"She could have easily handed me off to Thaata. It became clear that he asked her to, enough times. It would have made her life, her work, her moods…everything easier. She could have just visited me when she had time. But she didn't. She loved me, as much as possible for her, in whatever way her mind allowed. She tried her best and that's all I needed."

He stared at her with such stark, naked emotion that

Nush looked away. It wasn't uncomfortable but it made her feel as if she'd suddenly bared all of herself to his gaze—every insecurity, every vulnerability—and he was rooting through it all.

Staring at her fingers, she struggled to bring back the topic to what plagued her. "She'd spent years brainwashing me to never give in to marriage and yet when I asked her if she wanted to attend the ceremony…she was beyond excited. I think it has something to do with you," she said, solving at least one puzzle.

Astonishment painted over his features. "What?"

"I think you're the one man who managed to win Mama over. She trusts you and…" Nush swallowed the hard lump of gratitude that lodged in her throat. "Thank you for always being kind to her, Caio. For always thinking of what's right for her, especially when I couldn't. I know that she felt threatened by Thaata to let him handle it."

"I didn't do it for your gratitude, Nush."

"Why did you?"

"Because she needed looking after. And so you'd be happy and settled and worry free. I told you before. You reminded me of myself at my most…powerless. And yet, you didn't…" he cleared his throat, "you don't let bitterness touch you. I'm arrogant enough to like it that I had a hand in keeping you like that. Untouched and innocent."

She scrunched her nose at that, not liking it one bit. Not liking it at all that he still saw her as some sort of fragile creature to be protected. "That makes me sound like fruit," she said, loathe to disturb the strange, tension-filled truce they seemed to have reached.

"Would it be better if I said fruit that is ripe and ready to be eaten?"

"You need work on your flirting. That sounds *ewww*."

Sitting down on the bed in front of her, he pinned her with that weighty gaze. His thighs straddled hers and the thick, hard press of them caging her felt deliciously lethargic. "What's truly bothering you, Princesa?"

"You've never even had a girlfriend for more than a week. It's hard to believe that you're doing this because you…want to."

Arms folded, he seemed to consider his words. "Just because I didn't mention marriage doesn't mean I don't believe in it. I had other things occupying all my attention."

"Like this acquisition?" she poked again.

He sidestepped her yet again by giving her a morsel of something she was desperate for. "My parents had a great marriage built on trust and respect and an unshakeable foundation of…friendship."

She had a feeling he meant to say love but left it out on purpose. And she wasn't sure how she felt about that either. Did she want him to profess love to her?

God, no, came the instinctive, immediate answer.

She wouldn't believe him to begin with. Love never had anything to do with Caio's actions. He didn't even let anyone close. Even now, even when he was giving her this commitment, she had a feeling she wasn't going to get anything more than what they already had.

Whether a relationship between them could survive with his conditions and her fears was anybody's guess.

"We already have the foundation, Nush. A commitment is all that's needed. And I'm making that to you."

It should have sounded arrogant, like he was issuing a decree and expected her to fall in line. And it was that partly. But all Nush could focus on was the solemnity to his words and the overwhelming urge to set some kind of boundaries on her own expectations. Self-preservation was a bitch.

"Will you promise that you'll never lie to me? That you won't stay in this arrangement for some sort of twisted honor that dictates that you can't desert me? That you'll see me as an equal—not Rao's granddaughter or the woman who gave you OneTech or the girl you rescued a long time ago?"

"Yes, to the first and second. The third…it's not easy to separate you from all those things, Nush. And stop calling it an arrangement."

"I need time, Caio. I can't just jump in like you. I…"

"I want you heading OneTech with me. I want you in my bed, beneath me, giving this your everything."

A full body shudder overtook Nush as that very vivid image hit her.

When he grinned in response to her reaction, Nush decided she'd like nothing better than to unravel him too, bit by bit.

Whatever path this took, she'd at least solve the complex mystery of Caio. She'd learn every inch of him, inside out, until her fascination with him was gone, until there was no unknowns left between them.

In the meantime, she was simply going to enjoy the ride.

Thick towels in the same navy blue of the sheets, a first aid kit and something else was dumped onto the bed. And then Caio was kneeling at her feet, squeezing his big body into the space between the bed and the chair.

His damp white shirt proudly displayed the hard musculature of his back, tapering down to a narrow waist. The man was too beautiful for words.

When he gripped her calf and tugged one stubborn

shoe off, she let her torso pitch forward and pressed her breasts to his back, as if for support. The sensation of those hard, jutting shoulder muscles and bones digging into her soft flesh was indescribable. Nush bit her mouth to bite off the moan that wanted to escape.

He stilled instantly, like a big jaguar scenting prey.

"So this…" she searched for something to say, something to poke his steel trap mind with, "trip is kinda like a honeymoon?"

"No." His fingertips were featherlight on her calf.

"Why not?"

"This isn't a proper honeymoon. More of a work trip. I will take you on a real one as soon as our schedules let up a bit."

"In all the years I've known you, you've never taken a day off," she said, half laughing, half shocked and all too overwhelmed at the matter-of-fact resolve in his words.

"I will do everything to seduce you into giving me this, Princesa," he said, as if he knew exactly what she was thinking. "You should know that."

Golden-brown eyes held hers and Nush trembled. But she refused to let her fears hold her back anymore. For so long, she'd wanted this right to touch him as she pleased. To run her fingers through those thick locks of hair and sift through them.

She did it now, shamelessly, tracing her fingers over the plane of his forehead, tugging at his hair. He bowed his head, as if he was a present to be unwrapped for her pleasure. A half growl, half groan rumbled up through his chest. "I'd protest more if it weren't for the happy pills numbing my chaotic thoughts."

His fingers busied themselves with the other shoe, gentle but firm and all Nush could think of was how those fingers would feel on other places that were desperate for his touch.

"I didn't think you were the type to delude yourself, Nush. The pills don't make you amenable to something you're against. They *maybe* lower your inhibitions."

He straightened on his knees, bringing his face level with hers. One thumb traced her jaw, moving back and forth, his gaze glittering with an intensity that burned through her. "But as set on this as I am, I will give you time to get used to it."

"What does that mean? Are you going to cockblock me again?"

The corner of his mouth lifted up in a parody of a smile as the pad of his wicked thumb danced at the edges of her lip but never really landed. "How did I not know that you had such a dirty mouth?"

"You don't know a lot of things about me," Nush said, trying to act coy and failing miserably. It came out husky and needy and...hoarse.

"You're right. I'm looking forward to being enlightened." Pushing up to stand, he drew her to her feet. "Now, let's get these wet things off you."

"Are you going to make us wait then?" Nush asked, arresting his hands that were busy with the waistband of her leather skirt.

"Wait for what?" he asked, looking just as distracted as she felt.

His fingers had located the side zipper on the skirt before Nush realized he was waiting for a reply.

It was impossible to string words and thoughts together when his hands were all over her. The leather skirt was gently but firmly being nudged off the thick curve of her hips. "Make me wait before we have sex?" she said, uncaring how petulant she sounded. "I guess it's not such a hardship for you to wait. You probably even think of it like a task to check off but—"

Suddenly, his fingers were on the parts of her ass that were exposed by the bodysuit and her lacy white panties and she was pressed up against him so tight that a hard, heated length pressed up against her belly. She gripped his bulging bicep as she trembled as the shape and weight of his erection pressed into her soft belly.

For a long, tormenting minute, he just held her like that with his fingers roving and caressing and kneading the plentiful curves of her ass. Up and down they went, tracing the creases, delving nearer but not close enough to the place between her legs that was clenching and releasing and dampening for his touch.

Nush opened her mouth to suck in a breath and tasted his skin. Salt and heat and sweat added to the combustible pleasure waiting to dctonate inside. She desperately wanted to move, to seek the friction she needed, but the damned man had her locked up against him.

Caio's mouth stilled against her temple as he held her in place with one hand on her hip. "Still think it's a task on a to-do list, Princesa? I'm thirty-seven years old and yet, every single time I'm near you, I'm in this state, Nush. Ever since you demolished every bit of decency I ever possessed."

Closing her eyes, she breathed in the warm, dark scent of him, let her other senses feast on his need for her. It was a thrumming melody in her blood. At least in this, there was nothing but brutal honesty between them. And still, she needed more. Wanted more. Demanded more.

"Tell me something you want to do to me."

She felt the tension in his body ratchet up. "You like it if I talk as dirty as you do?"

"Yes. And you owe me this, Caio."

A rough bark of a sound that was a cross between a groan and a protest enveloped her "God, you're an insatiable little thing, aren't you?" One finger made a detour down her ass cheek, and stilled. "But I don't owe you anything. Not when you think this is all a filthy transaction, Princesa."

The blasted man and his mind games. "Fine. Think of it as a wedding present."

"So it is a wedding when you can use it to get something you want?"

"Yes. I learned negotiation from the best."

He laughed then. And it was a sound different from anything Nush had ever heard before. Desire and want and…joy twined through it, tugging her closer. "I want to lick your nipples, *querida*. Roll them against my tongue and suck them into my mouth. It was all I could think of when you sat across from me after the ceremony today. All pretty and placid and poised, all that fire and passion packed away where only I could reach it. Unraveled only for my pleasure. I wanted to throw everyone out and rip that dress off and take you on the desk."

Just as suddenly, as if he'd revealed too much, he released her.

Eyes wide and breath choppy, she stared at the tight set of his features. He didn't betray by breath or look that he was sporting an erection that made her tingly all over, his control a thing to watch, to marvel at. And Nush wondered what it would take to undo it. To make him as confused and volatile and unraveled as she felt. Not only at a physical level but deeper. Or if that was even possible.

"That thing is going to be tricky," he said in a matter-of-fact voice, pointing to her bodysuit top. "Where does it come off?"

Sticking her fingers between her thighs, Nush undid

the press button. The little contact of her fingers where she was desperate to be touched, while he watched, was a trip on its own.

The lower edges of the bodysuit rolled up, the stretchy material released.

His gaze stayed at the juncture of her thighs. With a hard swallow, Nush followed it. She liked his gaze on her—mesmerized, caught, still. The lacy fabric of her panties barely hid anything from him. Thank God she'd let Yana talk her into the spa day. She hated the idea of going completely bald down there but she was all trimmed and tidied.

The sight of his hard swallow made liquid desire thrum through her.

"Let's keep going, shall we?" he said a minute later and she definitely heard the crack in his voice then.

His control was there but it was also paper-thin. She smiled like a clown.

"What are you smiling at?" Caio asked, fingers busy rolling up the fabric of the bodysuit, baring more and more of her.

Nush shrugged and released the tension in her stiff arms. Let him move her until one arm was free of the bodysuit. She stood with her side pressed into his middle as he pulled the top off her head. Now it was just a matter of getting her injured arm free.

"Do you think you can manage if I remove the sling for just a few minutes?"

"The sling is mainly so that I don't forget about my wrist and jostle it."

"Here goes." With slow, light movements, he removed the Velcro from around her neck, all the while cradling her wrist with one hand. "Is that okay?" he asked, releasing her left wrist very gently.

Nush shook her head.

His thick brows drew into a frown, as if outraged by the fact that her body didn't listen to his dictates. "What do you need, Princesa?"

"A kiss would make me feel a lot better."

His nostrils flared, a wicked light dawning in his tawny gold eyes. "Let me get these wet things off you, Princesa, and you can have whatever you want."

"I want it now," she demanded sulkily, tipping her chin up. "I got married, lost a fortune in stock to my greedy fake husband, then got sent out while he hung out with his ex for hours on end behind closed doors with everyone giving me pitying looks, then I got hurt and then I got wet and then I got kidnapped and it's really not a stretch to want some kind of compensation for all the—"

His mouth swallowed her complaint.

Fingers gripped her head while he...*devoured* her. This kiss was rough, demanding, hard. Full of teeth and nips. His long fingers tangled in her hair, gripping it, twisting it, and Nush moaned. If he'd been gentle with her, she might have fallen apart. But he wasn't. He let her feel his hunger, his threadbare control, his raw need and that was the best present he could've ever given her.

Nush pressed into him, loving the scent and feel of him, craving more and more. Every inch of her throbbed, every inch of her needed. He tasted and smelled like all the decadent things in the world, of long, cozy winter nights, and bright sunny afternoons and everything in between.

Dragging his mouth away from hers, he trailed soft kisses down her jaw and at her neck and before she knew it, he was moving away. Still reeling from the dizzying sensation, she looked down to find him kneeling at her feet. Dampness made her sex ache and she couldn't help but press her thighs together.

"What…what are you doing?"

"Giving you a kiss to make up for all the hardship you had to endure today."

"But I meant…" Cheeks reddening, Nush watched helplessly as his big palms cupped her hips, steadying her. She wanted his mouth there but she also…

"This is the kiss I want to give. The taste I want from my new bride."

Devilish man and his damned games!

"If you're not ready for it, if you're too…tired for it," he said, his voice honey smooth, "I'll put you to bed, *querida*."

The wicked twinkle in his eyes tore through her inhibitions. How dare he insinuate that she wasn't ready for this? For him?

"No, I want it."

"Say it. Beg me for it."

"Caio, will you please go down on me?"

He gave her a smile that was so full of heat and promise that Nush swayed. "Hold on," he said, pulling her other hand to his head.

"I'm fine."

"You won't be when I get started and I don't want you to get hurt more."

She relented and clutched his thick hair.

Hands on her knees, he made her spread her thighs a little more and then he was nosing through her folds, the lace of her panties no barrier.

"You're so pretty all over, Anushka."

And then her panties were ripped off and then he separated her folds and then he was licking her…there.

The differences hit her first.

She was only used to her fingers and even then, she'd always needed lots of help but Caio's tongue… Jesus, he was thorough. He licked her up and around and then stabbed her opening with the tip of his tongue.

Nush thought she might pass out before she came.

"Is that good?"

"Please don't stop."

He chuckled and Nush wasn't beyond begging.

Seeing his dark head between her thighs added its own fuel to the fire he lit with soft, tentative licks. Nush was melting, coming undone, turned inside out. He wasn't applying some practiced technique. He wasn't using whatever experience he had.

He was learning her—every clench of her abdomen, every moan and rasp that escaped her, every shiver that went through her thighs—and he kept up a running narrative, asking her to tell him what felt better, where she wanted more, how fast or slow she wanted it, and God, it was a whole experience.

And then he applied all of that knowledge and Nush thought she'd drown but he didn't and then he was sucking at her clit and she was panting and then he was working his broad finger into her, and the wicked light in his eyes when he met hers for a fraction of a second, the shuddering inhale he took as if he needed the scent of her in his lungs and then more sucking of her tender flesh and she splintered apart. Hard. Shaking. Sobbing.

She screamed his name and even the momentary mortification that everyone on the flight could hear her didn't stop her.

Caio stayed on his knees, steadying her and holding her, kissing her and whispering praise, as if she'd done the work, until the last flutter died down.

Nush ran her fingers through his hair, a fizzy smile on her lips. "I'll make you one promise."

"And what's that, Princesa?"

"I'm willing to give this a temporary try if that's on the menu regularly."

With a growl of laughter, Caio shot to his feet and kissed her and she could taste herself on him and she wondered if it could truly be like this—full of laughter and pleasure.

It wouldn't be, the sensible part of her replied. It was just pheromones talking.

But if it was all she could get out of this for now—his kisses and his caresses and this intimacy with him—then Nush would take it. And cherish it when it was over. When things fell apart and when Caio realized he didn't need this arrangement of theirs anymore.

CHAPTER NINE

NUSH HAD NEVER believed in love at first sight. That was until she'd seen the house on the island that Caio had personally overseen the restoration of in the last few months by his own admission.

Everything that had stood before had been razed to the ground, he'd told her, because the very foundation of it had been rotting from the inside. And what he'd had built in its place had stolen a piece of her heart.

Three floors of honey-colored, hand-grained hardwood floors, huge open spaces with exposed beams and sloping ceilings and loads of light, three-hundred-and-sixty-degree glass walls with views of the ocean and a few splashes of color in the form of local art, the house was an architectural marvel. An infinity pool, a second-level deck with a hot tub, and on the beautiful grounds, an orange grove, there was so much to explore. White walls and white furniture and simple but elegant touches made the house warm and welcoming, even in its austerity. Like Caio himself.

We can live here part of the year if you like it, he'd said, eyes dancing with pleasure when she'd gushed over the sloping roof and the orange bougainvillea creeping up and covering all of one side of the house. *We need only return to your grandparents' house when Mira or Yana are visiting*, he'd added.

Nush had simply smiled, excited to explore rooms upon rooms but loathe to give her assent to his determined plans for their future. Not even to please him in the moment could she give in.

Though it was far from easy to resist.

He kept dangling such scenarios in front of her, drugging kisses laced with whispered demands that she take that final step with him—pretty much her fantasy and dream future rolled up into alluringly aching promises, and she tried her best to not react, to not reach for everything he offered. To retain some sense of self-preservation.

•

The first couple of days, she'd been sleeping and eating as her wrist had been hurting a lot more than she'd expected. Then she explored the house, one expansive enough to raise the big, boisterous family she'd always dreamed of having. Which led her to wonder if Caio felt the same.

How could he when he was tight-lipped about his own family, when in the fifteen years she'd known him, he'd never even mentioned them except for his father? Even then it had been to draw her out. As many times as she'd probed about the acquisition, he'd batted away her curiosity by distracting her.

She had let it go. For now. Especially since she'd barely seen him in the week since they'd arrived. He'd even apologized for leaving her alone for so many days.

Having fended for herself during her childhood and early adolescence, the quiet solitude didn't bother her one bit. She'd simply got back to work on the pending software model. The rest of the time she explored the grounds and the beach and kept in touch with her sisters.

She called Mira, who was in Athens, daily and was glad to hear that she and Aristos were giving their marriage a second chance. Which had been a love match.

At least that was what she and Yana had assumed when their reserved, practical sister had turned up married after one weekend in Vegas to a man she'd barely known.

Yana was harder to pin down as she traveled for shoots all over the world. Still, she texted whenever she could, sometimes in twenty to thirty strings of one-sided conversation, and Nush loved seeing her sister's naughtiness come through.

So Nush would've been content. Except for Caio, who seemed determined to control how much he was prepared to open up to her. Though to be fair, he was gone before she woke up and when he returned, she was knocked out by the pills.

On the couple of occasions that she'd been awake when he'd crawled into bed, freshly showered and in silk boxers she'd barely got a peek at, he'd peppered her with questions about the day, about design elements for the model she was currently working through on paper, about Mira and Yana and any number of things. All about her, while venturing nothing about his day or himself.

And Nush was beginning to see how easily he distracted her every time she asked after his family or his past or even the acquisition that had been so important to him.

Soon, Princesa. Once I have everything in place, was all he would say.

Another time his abrupt taunt had been, *When you give me your commitment, when you promise me you're with me for the long term, Anushka, you'll know all the dirty details of my past.*

Even in her half-asleep state, she'd wondered at what he didn't want to share with her.

Worse, only now, in broad daylight, did she realize that he was both surprised and displeased that she was holding out on him, could she see how he used her artless desire for him as a tool to distract her.

Just last night, she'd been awake enough for once to see the bleakness in his eyes, the hard twist of his mouth when she'd walked into the bathroom and found him staring at his reflection in the mirror.

Her heart had ached for the pain stamped all over him. And yet when she'd hugged him from behind and begged him to tell her what was eating at him, all he'd said was that he needed her. And she'd felt him channeling all of that pain into his caresses as he'd carried her back to their bed.

He'd kissed her and teased her with those clever fingers, his hard chest pressed against her back and her legs raised and open in an indecent but utterly erotic position that had made her sex clench greedily.

It had been the most gloriously slow climb to the peak, as he touched her slowly at first, then fast, then penetrated her with one, two and then three fingers, introducing her to a sweet, painful burn that made the pleasure he doled out in controlled measures all the more lush and welcoming. Like he was in every other walk of life, the man was extraordinarily thorough with her body, and the cues she gave, driven by some feral need that he'd learn every inch of her body and what turned her on, what made her sigh and groan and scream, that had driven him to drag out her orgasm for so long that when it had hit her finally, it had left her fractured and sobbing at the intensity of it.

Caio had held her with a tender reverence that had calmed her, coaxed her down from the volatile energy of her release, pressed soft kisses to her damp brow all the while whispering to her that her willingness and vulnerability were a gift he'd relish unwrapping again and again.

But even in the part Vicodin and part orgasm-fueled molasses that had been her mind, she'd known that he hadn't let her touch him.

As if whatever had chased him during the day needed to be cleansed by splintering her apart and putting her back together all over again.

If she hadn't felt him, thick and hard against her behind, she'd have thought he wasn't affected at all. But he'd been. There had been a desperate intensity to his caresses but he asked nothing of her.

Nush might have let it go until she'd seen the email that had popped up in her inbox by accident. Until she called Peter Sr. and inquired after the acquisition Caio was working on and learned that Thaata had been expressly against the very thing. Which explained why he hadn't left the stock to Caio.

Caio hadn't lied to her and yet he'd hidden something big from her.

Every question of hers about the acquisition had been unanswered. Worse, he'd distracted her, used her own desire against her.

Even now, as she walked back into the house after an early evening stroll through the orange grove and donned a swimsuit for a soak in the hot tub, she decided things would have to change.

Caio walked into the deck that provided a spectacular view of the sunset over the dark waves of the ocean providing a symphony. With the orange horizon behind her kissing the silky golden brown of her bare shoulders, and the flimsy triangles of her bikini top drawing his attention to the swells of her breasts, she was a sight he wondered if he could ever get used to. Jets of water bubbled around her, kissing all that bare skin and it was all he wanted to do.

The first few days, it had been extremely disconcerting to find Nush in his bed, tangled up in the sheets, arms and legs thrown akimbo, thick wavy locks of her hair spread over his pillow. Smiling in the dark, he'd collected various arms and legs and bed covers and slowly tucked her to his side, making sure she didn't jostle her wrist.

He didn't remember the last time he'd had a woman sleeping in his bed. Probably never. Even when he and Sophia had been together, it had been all hush-hush, a dirty secret she hadn't wanted to reveal to anyone. Being led by his groin and by the idea of thwarting his stepbrother, his nineteen-year-old self had found it intensely satisfying. He'd been a poor, gullible bastard.

It hadn't taken longer than a day for him to get used to Nush there. And worse, every evening he returned wondering if she would still be there. His rational mind knew she didn't know of his activities during the day and yet, with her probing questions about his family, about the acquisition, it wouldn't be long before she'd know what he was up to. Before he couldn't hide the reality of who he was from her anymore.

And the more she resisted giving him her commitment, the more he resisted giving her the truth, and the more he didn't want to let her go.

Because for all the years and strategies he'd spent to corner his stepfather like a hunted animal, Caio hadn't calculated how he'd feel when he'd arrived there. Of how empty and dissatisfied and purposeless it would all seem. How his half brother Javier's face as Caio refused to see him again would torment him.

Cristo, it should've been a celebratory moment. He should've felt free. Instead all he felt was…this feeling of betrayal.

Neither did it escape his notice that he was using Nush as a balm to cover that emptiness, that she deserved more, but he couldn't bring himself to care anymore.

Finishing his drink, he started unbuttoning his shirt when she became aware of his presence.

A fine tremor went through her shoulders as she turned to look at him, and wiped at the steam on her face. Her gaze landed on his bared throat and skidded away. "You're back. Before the middle of the night."

While the idea of aggravating her to the point where her explosive temper let him tease out that passion of hers was incredibly tempting, he didn't want to manipulate her. Not today, when he needed something real and raw like only Nush could give him, to bring him back to balance. To rid the aftertaste of what he'd done. "Shall I join you?" he asked, the wariness in her eyes playing havoc with his need.

"No." The weight of the single word had his fingers stilling on the buttons. "I'm ready to get out and if you want to take a shower, we can have dinner together after."

"You still haven't eaten?" he said, checking his watch, which said a quarter to eight.

"Nope," she said popping the *p*, which confirmed she was indeed mad about something. "And really, Caio, just because my wrist is broken doesn't mean I don't know how to look after myself. I've done it for ages."

He raised his palms in surrender.

Her mouth, in turn, pursed tight in a way that was just unnatural for her. Fighting the urge to tease it open with his fingers and then something else—God, she was nowhere near ready for that particular fantasy of his—he cleared his throat. "Did Maria leave anything in the refrigerator?"

"No offense but I don't know how you can eat her cooking," she said, pulling up to her knees, giving him a better view of the bikini top hugging her breasts.

His hands itched to cup their delicious weight before bringing them to his lips. Her nipples tightened to stiff points, making his mouth water for a taste.

"Her food is bland and boring. Is vegetarian lasagna okay? Or does not eating red meat for an evening offend your delicate masculine sensibilities?" she asked with a sniff that made him laugh until tears burned his eyes.

She stared at him, rapt. "You're gorgeous when you… laugh. When you just let yourself be…real."

"As opposed to what, Anushka?"

"As opposed to employing strategies and distractions with mc, as opposed to treating this thing between us like some kind of deal you're finessing," she finished in a soft voice that only underlined her anger.

"Let me help you out of there and we—"

She scooted away in the hot tub when he reached out to help her. The edge of his own temper flared, like a little boy denied his favorite toy. He wasn't unaware of how…invested he was getting in this, in her, but it only a warning at the edge of his consciousness. Nothing but a vague, discordant threat drowned out by his current obsession with pleasing her, making her smile, making her explode with his fingers and mouth.

Whatever she saw in his gaze, she offered a mollifying "I can manage it. Go ahead and shower."

"Is there a problem if I want to help my injured wife out of a slippery hot tub?" he asked, undoing and pushing the cuffs of his shirt back.

Her gaze dipped to his bare chest and lingered. Before

sweeping down onto his abdomen and then she licked her lower lip. Heat poured through him like thick honey at the stark desire etched onto her features. "Nush?" he said, incapable of teasing her. It felt like his control was hanging on by its last, frayed thread.

She looked up and blushed fiercely. "We've barely talked in the last week and I'd prefer it if we—"

"Is that why you're angry? Because I was gone so much?"

"Of course not," she said, genuinely confused that he'd think so. "You told me you'd be busy and contrary to your preconceptions, I handle solitude better than most. But for tonight, I have some ground rules."

"And what are those?"

"For starters, you're not allowed to touch me."

His curse could have been heard at the beach. His own anger flared to match hers. "That's not a rule. More like personal pettiness that's not worthy of you." Suddenly, he'd turned into the man-child that still remembered the shattering pain of his mama abandoning him, casting him out into the world. Choosing his stepfather and his half brothers above him. "And you know what, Princesa? Fine. I don't care. I won't touch you if that's what you want." Somehow, he arrested the hurtful words that wanted to clamor out of him.

But the damned minx didn't back down one bit. "Okay then. If it's that much of a deal breaker for you to let me have some say in this, there's no point in me pretending that I belong here. You already got what you wanted, yeah? So let me go, Caio. Let's call this farce what it is. I want to go home first thing tomorrow morning."

"No," he said, his mouth twisting in a wounded snarl. "Your home is with me."

Her gaze held his—not just defiant but beseeching too.

"Choose, Caio, then. Choose me. Right now. Choose me because you want a future with me. Choose me for myself, not for the stock in the company or to save your face or to acquire something else you've been coveting for years. Choose me because you can't let me go."

"Jesus, Anuṣhka," he said, staring at her. Cristo, the woman had a multitude of weapons against him and yet, for once he didn't mind losing. Even as she dictated terms to him, he found himself wanting to kiss that mouth, to taste that fierceness. "When did you turn so blood-thirsty?"

"You're not the only one who can be determined and aware of their power in this relationship."

"For once, I've no idea what you're thinking." He rubbed a hand over his forehead. "Why am I not allowed to touch you?"

Her smile was full of a wicked triumph he wanted to taste despite his own fury coursing through him. "I want to talk tonight and if you touch me, we'll go off-script."

His mouth twitched, his anger leaving as fast as it came. "How's that?"

"Hmm? You'll touch me to lift me out and then I'll want to kiss you and you'll oblige and I'll sweetly beg for an orgasm and you'll make me work for it, prolonging every caress and kiss and by the time I climax, I'll be so exhausted that I'll want to crawl into bed and you'll pat me and tuck me in as if I've been a good little girl and out the window go all my intentions…" She let out a long breath, a line appearing between her brows.

"That you can't keep your hands and mouth off me is the biggest turn-on I've ever known. Don't take that away from me, Princesa."

"It is when you use my desire for you like a weapon

against me," she said, her voice thick and full of unshed tears. "That has to stop. Now."

Twin flames danced in her big eyes and he found himself floundering in them. How had he not realized that the quiet, shy teenager he'd teased had turned into a magnificent woman who could hold her own against him? How could he tell her that it was only with her that he felt even this much?

"You have to stop treating me as if I'm some imbecile teenager with a crush on you."

"You know me more than I have ever let anyone else know me, Princesa."

"I'm not in a competition with others in your life, Caio. Neither am I some kind of complimentary prize you're letting yourself have. Because if that's how you see me, then..." she swallowed and looked away, "then this is over. Now."

Caio flinched at how close to the truth she'd got. "Threatening me, Princesa?"

"No. Setting some ground rules." An ache he hated seeing glowed in her eyes. "I should've known that that's the only way to get anywhere with you."

"That's unfair."

"As unfair as hiding that you went against Thaata's express wishes when you used your executive power to push through that acquisition? Or the way you distract me every time I get close to the truth?"

"I thought your loyalty was to me, Nush."

If he thought the bitterness in his voice would shake her, he was wrong. "It is to you, Caio. I don't care why you did it or even that you went against Thaata, to be honest. But you...you don't respect me enough to let me—"

The clamor in his chest quieted as fast as it had begun. Ignoring her squeals of protest, Caio locked his hands at her back and lifted her out and when she could kneel on the edge of the tub, he kept her there. Miles of bare, wet skin greeted his hands and he stroked and petted every inch shamelessly. "You're wrong if you think I see you as any less than the magnificent woman you are, Nush. Why the hell do you think I've let it come this far? Why do you think I jumped on the chance to make you mine forever?"

Her eyes widened in her face, her mouth trembled. "You're not lying."

"No. I choose you, Nush. Never believe anything else. And if it's truth you want, then you'll have it. In all its ugly glory."

She stared at him, her mouth glistening, her eyes full of those unshed tears again. "I'm getting you all wet," she whispered hoarsely, her breasts crushed against his chest.

"I don't care," he said, and then he kissed her.

It was a rough claiming. A branding, even he couldn't deny it. An arrogant declaration that she was his to kiss, to rumple up, to tease and taunt as he pleased.

He poured every ounce of heat that had been simmering through him all day into the kiss. Fingers twisting in her hair, he laved at that lower lip until she opened up with a groan. He scored his teeth over her neck and licked a trail over the marks. When her spine arched and she pushed into his touch he took her nipple, covered by the flimsy fabric of her top, into his mouth and sucked at it. When she sobbed, he dragged the cup down and laved the aching bud with reverent strokes. When she grabbed his face with shaking hands, he plunged into the warm cavern of her mouth, as if he were a parched man finally reaching home.

And to him, after everything he'd put in motion today, Nush was coming home.

With a growl that made him impossibly hard, she bit

his lower lip and that in turn gentled and calmed the ravenous beast inside him.

Drawing his fingertips down the line of her spine gently, he let her claim him in return. The twin swords of her innocence and her sensuality were like a cleansing fire that left him shaking. Her own aggression died down in a few seconds, like his had. Fingers clasped at the nape of his neck, she pressed her face to the hollow at his throat. Even then, her tongue flicked out and licked him there and he let out a guttural growl.

She hid her face again and a wave of tenderness shook him. "Why haven't you slept with me yet then?" The question came out in a soft, cloaked whisper as though it had somehow slipped out before she could intone it better.

"I sleep with you every night, Princesa," he said, keeping his own words free of tease. "In fact, I think it should be one of the primary tenets of our marriage. We always go to bed together, no matter what."

Looking up, she searched his gaze as though to check if he was being facetious. "That's a good rule. But I haven't agreed to calling this a marriage yet."

"Why didn't I know how stubborn you can be?"

"Why didn't I know how manipulative you can be?" she returned on the next breath.

Caio laughed and the sound was full of a relief that filled him. Hope sprung in his chest despite the bitter ground his mother had left behind. Could Nush see him for who he was and still want him?

"On an intellectual level, I know that it's not because you don't want me. But on another level, I know that you're playing a game with me. Holding out on me. I might even call it sexual blackmail because I didn't immediately fall into line with your plans."

He tilted her chin up to face him. "I am surprised by

your resistance, yes. But you give me diabolical motives I'm not guilty of. You know I've been too busy to even have dinner with you. And I wanted to give you time to get used to this."

"So no sex until I give in to your permanent partnership deal?"

Smiling, he ran his fingers over her cast. "You've been using that hand too much with work and now cooking. I also…" he cleared his throat, searching for words so that he didn't embarrass her, "know that you haven't done this before, Nush."

"Done what?"

"Had sex."

"Oh." She blushed then, so prettily that he couldn't help grinning. "Of course, you could tell with how busy your fingers have been."

His chest shook with mirth. "I wasn't going to be all over you, demanding my marital rights after realizing that."

She giggled and it was the sweetest sound Caio had ever heard.

"It's not a big deal, Caio. Yes, some of it was that I was hung up on—"

He pressed a hand to her mouth, his heart thudding as if it had been slammed hard against its cage. "You don't have explain anything to me, *querida*. It just…made me put brakes on how fast I was driving this, that's all."

"I like fast, Caio. I love your speed very much. And you should know that if you were going too fast, I'd protest quite loudly." Then she rubbed the tip of her nose against his in a tender gesture that burned him. "You have to stop making accommodations for me, Caio, as if I were not strong enough to handle you. You've got to trust that I know my own mind."

He nodded, wondering what benevolent god had dropped her into his lap. Because he sure as hell didn't deserve her. "It might hurt, Nush. However much I try to make it better."

"Then isn't it better to get the first time out of the way so that we can get to the better times?"

He shook his head and pulled her up. "Wrap your legs around me."

"Why?"

"You're tiring, Princesa. Let's get you into the shower."

That she didn't deny it told him he was right. "How'd you know?"

"The more it bothers you, the more you cradle your wrist to your chest like a shield." He hefted her into his arms and walked through the house, her outraged giggles that they were ruining the hardwood floors by getting everything wet ringing in his ear. Her laughter reverberated through the empty, desolate house as did her breath through him.

And that small part of him he could never quite shut up asked if she'd let him hold her like that if she knew of the destruction he was wreacking, if she knew how close to the truth she'd come when she'd called him manipulative and controlling and arrogant and how he could lose the battle to win a war.

CHAPTER TEN

I CHOOSE YOU, *N*USH. The words reverberated through Nush like temple bells, restoring her faith in their relationship at a deep, core level where all her insecurities dwelled like sleeping monsters.

By the time she emerged from the shower, hair still mostly damp because she didn't have enough strength in her one weak bicep to dry her thick hair, Caio had arranged everything outside in the patio off the kitchen.

A soft melody belted out from cleverly hidden speakers, the words in Portuguese. Running a hand over her dress, she reminded herself to ask him to teach her the language. She wanted to be able to converse with him in his mother tongue, which was a long-term project for her brain. But more than that, she wanted to understand all the things he muttered to her when he touched her.

He'd set the plates already served with lasagna she'd made, a salad he seemed to have whipped up, a bottle of wine and glasses. A couple of sleek solar heaters kept the space toasty even as a breeze from the ocean tickled its cold fingers once in a while.

Beautiful, rare black roses sitting in a crystal vase at the center of the small table sent her pulse racing all over her body like a loose electrical wire. That he'd remembered what Yana called her morbid fascination with all things dark and decadent made her dizzy with joy.

His hair, like hers, was still wet from the shower and slicked back. He'd dressed in dark jeans and a gray Henley that seemed to span an endlessly broad chest. The sexy casual attire made the dinner feel even more intimate. Like here was another side of Caio Oliveira revealed just for her and only for her pleasure. And God, what those jeans did to that ass.

Feeling suddenly self-conscious, Nush wished she'd taken the time and patience to dry her hair properly. All she'd done in terms of dressing up had been to pull on a loose, sleeveless pink gown with a deep V at the front and slap a little lip gloss onto her lips. After all the fuss she'd made about dining together, maybe she should have…

"Princesa? Have I missed something?"

"No. I just…" Nush swallowed her silly doubts at the possessive gleam in his eyes when they swept over her, lingering everywhere it fluttered. "It's perfect."

"You're the one that is perfection, Nush."

She bit her lip and smiled, fighting the urge to smooth her hair down. Longing twisted through her for something more. Even though she kept begging her greedy heart to stop its needy clamor. "Thank you."

"Shall we eat then?"

Nodding, she joined him at the table. He'd arranged the chairs closer together, looking out into the ocean, instead of on opposite sides of the table. Her belly swooped at how romantic it looked.

When they'd settled into the chairs, he poured himself a glass of wine and produced sparkling water for her. "I'd like wine too," she said, forking a piece of the flat noodles into her mouth.

"I thought you couldn't mix alcohol with your meds."

"It's one glass, Caio. And I'm not really planning to drive myself anywhere."

Nush took a sip after he poured and made a face. The dry bitterness drew a caustic trail down her throat. "That tastes…awful."

"That's a ten-thousand-dollar bottle, Princesa," Caio said, looking suitably horrified by her comment even as his mouth twitched. "Maybe you need a discerning palate to enjoy it."

She stuck her tongue out at him. "I think my dad took care of our palate when it comes to enjoying alcohol one way or the other. After seeing him in one of his binges, none of us can stomach alcohol in any form."

He stared at her. "Then why did you insist I pour you some?"

"Because you decided I couldn't have any," Nush said, biting her lip.

"Stubborn minx."

"Arrogant, high-handed stud."

His laughter provoked her own and they busied themselves with the cutlery.

"I didn't realize how it must affect you, or Yana or Mira, to see him like that."

Nush shrugged. "Mira's the one who's seen him at his worst, who's terrified that that kind of addiction runs in her veins."

"You?"

She shivered and instantly, Caio placed a jacket over her shoulders. "My fears lie in a different place."

His fork clattered to the plate with a loud clank in the silence. "Where?"

"It's not a big deal. Neither is it something you can immediately fix for me."

His brows tied together in a dark scowl. Breath hitching in her chest, Nush watched him.

The wineglass turned round and round in his large hand. "But you know that I'd try anyway, don't you? To fix them for you?"

She swallowed, an overwhelming sense of affection surging through her. Turning away, she took a bite of her food, knowing that any of her attempts to hide from him were only half-hearted. She couldn't play games like him, couldn't control her thoughts and feelings around him in some kind of transaction. A sigh left her. "Promise me you won't think me less for it?"

His golden-brown gaze held hers in a solemn promise. "There's nothing in the world you could tell me that would make me think less of you."

"Mama's mental health problems…are hereditary." She touched his wrist when he'd have spoken up. "I know it's not a guarantee that I'll get them, only that there's a probability higher than…yours, for example. My fear is not even that I'll inherit them. But more irrational…"

"Like what?"

"My recurring nightmare is that I'll be left alone in some clinic, forgotten, with no one to visit me, that I'll just fade away under the kindness of strangers."

With a soft curse, Caio gathered her to him, his arms a steel band around her. "It's never going to come to that, Nush. You're never going to be alone like that. Never."

"I loathe the idea of becoming some kind of burden on you."

"Is that how you think of your mother?"

"Of course not," she said, recoiling at the very thought. "I just… I have a hard time, still, believing that this is all real, Caio. That you want to spend your life with me. That it's not a…"

An angry growl escaped from his mouth, making her pull back from the pit of her own insecurities. "What do I do to prove to you that I want this?"

"You don't have to prove anything to me," she said, alarmed by the hard edge of anger and something more in his voice. "Proofs and transactions and contracts… those won't bind us."

"You're being purposely stubborn about this. Turning this into a battle."

"I'm not, Caio, believe me. Choosing the hard way is Yana's style. Not mine. I just…want this, have wanted this for too long, with everything in me, to let it be anything but real. I'm not holding out on you because I don't want this. But because I…want it too much."

Even out of her periphery, she could see the tension around him deflate at her honest confession.

Hard knuckles dragged down her cheek as he said, "Okay, let me ask you something. Would you turn back on me, desert me if you discovered a new facet to me? If you learned that I…have a real deficiency? Not a mental health problem like you worry about, which makes no woman or man less. If I have a weakness that has been bred into me as a product of cruel circumstance?"

It was her turn to stare at him. There had been something in his voice as he said that, a certainty that there was some dark facet of him that he'd never let her see. Yes, he was ruthless, and ambitious and had an armor that was probably made of platinum but… And even the question was more dare. As if he was playing with her concept of loyalty and commitment.

"If it's some kind of test, it's a horrible one," she said, reaching for the wine. Wanting to wash away the taste of fear from her mouth.

"It's not, Princesa."

"Of course I wouldn't desert you."

"Then you also know that I'd never let you be alone like that, Nush," he said, "no matter what happened between us."

Nush blinked back tears, his promise taking the edge off her deepest fear.

Throwing her own rules out the window, she nuzzled her face into the side of his neck, loving the scent of him, the rough texture of his skin even though he'd just shaved. When she pressed a soft kiss under his ear, his fingers on her arm tightened. With a smile, she catalogued his reaction away.

Her erratic heartbeat settled back into a slow rhythm as she pulled back into her seat.

For a while, they ate in silence, his vow taking on a new depth and breadth between them, morphing into another concrete layer in the foundation of their relationship. Not that everything had been addressed, she knew that.

But it was progress and she reveled in the quiet joy of sharing the moment with him.

"How did I not know that you're such phenomenal cook?" he asked, patting his flat abdomen.

Pleasure filled her like colorful bubbles in a jar at the sight of his empty plate. "I'm full of untold delights like that."

"No arguments there." He kissed her knuckles. "You're like a present I'll unwrap forever, Princesa."

Heat crested her cheeks and Nush cleared her throat. "If you keep saying things like that, I'll melt into goo, and you'll have to scrape me off this lovely patio."

Elbow on the table, he leaned toward her and licked her upper lip. "How's it that you exchange filthy talk like a pro but blush fiercely at simple compliments?"

She bunched the neck of his sweatshirt in her fingers and licked him back, inviting him to do more.

No, she didn't have to wait for him to do anything. He was hers for taking, for mussing up, for reveling in, to do as she pleased. For now, at least.

Bolstered by the thought, she took his mouth in a hungry kiss, pouring every ounce of her need into it.

She moaned when he nipped her lower lip and his tongue swooped into her mouth. The kiss intensified yet again, as if there was nothing but heated embers between them to be stoked into life at the barest contact. Flaring hotter and higher with each day that passed, each layer of vulnerability that was ripped off.

His mouth came back for her—nipping, licking, demanding. Demanding so much that Nush felt like she was nothing but a mass of sensations. God, the man kissed like a hungry beast. As if only devouring her would do. As if she was the only thing in the entire universe. And still, this kiss was different from the other ones. As if there were a million different flavors to be yet discovered between them.

He growled when she pulled away to whisper, "God, Caio. We could be together for seventy years and I'd think I'll want you with this same desperate need."

"Give me your vow, Nush. Give me what I want."

Burying her face in his chest, she whispered, "I'm yours, Caio. And not just because those papers say so."

He held her tightly then, with more affection than passion, she thought. Just like their kisses, this embrace was different from all others.

"How did you learn about the acquisition?" He asked then, and Nush felt the instant change in the tenor around them. His arms around her stiffened. And his embrace went from warm Brazilian coast to Arctic frost in one second. He didn't push her away as much as he slowly untangled them and turned to face the spectacular view. Was that all it took? Her word that she was in?

"The paperwork… I got cc'd on your email by accident."

Nush watched him guzzle down his wine in the periphery of her vision. She turned in her chair, playing with the edges of her napkin. "I looked it up and noticed that it was your father's company that you mentioned. The small start-up he began at the same time as Thaata did with OneTech. Then I called Peter Sr. and he was all too happy to enlighten me that Thaata was against the buyout too."

For a long time, he said nothing. Nerves stretched tight, Nush simply waited.

"He was," he said, rubbing a hand over his face. The wet slosh of the wine as he refilled his glass felt like a boom around then. "Enough to block me from beyond the grave."

"I thought you needed majority because you wanted to reign as king over those vultures on the board. But you needed the executive power to push through the purchase for a…problem-riddled company."

A dark smile flashed at her. "I like being a king who lords it over them too."

"Why didn't you just tell me it was once your father's company, Caio? I don't care if Thaata thought it was a lost cause."

"You'd have taken my side even if it were a complete loss," he said as a statement, a little warmth coming back to his eyes.

"Yes. Do you know how happy I feel that our partnership has enabled you to buy your father's company back?"

"Don't be so eager to celebrate, Nush," he said, with a

sneer that didn't seem to be directed at her. "It's not the happy ending you always want."

The unease in her gut solidified. But Nush refused to let him scare her off the topic. Push her off a subject that had shaped the man she'd married. "Tell me about the company. Please."

He tapped her lips with his fingers. "What a tantalizing puzzle you are, *minha esposa*."

"I don't know what you mean," she said, cheeks heating up.

He leaned down, and took her mouth in a rough, animalistic kiss. It was full of dominance and ego, full of technique and skill employed to leave her panting. To assert his mastery over her senses. Knowing that, she still quivered, a telling dampness at her sex. "Is *handling* me another one of your secret powers, Nush?"

"All I want is to know about the man who shaped you. About your family. About..."

"Do you really need to know, Princesa? Or are you using my reticence as a weapon against me to deny me what I want?"

"You know the answer to the question, Caio. I told you a real marriage is sacred to me. It means being real in the present. But it also means building a future, a future that encompasses so many things that we haven't even touched."

He rubbed the pad of a finger over her lower lip, setting her on fire. "Like what, *querida*?"

"Like kids, Caio. I want a big, boisterous family. I want my kids to be surrounded and loved by family. I want family vacations, school recitals, story times. I want my kids to know that they're loved by their parents, unconditionally. I want them to have everything I didn't as a kid."

His gaze gleamed with emotion as he placed a tender

kiss to her lips that made her emotional all over again. "That sounds like…a future I want to be a part of too, Nush."

Nush exhaled roughly. "Right now, you're no more than a stranger to me. A stranger who carefully filters out what information he'll let me have. A stranger who demands I give everything without giving me anything back. That's not the beginnings of a healthy relationship. That's just a transaction."

His mouth flattened as if her words were a direct hit. She wondered if she'd gone too far. With a rough groan, Caio rubbed his hand down his face. "What do you want to know, Nush?"

"Tell me what this acquisition means to you. This company…"

"My father poured his blood and sweat into it. At the height of his career, it was one of the most successful companies in Sao Paulo. And not just by its workforce or market worth either. It prized financial ethics and family values and had a community with shared values at its core. Papa was its beating heart."

The pride and ache in his voice filled her throat with sudden tears. She took his fingers in hers, wanting to provide him with an anchor in the moment. Wanting to ground him here in the present even as he went away to visit some painful place in the past.

He didn't return her clasp like he usually did, nor did the tension in him abate. But Nush held on. "He sounds like an amazing man. I'd have loved to meet him."

He met her eyes then and she saw that he knew that she meant it with all her heart.

"He'd have loved to meet you too, Anushka." He frowned, studying her as if she was an interesting equation he hadn't seen clearly until that precise moment. "In fact, you're both a lot alike."

"How so?"

"Integrity. Generosity. A seemingly infinite well of quiet strength beneath it all." He rattled them off in a matter-of-fact tone. As if he had to distance himself from Nush too as he'd clearly distanced himself from the memories of the man he'd adored. "A distinct lack of self-preservation or cunning required to survive in this cutthroat world."

"Hey," she said, swatting his arm in mock outrage.

"Just speaking the truth, *querida*." And just like that, she understood the deeper significance of his protectiveness of her.

A long exhale made her chest rise and fall. "What happened to him?"

"He died of heart disease when I was thirteen."

"Oh." She didn't utter any trite comforting words. It was clear that it had devastated him as a child. That it continued to wreck him even now. "Is that when the company fell apart?"

"No. It fell apart, year by year, one underhanded contract after another, one corrupt scheme after the other, once his partner took over. When he realized he didn't have long left, Papa signed over the power of attorney to his partner Carlos. My mother…" such stark anguish crossed his features that it froze Nush in acrid fear, "was a simple soul. She never cared about business or politics or wealth. Papa's partner took advantage of her grief, of her loneliness, of her ignorance, married her within a year of Papa passing. Then he proceeded to drive a wedge between her and me, until she asked me to give up my right to the company. By the time I left to live with Rao, she and I…had become strangers to each other."

The carefully dispassionate way he spoke of his mother…only made the truth that much clearer to Nush. It hid a well of unhealed, festering wounds made of nothing but hurt and pain.

She wanted to throw her arms around him then, to simply hold him. But there was a forbidding quality to him, a brittleness that threatened to shatter everything that was new and fragile between them if she so much as touched him.

"When did she die?"

"Two years after I left. I begged her to join me." Such pure bitterness spewed from his words that Nush wouldn't have been shocked to see them land like acid drops on the air. "But she kept saying her sons needed her."

"Her *sons*?" She wasn't able to keep her shock out of it.

"She has two sons with him. Twins. Jorge and Javier."

Shock turned her words into a whisper. "Your brothers, you mean?"

Another shrug.

Her chest was so tight that she had to force herself to breathe. "You never saw her again?"

He shook his head and upended another glass of wine down his throat.

"I'm so sorry, Caio. I can't imagine…not being able to say goodbye."

"It is what it is, Princesa. Her priorities were different from mine."

Nush wanted to argue, to say she didn't agree with that. She wanted to delve but was it for anything other than to satisfy her curiosity? Was it for any reason other than to poke her finger into an unhealed wound and make it spill forth more poison? But if he didn't talk about this with her, if that hurt wasn't purged…

He's shared this much, Nush. Give it time. That voice

distinctly sounded like Thaata and Nush pushed away the more intrusive questions.

"But you've bought the company now," she said, infusing a lightness she didn't feel into her words. "You can build it up bigger and better than before. Bring back all those principles your father valued. Make it a monument to his big heart and values."

Caio stared at her as if she'd suddenly grown two horns, his sensuous mouth twisting into a distasteful slant. "No."

"What do you mean no?" she said, any semblance of remaining the steady, sensible one in this difficult conversation shattering at the resolute will of that single word.

"There's nothing of my father or his legacy left in that company, Nush."

Nush got to her feet, startled by the vehemence of his words. "You bought it to destroy it?" Clarity came like a veil being lifted permanently. "You set your stepfather up to fall, to lose everything, didn't you?"

"Carlos already destroyed everything good about it, Princesa." By the way he spat that name, Nush knew it was his stepfather. "Lured by the idea of more and more profits, he made one bad deal after the other when he had no resources to deliver. His son Enzo embezzled the pension funds of the employees. Carlos is in crippling debt, all the livelihoods under his care ruined, and he was still looking for a payout. All that's left to do is to pull out its very rotten foundation and grind it to nothing, to reduce the rubble to ashes."

Emotions thrashing in her chest, Nush stared at him. She'd always known there was a well of anger and pain under Caio's smooth facade. Had realized, even as a teenager, that something dark fueled his every move. But to know it as vague speculation and to see it were different.

To stand in its direct path was terrifying at a soul-deep level. "And you've been planning this for how long?"

"More than a decade."

"That's…horrible." Agitation pushed her words out. This was why her grandfather had been against Caio going ahead with this. Because if he did this, he was permanently shutting down any connection left to his past. With the bad, he was burning down the good too. "To work toward that kind of destruction for years…you'd have to be…empty of all good things."

"Are you already regretting your promises, Nush?" he said, taking in her defensive posture with her arms around her waist. The distance she'd imposed between them.

She pressed a hand to her forehead, refusing to let him make this about her. "I'm just sad that all of his good name, everything your father stood for, it has to come to dust and ashes like this. That everything you…" She plunged her fingers into his hair, feeling as if her own heart suddenly had a crack in it. "This can't be it, Caio. Tell me the truth. Tell me that's what has been hounding you for the past week. Tell me it feels like a defeat."

He pushed away from her touch. "I have everything I've ever wanted—OneTech, you, this house, the whole bloody island—while Carlos will be left with nothing."

Nush didn't point out that his reassurance sounded painfully hollow and empty. "You've clearly thought this through," she said, forcing a semblance of acceptance into her words. Into her heart. For now, at least. This wasn't a wound that would heal immediately, or pain that would wash away from one conversation with her, however much she wanted that for him.

"Don't waste your bleeding heart on this, Nush."

And that felt like a premonition more than a warning. Nush took her another step back, knowing that both of them needed space to process this. That the threads binding them were still too fragile to bear the heavy weight of her dissent right now, as much as she wanted to scream it at him.

"I'm going to bed."

He didn't look at her then and it felt like this was a defeat too. Like the bridge they were building to each other was already wobbling. "Don't forget your pills, Princesa."

Nush walked away. But she stopped when she reached the massive living room because she couldn't bear to leave him like that. As if he were all alone in the world, even if he didn't say it.

And where it mattered, in the vulnerable places that lived in all of them, that some of them covered up better than others by hiding and shying away in the margins of life, drenched in fear of loss, that some of them replaced with ambition and success and material possessions they didn't even want, Nush knew Caio was less for the loss of his family. Less for not knowing his brothers. Less for shutting down parts of himself. Less than the great man his father had been.

Which meant he had less of himself to give this thing between them, to give her, whereas she'd already given more than she could afford, all that she had.

All in, as always, Nushie-kins? she could almost hear Yana say in her admonishing voice. *Tsk-tsk...learn how to play the game.*

But it wasn't over. Neither Yana nor Caio understood that part. As afraid she was of who Caio was becoming and what was in thefuture for them, she couldn't simply abandon him when he needed her. It wasn't in her.

Only what if he didn't even admit that he needed her? What if he pushed her away like he'd done with the memories of his mother or the future he could have had with his half-brothers? What if she didn't agree with him and he decided he'd had enough of her too?

Could she walk away from him tonight knowing how closed off he was? Knowing he was choosing destruction and more pain when he could have something else?

No.

But it couldn't be finished as easily as that. Not when their story was just beginning. Not when he'd stood by her side through all her hard times.

"Caio?"

Her breath came easy when he turned and met her eyes.

"Was that our first big fight?" she said, half laughing, half crying, throwing him a rope and asking him to grab it with both hands.

His head dipped, his forearms braced on his knees, his wineglass dangling precariously between his fingers. "I don't know." Looking up, his gaze pinned her where she stood. Hunger and heat arced into life between them with a snap like an electric whip. "But you got what you wanted, Princesa," he said with a soft growl. "You know now what I'm made of. If you want to break your word, Nush, now's the time. Before I—"

"I think it was a fight," she said, shutting down his line of thinking. She smiled then, through the tears in her eyes, and the furrow between his brows cleared. "When you're ready to make up, you know where to find me."

His golden eyes gleamed again, that faraway look dissipating instantly. "Yeah?"

"Yeah. I want to make up the fun way. I hear that's the only good thing about fighting as a couple. And Caio?"

"Yes, Princesa?"

"I want to be your wife. Tonight, in every way that matters." Finally, she was beginning to understand him. Was beginning to know the real him—hard, cutting edges and all. And if he wanted her in his life, then he'd have to know her as her too. And that was someone who wouldn't let him make a wrong decision, someone who hated seeing him in pain. "Don't make me wait."

"Is that a threat?" he said, back to playing that wicked game of his.

"Yes," Nush said throwing herself all the way in. "But it's also an entreaty."

She didn't wait to see his reaction but she heard his pithy curse and she wondered that for all the games Yana had played all her life, her sister had never managed to understand the subtle tactic that sometimes to win, one had to surrender completely first.

CHAPTER ELEVEN

THE SOFT BUSS of lips at her cheek instantly awoke Nush from a restless slumber. "Caio?" she whispered, her hands reaching out for him automatically.

His rough, calloused hands took hers, as her eyes got used to the darkness of the bedroom. He'd been standing by the bed on her side, bending over to kiss her. A thread of fear wound through her and words rushed out through a dry mouth. "Are you leaving?"

"No. Of course not. I only meant to check on you, make sure you didn't tangle yourself up in the sheets. You're the most violently active person in sleep."

"Oh," she whispered, feeling a flicker of joy at her chest. In the big scheme of things, it wasn't a big deal that he knew her sleep habits or that he'd wanted to check on her. But to her silly heart, it was a huge thing.

"I didn't mean to disturb you. Go back to sleep, *querida*."

When he'd have pulled away, Nush tightened her grasp of him. "No, wait."

His white smile flashed in the darkness and she breathed out in relief. She saw him thrust his hand through his hair, and sigh. "I demolished the entire bottle of wine, I'm in a sullen mood and sleep is far away for me, Nush. I'll only disturb yours."

Swallowing, Nush pushed up until she was half sitting, supported by her elbow and his tight grip. “I didn’t mean to upset you by raking up… Earlier, I mean,” she said, wanting to soothe him.

Caio rarely ever let her see him in a dark mood and clearly, she’d breached some invisible boundary she hadn’t even known existed.

“You didn’t upset me. It’s not something that’s…ever far from my mind.”

Nush swallowed the urge to say that that was by design. His ruthless pursuit of the company, this house even… he’d made the loss of everything a part of himself. He’d turned it into the fuel that drove him. And like a virus, it thrived inside him.

His thumb traced the plump veins on the back of her hand, the touch infinitely gentle. “It’s okay if you do upset me.”

“I know that,” she said, grinning cheekily. “I just meant that I didn’t mean to upset you tonight. Especially not when I want you in a favorable mood.”

His grin made her feel as if she’d won the biggest prize in the world. “And why did you want me in a favorable mood?”

“I’m bad at this, Caio,” she said, hiding half her face in the pillow. “Fighting with you, I excel at. Throwing dirty talk in your face to rile you up, give me a diploma already. But this…the real thing… I need you to drive this.”

His palm covered the other half of her face, encasing it completely. Nush had imagined all kinds of scenarios between them and yet she’d never expected the tenderness with which he constantly touched her. And that made her realize that he did touch her a lot. Outside of sexual context. As if it were as necessary as breath.

Her chest felt like an enlarged balloon, full of wonder and joy and more.

"You're better at it than you think you are."

"Then stay, please." She placed a kiss at the center of his palm, and then licked the spot. His indrawn breath filled the air around them. Egged on by it, Nush dug her teeth into the thick pad of his palm and the tension radiating from him increased a hundredfold. Then she blew on the hurt she'd given him, pressing soft kisses to his wrist.

His thumb traced her lips and then plunged into her mouth. She gave it the same thorough treatment, nipping and biting and licking, sucking on it, until his harsh breathing was a symphony in the room.

"I am a little drunk, Princesa. I might not be—"

"Jesus, Caio, when will you understand that I trust you more than I've ever trusted another person? Even myself at times." Her voice had risen, something electric arcing through her words.

Bringing her hand to his face, Caio buried it in her palm. "That's what makes this so hard. I'm not sure I deserve it."

"I told you. That's not how any of this works. There's no deserving when it comes to…" She swallowed the words that automatically rose to her lips, feeling as if she'd suddenly been plunged into ice-cold water. "Stop making me beg you."

"Turn on the night lamp," he said, command and desire in it making his voice deeper and heavier than she'd ever heard before.

She remained silent, and unmoving, suddenly nervous at the prospect of what she'd wondered for years. It wasn't that she was insecure about her body so much as she wanted to please him. Having tried multiple times with not-quite-unpleasant partners, and then freezing halfway through, she didn't want to face the same mental block again with Caio of all people.

The lamp turned on and she blinked. When she lifted her eyes, Caio was leaning over her, his broad chest tantalizingly bare and within reach. He bent and took her mouth in a gentle, soft kiss that made her heart crawl up into her throat. "I will be as gentle as you need, Princesa."

"Tell me what you like, please," she whispered against the tug of his teeth, her body arching off the bed toward him like a magnet.

"Touch me. Whatever you want to do to me will please me, Nush. That you want me like you do makes me half-hard most of the time."

Nush didn't have to be told again. She ran her hands over his chest in mindless circles, relishing everything about him. Christ, every inch of him was delineated and defined. The hard, defined pecs, the springy hair sprinkled throughout, the rippling definition of his abdomen muscles, the taut musculature of his back and the dark trail of hair lower that disappeared into his jeans…everything about him appealed to her starved senses. Every cell in her arched up to feel and absorb as much of him as possible.

His rough growl at her mouth when she raked her fingernails down his stomach egged her on. Everything was contrasts—the roughness of his kiss and the softness of his lips, the light bursting behind her eyes and the darkness that surrounded them, the bubbling lightness that spread through her that she was finally, finally, doing this with the man she'd wanted for so long.

Her eyes drew closed even as the kiss morphed from lazy, tender exploration to something else. Something hungry and needy and dirty.

"Let's get this off," he said, placing one knee on the bed, right between her thighs.

Greedily, Nush scooted closer as he reached for the hem of her sleeveless tee. His laughter surrounded her as he realized what she'd been trying to do and he pulled her onto his thigh.

Nush threw her head back, clinging to him as his hard thigh gave her the friction she desperately wanted. She didn't know how he managed to get the tee off or when he'd climbed onto the bed and lifted her atop him until she was straddling him or when he'd got her panties off.

All she knew was that he gave her everything she needed. His calloused hands roaming her bare skin, cupping and kneading her breasts, his fingers drawing mindless circles around her nipples, and his thick erection nudging against the folds of her sex.

"Open your eyes, Nush. Look at me."

If he asked her to follow him the through the gates of hell just then, Nush would've happily done so. The sight that met her eyes tightened the fist tugging down in her lower belly. He still had his jeans on even though the button was undone and her sex was indecently open and rubbing against the hard ridge of his abdomen, while his erection nudged at her buttocks.

Heat crested her cheeks at the wetness she'd left on his bare skin. As she watched, he rubbed the dampness onto his skin with one long, elegant finger, the act downright filthy and erotic. And then he brought the tip of his finger to his mouth and licked it away.

"How do I taste?" Nush asked, any nervousness she'd felt earlier misting away at the dark, hungry gleam in his eyes. It was liberating that she could say anything that came to her mind and he only found it arousing.

Hair mussed by her fingers, mouth swollen from her

greedy kisses, he looked like the stuff of her wet fantasies come true. He gave a thoughtful hum, as if considering the question before he said, "Like you're mine."

Nush arched into his touch, her spine elongating like a cat stretching, desire vibrating through her body. And Caio played her perfectly.

Touching her everywhere but never lingering long enough.

Over and over, bringing her to the edge and talking her down.

Asking her to trust him when she protested.

Filthy curses flying from his own mouth when she dug her teeth into his shoulder, encouraging her to do to him as she pleased.

It was like waiting for a storm and yet not knowing when it would hit.

Tongue and teeth licking and tugging at her nipples, those clever fingers learning and relearning her folds, his thumb playing decadent peekaboo with her clit, he pushed her toward the peak all over again. Soon, every inch of her was damp with sweat, muscles tense and tight, skin oversensitized.

She ground down on his fingers when he penetrated her, cursing at him to go faster when he barely moved them inside her, screaming that she hated him when he edged her once again, and then finally, he gave it to her with a gleaming smile and a whispered "You're achingly perfect and you're all mine, Princesa."

The orgasm caught her by surprise and ripped through her, stealing her breath, making her sob incoherently, while she chanted Caio's name like it was a benediction. She should've been used to it—to the physical and emotional cleansing it felt like every time he made her come.

Like he'd smashed her into pieces and put her back together again and every time, she emerged a little different. A little less scared of her own heart.

It was minutes before Nush could form some kind of coherent thought. She was on her back, Caio's fingers lazily drifting up and down her side, her breaths still shallow and too fast. The cold of the damp sheets was a welcome contrast to the pockets of heat still tingling over her skin.

"I thought I died," she said, tasting salt on her tongue.

"I wouldn't let anything happen to you, Princesa." He asked, a sudden gravity to his tone, "You okay?"

"You know when I went on all those dates with all those men over the last year?" she said, her throat hoarse after all the moaning and sobbing, her words shooting out of a place she hadn't even known she wanted to visit. Especially in front of Caio.

Maybe the orgasm had undone not only her body but unlocked her heart too.

It's just damn good sex, Nushie, she could hear Yana say with a roll of her eyes. *Not magical healing.*

But neither could Nush discount the fact that this intimacy hadn't been possible for her with any other man except Caio, because she was emotionally invested in him already. Because she'd needed this real intimacy to go further.

The sudden tension that gripped Caio was a tangible thing in the air that plucked at Nush's wooly head. "Is this punishment for stringing your release along for too long?" His voice was only half joking.

But it didn't stop Nush. It seemed nothing could now.

"I was trying to get you out of my head. It got distressing to see you every day, every minute, to be so close and not tell you that I… I was determined that I'd prove to myself that it was just attraction. Lust. I'd idolized you for so long and somewhere along the line, it morphed into this…desire. I desperately wanted you to see me as a woman. I built up all these insecurities about why you didn't and I drove myself nuts."

"You're the most beautiful woman I've ever seen, Princesa."

To her pleasant surprise, Nush found that his words sank deep, that she believed him wholeheartedly. He saw beauty in her, conveyed it in his words, his touch, his kisses, and who was she to question that? All the ways he made her respond, the pleasure her body sang for him, what they had together was beautiful and powerful in itself. More than simple chemistry.

"Thank you," she said, running a finger over the furrow between his brows.

He held her wrist and again, pushed his face into her touch. "We don't have to talk about this. Now or ever."

And that sent a niggle through her. He was so reluctant to hear about her feelings for him, even as he demanded all that she had to give. "I'm not ashamed of how I feel, Caio. It's just that I think I see it finally. Why it didn't work with any of them. Why even when they were nice and pleasant, I couldn't go through with it. I used to think it was a mental block to do with how…everyone called me weird for so long."

His silence, instead of discouraging her, prodded her on.

"It was a block but not that. I simply didn't want any of those men even if I convinced myself I did. I've been in love with you for so long that…it was the last thing I wanted to admit to. I tried to purge it by going out with others. But my heart wasn't in it. And I backed off every time and my reputation grew even more bizarre."

As wrapped up as he was around her, Nush felt the

tension that gripped him. What was heartfelt on her part gave way to an awkwardness she couldn't seem to dispel. Still, she tried. "That I love you…it's as natural as breathing for me, Caio. It's not a demand or a price or a weapon. It simply just is."

Caio kissed her shoulder, gathering her to him with tender reverence that plucked at her heart. "You're a gift I don't deserve, Nush."

And then he kissed her again, before she could argue with his questionable concept of deserving again, pushing her back into the sheets.

There was an urgency and something more to his kisses, a sense of determination. As if he wanted to make up for something he couldn't give.

The final piece of puzzle in place, Nush let herself float on the cloud of pleasure he pushed her onto. Already, all of her was addicted to him. And now she tested the words on her lips, of the truth she'd fought for so long.

She was in love with Caio. That was her truth. Her vulnerability. Her strength. And there wasn't much she could actually do about it. Her past and her present and her future all irrevocably tied to him who only dealt in absolutes. In words like *loyalty* and *commitment* and *deals.* In the past that was full of pain and ache and hatred.

She'd been in love with him for as long as she could remember. She wondered if she should be scared, if she should worry that he didn't feel the same but all her *shoulds* melted as he worshipped her with his mouth.

There wasn't an inch of her he didn't kiss, an inch of her he didn't learn. An inch of her he didn't bring into sharp clarity, teaching her new, exciting things about pleasure and her own body and how he could make her addicted to it all.

His hands were everywhere but stayed nowhere. Never

long enough or lingering enough. On the bare swells of her breasts. Over one of her peaked nipples that was wet and glistening. Over her hips that bore his fingers' imprints. Over her thighs that she'd compulsively wrapped around his hips. Only inciting her further, only driving her toward that peak that she'd already thrown herself off.

He built her all over and all the while Nush was aware of the press of his thick, hard length against her outer thigh. "Can I touch you?"

His answer was a grin against her mouth before he drew her hand to his shaft and guided her fingers.

Turning on her side, unable to see him, Nush let touch and sensation speak to her. He was hard and thick and pulsing in her clasp. She traced the tip of it with her finger and found a drop of liquid. Her sex clenched, hungry for him all over again. Dampness fluttered even as her clit felt swollen and sensitive. "Is this okay?"

"Everything's okay between us, Nush," he said, thrusting his hips into her clasp as she moved her fist up and down.

Releasing his erection, she brought her finger to her lips and tasted him. He was unlike anything she'd ever tasted and the dark gleam in his eyes made her want to lick him up all over. "I'm not ready to swallow yet, but that's my goal. Just so you know."

A filthy curse from him echoed around them. "I don't know whether to mar you or worship you."

"Why does it have to be one or the other?" she said, sending her hand on another foray. His shaft twitched in her hand, and the more she fisted it, the more Nush could see the tension vibrate through him. A displeased growl fell from her mouth as she could only do so much with one hand out of commission.

She fell onto her back and he followed, and finally,

oh, finally, he bore down on her. Not giving her all of his weight though. Nush panted at the delicious weight of him and her thighs instantly fell open for him. Like a cat in heat, she rubbed her bare breasts against his hair-roughened chest and the erotic shock of that sensation made her roll her eyes back.

Nush nudged her hips upward, following instincts she didn't know she possessed and it was the most delicious feeling she'd ever known. And then he was there, running the head of his cock through her folds, drenching himself in her wetness, igniting a thousand sparks all over again.

"Hold on to me, Princesa."

Nush did, breaths coming helter-skelter now as the fat head of his erection dipped into her heat. It was tight and hot and her heart felt like it would beat out of her chest if he didn't continue.

"Look into my eyes, Nush. Keep touching me and yourself. Give me everything you've got, *minha esposa*."

Nush followed his order, melting at the gravelly command. Melting at the taste of him. Melting at the feel of his taut, tense muscles rippling as she raked her fingernails down his skin. Melting as sensations she'd never known before, pain and pleasure, suffused her.

Caio drove into her inch by merciless inch, going impossibly slow and she knew from the concrete set of his jaw that it was costing him every bit of his steely control.

Arching up, she rubbed herself against his chest. Touched him everywhere, whispering to him that she wanted all of him. And then with one merciless thrust, he penetrated her so deep that he was a part of her.

The pain was intense, cleaving through her pelvis, but fled as fast as it came. She gasped in air through her mouth, willing herself to breathe through it. Eyes closed, fingers digging into his shoulder, she tried not to betray her shaking. Not to give in to fear and push him off.

"I'm sorry, Nush," Caio breathed out. "Taking longer would only prolong the pain."

A drop of sweat hitting her shoulder made her look up. Golden eyes darkened impossibly, his jaw was so tight that a muscle jumped violently in his cheek. The regret in his eyes was like a balm to the pain that was already fleeting. Giving way to an achy fullness that she wanted to explore.

Nush clasped his cheek, pushed up and kissed him. Even the little movement made her gasp, her pelvic muscles clenching and releasing in an instinctive reaction. "I know," she said, rubbing her cheek against his like a cat.

"Don't, Anushka," he gritted out as a warning making her giggle. "Let me catch my breath."

His lips were soft and gentle, a sizzling contrast to the impossible hardness of him inside her. Wrapping her legs higher on his hips, Nush clung to him with one arm around his back. "It's almost gone, Caio."

He licked into her mouth with a groan. "That was the worst, Princesa. I'll make it better and better every time."

"I know." She stretched as he drew a line of kisses down her throat, wondering if it would ever stop feeling so new, so fervent. If she'd ever have enough of him. "Hey Caio?"

"Yes, Nush?"

"Do you think we can be ambitious enough to try and make me come again?"

He laughed, just as she'd intended and Nush fell in love with him all over again.

He was hers, irrevocably, and the simple fact terrorized her as much as it made her want to fly.

Her laughter and her wanton request were as arousing as the tight clutch of her sex. It had taken everything Caio had and more to be gentle when her wet heat had begun swallowing him with the same greediness that Nush showed in her words.

Sex was all he'd ever known but with Nush, it was making love, as much as he wanted to deny it. In this, he yielded the fight with grace.

This woman he'd married for all the wrong reasons demanded to be made love to, so he did it. Showing her with his mouth and fingers and his kisses and caresses that she was already invaluable to him. Making love to her because it was the only thing he could give her.

Not for a second did he forget the utter disbelief and horror in her eyes when he'd told her about his intentions for his father's company. If it could even be called that anymore.

But how could he stop now? How could he have any peace if he didn't see this through? How he could start a new chapter of his life with Nush if he didn't destroy the ugly pain and ache he'd stored up as if it were life-giving elixir?

If he didn't burn it all down and start afresh—the humiliation he'd suffered at Carlos's cruel taunts, the pain he'd suffered at his bullying son Enzo's fists, the agony of knowing that his mother had no strength to defy the man she'd married in haste, not even to protect Caio, the shattering of his heart when he realized she'd simply cast him out to protect her other sons, the loneliness, the pain of being ripped from the only home he'd ever known, of losing his father's legacy… He had to burn all the pain and bitterness away. Only then Nush could have what little was left of him fully, without those demons haunting him. Without the need for revenge hollowing him out. Only then could he break free and build a future she'd brought to shape.

She'd always known him as this hard shell of a man. She'd picked him, had chosen to tie her life with his, knowing this was all he could give her. She'd confessed her love for him, knowing he wouldn't return it, he reminded himself.

No, his path was made.

It was only her easy declaration that had shaken him. That had planted all these doubts in his head.

"Caio?"

"Yes, *querida*?"

"Are you…is everything okay?"

He looked down and his heart ached at the picture she made. Wide eyes that demanded all his secrets, wavy hair spread out behind her, silky skin sweat dampened, mouth glistening pink…she was his every fantasy come true. "Yes. It's more than okay, Nush. You, me, this… It's better than I could've ever imagined."

She smiled then and it felt like basking in the warmth of a sun after a long, dark winter. "It doesn't hurt that much anymore. Can you…? Can we…?" She gave an experimental thrust of her hips and fire rippled down his spine, pooling low.

He groaned, licked the drop of sweat dripping down the valley between her breasts.

Pushing away any other doubts that threatened to mar the sheer bliss of this moment for her and him, he kissed her gently.

Just a few more days and he would be…ready for this. Fully ready. Fully free.

Amassing all the patience and reverence and his experience, he applied himself to giving her the one thing she had asked of him.

Holding himself off her on one elbow, he plucked at the taut nipple calling for his attention. He licked it, before sucking into his mouth and beneath him, Nush trembled, arching off the bed into him. Demanding more.

More, more and more, even as if he gave her everything.

Even as she clung to his neck with one arm, she sent her other hand on a quest of his body. Fingers like butterfly wings explored his neck, his pecs, his abdomen, and Cristo, where they were joined even.

The woman was analytical and there was no stopping her curiosity.

A growl escaped his mouth as he felt her fingers flutter over his balls, traced over the root of his cock, following to the folds of her sex. “Touch your clit, Nush.”

“Yes sir,” she whispered cheekily and drew circles over her clit. Seeing her fingers move over that swollen flesh, Cristo, that was an image that would haunt him forever.

He pulled out, and thrust in, a deep heat gathering at the base of his spine.

Her own growl joined his. “I’m getting there, Caio. God, please push me off. Now.”

Lifting her hips off the bed, he thrust in and out at an angle, his own climax reaching and roaring for him.

“Oh…” she whispered, head thrown back as he hit her clit on the way in and out. “Caio, I feel it. I feel it here,” she said, touching the slit of her sex when he’d almost pulled out completely.

He grinned and their eyes met. “Collecting all the data, Princesa?”

“You know it.” Sweat-dampened brow, lush full lips, and chest covered in his stubble burn, she was the most erotic thing he’d ever seen. “Now, harder. Caio. Please, faster.”

“Keep touching yourself,” he whispered and then his rhythm became something else.

It became madness. It became a hungry bellow from his chest. It became a hungry claiming like he'd never known before.

She got her wish, screaming out his name as she climaxed and her clenching muscles tipped Caio over. He came with a hard burning rasp wrenched from his throat, heat invading every limb and muscle and leaving him shaken. For a few seconds, he allowed himself the luxury of feeling her under him, burying his face in her neck and inhaling the scent their bodies coated the air with. In his arms, she felt small, fragile and yet there was such power in her to…shatter him if she wished.

The thought made his chest cold and he moved to lift away from her.

Her hands on his shoulder, she stopped him. "We did it," Nush whispered, eyes gleaming, and his heart thumped unsteadily in his chest.

Suddenly, his life without Nush in it didn't bear thinking about. Maybe this wasn't something he'd imagined his life to play out, but he wasn't foolish enough to reject a gift just because he hadn't recognized it immediately for what it was. But would her love for him last when he didn't return it? When it would always be marred by a shadow of disbelief and fear that she'd take it back?

Would she realize one day that he didn't deserve it?

CHAPTER TWELVE

IT WAS LUNCHTIME when Caio jumped out of the helicopter and signaled his pilot to leave. He'd been terse and short and unsettled all day and most of his team had sighed out in relief when he'd announced that he was taking off for the day.

As the chopper's wind blew at him, playing with his hair and clothes, Caio admitted the truth he'd been fighting all week.

His heart was not in it anymore. In seeing his plans through—the very plans it had taken him more than a decade to set in motion.

Seeing his stepfather Carlos's face turn frightfully purple as Caio had walked into his office two days ago to reveal to him that he was the designer of his destruction had not been as satisfactory as he'd expected. Not when he had to face the diseased spirit of employees who had been with the company from his father's time.

The last decade and more had not been kind to Carlos. In fact, Caio wondered if his ruin had begun from the day Caio's mother had died.

It had only left him with disgust as to how many lives Carlos had actually ruined. And neither had there been satisfaction in seeing his stepbrother Enzo dragged away by the police for embezzling pension funds, for all the Ponzi schemes he'd run using Caio's father's name. Not when Caio had also been witness to Enzo's wife's tears—a woman Caio himself had once liked. In the battle that had resulted between him and Enzo, Sophia had chosen Enzo, knowing of Caio's imminent ruin, and expulsion from his own father's company.

But nothing in him today had liked the misery on Sophia's face or seeing the framed picture of her three kids on her desk whose futures had been shattered by everything Caio had unleashed.

All he had known then was that he had to leave. Nothing was going as he'd planned. It hadn't felt like freedom from the fury that had coursed through him, corroding him for years. It hadn't felt like relief from the isolation he'd felt, from his family, from his own identity as the son who'd been loved by his parents.

He'd thought he'd feel redeemed, different, maybe even renewed.

But all he'd felt was…this gnawing, aching sense of loss. This emptiness, as if revenge had scoured him and left him with nothing.

Only the thought of returning to Nush had energized him.

He needed to see Nush, needed to touch her and hold her. He needed to make sure she was still there, to reassure himself that she was the only certainty left in his life.

He heard the laughter long before he saw them, as he walked around the house. They were sitting at a table next to the pool, heads bent together, and laughing. The woman was Anushka, Caio knew that. He would know that laughter anywhere.

Finally, he could see them.

She was dressed in a pink top that dangled off her shoulder, and black shorts with her legs kicked out. The man…his profile seemed familiar. Even as Caio frowned, the man pointed to something, Nush laughed and swatted him on the shoulder.

Another step, another hard breath and Caio knew.

He knew who the man was.

As if punched by an invisible first in his gut, every inch of him stilled. It was a wonder he hadn't put up his fists to defend himself. That was how painfully real that hit felt.

Thoughts and questions swirled through him, like lines in a complex algorithm that flashed across the screen when the program he and Nash built together ran. He couldn't pin anything down. He even made a half turning motion, some primitive instinct part of him urging him to flee.

It felt like betrayal—her sitting with him. Her talking with him. Her laughter with his brother. Her going behind his back.

"Caio? You're back."

Caio hadn't seen Javier since he had arrived in Brazil. If he was completely honest with himself, he'd been avoiding Javier.

Even though Javi had called his assistant several times, requesting a meeting. He'd even showed up once outside of Caio's temporary HQ but he'd pretended to have not seen the younger man. Just like he hadn't set foot in the headquarters of his father's company.

It wasn't Carlos or Enzo or his other brother Jorge that he had wanted to avoid. But this young man in front of him, who reminded Caio the most of their mother.

Caio watched him now with the greediness, all the limits and restrictions placed on himself blown to smithereens by his conniving little wife. It was another punch to his gut—how much Javier looked like Caio himself.

He counted to some arbitrary number before he let his gaze touch Anushka.

As if aware of this microaggression, she raised her brows and glared at him, instead of looking even remotely guilty.

He let her see his fury.

She sighed, her large eyes drinking him in greedily. "If you have something to say, Caio, please feel free to do it."

"We will deal with our…issues in privacy, *minha esposa*," he said, enunciating the endearment. He was blazingly angry and yet the anger seemed to wash away resentment and the sense of betrayal that he wanted to hold on to. Because anything he felt around the blasted woman was far too real and welcome. Even his body seemed to know that but not his rational mind. "After I deal with the unwanted guest."

"Caio, I apologize—" his brother began.

Hand on his shoulder, Nush defended Javi as if he were her cub. "No, Javi. Don't apologize," she said, standing up. "This is not just his house. It's mine too. My home. And as such, I'm allowed to have guests. If Caio doesn't like that, then he can go inside and take his black mood with him."

Caio couldn't remember another occasion—not even as a boy—when someone had so outrageously provoked his temper. Not only had she gone behind his back and invited his brother here, but now she dared to defend Javi, to throw herself in front of him as if Caio would eat him alive…

"What the hell are you smiling at, Javier?" The question burst out of him before he had consciously decided that he would speak to his brother. A part of him wanted to dismiss him, have him thrown out of this house, this new life he was building for himself. A part of him wanted not even the shadow of his brother to touch Anushka. But clearly, it was too late for that.

The diplomat he always was, Javi just shrugged. "Congratulations on your wedding, Caio. Your wife is…" His mouth twitching, he cast Nush a sideways glance, and even in just the flash of a second, Caio could see how smitten Javier was with her, and he had to swallow down an irrational spurt of jealousy. "She is delightful," Javier finished. "I'm glad to see you settled and happy, finally." There was such genuine emotion in Javi's words that Caio's own anger ebbed as fast as it had come. And he wasn't ready for that.

"I've been happy for a long time, Javi," he added, like a petulant schoolboy. Even though he knew his words were false.

"Can you really say that?" Javier demanded in a soft voice. "Because if you've been so happy, why have you been hiding from me? Why carry out your elaborate charade of stripping everything from Carlos but avoid me and Jorge?"

"Get out," Caio said finally in a soft whisper.

"No," Nush said, defiance shining in her gaze. "Not until you listen to what he has to say. Please, Caio… I went to a lot of trouble to get him here."

"I told you it was useless, Anushka," Javi said, his eyes on Caio. "He has turned his back on us a long time ago. It is only you who holds impossible dreams and hopes for him."

Ire flared in Caio's depths. "Don't talk to my wife like that."

"Why not? The foolish woman thinks the world of you when you can't even—"

When Caio would've punched him in the face, Nush stopped him with a hand on his chest. "Jesus, Caio. Can't you see that he's provoking you?" She pressed her forehead into his chest, wrapping her arms around him. "Just give him a chance."

"You shouldn't have interfered, Princesa. This is none of your business," he said, tucking his hands into his pockets and turning away from her. He closed his eyes when he heard her soft gasp. And he had to stiffen himself, stop himself from soothing the hurt.

"Everything that concerns you is my business. This path of destruction you're on is my business."

He turned toward her, feeling like a cornered, wounded animal. "Walk away if I'm not good enough for you, Nush. But please, don't assume to know my pain."

Nush flinched, and still, she didn't walk away. "You don't mean that?"

"Whatever you think this will do, you're wrong," he said, gentling his words. "I have had more than a decade to nurse this resentment and anger and pain. Nothing Javier tells me today is going to get rid of it."

Clasping his face with her hands, Nush pressed a soft kiss to his lips. "This is not a quid pro quo. My promise to you is unconditional. But I can't see you ripping yourself in half either. Please, Caio, do this for me. I've never asked you for anything before."

She walked away, leaving him feeling alone in the entire world all over again.

Hands tucked into his pockets, Caio turned to his brother. "What's there for us to discuss, Javi? What can you feel for me after I've destroyed your father and brother? Because I won't take that back for anyone. Carlos and Enzo deserve to rot in jail."

His brother scowled. "You think I'm here to beg for mercy on their behalf?"

"Or to curse me for ruining them?"

"I know you have had a long time to hate all of us, Caio. And I can't even blame you for any of it. It took me and Jorge a long time to see Papa's true nature. It took me a long time to catch up to how Enzo was bullying Jorge right under my nose. The same thing he did to you..."

A feral sound escaped Caio's mouth but it wasn't because of the past. It was at the thought of their gentle, quiet, artistic brother Jorge being Enzo's new victim. He rubbed a hand over his face and found it shaking. "Enzo bullied Jorge?"

Javi nodded after a hard swallow. "I did my best to stop him, to remove Jorge from his presence. I used all the money you kept sending us to protect Jorge."

"Why didn't you just leave?" Caio thundered, guilt a fresh thorn under his skin.

For so long, he hadn't even looked back and now, to realize that he could have put an end to all this, that he could've stopped Jorge from being hurt as he had been once.

"You never once looked back," Javi said, pain and even resentment etched into his own face. "You just left one day, Caio. Without goodbye. Without uttering a word to me or Jorge. And then Mama fell sick. I looked after her while she pined over you. She died of a broken heart, Caio. And all the time, Enzo and Papa kept telling me and Jorge lies about you. Who do you think I'd believe first?"

Caio closed his eyes, a part of him shying away from meeting his brother's gaze. "I sent you money."

"And that was the first sign that you even cared about us, the first communication I had from you after years." A bitter laugh escaped his brother's throat. "We needed you, Caio. Not your money. When Anushka called," he said, casting a glance in the direction of the house, "I grabbed the chance to come see you. Jorge didn't want to but I did."

"It's too late to save them, Javi—"

"You think I couldn't have told Papa that it was you who was masterminding the whole thing from behind the scenes?" Javi shook his head. "I haven't come here to ask you for anything, Caio. Not for me, not for Jorge, not for

Papa. I came to tell you that Mama loved you. That she thought of you every minute, every day after you left. That it broke her heart that she had to let you go."

"She had a choice, she could have—"

"She had me and Jorge to look after. You think Papa would have let us go with her? Can't you see this from her point of you, Caio? She did her best by us and by you. Did you know that she called Rao and begged him to give you a new direction?"

Caio felt as if someone had delivered another punch. "She asked Rao?"

Javier nodded. "When he did his monthly checkup, yes. She knew the best thing for you was to leave that toxic environment." His brother sighed. "I…thought you should know. Jorge and I are your brothers, your family. She'd have wanted me to take this step. She'd have…"

His brother broke off, overwhelmed with emotion and left without another word.

Caio stayed by the pool long after darkness swallowed his shadows, wondering at how much his revenge had robbed from him. How much he had willingly lost. How many years he could have had with two brothers.

And he had hurt the one woman who'd cared enough to help him see the truth, despite his bullheadedness.

When Caio returned to the house, a tightness in his chest that he couldn't swallow past, the living room and the kitchen greeted him with silence. He made his way to the bedroom to find Nash methodically packing her new clothes into a bag on the bed. Fear crawled through him like spider legs skittering all over, fisting his chest in a vise grip.

"What are you doing?" he demanded with his usual arrogance.

"Yana's agent called me. She fainted yesterday during a shoot. Mira, as you know, has just returned to Aristos. I want to spend a few days looking after Yana. You know she's not that great with managing her type one diabetes."

"I thought you would at least tell me the truth instead of using what seems to be the perfect excuse."

Nush whirled to face him. "Perfect excuse for what?"

"To leave me. What else?" Caio didn't think he had ever felt as hollow and empty as he did then.

"Leave you?" Nush said, her brow tying into that frown that he loved to kiss. Arms folded, she considered from beneath those thick glasses, her hair in a messy knot he wanted to unravel. "You think I'm leaving you?"

"You were right. I set up my stepfather using his own greed to fall. I used all the information I had against Enzo to get him behind bars. For more than fifteen years, all I tried to do was to pay them back for what they took from me."

Nush stared at him as if she had never seen him before. He wondered if he would see disgust in her expression finally. "Did it feel good?"

It was the last question he had expected and he had no self-preservation left to hide it from himself or her. He sat down on the bed next to the suitcase, leaving enough distance between them so that she didn't have to step back if she didn't want him near her. "No." He thrust his fingers through his hair. "I've been struggling with it for weeks, waiting for it to feel good. Then, I was waiting for it to feel less horrible, less dirty. I thought bringing them down, showing them what I had made of myself, how powerful and wealthy I was…" he couldn't help the laugh that escaped his mouth, "would take away the pain and loss I felt all those years ago. I thought destroying them would help me gain something of myself back. Instead, it felt like it was tainting me too, all the innocent lives I was walking away from, in ruins. It was their fate with Carlos, sooner or later, but still… In the last day, I've been wondering if you were right. If I should be saving the company instead. If I should save things instead of ruining them."

She didn't say anything for a long time and Caio wondered if there was nothing left to say. She mirrored his pose and sat down on the bed leaving the bag between them. It felt like an ocean between them, taunting him, mocking him for everything he'd failed.

"I know it was sneaky to go behind your back and find Javier but I had to," she said finally. "The more I dug about your father's company, your stepbrother's embezzlement, all the shady deals Carlos has been making…it dawned on me what you meant to do. I could see it in your eyes, Caio, what it was costing you. And then of course my curiosity wouldn't stop there. I found Javier and called him. I don't know what I was thinking I'd do if he turned out to be like your stepbrother. But I had to take the chance."

"A chance on what, Princesa?"

"A chance that you might gain a brother or two back, Caio. A chance for you to have a family again. You brought me to mine when I was struggling. You helped me make right decisions for Mama. You were my strength, my rock when Thaata and Nanamma died. Why wouldn't I want to do the same for you?"

Caio scoffed. "Are you saving me, Nush? Because I've lived with this rage for so long that I don't know what I would be without it, Princesa."

She scoffed back. "Save you? You think this is some debt that I'm paying? I told you I love you, Caio. To see you unhappy, to see you miserable and angry, to see you hate yourself…it hurts me. What kind of a life would you and I have if this path of destruction you've been on destroyed you too?" She shook her head. "This was purely selfish. I want a future with you. I want to have kids with you. I want my kids to have a father who loves them with his whole heart. I did this all for myself. For my future."

Throwing the bag between them down on the floor, Caio rolled Nush underneath him on the bed. "Letting go of all that poison, all that hatred after all these years… it's terrifying. I'm afraid that there will be nothing left in me. That it has eaten away at anything good and whole."

She pushed his hair off his forehead, her big eyes stinging with gentle strength. "You already know that's not true. That's why Thaata wanted to stop you too. You're your father's son, Caio. You're Rao's protégé. You're my fairy-tale knight. You're the big brother Yana's always wanted. You're the steadfast friend Mira said she'd always needed. You couldn't be all these things to all of us if there was nothing good in you. There's a reason you've been fighting yourself the last two weeks. A reason this was eating away at you."

"Then you're my saving grace, Princesa."

Pushing up on her elbows, she leaned her forehead against his, her cheeks damp with tears. "No. You just needed a nudge. You… I love you so much, Caio, that it terrifies me every day. I trust your word that you wouldn't abandon me but I wanted to do it because you love me, because you need me as much as I—" A sob burst through her words.

"Shh… Princesa. No tears. I'd hate myself if I made you cry."

"I thought I could stick it out, be happy with what you give me, but I can't." Her open eyes held his. "I want it all, Caio. I can't—"

Pressing his face into her throat, Caio said the words

that had been battling to be let out of his chest for quite a while now. "I don't know what I did to deserve you...but don't walk away now, *Princesa*. I want that future you're promising me. I want to be the husband you deserve. I want our kids to be surrounded by aunts and uncles like I was once. I can't imagine a single day without you in my life, Nush. I'll spend the rest my life proving to you how much I love you. How much I need you."

Her hand in his hair tugged his head up and he saw that his clever wife hadn't missed anything. "You'll reconcile with Javier and Jorge?"

He nodded, swallowing the tears that had hardened in his throat. "Yes. Javier made me face some choice truths I was too angry and hurt to see. He told me that Mama was the one who asked Rao to take me away."

Joy bloomed through Nush's chest at the thread of hope in Caio's eyes. "She did?"

"It was the only choice left to her. Carlos would've taken Jorge and Javier from her if she even tried to...so she made sure I got out of there. And she..."

Hand in his hair, Nush held him as Caio buried his face in her chest, his big, broad shoulders trembling. Mouth at his temple, she kissed him and calmed him and whispered all the things she could.

"I'm so sorry you never got to see her again, Caio. I can't..." Her own tears beckoned. "But she loved you. And all the anger and rage and pain...it hasn't tainted you, Caio. It's hardened you. It's..."

He looked up then. "You think there's hope for me then, *querida*?"

"Hope, Caio? You're my hero, my knight, my everything. I'd have never fallen in love with a man who found pleasure in hurting others. You and I both know you were already struggling with this. I just wish..."

"That's because of you and Rao and Mira and Yana and all the love you showed me. If you hadn't proposed our wedding—" A shudder went through him and Nush giggled.

"Laughing at my pain, Princesa? That's a cheap shot."

Any sweet words she wanted to offer evaporated when Caio shifted on top of her completely and proceeded to punish her with hard, demanding kisses. "I love you, Caio," she whispered, her heart and body both soaring.

"I love you, *minha esposa.* And if you need to visit Yana, I understand."

"A part of me doesn't want to leave you so soon. I'm afraid that—"

"No more than five days, Princesa. You can't be her keeper. Not when you have a husband you have to keep on the straight and narrow."

Nush giggled then. "What will you do?"

"I have a lot of reparations to make. Starting with convincing my brothers that I want to be a part of their life. And then, when you are back, you and I will make a plan to rebuild my father's company."

"Then we better get busy then."

"With what, Nush?"

"We need to have five days' worth of sex before I leave. Or else I might go into withdrawal."

His hands were moving before Nush had finished talking. She gasped as those fingers began weaving their magic as Caio whispered, "Fast or slow, Princesa?"

"Hard first and then slow," Nush whispered, taking his mouth in a rough kiss.

Her heart stuttered with joy as Caio drove her body all the way to the peak again.

* * * * *

THE PRINCE'S ROYAL WEDDING DEMAND

LORRAINE HALL

MILLS & BOON

For Flo & the Ms

CHAPTER ONE

THIS WAS NOT the "simple dinner" Ilaria Russo had been expecting.

It was supposed to be straightforward. Pretend to be Sophia, her cousin, have a long, boring dinner with some lord or duke, and then when he inevitably proposed, turn him down.

All the while Sophia would be escaping and eloping with the man she really loved—a sailor her father did not approve of.

Giovanni Avida might be Ilaria's uncle—the man who'd married her late mother's sister—but Ilaria considered him one of her few enemies in life. His grasping, conniving accumulation of wealth had created terrible conditions at the mine her father had worked and subsequently been killed at. The disaster had taken the lives of not just her father, but twenty other men from her village.

And instead of receiving any punishment for his actions, Giovanni had been given a job in the King's ministry. Instead of helping his orphaned niece, he had refused to let Ilaria visit his home in wealthy Roletto. The only "kind" thing he'd done was allow his wife to sometimes bring their daughter, Sophia, to Accogliente to visit Ilaria. Ilaria had always assumed it was the one thing her aunt insisted upon.

While Ilaria had maintained a close friendship with her sweet cousin, Giovanni had spent the past ten years amassing yet more wealth and influence, and desperately trying to get Sophia married off to a title so he could have one himself.

So, when given the opportunity to thwart *him* and help her sweet cousin who deserved escape from her father's ironclad control, Ilaria had taken it.

Now she was here in Roletto, the capital city of Vantonella, using her considerable likeness to Sophia to take her cousin's place.

While Ilaria was certain of her purpose, nerves had set in when she entered the sparkling city nestled between the towering European Alps and the shining Lago di Cornio. There were so many buildings. So many people bustling around the train station. She'd spent the entirety of her twenty-four years in the little cottage built by her ancestors centuries ago, deep in the Pecora mountain region of Vantonella, farming and sheep herding and helping her grandfather until his death last year.

She'd had a brief moment of panic in the train station when she'd considered turning around and running home, but Sophia and her sailor had found Ilaria in the crowd. Though Sophia had acted somewhat strange, they'd exchanged clothes, identification and hugs. Ilaria had wished her cousin well. The meeting with Sophia had returned most of her courage.

Until Ilaria had reached the address Sophia had provided and found an ancient cathedral instead of a restaurant. Until she'd been gestured inside by a soldier in full military regalia. Until she'd looked down the aisle to see a tall man in the shadows. Presumably waiting for her.

Something about the incredibly ornate altar made Ilaria very, *very* nervous. The soldier who'd opened the door and now stood there watching her did not help. She wiped her sweaty palms on the hips of her borrowed dress.

"Your purse," the soldier intoned, holding out a hand.

Ilaria looked down at the small purse she clutched. It was Sophia's, like everything she wore, and it felt wrong to give it up. The soldier did not seem impressed with Ilaria's hesitation, however, and Ilaria knew she had to do her best not to act like the country mountain girl she was.

For tonight, you are well-to-do, well-trained Sophia Avida. You will firmly turn down whatever marriage proposal is made here. And you will give Sophia the time to disappear, never to be found by her controlling, scheming father again.

Tomorrow, once she was certain that Sophia was married and safe, Ilaria would go home to her farm. She had left it in capable hands. After the mining disaster ten years ago, her grandfather had begun to hire orphan children to help tend the sheep. Ilaria had worked with him to create whatever opportunities they could for those children and their widowed mothers to stay in their home village, rather than be shipped off to orphanages and workhouses in the city and lose their homes on top of everything else they'd lost.

Because *that* had been the King's and her uncle's grand plan for disaster relief.

Ilaria and her grandfather had done what they could with tragedy. And now those children were coming into adulthood with a set of skills, and small savings, to rebuild their own lives. Those widows had been able to feel as though they'd taken good care of their children, even in a village with few financial opportunities outside generational farms, with the mine now shuttered.

It was not quite the same scale, but Ilaria liked to think that by stepping in to help Sophia, she was doing what her grandfather would have done. Given someone an alternative that would allow them freedom and happiness.

She had not been able to protect her father from the mining disaster. She had not been able to stop the slow decline in her grandfather's health that had ended with his passing last year. But she could save Sophia from a sad, manipulated life in the titled circles of Roletto.

"Sophia, please move forward," the shadowed man instructed from down the aisle.

Ilaria did so, compelled by the authoritarian voice. She had to swallow down the nerves, straighten her shoulders, and not wilt at the depth and certainty in the voice that beckoned her forward.

Down the long, intimidating aisle. She looked back once, but the soldier now stood in the middle of her exit. Like he was blocking it.

This is all wrong.

Still, she moved toward the man at the end of the aisle.

For Sophia. And, in a way, for Uncle Giovanni.

Each footstep echoed in the grand marble building. Dim lights cascaded through bright stained glass, and gold and silver seemed to shine and glow everywhere she looked.

She'd never seen anything so opulent in her life. It likely rivaled the inside of the royal palace. She was used to patched roofs and muddy roads and the sound of farm animals in the distance.

As she reached the end of the aisle, she realized two terrifying truths at once. First, there was a second man here. Shorter in stature, standing behind a pulpit, a Bible opened in front of him.

Second, and more importantly, the man who'd beckoned her closer was not a duke or a lord.

He was *Prince* Frediano Montellero, the direct heir to the Vantonella throne.

Ilaria was sure she gaped up at him. Her shock had to be evident in every slack muscle on her face. Even in her small village she'd seen pictures of the famed Prince. The *heir*, who was nothing like his wild and impetuous parents who'd died at a young age *free*-climbing the intimidating Monte Morte.

Prince Frediano was said to be as proper and *honorable* as his grandfather, the great King Carlo. Ilaria had never understood how anyone could call the monarchy honorable when they gave schemers and all but murderers places in their ministries. When they were so out of touch with people in need that they suggested things like moving those who'd lost everything to cramped rooms and orphanages in the city.

That did not mean she was *immune* to her reaction at standing *next* to Prince Frediano, with his stunningly sculpted face, surprisingly broad soldiers and a dark suit that no doubt had cost more than her entire *life*. His hair was a glossy black, kept cropped short in such a way he gave the impression of some kind of *warrior*. No doubt even the whiskers on his chin sought permission before they grew.

Everything about him seemed to scream *don't touch*, and surely there was something wrong with Ilaria that her fingers itched to do just that. Test out the sharpness of that chiseled jaw, or if his hair had any of the soft give of mere humans.

Because surely he was something *unearthly. Unreal.*

She should *want* to spit on his shoes, treason be damned, but she could not stop staring. She could reach out and touch a *prince* if she wanted to. The world had been flipped on its axis.

Prince Frediano nodded to the man with the giant, ancient Bible. "You may begin," he said.

His voice was like a terrible strike of thunder, vibrating deep within her, making something completely unknown pulse with heat, rendering her mute. She was rather used to being in charge in her village, though she always gave her elders the appropriate respect. She did not understand this *muteness* she couldn't seem to control.

The priest began speaking in a slow, monotone voice. Talking about the sanctity of marriage and the sacredness of vows.

The noise Ilaria made when the priest directed the "Do you take this woman to be your wife?" question to the Prince could only be characterized as a squeak. Her head whipped from the priest back to the Prince. She opened her mouth to say something—anything—but only another squeak emerged.

And the Prince said *yes* with shocking ease, as if this made any sense. As if he would have married any woman who'd stumbled inside the cathedral at this particular time.

The priest started speaking again. Ilaria was shaking now, knowing she needed her vocal cords to work but something like terror held her resolutely speechless.

Until the priest looked at her, as if it was her turn to answer.

She still couldn't speak, but apparently she could laugh. Slightly hysterically. Because not one moment of this made sense. Some odd…prank. A clear, *wrong* mix-up. It was supposed to be a dinner. A proposal.

Not a *wedding.*

"I'm sorry" she managed, though the words came out as a croak. "There's been a mistake."

For the first time, the Prince's gaze turned to her. His dark brown eyes—so dark they were nearly black—met hers with such cold, frigid disdain she couldn't form words. But her body trembled—inside and out. She could not fathom *why.*

"There is no *mistake,*" he said firmly. "I do not *tolerate* mistakes."

Well, that was suitably terrifying. But she could hardly just *agree* to marry him when he must think she was Sophia. When he was a *prince*, the grandson of the man who'd vaulted her uncle to new heights when he should have been thrown in prison. When, *honestly*, this had to be some kind of hallucination. "I'm not—"

"You are here, are you not?"

"Yes, but—"

"There. She has said yes." His gaze moved back to the priest. "Proceed, Padre."

"No! I didn't say yes to the vow. I'm not—"

But the priest did in fact go on. Why wouldn't he? A prince had told him to. The man with all the power in the room.

"This has to be a dream," Iliana muttered. *A nightmare.*

"I assume you mean that all your dreams have come true. You are most welcome." He even gave a little bow, though she got the impression that impatience simmered beneath every move. "Now the formalities are finished. Let us proceed to the palace." His gaze raked over her. "We'll need to do some work prior to the public introduction tomorrow."

"Work..." She didn't know what that might mean. What *any* of this could mean.

The Prince strode down the aisle. No doubt expecting her to follow. She scurried after him, practically tripping in the borrowed shoes. Sophia's shoes.

She just needed to find the words to explain. To fix

this. She could. When the men had come to tell her grandfather of her father's death, *she* had handled Grandfather's emotional collapse. *She* had suggested he take in the orphans to help at the farm. *She* had handled the rapacious men at the door trying to buy their farm for a pittance.

She knew how to handle tragedies. Surely she could handle this blunder. *For Sophia.* "Wait," she called after him.

He did not wait or even acknowledge she'd spoken. When he came to a side door of the cathedral, he held it open and finally looked back at her.

His dark gaze studied her with such intensity she didn't know how he carried the weight of it. She wanted to stoop, hunch in on herself.

She swallowed and forced words out of her tight throat. "I'm very confused. I don't understand what just happened."

"I would have thought it quite self-explanatory."

"Well, a wedding." She laughed a little breathlessly. Honestly, how wasn't *he* laughing? This was beyond absurd. Then again, looking up at his cold expression it was hard to imagine him laughing *ever.* Did royal mouths even curve that way? She'd only seen dour portraits of him and his grandfather. Suitably proper and royal, but with no hint of mirth.

He pointed out the door. "After you, Princess."

Princess. She was going to start laughing again, and this time she might not stop until she was crying. Or screaming. "There has been a mistake," she said firmly. The same way she'd spoken when she'd told Sophia she would take care of everything.

You've certainly taken care of things, Ilaria.

"Even if you don't like them, there has been one," she said before he could stop her. "Sophia told me she was meant to have dinner with a duke or a lord. I was only going to go through with the dinner, refuse the impending proposal, then go home to Accogliente and—"

"Silence."

Ilaria immediately clamped her lips together. It was as natural as breathing, following his sharp order.

"What exactly are you saying?" the Prince demanded, his voice vibrating with something Ilaria couldn't name, because he clearly kept the emotions behind them locked deep within. But there was *some* emotion there. And it wasn't good.

Still, she had to muster all her courage and set this to rights. Her heart pounded, and her hands shook even as she clutched them together. But she held his dark, intimidating gaze. "My name isn't Sophia. Sophia is my cousin. You've married the wrong woman."

Frediano did not respond immediately. He had learned to temper *all* his baser urges—whether they be anger or greed or lust—by taking his time. He had spent the better portion of his life learning control at the feet of his grandfather, the man who had ruled Vantonella honorably and justly for forty years. The man who had given him safety and purpose and had saved him—literally and figuratively—from the careless neglect of his impetuous parents.

And now that prodigious man's heart was giving out. Doctor after doctor had told King Carlo that if he did not step down from the throne, have the recommended surgery, avoid stress, and *rest*, he would not live to see his next birthday.

Frediano intended to make sure that the great King Carlo lived to see at least twenty more such celebrations. Which was why he had set out to find himself a wife, knowing very well his grandfather would never consider retiring until Frediano was married to an appropriate, sensible woman who would not upset the order of things.

No matter how his grandfather trusted Frediano, Carlo would never risk what had happened before. Not when it came to his only remaining heir. So Frediano had sought the perfect wife. Not a story, not the selfish, press-seeking disaster Frediano's mother had been.

Frediano kept his entire body still as he collected the information this…creature had just laid at his feet.

He had not married Sophia Avida—whose father was a wealthy merchant and the crown's Ministry of Energy, neither titled nor poor, and thus as uninteresting and biddable as any potential princess could hope to be in his eyes—but instead her…cousin.

He had only met Sophia briefly because this union was not about attachment or feeling. It was about being master of the situation he found himself in. It was about convincing his grandfather it was time to step down.

So he'd had a wedding with no guests, and no forewarning to the public. Nothing that spoke of his parents' outrageous, attention-seeking behaviors. He'd chosen a bride who would be pliable, bland, and of no real interest to anyone, so that his grandfather could be certain there would be no embarrassments of the kind his father had heaped on King Carlo's shoulders.

But this woman… "I am supposed to believe that despite looking exactly like Sophia, you are not she?"

The woman clasped her hands so tightly together her knuckles went white, but she held his gaze and did not wither at his accusatory tone.

"I wouldn't say we look *exactly* alike."

Enough alike, if this were true, for him not to tell the difference. Of course, the lighting in the cathedral had been suitably dim and shadowed, all in a nod to keep the public and press from stumbling on that which he would announce tomorrow.

He studied this woman who still stood inside the door, the glow of a sconce highlighting her features. She had the same dark hair as Sophia. Green eyes with flecks of blue. Taking stock, he noticed this woman had freckles dusting her nose and he doubted the sophisticated Sophia spent much time in the sun. Her dress was modest, but expensive. Though a bit ill-fitting around the shoulders.

Borrowed. No doubt from the traitorous cousin. Who'd *known* she was meant to marry a prince this evening. And had instead sent her look-alike *cousin*.

"You are from Accogliente?"

"Yes," she said.

A tiny mountain village of little consequence, far to the north. Sophia had been raised in Roletto, and though not from a royal family, had obtained an education in both scholarly pursuits and in etiquette. Her father was desperate for a title association. Frediano had considered that an asset—something to hold over the man and keep him and his family in check.

This woman from Accogliente would know nothing of how to handle herself in Roletto. She had all the trappings of being an embarrassment. Or a story. Worse, both.

This was a mistake. One he could not afford. Sophia had been the perfect candidate. She was nothing like his mother. She was quiet, pretty and wholly uninteresting. She would not draw attention. She would do as she was told and not be the source of mortification his mother had been. She would not abandon…

Well, that was neither here nor there.

He could demand silence from the padre and the soldier, even from his staff who had the next steps ready at the palace. He could track down Sophia. Demand she marry him. This could be fixed.

But it would take time, and allow for the possibility of too many leaks, too many complications. And the longer it took, the more his grandfather's health stood to suffer.

Frediano had promised his grandfather a perfect bride with a public announcement *tomorrow*, and he would not go back on this promise. He could not return to the palace empty-handed. In the end, he did not care *whom* he married as long as the end result was what he wanted.

Frediano struggled to rein in his temper. To keep the lid on all that seethed and bubbled within him. Someone had thwarted his plan. Had put their own needs ahead of everyone else's. It reminded him too much of a childhood often spent fending for himself while his parents courted the press and performed their outrageous stunts. All their self-absorption had made them perfect for each other. Their "love" for each other had caused wreckage for everyone in their path.

But he was no longer a child, frozen and alone at the base of a mountain his parents had tumbled to their deaths from. No, he was an adult. A prince. A future king.

He eyed his unknown wife.

She would be as boring and biddable as her cousin, he decided then and there. Surely, if she'd had skeletons in her closet, the detailed investigation into Sophia would have brought those to light.

This girl could learn manners. She could learn how to handle herself. He had, once. Perhaps it was better this way. She was new, unmolded clay.

He would turn this *mistake* into a triumph.

It was what he did best.

He, once more, pointed out the door. "We will proceed."

"Proceed?" the woman repeated, her eyes widening and her hands dropping to her sides.

"We are married. You are now Princess… What is your name?"

She blinked down at his hand when he took her by the elbow and led her into the cool evening. She stuttered over her name as he walked her quickly to the unassuming sedan he used when he wished to travel unnoticed. "I-Ilaria Russo."

"Princess Ilaria Montellero. We will go to the palace and prepare for tomorrow's wedding announcement. You have much to learn before then."

The driver had the back door open as Frediano pulled the stuttering Ilaria toward the vehicle. But she jerked her arm out of his grasp and turned, stubbornly refusing to get in the car.

"The priest said *Sophia*, not Ilaria," she said, holding his gaze, her fingers curling into fists as if she meant to fight him off.

He might have laughed if time wasn't of the essence.

"You only tricked me into saying yes," she continued, keeping those fists wisely at her sides. "We don't know each other. I have a home and people who depend on me and absolutely no desire to become a *princess*."

"The priest will correct any name mistakes *he* made. Knowledge is not necessary for marriage. As for your home, if there are mementos you'd like, I'll send someone for them at once." He did not address the no-desire-to-become-a-princess part.

Honestly, everyone was so against becoming a princess these days.

"I have a farm. I have responsibilities."

"You may sell them." He considered this *more* than fair, if it would expedite this process.

"I don't *want* to sell them. People depend on that farm." Her eyes flashed with temper, which stirred his own.

He squashed the feeling, encased it in ice as she continued.

"You cannot sweep in because you're a prince and take everything away from me."

"I think you'll find that's exactly what I can do."

"This is *madness.*" Color had risen on her cheeks, and her green eyes seemed to change with her moods. Perhaps she was right, she didn't look *exactly* like her cousin. She might be a bit prettier—when she was angry.

But Frediano could risk neither anger nor beauty. Only control of the situation mattered.

"I was protecting my cousin from a proposal she did not want and feared she could not refuse. I'm sorry you somehow misunderstood and got caught up in this, but—"

"I do not *misunderstand.* I think you do. Your cousin was not expecting a *proposal* this evening, Ilaria. She knew she was meant to *marry* me. Here. She has deceived me, and *you.*"

The woman's mouth dropped open. But it wasn't just shock. There was denial in her eyes. She did not believe him.

Frediano did not need her to, but she had given him a glimpse into the tools he could use to mold her to his will. If she cared for Sophia, fancied herself the protector, she would continue to act toward that goal.

"Her deceit will be avenged, I assure you, but what has transpired cannot be changed. You are my bride, my princess. *That* is final."

"And if I refuse?" she demanded, eyes flashing, those fists tighter now.

Frediano's gut tightened, an unwelcome heat at war with the ice. But the ice would always win. "I could always track down your cousin, if you prefer. Bring her to the palace, willing or not. Make her my princess instead. Because I assure you, *tesoro*, I am not going back to the palace without a wife."

CHAPTER TWO

ILARIA SWALLOWED AGAINST the terror in her throat. Against the betrayal she couldn't help but feel. She did not want to believe the Prince. There was no way Sophia would have used her in such a way.

But, she remembered, Sophia had acted in an odd manner at the train station. Ilaria had chalked it up to fear over defying Giovanni, and excitement over marrying her love.

Now she wondered if it was guilt.

But this was all secondary, because in saving Sophia she had somehow made a terrible mess of things for herself. She could not be married to Prince Frediano. The grandson of a king she loathed. The priest had said *Sophia* while reading the marriage vows, and Ilaria had not truly said *yes*. They were *not* married.

Inexplicably, the Prince seemed to want them to be. Which she knew meant neither legality nor her own wishes mattered.

"What choice do you prefer?" the Prince asked, silky smooth. It should poke at her temper, it should offend her, but his voice caused some physical reaction that was none of those spiky feelings. She did not understand how a voice could make her insides feel warm, make her heart beat so heavily against her chest.

She wanted to run, but she had a *choice* to make.

Neither was a real option, but one would protect Sophia. Perhaps Sophia had knowingly thrown Ilaria to the wolves, but she must have had her reasons. Or maybe she still needed saving. Yes, that was most certainly it. Ilaria could not give up now. She had to be strong. And smart. She would not fail her cousin after promising to help.

Ilaria knew that kings and princes did not care for anyone else's wants or needs. She might have been able to ward off grasping businessmen who wanted her land and government officials who'd wanted to send those poor children off to Roletto orphanages, but she did not know how to convince a *prince* he was wrong.

She could feel the strain of Frediano's patience. Her only *choice*, in this moment, was to go along with this for the time being. Once she was certain Sophia was far enough out of the city, legally married to her sailor, then Ilaria would figure out her own escape.

So, chin held high, Ilaria moved into the car. Though it was dark inside, and smaller than anything she'd expect for a prince, it was still nicer than anything she'd ever *seen*, let alone been in.

The entire inside of the car seemed to warm when the Prince slid in next to her, like he himself was a heater. Though she could not see him as anything more than a shadow, it was as though she could *feel* his gaze, like fingers along her skin.

She suppressed a shudder. She was not well versed in the ways of men and women, but she knew what it meant when a man and woman married.

Surely he wouldn't expect… Well, it did not matter what he expected. *That* was a bridge she would not cross. Even to save Sophia.

"So, tell me, Ilaria Russo," the Prince said, drawing her name out like it was a morsel to be savored. "Would you have come to protect your cousin if you had known a wedding was at the end of the aisle?"

Ilaria didn't have an answer, and she hated that he posed the question. Even reeling, even hurt, Ilaria wasn't sure she would have refused her cousin if she'd known. She'd always wanted to protect Sophia, hurt Giovanni. She likely would have charged in thinking she could handle the situation.

Would you have been able to?

At the end of the day, it did not matter, because Sophia had not told her the truth.

Ilaria looked at the shadow that was a prince and doubted herself, something she did not care for at all. So she turned away, instead watching the lights and buildings get farther and farther apart as the car wound its way up a hill. She tried to come up with a plan. A response. Anything that would keep her *and* Sophia out of this man's clutches.

When the car pulled up to a tall, winding stone wall, she thought perhaps the driver had gotten lost. Or maybe the great stone wall would simply *open* for them, because a prince wanted it to.

Her mouth dropped open as it did just that. The wall *moved,* creating an opening large enough for the car to drive through, and then there it was. Even in the dark night she knew the looming shadows and flickering lights were the palace.

She was going to the palace. She had never even *dreamed* of going inside the palace. The only dream she'd ever had about this symbol of royalty was picketing outside the thick stone walls.

"As the days move forward…" Prince Frediano said, his voice a sardonic blade in the dark shadows of the car. Sharp and cutting, yet it did not feel like pain when he spoke. It was a caress, deep inside of her. "…you'll be given many lessons in how to comport yourself, but may I offer lesson number one here and now. Gaping like a hooked fish is *not* how a princess should behave. Ever."

There was that word again. It was baffling enough to accept she was speaking to Prince Frediano Montellero, that she was in a *car* with the *heir* to the Vantonella throne. That his voice seemed to dance along her skin like fingers. But the cherry on top of all that nonsense was the fact he kept calling her a *princess.*

She tried to study him, to convince herself he was perpetrating some bizarre ruse, but the back of the car was dark and he was only an intimidating shadow of a man. She fought off a shiver—of foreboding, surely. "You cannot honestly want *me* to be the Princess of Vantonella."

"Why not?"

"I am no one. I'm surprised Sophia was even an option, but at least her father is wealthy." *If the devil incarnate.* "I'm an orphan farm girl from Accogliente. I was raised by my grandfather in a little cabin on a very small sheep farm. I know next to nothing about…anything. Except caring for a home and raising sheep."

"You needn't remind me," he returned. Disapprovingly.

His little jab, no matter how she agreed or had pointed it out herself—made her voice sharper than was likely wise when talking to a prince. "No. This is simply impossible. Turn the car around. Take me to the train station. I promise you, it's best for the both of us. We are not married, and we will not be. Beginning and end of this strange little story."

Silence stretched out between them, seeming to throb with portent. When he spoke, though, the words were calm and slow. But unyielding, definitely.

"You seem to be under the impression that my mind

can be changed, when I assure you it cannot. I will return to the palace with a bride. It will be you, unless you'd like it to be your cousin."

The way he said it—so final, so cold—it was like a prison sentence. Panic didn't just beat dully under all her other conflicting emotions now, it pounded hard against her chest. She struggled to breathe, to think straight.

She couldn't let him interrupt Sophia's chance at freedom and happiness. But she did not wish to sacrifice her own. She contemplated the only possibility: escape.

Even if it meant jumping out of the moving car.

She reached for the car door handle before she fully thought the action through. She would…jump out. Escape. She would. She *had* to. Surely it was an option no more ridiculous than the situation she found herself in? And if he was chasing after her, he couldn't chase after Sophia.

But he trapped her hands with his before she could complete the movement. Was he that fast? Had she hesitated? She was afraid she didn't know *anything* in this moment, when she'd always prided herself on being ready for *any* moment.

His hands were very, very large. Warm. All-encompassing. This time when her heart thundered in her ears, it felt less like panic and more like something…deeper within. Something she dared not examine too carefully.

"Would you like to tell me where Sophia is?"

"No," she returned, vehemently.

"I could, of course, have her found. In a matter of minutes, my people would be able to drag her back—"

"No!"

He shrugged. She could feel it, as he still had her hands trapped. "Then I'm afraid you are the bride I shall present before my grandfather and our people tomorrow."

Ilaria inhaled sharply. She had to get a hold of herself

lest she make an irrevocable mistake. This was a disaster, yes, but not a tragedy. Losing her parents and her grandfather had been *tragedy.* This was simply…a mistake. She had made a mistake. A few, maybe.

She took a deep breath. She needed to regroup. No panic, no attempts at jumping out of cars. She would not get through to the Prince with words or foolish attempts at escape. He had made up his mind—for reasons she would never be able to understand.

Like Mother Nature, he was incomprehensible, unpredictable. She would have to handle him as any good farmer handled the fickle weather. Biding her time, riding out the storm, then cleaning up the mess. But never surrendering to the storm. Never letting it make her give up, no matter how painful the results.

Him holding her hands in his felt like some kind of storm.

"Your hands are rough," he said, as if the fact of the matter surprised him. Or offended him.

She hadn't been expecting poetry, but she didn't particularly expect to be insulted, either. She tried to snatch them away, but he held firm.

"Of course they are," she shot back, trying for firm and disgusted over alarmed and out of her depth. Revolted instead of stirred. She'd pretend he was a boy from the village who'd tried to get his hands on her sheep…and other things. She had no problems rejecting those boys with a stern look and a few sharp words.

The problem was, they were boys. Not even men, let alone princes. And nothing they'd ever said or insinuated had come close to making her feel as though she'd melted from within.

"I've *labored*, which I'm sure is more than you can

say." It did not come out strong or scathing. It came out with a shake. "I know how your family views *labor*."

He made a noise, neither confirmation nor denial. Just as though he accepted she'd said words.

The sheer audacity of this man—because he was a man, she had to remind herself. Princes were just men. Human. With so *many* failings. Though at this point she wouldn't be surprised if he turned into a literal dragon right in front of her eyes.

She tried to picture that, rather than react to the way he still held her hands, like they were stress stones. His fingers moved patterns over her palm, then the backs of her hand. She tried to breathe normally, but there were hitches every time his fingers moved. She tried to pretend her entire body hadn't been engulfed by something she had never experienced before. But she was very afraid she'd read about.

You will not be attracted to this man. He is your enemy.

It seemed no matter what she told herself, her body had other ideas. Completely other reactions. His thumb brushed across the inside of her wrist. She jolted, heat slamming into her body as though she'd been struck by lightning.

She could not see him, but somehow she knew his mouth curved in dark amusement.

Still, she could not manage any stinging words of rejection. No, she seemed to lean forward as though she were magnetized to him, helpless to the sensations his fingers brought out. His hand smoothed up, over her wrist and to her bare forearm.

Her breath caught, though it shouldn't. He was not touching her out of any kind of interest or gentleness. Perhaps he was testing what she was willing to do, and surely she was willing to do *nothing*.

"Let me impart another lesson, Ilaria." He was closer now, and the way he sounded out her name with his cultured voice had goose bumps breaking out down her arms. He smoothed them away, from elbow to wrist, then back again. "The world is cruel and does not care. Whether you tend your sheep or marry princes. None of it matters in the grand scheme of things. But I am inevitable, and what I deem necessary is inexorable. You can fight me, if you must, but I will not bend."

He let her go, somewhat abruptly. He even managed to create some new distance between them, even though the car was small and the back seat gave him no quarter to move away. Her hands fell to her lap and she suddenly felt…cold. Slapped at. Which jabbed at her temper once more.

"Do you know what they say about things that will not bend?" she shot back.

"Commoners break. I, on the other hand, am a prince. A future king. *I* get what I want, no breaking required."

Ilaria thought that sounded an awful lot like tempting fate, but princes no doubt controlled fate, too. They controlled *everything.*

Not me, she vowed. Somehow, someway, she would get out of this. With Sophia happily married to her sailor. Her uncle incapable of extorting a title. And Ilaria back with her sheep.

She simply had to weather the storm.

The car came to a stop and when he spoke, that deep dark voice sliding around her in the dark, she wondered if that was precisely true.

"Welcome home, Princess."

Frediano did not often find himself puzzled. Oh, there were a great many problems and challenges in his life, both from being *a* prince, and being the Prince that he was. But these were a bit like war. One developed a strategy, a master plan. One twisted the world to suit the outcome one wanted.

He did not know how to twist Ilaria to what he wanted. The threats against her cousin would keep her obedient for a period of time, but it would not last forever. He would need more leverage.

If she could be the simple mountain village girl, that would be workable. Not ideal, but he'd worked *not ideal* into exactly what he wanted over and over again.

It was her loyalty that puzzled him, maybe even startled him. Her cousin had clearly lied to her, used her, and not considered the lifelong consequences for Ilaria.

And still the woman would trade her future for her cousin's.

Frediano didn't understand it. No more than he understood his fascination with the way Ilaria's hands were rough, her wrists soft. She had flashes of temper, but it was hidden under a softness that made the blade of it all the sharper. Her eyes were intelligent, working through the problem quietly.

A trait he recognized.

He could have dealt with all that, too, and easily. He was not to be outdone by anyone simply because they knew the power of patience and silence.

It was the way she reacted when he touched her that truly concerned him. As if simply holding her hand in his had been a naked grappling in the dark. She was *responsive*, and he found his own needs stirred far beyond his comfort level. She was *nothing* he should find himself having an intense reaction to.

He had chosen Sophia Avida because she was simple. Bland. She would have been the kind of princess no one cared too deeply about, nor sought to make stories out of. He would have been immune to the hitches in her breath, surely.

Or, maybe this odd attraction might have snuck up on him with her as well, if she had appeared. After all, the two women looked disarmingly alike.

In the end, it did not matter if it was Sophia or Ilaria. He would not lose himself in another person as his father often had. A slave to his wife's whims and desires nearly as recklessly as he was to his own. Both at the cost of all else.

The crown. The country. King Carlo's health.

Frediano would never risk anything that might hurt his holy trinity.

So he would mold his wife into what the situation required. Maybe it would be a more difficult task than he'd originally planned, but he was equal to it. And if all went well, his grandfather would step down within the week. Because time was running out.

Frediano emerged from the car, then waited for Ilaria to follow. Attraction would make the act of producing heirs pleasant, he supposed, but that was not the express purpose of heirs. Nor his goal.

His goal was all the respectability his parents had tried to destroy with their reckless choices and disdain for the rules and traditions that had allowed them that recklessness. All they had done had been direct causes of his grandfather's current health problems, even as his grandfather had bent over backward in an attempt to give them all they wanted. Until their actions had almost been the death of Frediano at the base of that mountain, all those years ago.

Ilaria was simply different than what he was used to, and once he trained his body to acclimate to different, he would once again control all his baser urges with his usual aplomb.

"Not getting out of the car does not change the inevitability of the situation," he offered when he had waited far longer than was appropriate for a prince to wait for anything.

He expected her to be contrary and delay even longer, but instead she appeared. She looked up at the palace much like she'd looked up at him when she'd reached the end of the aisle.

The jolt he'd felt then should have been his first clue that all was not right, but he'd been determined to see his plan through.

"It's beautiful," she said, and he knew she was not speaking *to* him, simply speaking. As she was a poor farm girl from Accogliente she had likely never been to Roletto. Never seen the grandeur of the palace that had been built centuries ago for the first King of Vantonella.

Though it was dark, lights shone from inside and out, illuminating the stone walls and dark red shutters, the turrets and spires reaching up for the starry night sky above them like the mountains they were tucked into on the west side. When the sun rose in the east, it would shine on Laga di Cornio, glittering brilliantly and beautifully.

It was a small country, of little interest to the outside world, but proud. Important to him and the name Montellero. He looked at the woman who was his wife in the shadow of the symbol of all he was.

She would not be an embarrassment. He simply would not allow it.

"Follow me, Princess."

"I wish you'd stop calling me that." But she did follow as he strode forward. They would go in the side entrance in the courtyard where he could take her to one of the rooms in his wings with minimal staff interference.

"I'm afraid you'll have to get used to your new title." He had a feeling she had more complaints or refusals on the tip of her tongue, but they reached the door—his aide already holding it open for them.

"Thank you, Eduardo. Is her room ready?"

"Yes, Your Highness."

"Excellent. Have her staff arrived?"

"Yes, sir. Would you like me to show the lady to her room?"

"No, I'll handle it from here. Please tell my grandfather that I have returned and all is as it should be. I'd like to take one last look at the approved press releases before we send them out in the morning." Because while few people knew what had occurred, and what would, there was a plan in place. Secret wedding this evening. Already written and bought announcements that would run in the paper tomorrow, and then the public introduction in the afternoon, as was tradition.

He just had to change the name of his princess before it was sent to print.

"Of course." With a short bow, Eduardo melted into the shadows. Ilaria clearly didn't notice. She was too busy looking around the grand hall. Lancet windows lined every wall, sconces glowed tastefully, but as it was evening and the hall wasn't in use, shadows crowded the corners.

She looked up at the ceiling, where it twisted in a beautiful painting of the sky, into the point of the spire one could see from outside. "It's simply amazing. Someone with very little technological or mechanical help built this place hundreds of years ago, with just ingenuity and their own bare hands, and made it so grand and beautiful that for centuries people have stood under here and looked up. And it has become an enduring symbol of the country. Of your family."

She had concisely put into words what he had always felt. About this room. About his country. His legacy. His role as a symbol. It felt dangerous.

Then she met his gaze, and any awe in her expression died. "No doubt you've never stopped to appreciate the *commoners* who would have actually done the work to build this."

He chose to ignore this comment as he had no plans to *prove* himself to her. "You are now part of that symbol, Ilaria."

Her eyes narrowed, but when she spoke, her voice was controlled. "I suppose it's a waste of breath to tell you I don't want to be."

"You are correct."

She sighed, looked away once more. "I'm tired."

"I will show you to your rooms. You may rest and then tomorrow you will begin your lessons."

"I can't possibly learn how to be a princess, no matter how many lessons you give me." But she followed as he strode through the hall and then to the entrance to his wing of the palace.

"I learned how to be a prince."

"You were born a prince," she returned.

When he glanced at her, she was taking in every last corbel and painting. Even if she did not love the term "Princess", she was clearly keen on the palace. Or perhaps the *commoners* who'd built it. "Ah, you have not kept up with the royal news, *tesoro*. Perhaps I was younger than you are when I learned, but I was not raised in the palace walls for those first few years. I was a captive of my parents' whims until their untimely demise."

Her silence in response was…odd. It made the words he spoke seem to land uncomfortably, as if she could read all the darkness behind them. The nights as a small child, hungry and alone while his parents were at some party, when they could have simply left him to his grandfather and the royal staff. But no, they had wanted to pretend to be above the throne, above its trappings.

And *he* had suffered.

Which was nothing he should be thinking about when he had his new bride to install in her rooms, press releases to change, and information to uncover about Ilaria Russo.

He would bind her to him in every way, so that she could not get out of this. He would find her every weakness. Because *he* was in control of everything these days. The marriage would be perfect—in his grandfather's eyes, in the people's eyes. There would be no disgrace of divorce, no hint of scandal. There would only be his princess, his future queen, and their serene—if faked—devotion to one another. So that his grandfather could step down and take care of himself.

Frediano walked faster down the halls, but she kept up easily enough. "I don't even remember my mother," she said, as if musing parentage. "She died having me, and my father was killed at Estraz."

Estraz had been a mining disaster over a decade ago. Something like twenty men from a cluster of small villages in the north—including hers—had been killed. It had been a national tragedy everyone in Vantonella was aware of.

Another angle to her story he did not care for. She was more pauper than he liked—the press would focus on this angle mercilessly. So he would have to use every last tool at his disposal to make sure the media did not try to make a story out of her. It would require a delicate balance. So much of this would. But he was, of course, equal to the task. He would make sure of it.

He reached the cluster of rooms that she would inhabit. As his princess. As his wife. Even though he'd been planning on it, albeit with another woman, the reality of installing someone here was disorienting.

He had been alone in this wing since the day of his eighteenth birthday. His grandfather did not come down here, and Frediano was not one to have staff continually about, so he had gotten used to the quiet.

She would upset it.

No. He wouldn't allow that. She would simply do what she was told. She would soon realize that was the best course of action.

He opened the thick door that would lead into her sitting room. He said nothing, walking through to the next door that opened up to her bedroom. He took a few steps inside to encourage her to do the same.

She looked around, not with the same awe she'd had in the great hall, but with a trepidation he did not fully understand. It was a finely appointed room, designed to make any woman happy. Surely finer than anything *she'd* ever seen?

But Ilaria did not look happy. She blinked a few times, then turned a guarded, green gaze on him. She put extra distance between them.

"This is…*my* room?" she asked, and if the hesitation did not give away her thoughts, the way her cheeks flushed an attractive pink would have.

He found himself darkly amused at the nature of her concerns. "Were you expecting something grander?" he asked, endeavoring to make his expression surprised.

"Don't be ridiculous," she returned, her eyebrows drawing together.

"Then what is your concern?" he asked silkily, moving closer to her, the small distance between them seeming to warm and dance with possibility.

She *was* his wife after all. He had been looking for a wife who was nothing out of the ordinary. She mostly fit the bill. So much of her was average, her height, her build in the ill-fitting dress, even the rather dull brown shade of her thick, wavy hair.

But her green eyes, their ever-changing shades and hues, were intriguing. Alluring. If she used them as weapons, they could in fact create chaos.

He would have to be certain she did not.

"I don't have a concern," she managed, though her voice came out strangled and her cheeks grew pinker, her breathing quicker.

Deep within him, he felt the chains of his control pull. He wanted his hands on the flush of her skin. Wanted to see if it covered the rest of her body. Would there be other rough parts of her like her hands, or would she be soft all over?

"I suppose in your village husband and wife share a room," he offered, taking another step so that they were nearly toe to toe. So that he could examine those eyes, that flush, and test her.

She stood, rooted to the spot, looking up at him. He did not know if it was courage or fear that kept her from retreating. It did not matter. Both could serve.

"I—"

"And a bed," he added, as if it had only just occurred to him. When quite frankly a bed had entered the equation when she had jolted under his touch. When she had leaned forward in the car, not away.

She should not intrigue him. This was not the plan—and he never made plans he did not stick to wholly—but here he was. With an altered plan, with an impossible attraction to the wife he had not chosen.

But he would not give in.

Perhaps she would, though.

She shook her head again. "I wouldn't—"

"We, of course, will." That too, was inevitable. And much like her eyes, all too alluring.

She made that same noise she'd made back at the cathedral. A kind of inelegant squeak. But she did not turn away. Did not *run* away. She held his gaze, as if trapped there. The woman *did* have a backbone.

Even if his was stronger.

"You are my wife, Ilaria."

She shuddered out a breath, and he could not speak for the surprising and disarming bolt of need that shot through him. The heat, the violent claws of it. He wanted her naked beneath him, in that big frivolous bed.

Now.

But that would not do.

He would control this lust. He could. If he enjoyed bedding her, so be it. She no doubt would enjoy the same.

But he would not be ruled by his traitorous wants that led to ruin. So he eased himself back. To the door. To somewhere he could get a handle on his control. There was time yet for the duty of making heirs, and he would make sure it was appropriate.

"But you need your rest tonight. Tomorrow you will be introduced to our people," he said through gritted teeth. "Sleep well, Princess." And with that, he left her.

And cursed himself for being a fool.

CHAPTER THREE

ILARIA HAD NOT settled for some time after the Prince left her. She was battered by feelings she did not want—all physical, all beyond her control.

She'd never felt that way before. At home, she had too many responsibilities to worry about things like *attraction.* She had long considered marriage out of the question. She had too many people depending on her to worry about finding love and partnership, and she had assumed attraction and chemistry were by-products of such.

Clearly, she had been very wrong. And it was hardly the only thing she'd been wrong about.

Sophia had *known* what fate she was condemning Ilaria to. Ilaria wished she could believe the Prince a liar, but unfortunately there was no logical explanation except his.

And still, Ilaria chose to stay. To protect her cousin. If she ran, Frediano would no doubt go after Sophia *and* her. If she stayed…

It was so unfathomable. How could she be married to a *prince*? The symbol of everything she blamed her father's death on. The grandson of the man who had no sense of her loss, of her people. Who believed Uncle Giovanni's cost-cutting measures and dangerous greed made him the perfect choice for Minister of Energy.

She could not become *part* of everything she loathed. Her father and grandfather would certainly roll over in their graves.

But how could she condemn Sophia to that fate when her cousin had someone who loved her, wanted to marry her, and get her away from her terrible father and a life she hated? If Ilaria ran, how would softhearted Sophia stand up to a prince when she hadn't even been able to stand up to her father?

Ilaria thought of the dark, foreboding Frediano. The way he made a woman, even one as strong as herself, feel. Not weak, never that, but unsteady. As if he willed earthquakes wherever he walked.

She sank onto the bed. It was like lowering herself into a cloud, and nothing like her rough sheets at home on her small, lumpy bed.

There had to be a way out of this without endangering Sophia's happiness. If Ilaria had to be married to a prince for a time, *she* could stand up for herself. Would. And somewhere along the way she would figure out how to extricate herself from everything she loathed.

She would just have to ride out this storm.

She flopped back onto the bed, looking up at the ceiling. It was a beautiful mural of angels floating above the mountains and a large alpine lake. Gorgeous. Everything about the palace was absolutely stunning.

And so very much not her home.

Exhaustion deep in her bones, she crawled under the silken covers, pulled off the uncomfortable borrowed dress, and fell into a surprisingly restful sleep.

She woke with a start to *people* in her room—marching around while sunlight streamed in from floor-to-ceiling windows, offering a stunning view of Lago di Cornio sparkling in the sunrise.

"Are you ready for breakfast, Your Highness?" A woman asked from a respectable distance away.

Ilaria's stomach growled as she pulled the sheets up to her collarbone. She hadn't eaten since the train, but she did not know how to proceed.

"Aurora, fetch the robe," the woman said without waiting for Ilaria's answer.

Aurora, presumably, walked over to a large wardrobe, opened it and Ilaria gaped at all the clothes inside. Then she remembered what Frediano had said about gaping fish last night and closed her mouth.

"I am Noemi, your personal assistant. If you need anything, you simply ask me and I will make certain it's done. Today, we have a very tight schedule."

Ilaria was handed a robe. She felt there was no choice but to pull it on. Much like the sheets it was one of the softest materials she'd ever felt. Reasonably she understood a palace and a prince would have the best of the best things, it was just she'd never even been able to *imagine* the best things.

"The Prince has sent up a breakfast for you in the sitting room." Noemi gestured at the door. Clearly a sign that Ilaria was to get up and stick to the schedule.

"I… I need to make some phone calls. There are people I need to speak to."

Noemi hesitated a moment, something flickering in her gaze and then disappearing before Ilaria could parse it. She nodded. "Of course. Why don't you come get settled in for breakfast? I will see about…obtaining you a phone."

Ilaria would have preferred to go to a phone right now, but she didn't feel comfortable ordering this woman around. Personal assistant or not, Ilaria was not accustomed to people waiting on her.

"Maybe you could just show me to a phone and—"

"Come. Eat," Noemi interrupted smoothly, gesturing Ilaria toward the door. "You'll want to keep your strength up today."

Ilaria got out of the tall bed as gracefully as she could manage. She followed Noemi into the sitting room. There were pretty, comfortable-looking chairs arranged around a coffee table filled with trays full of more food than could feed her, or even the two new people in this room.

Her stomach rumbled, but she did not sit. "This is… far too much. Far too elaborate." It could feed her entire village.

But Noemi chuckled. "Nothing is too elaborate for a princess on the day of her royal introduction."

Royal introduction. Ilaria desperately needed that phone. Needed to make sure Sophia was safely married. Safely hidden away somewhere.

Then she'd get out of this place. Dig an escape tunnel out if she had to. Swim across Lago di Cornio. *Anything.*

"I'm not sure I can eat until I can make a phone call and check on things at home."

"If you sit and eat, I'll go fetch a phone for you. If I'm not back by the time you're done, Chessa here will begin the fitting." Noemi gestured at one of the two women in the room. They flitted around a rack of gowns, a platform and a full-length, three-paned mirror that faced it.

Ilaria wanted to argue. Or run screaming, but she had promised herself to ride the storm. So she swallowed down her objections and took a plate and put some food on it.

Noemi smiled. "I will go track down a phone for you." Then she left the room.

The seamstress studied Ilaria with speculative eyes. Ilaria was not used to such attention. She managed a smile and took a bite of a soft cornetto filled with chocolate cream so good she worried it might ruin her for all other food.

"These are beautiful," Ilaria said, gesturing to the gowns, attempting to make conversation. "What are they for?"

Chessa and the younger woman, maybe an assistant or apprentice, exchanged strange looks.

"Surely the Prince..." Chessa trailed off, then smiled brightly as if that could erase the words. "An announcement of your marriage to the Prince will be made, and you will appear before the people of Vantonella as an introduction. You will need a gown, of course."

Right. That.

"So we must get the dress ready. Quickly."

"And then Noemi will help you prepare your speech," the assistant added helpfully.

But Ilaria felt the cornetto turn to ash in her mouth. "Speech?" she repeated. She was sure she paled as well. Frediano had mentioned an announcement, an introduction. But not speeches.

Chessa waved this away, as if it was simply of no consequence when she was expected to stand up in front of *all* of Vantonella and *speak*. "Not so much a speech as a few words. Mostly waving. And the kiss, of course."

"The...kiss."

"For the official marriage photograph printed in the papers."

Ilaria looked from Chessa to the assistant and tried not to feel as though they were speaking a foreign language.

Official marriage photograph. Pictures and speeches would make it much harder to escape this. It would make her known, complicating any escape once she knew Sophia was safe. Complicating everything, because everyone in the *country* would know.

That she'd married a prince. That she had stepped into the world she had spent most of her life railing against.

She desperately needed that phone. "When does all of this happen?" Ilaria asked, hoping she sounded casually curious and not hysterical.

"Three this afternoon, Your Highness."

That did not give her much time to convince the Prince she was unsuitable, while also convincing him Sophia was beyond his reach. There had to be some third option. A compromise.

"I must insist you finish your breakfast," Chessa said. "I'll need time to accomplish alterations, and the Prince will have my head if I do not."

"The Prince should worry about himself," Ilaria grumbled, then winced, because obviously this woman was *employed* by the Prince, and loyal to him. Not her.

"The Prince worries about everyone, Your Highness."

Ilaria felt suitably chagrined, though it was ludicrous. Why should she feel shame for speaking poorly of the man who'd all but kidnapped her? Quite frankly she deserved a few angry words. And an *escape*.

She definitely had to escape before there was any kind of speech.

Or kiss.

She shivered—the bad kind, surely, because though the Prince was handsome, he was her captor, and she did not *want* to kiss him. Truly.

She'd never kissed *anyone*, and now she was meant to kiss a prince? In public?

"Let us begin." Chessa pointed to the platform.

A dress was simple. Certainly not irrevocable. And Noemi would be back with a phone she could use soon. And then she could speak to Sophia…

What? What then?

She'd figure something out. So she stepped up onto the platform, and then had to fight discomfort as the assistant pulled the robe off her. As the two women commented on her body and slid a dress off the hanger and then helped her into it.

When Noemi returned, she was empty-handed. But she smiled brightly, likely at Ilaria's obvious dismay. "A phone is on its way, Your Highness."

From behind Ilaria, Chessa spread out the skirts of the fine dress. "These colors aren't right at all. Not with her coloring."

"I'm afraid the Prince was very clear that these were the types of dresses he preferred," Noemi returned.

The seamstress muttered a string of rebuttals, then spent the next half hour putting Ilaria into and out of dresses. The gowns themselves were no hardship to wear. Each was more beautiful than the last. And so surprisingly comfortable. The beige ones stayed on the rack and Noemi's frown deepened with each jewel-toned addition Chessa offered.

Just as the tension in Ilaria's stomach doubled with every minute a phone did not appear.

The last gown was made of dazzling beading that glittered like jewels. It was stunning. Like nothing Ilaria could have ever imagined. Yet it hugged every curve and dipped dangerously low so that she held her hands over her chest while the seamstress tugged and pinned and muttered to herself.

"This is the one," Chessa said without hesitation. "The others are far too plain."

"The Prince requested a beige dress," Noemi cut in. Repeating herself.

Clearly, Chessa did not fear the Prince. "Nonsense!

He'll want his princess a glittering jewel. Men know nothing of fashion. We shall alter the beaded gown."

Spitefully, Ilaria wanted to agree with Chessa. If the Prince would hate it, this was the dress. But she was deeply uncomfortable with the cut. "Isn't it…" Ilaria trailed off as three sets of eyes looked at her, as if surprised to find her a breathing human being and not a lifeless doll. "It's rather revealing, isn't it?"

Noemi smiled kindly. "You look beautiful in all of them. However, the Prince—"

Before Noemi could finish the sentence, the door to the sitting room opened—no knock, no hesitation. Because princes likely never knocked or waited to be given permission to do anything.

Frediano opened his mouth but did not immediately say whatever greeting he'd been planning on. He paused. Ilaria felt his gaze move over her, like a flame being held to every inch of her previously cold skin. He had looked at her like this last night. Like he might devour her whole. Like, inexplicably, she might be attractive to a *prince*.

Which she surely did not want, no matter how her body reacted.

Then the heat went out of his eyes, just like last night. Cold. A switch that could be turned off. She should be happy that he could and would.

But she found herself yearning for things she did not fully understand instead.

"This is not the correct dress," he said.

"No, Your Highness, but it suits her much better," Chessa replied, chin held high.

The Prince looked at the seamstress with such frigid disdain that Ilaria nearly wilted *for* her, but the woman simply held his gaze.

"I did not request one that *suits* her. I requested the one

I required." He turned to Noemi, effectively cutting off the seamstress. "You will correct this error immediately."

"Yes, Your Highness." Noemi curtsied quite gracefully, and immediately disappeared with the seamstress, her helper and the beige dress.

Leaving Ilaria behind in the sequins, and far too much skin showing.

"I have requested a phone," she said so she'd stop thinking about the dress. And the way he looked at her with heat in his eyes. "I need to make some phone calls."

Frediano looked around the room, not responding. There were two people cleaning up the breakfast trays. "Leave us," he ordered with a flick of the wrist.

They scattered. No, that wasn't fair. Scattered suggested something *she* would do, or sheep might. The staff *melted* away as if they'd never been there in the first place.

Then, he pulled a mobile out of his pocket. He even smiled as he held it out to her.

She did not trust that smile. When she reached out, it was gingerly, but before she could take the phone, he continued.

"I'm sure you will want to speak with Sophia, but you needn't bother. I have already done that for you this morning."

For a moment, Ilaria felt as though her knees might give out. But she stiffened them. She could not stiffen her arm. It fell to her side.

"It turns out that, strangely enough, she did not make it across the border with her...sailor last night." Frediano frowned and shook his head, as if it was too bad. "She and Tino were, shall we say, very kindly detained."

Ilaria wished she could have absorbed this information as casually as he delivered it, but her breath caught with a stab of pain. Because she understood what he was telling her. What he was doing.

It was a threat. No, it was *blackmail.*

"Now, as the Prince, I could let them go, of course. Across the border, to marry and live whatever lives they've planned."

"Yes, you could," Ilaria managed, trying to keep her voice caustic instead of despairing. She was quite certain she failed. "Why did you bother with a wife when what you want is a prisoner?" she demanded, impotent anger coursing through her.

"You are not a prisoner," he replied with a laconic shrug.

"You're blackmailing me!"

"No, *tesoro.* You have a choice. You just don't like the choices."

He was arguing semantics, so there was no point continuing the verbal argument. He was right in a way. Two options. Hurt her cousin or hurt herself. Give her uncle what he wanted by handing Sophia over to the Prince, or lose everything that mattered to her, when she'd already lost so much.

Frediano had effectively trapped her. Into gowns and speeches and kisses for royal portraits.

They faced off in silence, Frediano with a small, satisfied curved to his mouth. Ilaria doing her best not to hurl her fists at his chest. It would do nothing, and no doubt she'd be thrown in a dungeon or something equally archaic.

And Sophia would not escape her father. Uncle Giovanni would get what he wanted.

No, it could not happen.

"But to show you how generous I am, I am prepared to offer you a gift of sorts."

She snorted, which was probably not the mark of a princess, either. All the more reason to indulge. "I find that very hard to believe."

"Believe in me always, Princess. As it only took a quick glimpse into your life to understand that jewels and furs and castles would not be the way to your heart."

"*Hearts* have nothing to do with this," she returned acidly.

"Indeed they do not. At least, mine does not. Yours does a little, according to your neighbors."

She felt thrown thoroughly off axis. "My…neighbors."

"They told my men many things about you. All glowing, of course. Excellent for a future queen. But mostly they spoke of your devotion to your under-the-radar and potentially illegal orphanage."

This time, her knees just didn't weaken, her vision blurred. He would threaten her home? The people in her care who had lost so much already? She had to stay strong. She had to fight. "It isn't an orphanage," she said, trying to remain cool.

"A work home?" he suggested, feigning an innocence he'd likely *never* had.

"It is *home*," she returned, and had to curl her hands into fists over the low dip of her dress.

"A home for some, perhaps, but there are four underage children, with no parents, living on this property. Neither you nor any of the other adults are the legal guardian of any of them, correct?"

"I knew your grandfather was a thoughtless fool, but you are a soulless—"

The calm, self-satisfied expression with which he'd been delivering his information fell off his face in a flash. He stepped closer. "You will never, ever insult my grandfather, your king, again," he said, so quickly, with that same frigid tone he'd used on the seamstress. But there was fury in his eyes—heat, not ice. He took a few moments to cool it. She watched it happen, fascinated against her will.

When he spoke again, he was calm. "Not *everything* is a threat. As I said, this is a *gift*. Insurance, if you will. I will not shut down your little organization. I will instead lend it some legitimacy."

"I don't need—"

"Upon the completion of the marriage announcement this afternoon, a trust will be set up to fund not just your operation, but an expansion of your farm in Accogliente. For every year you do not cause a scandal in our marriage, an increasingly large amount of money will be placed in this trust. When you supply me with an heir, the trust will be moved into your name and theirs and be completely under your control. You can help your village, your orphans, whatever you wish, however you wish."

Ilaria was shaking. She tried to control it, but this was some sort of…devil's offer. It was so much of what she wanted.

And it would bind her to him. Forever.

"How do you know that's what I want?" she managed to ask.

"My men are very thorough, Ilaria. And your little orphans are very forthcoming when people ask the right questions. You should probably teach them a better distrust of strangers."

A violent wave of reaction went through her. That he would use everything she loved against her. So quickly. So easily. Because *this* was what royalty was. Cruel and selfish and only interested in their own incomprehensible whims.

"I hate you," she seethed.

"Do you?" Frediano returned, unbothered and unsurprised. "When I am making you such a generous offer? That doesn't make much sense."

It was generous, maybe, but certainly not selfless. At best, it was a payoff. At worst, it was another layer of blackmail.

One that would help so many. Help the village. It would help *everyone*.

Except her.

She closed her eyes against a wave of grief.

"You may thank me."

Ilaria opened her eyes, meeting her *husband's* cold gaze and vowed to herself that *someday*, she would find a way to get revenge on him. *Someday* he would wish he'd never said *yes* in that cathedral.

But when his dark, impenetrable eyes settled on her dress, thoughts of revenge scattered. She wanted to back away. Run away. But she was held still by the sheer force of his gaze.

"Drop your hands," he ordered.

Some part of her felt compelled to obey immediately, but the thought of him seeing so *much* of her… She shook her head, cheeks flaming with heat.

"I'm afraid I must insist."

"You're not afraid of anything." Was he? Surely even a prince feared something?

"Would you like me to drop them for you?" He said it silkily. Like it was a promise, not a yet another threat in what felt like an avalanche of them.

But she found her hands dropping nonetheless. It was his voice. Perhaps there was some sort of drugging quality to it. It reverberated inside of her until she lost herself, when she could not afford to lose herself.

"You are surprisingly beautiful, Princess."

"I…" She had never considered herself *beautiful*. Her life had not been about how she looked, ever. It had been about what she could do. For her grandfather. For her farm and the children. For Sophia.

His gaze was on her eyes—but she could not help the feeling that he took her *all* in. Over and over again. The more her pulse beat, the more she did not wish to cover herself any longer. She felt like her whole body was becoming a pulse of something. A good something. An exciting something.

Her body seemed determined to betray everything she was.

"Now that we have successfully determined what *appropriate* dress you will wear," Frediano continued, "we will go over what will be required of you to say. And do."

"Do," she repeated.

He smiled then, not mirth or blackmail, but something…wicked. "Indeed, Princess. I will introduce you to our people. You will read Noemi's carefully prepared speech. Only a few lines. And then we will share a kiss."

She was not sure how he could say the word and make her feel like he had touched her. When she had never once been kissed before. Had never had time to think about wanting to be kissed.

"It is a tradition going back centuries—paintings and then photographs. Only my parents have broken this tradition. I do not intend to follow in their footsteps. In anything."

That he said seriously. As seriously as any vow.

This was all so overwhelming, and what made it so much worse was *him*. The way he looked in his dark suit. The way his gaze made her feel like she was ablaze. The way her mind kept going back to the thought of *kissing him*.

Kiss this man. As if she were his wife. His princess. A future queen.

When she only wanted quiet and her farm and the old life where she was the one helping people and wanted nothing for herself.

But there was a want inside of her now she was afraid to name. It grew with every moment they were alone. With every moment he regarded her and did not look away.

She could not go back in time. She could only go forward with what tools she had. She had learned that after her father's death, and it had served her well. It had turned her into a strong woman who figured out how to handle the challenges life threw her way.

If she did as the Prince said, Sophia would be safe, her people back home protected, maybe even elevated. And if she was miserable in the process… Well, she would rise to that challenge. Find a way to turn this strange and awful turn of events, this misery, into a positive.

Ride out the storm. Somehow, she would.

Frediano could all but *see* her thinking, pulling herself together and readying herself for the war ahead. Admirable, but she would need much more of a poker face if she was going to survive being royalty.

So she would, because he had found the key to keeping her under his thumb. He had been surprised to learn of her little farm/orphanage operation. It was impressive, he could admit, what she had done with so little. And how well liked she was in her village, according to his men's reports. Her kingdom was tiny, but loyal. He could appreciate that on its own merit, philosophically.

But this was reality, not philosophy, and in reality, her reaction to him spoke volumes. She was horrified by the lengths he was willing to go to ensure her obedience, but she was not horrified by the heat between them.

He knew better than to play with fire, but surely he could handle a little spark? "Which part concerns you so, Princess? The speech?" He stepped closer. "Or the kiss?"

She held his gaze, chin jutted stubbornly. He was tempted to smile, though her challenge should frustrate not amuse.

"I have no concerns, Your Highness," she said, and then she smiled. Or tried. The bitterness in *Your Highness* was a little too clear to believe smiles. "Perhaps you should tell me yours."

He laughed. If only such a challenge fit into his life, but all that mattered was molding her into the perfect princess that would convince his grandfather to step down and focus on his health.

She frowned at his laugh, and then deeper when he put his finger under her chin and raised her face so she met his gaze.

"We are adversaries, *tesoro*. I will not be *confiding in you*. Ever. This is a marriage, and it is a battle. I intend to win." No one's wants would threaten his grandfather's health, most especially his own. He would control this as he had controlled everything for so long.

She struggled with something. Her innate need to challenge him, no doubt. But she did not immediately argue. Did not childishly state her intent to win instead. She sucked in a deep breath, which brought his gaze down to the low dip of her dress.

Yes, she was quite beautiful, and it would not do for anyone to know just how much. The beige dress, the boring newspaper article. Any spark of how interesting she truly was hidden so no whiffs of similarity between her and his mother were made. King Carlo had to think her wholly different.

"I think it only fair we try to reach a compromise." She tried to smile again. It did not reach her eyes. "I can give a small speech, but we could abstain from any kissing as there are no romantic feelings between us and never will be."

He slid his thumb across her jaw, almost without thinking about it. Like his fingers had a mind of their own. But her skin was so soft. "This is not a negotiation. It is tradition." He smiled at her then, wanting, perversely, not her sad attempts at compromise, but her challenge. "Don't tell me you're afraid."

She jerked her chin from his fingers. And his smile widened.

"Perhaps the real concern, Ilaria, is that hidden away in your little village, taking care of other people's children, you have never, in fact, kissed anyone privately let alone publicly." She sucked in such a breath he knew he was right. The reports on her had unearthed no suitable men in her life, but one never knew exactly what was done behind closed doors.

She made it clear *nothing* had been done.

"Do you worry you will bungle it?" he continued. "Or do you think perhaps a kiss from a prince might be so different you are afraid of swooning in front of our people?"

Her struggle was valiant, to not let her surprise or irritation with his words show. But she failed.

"There is that gaping I warned you about."

Her eyebrows furrowed again, anger causing those green eyes to turn a stormy gray. Fascinating, really. Perhaps she was some kind of mountain witch.

But she did not speak any more. No vehement *I hate you.* She was silent. He had given her two very strong reasons to hold herself back. He had twisted *her* world to make sure it *had* to suit his.

As *kings* did.

"Perhaps you are worried that you will jolt at my touch, as you did last night." He'd relived the simple pleasure of dragging his thumb against the soft, velvety expanse of her wrist, over and over in his bed last night.

His body tightened—the dreams he'd had of possessing all of her on that ridiculously frivolous bed in her bedroom were too close to the surface. *Playing with fire will always get you burned*, his grandfather had warned him often as an adolescent.

So he had learned. You could not *control* fire, but you could learn to *endure* anything. So he had.

His control was his armor. It was who he *was* and how he survived. And in this *battle*, it would see him winning yet again.

"I worry about none of these things, *Your Highness*," she said, managing to make the honorific sound like some kind of insult. Her voice was cool, composed.

Impressive.

Everything about Ilaria Russo was turning out to be surprisingly impressive.

The way she seemed to glisten like the sea in this sparkling dress. The ill-fitting fabric from last night had not accounted for the way her body curved. He had trouble trying to not imagine his hands gripping the flare of her hips, her rough hands on him—

She was a *temptation*, but he reminded himself he liked proving his control, time and time again.

He stepped back from her, offered her a cool, polite smile. He put the mobile on the table next to a breakfast tray. "The phone is yours, Princess. Feel free to contact whomever you wish. Once the introduction is made this afternoon, I will instruct my men to let your cousin go. Should you need anything, you need only ask Noemi."

He gave her a little bow, smiled at her with just enough princely courtesy to have her frowning outright.

And then he left to prepare to introduce his princess to his people.

CHAPTER FOUR

ILARIA WAS POKED, prodded, moved about and basically treated like one of her sheep. She was not a woman with her own thoughts or opinions. She was *livestock.*

And there was nothing she could do about it as long as the Prince held her cousin captive.

Three o'clock loomed closer and closer. Women came in and out of her rooms to prepare her.

She was dressed in a gown nothing like the jeweled one from this morning. It was beige and, though clearly elegant and expensive, plain. Her hair was done in a similarly simple manner. An army of people lathered and painted at her face and somehow made it look…different. Not glamourous or like a princess, but more like a slightly shinier, less freckled version of herself.

She looked at herself in the mirror and did not know how to feel. On the one hand, no one would find her interesting if she looked like *this*. Except to question perhaps why the Prince had chosen her. And she did not wish for anyone's attention, so it seemed…right.

But part of her wondered why she couldn't at least *look* like a princess, even if she did not wish to be one.

"Are you certain about this?" she heard one of the makeup people ask Noemi.

Ilaria met Noemi's gaze in the mirror. The woman's slight frown immediately turned into a reassuring smile.

"This is exactly what the Prince requested," Noemi said brightly. Which was not an assurance that she looked particularly beautiful, only that she met the Prince's requirements.

"Maybe the Prince shouldn't always get what he requests," Ilaria muttered, causing the young woman straightening the *beige* collar of her gown to giggle.

Noemi began to gather up all the staff, giving them soft orders. Ilaria found she couldn't think of anything to do but sit here and stare at herself in the mirror.

She was reminded too keenly of that first day after her father had died. How she'd been lost, powerless to stop a relentless chain of events.

And then you pulled yourself together and figured it out.

She had to find some kind of faith that she could do the same in the midst of this unfathomable string of events.

She had called Sophia four times on the mobile Frediano had given her. Each time she had left a message. Sophia had not returned any calls. Ilaria couldn't help but think that if Sophia would at least call her back, she might find that faith.

"Is there anything I can do to help you feel any more prepared?" Noemi asked.

Ilaria looked up at the woman—her *assistant*—and blinked at the tears that threatened. She was stronger than tears. "You've been wonderful." Ilaria did her best to smile at Noemi. But she was sure it failed because there was *nothing* to smile about. "Thank you for all your help."

"It is only my duty." Noemi looked at the piece of paper Ilaria hadn't touched since Noemi had handed it to her. "Perhaps you'd like to practice your speech?"

Ilaria hadn't even been able to bring herself to look at the words. Almost as if seeing them would make this real.

It's real all right.

She lifted the paper. *Good afternoon, citizens of Vantonella. I am so happy to be here this afternoon. Thank you for your most kind welcome into the family Montellero.*

She closed her eyes against the words and resisted the urge to crumple the paper. She was *not* a Montellero. She was a Russo. Her grandfather and father had been proud of their family name, and with the orphans and farm under her care, Ilaria had never given any thought to changing that. Marriage had always seemed a luxury meant for other people with fewer responsibilities and more time.

But this was not a real marriage. It was a rescue mission. It had been her father who had always told her she must look out for Sophia. That while it might seem her cousin had all the things Ilaria did not, the Avida home was not a warm or loving one. And it would make her mother proud if Ilaria did all she could to forge a relationship with her cousin and protect her in whatever small ways she could.

So maybe this was a disaster, but at the very least she was making her parents proud.

Ilaria swallowed the lump in her throat. The pain she felt was not new. It was an old loss. Grief that never fully went away.

"It is time for us to meet the Prince, Your Highness."

"I don't suppose you'd point me to the nearest exit and not sic the guards on me when I run?"

Noemi's eyes went wide in alarm. "I'm sure that won't be necessary."

Ilaria had to laugh at the woman's discomfort. "I'm

sorry," she said, putting a hand on the woman's forearm. "It was a joke."

Noemi smiled tightly. "Of course." She clearly did not find it in the least bit funny.

"Follow me."

Ilaria was led through the maze of hallways that made up the palace. In order to calm her nerves and keep her mind busy, she began to make a to-do list. One would be to get a map of the palace so she could memorize it.

Or figure out the best exits anyway.

She was ushered back into the gigantic room she'd first entered last night, with its gleaming windows and amazingly impressive ceiling, built centuries ago.

For all the ways she did not want to be here, for all the ways this was a nightmare come to life, this room simply *awed* her.

And very much against her will, so did the man standing in the middle of it. She hated him. Truly and totally.

But he was so very handsome. He stood next to another man, whom she would have recognized—even at this distance, and even if he wasn't the King of her country—as Frediano's relation. They shared broad shoulders, dark hair—though the King's was sprinkled with gray—and an unsmiling mouth that could easily be called cruel.

Holding themselves in the exact same manner, ramrod straight and hands clasped behind their backs, they studied her approach as if she were a lifeless piece of art.

She wished she was.

She glanced back once, to find that Noemi had disappeared. Melted away like all the palace staff seemed to. It left Ilaria feeling adrift. Abandoned.

But there was no choice, at present, except to move forward. To stand before the King and Prince and somehow behave as if this was *normal.*

Frediano inclined his head in a kind of bow as greeting, though there was no deference in the gesture. "Grandfather, I would like to introduce you to my wife. Ilaria, this is my grandfather. Your king."

He is not my king. Ilaria knew she was meant to curtsy. Even a country girl who'd never had any dream of meeting the monarchy knew this was the sign of respect required.

But she didn't want to, couldn't seem to force her knees to bend. She stood, silent and still, working so very hard not to do the one thing she so desired: spit on the King's shoes. For her father. For Accogliente and Estraz.

"Ilaria." There was warning in Frediano's tone, but she could not seem to heed it. This man had *promoted* her uncle. Rewarded him for all the ways he'd put his own wallet over the hardworking men in her village.

"She is shy, Grandfather," Frediano said, with some humor she doubted he felt. "And not accustomed to the ways of the monarchy just yet. But I will ensure she has all the proper training."

"Excellent," King Carlo returned, nodding. His voice was as deep as his grandson's, with a hint of gravel. But that was not what Ilaria couldn't help but notice or study. Frediano spoke differently to his grandfather. Not just deferentially as required by title, but almost with…true warmth. There was a softness in his dark eyes when he smiled at the man who'd all but sentenced her father to death.

"Do you have a voice, girl?" the King asked her, but he did not sound angry. Not even impatient. There was no inflection whatsoever.

But him calling her *girl* certainly had her emoting. "Yes, Your Majesty," Ilaria replied, telling herself to bite her tongue, and losing the battle. "And, as I'm twenty-four, I'm hardly a girl. Which is good news for your grandson as I'm not sure a child bride would suit the image you're trying to curate."

The King's eyebrows rose, but he did not offer any kind of scolding. Of course Frediano's frigid gaze warned her she'd likely get one from him later.

She inclined her chin. Frediano had said she could not create a scandal if she wanted to ensure her cousin and farm were taken care of. He had *not* said holding her tongue was a condition of the deal.

It's blackmail, not a deal.

And she'd do well to remember it.

Frediano prided himself on being able to read people quickly and accurately. His one and only challenge these days was his grandfather, who had keeping things close to the vest down to an art form.

Frediano hoped that in the years to come he could find his grandfather's level of detachment, but perhaps there was simply too much of his mother in him. Perhaps he could not completely hide his emotions, but he could control them. So he did not reprimand Ilaria or ask her what the hell she thought she was doing talking to the King in such a manner.

He took her arm instead and followed his grandfather down the hall at enough of a distance that Carlo would not overhear their hushed conversation. "You look lovely this afternoon, my wife," he offered, smiling pleasantly.

She offered him the same smile, though her eyes flashed. "No need for dishonest flattery, Your Highness." She looked at his grandfather's back, then up at him. "My cousin is not returning my calls."

"I assure you it is no fault of *mine*," Frediano replied. "Perhaps she is too embarrassed or guilty to take your call."

Ilaria's dark eyebrows drew together, as though she

wanted to argue with him but could not find the words to do so.

"You must let her go," she said instead.

"And I will. The moment we are done with your introduction." He smiled down at her. "You have my word."

"Your word means *nothing* to me."

Frediano's temper flared, but he had been watching his grandfather too long to let his emotions show. He kept his arm relaxed, his expression bland, and any of the rage he felt was allowed to burn and bubble deep inside, but only there.

They walked side by side down the long hall. At the end were the double doors to the terrace, flanked on either side by staff who would open it for them at the appropriate time.

Outside, the King's aides would be setting everything up and would signal when it was time to make their entrance.

King Carlo turned his dark gaze to Ilaria. He surveyed her, but Frediano could not hope to gauge what his grandfather saw. Hopefully, the kind of quiet, obedient princess that would allow him to feel comfortable in stepping down.

Not the woman so *disgusted* by the idea of him giving his word.

"You have been apprised of what is expected of you today, I hope?" the King asked Ilaria.

"Yes," Ilaria replied. Through gritted teeth.

There was a long stretch of silence where both Frediano and his grandfather waited. And waited. And waited.

Frediano had to give himself a moment before he spoke to make sure his tone came out measured. "When speaking to your king, Ilaria, it is customary to use 'sir' or

'Your Majesty'. To curtsy when you first approach and when you leave."

Ilaria remained stubbornly silent, making eye contact with neither of them. She looked straight ahead at the doors.

"She will need that etiquette training as soon as possible," King Carlo muttered.

Torn between frustration and boiling fury, Frediano forced his mouth to curve ever so slightly at his grandfather. "Yes, sir. I wholeheartedly agree. No need to worry for this afternoon, though. Noemi has prepared her thoroughly. Hasn't she, Ilaria?"

For a moment, those stormy green eyes met his. "Of course. *Sir.*"

This time the heat boiling in his gut had very little to do with anger, but both responses were dangerous, so he looked forward. At the ornately carvcd door and shining gold knob. She wished to be challenging. Unfortunate, but not impossible.

Nothing was impossible.

"They are ready, Your Majesty," one of the doormen said, bowing at King Carlo.

The King lifted a hand. "Go ahead."

Each man pulled open a door. King Carlo moved first, out onto the ornate royal terrace that looked down over the large courtyard in the front of the palace. As predicted, hundreds of Roletto citizens stood below, eager to hear their king speak. To catch their first glimpse of the new Princess who had only been announced this morning.

Frediano stepped forward, Ilaria's arm in his. She took the first few steps easily enough, but as they moved into the sunlight, as the crowd came into view, she stiffened.

She tried to pull her arm from his grasp. She even moved to take a step back, so he held on to her more tightly. "There's no turning back now, Princess," he said into her ear, quiet enough his grandfather wouldn't hear as he used the microphone to greet the crowd.

Ilaria's breaths began to come in pants. He looked down at her, noting the way her eyes darted over the crowd. She was…terrified.

Against his will, he remembered his own first time here. After his parents' death, he had been in no shape to be shown to the public. His grandfather had secretly purchased a remote mountain chalet and taken him there. For three months, he'd given Frediano the space to recover and prepare for his new role—far away from all these eyes.

But eventually, Frediano had needed to face his future. He had been placed on this very stage three months later. Eight, nearly nine. Terrified that so many eyes were on him. He knew, too well, what it was like to step out onto this terrace, being wholly unprepared for an entire capital city interested in *him*.

He had *felt* wholly unprepared, but not as out of his depth as she must be—he'd known he was royalty, even if he'd never known his grandfather prior to his parents' death. He'd been used to paparazzi, to a certain amount of *attention*. He had been given three months to prepare as his body came back from the brink of death.

He'd been terrified, and a child, but he had not walked in totally blind.

Ilaria came from nothing. A small mountain village with fewer people in the entire town than were gathered in the courtyard. She was from a family with no connections—save an uncle by marriage—who, as far as Frediano had been able to surmise, had no connection with the Russos.

Ilaria tried to step back again, but Frediano held her

firm. There was no going back now. He remembered what his grandfather had whispered to him all those years ago.

And thanks to those words, and his grandfather's support, he had gotten through it.

So would she.

"Count your breaths, *tesoro*. It will do no good to faint. In, one-two-three. Out, one-two-three."

He was surprised that she listened, breathing carefully and no longer attempting a retreat. Perhaps fear was stamped all over her features, but she breathed. And as she did, she became less rigid.

Oh, she looked like a terrified gladiator about to be thrown into a coliseum full of lions. But she no longer seemed about to run.

She was brave, this mistake he'd made. Strong in the face of the unknown. Unwilling to let her terror win. A strange feeling wound its way through him. Something almost like pride.

When his grandfather turned and signaled for him, Frediano…hesitated. He did not for the life of him understand why, but it felt like a betrayal to drop her arm like he was supposed to.

When the only betrayal would not be accomplishing his duty. Still, when he stepped forward, for the first time in his life, he did not follow tradition—in this case approaching the microphone and the crowd alone before bringing his new bride to his side.

He found he simply could not let Ilaria go when she gripped his arm like it was an anchor.

So, as he stepped forward, he brought Ilaria with him.

CHAPTER FIVE

It worked, somehow. Counting. Breathing. The crowd was still overwhelming, but Ilaria didn't feel the need to run. She breathed. She counted. She held on to Frediano as he spoke, though she heard nothing of what he said.

He had become her anchor in a sea of panic. She didn't know how or why. Usually she only had herself to grab on to. Her sense of right. A *cause.*

Your cause is Sophia. You make it through this, and she gets a life. Your cause is your farm and the things you could do to help them with all that money he has promised.

Right. That helped, too.

She felt Frediano maneuver her closer to the microphone, and that was when she was finally able to concentrate on the words he was saying.

"I hope you will all warmly welcome your new princess. My wife. Ilaria Montellero."

My wife. Montellero.

The panic returned, doubled, tripled. But she thought of Sophia being free to marry her sailor. She thought of her uncle's face out there somewhere—it would kill him, that she had taken Sophia's place. That he would not get his title. It was revenge. If everything else was terrible, and, *oh, it was*, at least there was that.

She was to hold the paper in a manner so that no one could tell she was reading from the paper, but the arm Frediano held was supposed to be how she did it and… She couldn't let him go. She could not explain it, but she would not have the courage to speak without his stabilizing hand.

Everything felt more like a buzz in her head than any words, but still she thought of what little she'd read. And then she thought of what she'd want to hear if she was… them. A citizen of Vantonella. A citizen of this country and this monarchy.

She looked out at the sea of faces. It was too overwhelming, so she fixed her eyes on the great Monte Morte in the distance. Its peak was white with snow, the rest dazzling, craggy grays. The sky so blue she had to squint.

"Hello." That wasn't right. What had the paper said? "Good afternoon, citizens of Vantonella." Her voice shook and she knew she had to get it under control. She was an expert in faking bravery when she had none. "I am…" Not happy. At all. If she said she was happy she might burst into hysterical laughter. "I am honored to be here today." It wasn't the right word, either, but at least it didn't make her laugh.

Even as she held on to the strong, warm arm of the Prince, she reminded herself she had *some* kind of power as a princess. Surely she could do something to make these people feel like they might be…important. Heard. She kept her eyes on Monte Morte, and as she spoke to the crowd, her voice got stronger.

"I hope that I can offer a new voice to the monarchy. One connected to those of you who work for a living. Who have suffered great tragedy. I hope I can speak for all of you, in my way, and offer you a voice here among those too far removed to understand." She dared a look at Frediano, at King Carlo. Neither betrayed a response. She wondered if she'd ever be able to build that kind of formidable stoicism.

She held Frediano's gaze as she said the rest to the people. "But I understand. I will always understand. Thank you."

Frediano's granite expression gave nothing away as she stepped back from the microphone. But he dropped her arm.

She had no idea why that felt like a loss.

Brief loss, though, as he put his hands on her shoulders then and pulled her forward. His gaze did not change, nothing about him *changed*, but she remembered the part she had been hoping to avoid.

The kiss.

He leaned down, close enough she could feel his breath against her skin. She could feel his warmth…everywhere. In his hands on her shoulders, in the darkness in his gaze. She forgot about the crowd, the King. Everything centered on his dark, fathomless eyes.

She did not want to kiss him. She desperately reminded herself over and over again she did not *want* this. Her body seemed to think otherwise.

Because she did nothing to stop it. She did not move away from the finger that brushed against the collar of her dress, making her skin prickle with electricity and warmth, making that deep throb inside of her so all-encompassing she could think of nothing else.

His lips touched hers, and yes, just like in the car last night she jolted. It was *electric*, what a simple touch could do. Hands or mouths, it did not matter. Her skin seemed charged with something that only came to life when they touched.

She did not understand it, did not *want* to understand

it. But she was helpless to it all the same. His mouth on hers, a gentle brush of contact that seemed to sweep inside her like light and heat. So she only wanted to lean forward and find more.

But his hands on her shoulders tensed, held her there and out of reach. He looked down at her, cold and forbidding.

"I hope you are happy, Princess," he whispered, making her shiver. "You have ruined *everything.*"

There was a great cheer, his grandfather waving at the crowd, and then the exit. Frediano thought of it in steps, instead of his reaction.

Out the door. Into the hall. Face King Carlo.

His grandfather's expression betrayed nothing, but Frediano thought his complexion had paled. He could not ask his grandfather if he was feeling all right in front of all these people, but he worried and would have to send a message to his doctor as soon as possible.

"Frediano. We will discuss this in my office. Young lady, I hope you are better prepared to follow tradition and protocol when we have the royal wedding dinner."

"Royal wedding dinner?" Ilaria blinked. "But we're already married."

King Carlo only sighed. "Frediano."

"I assure you, sir, she will be thoroughly prepared for the dinner. You needn't worry. She will be perfect."

King Carlo looked at Ilaria with a hint of disbelief but said nothing. Just nodded to his hovering aide and then turned and walked away.

Frediano held himself perfectly still. So many different things roared through him. Fury that she'd *dared* to say whatever she wanted—creating a story no doubt the press would eat up like candy. A voice of the people. A princess ready to fight for the common man.

Exactly what he'd been looking to avoid with someone as bland as Sophia Avida.

His grandfather now questioned her suitability, and this would ruin the timeline. It would jeopardize his grandfather's health, and it was too late to go back now. She was his wife, introduced to all of Vantonella. He could not discard her and go demand Sophia marry him. That would be a disgrace as damaging as his parents' scandals.

And if that were not disastrous enough, he'd wanted more than the chaste kiss on that balcony. He'd wanted to kiss her until those misty green eyes were bright with passion. He'd wanted to feel the gentle shiver of her body everywhere. He had *wanted* so much that it had almost overridden everything else.

He had resisted his wants for decades now. They did not matter. They did not factor. His wants were nothing to the needs of Vantonella. To his ailing grandfather.

Because that was all she was—a *want*. Not a need.

No matter how his body wished to betray him and present her as one.

"Let me escort you to your rooms, Princess," Frediano said, offering his arm.

She gaped at him, but then seemed to remember his warning about doing so and snapped her mouth shut. She looked at all the people around them as if deciding who might help her escape.

But there was no one. She took his arm and walked back to her rooms in complete and utter silence. With every step he felt her tense, more and more until by the time they stepped into her sitting room she was like a wound top ready to explode.

He dismissed everyone, shut the door, and then looked

at her there in the boring dress she'd somehow managed to make look beautiful anyway. Made herself interesting with her words *anyway*.

She whirled on him. "I never want to do that again."

He raised a brow. "Which part? The kiss or the part where you went off script and ruined everything?" He congratulated himself on how bored he sounded when what he wanted to do was rage.

She looked up at him, eyes wild, doing enough raging for the both of them. "All of it," she said fiercely, her hands curling into fists as they had last night and again this morning. "I have been introduced as you desired. Let my cousin go and…and…lock me in a dungeon or something. I never, ever want to stand in front of a crowd that size again. I do not want anything to do with this dinner, your traditions or your protocols. I would rather be alone in a…prison. Forever."

He looked down at her, surprised by this reaction. She had panicked initially, but then she'd spoken quite beautifully to the crowd. Even if it wasn't what he'd wanted or could tolerate, the crowd had been rapt. Now she looked like she was panicking all over again.

"I did not expect theatrics, Ilaria."

She looked up at him, defiant and angry but still with that edge of desperation he did not care for, because it made him wish to reach out and calm her.

When she *should* panic. She had caused a mess.

She whirled again, began to pace. "I hate it. I can't do it ever again. How does anyone stand it?"

"Perhaps there are people out there who crave to be dissected by all and sundry, but I am not one of them. Still, I am a Montellero. It is my duty." He looked down at her, fighting too many urges to name. "You get used to it." Was that gentleness in his tone? He needed to harden himself. Make sure she understood that she could not cross him. Not ever again.

"I am a Russo," she returned, fiercely. She came to stand in front of him, like she might jab a finger or fist in his chest. When he raised both eyebrows at her, her hand fell, but she did not shut up.

"We mine. We herd sheep. We do not *speak* to crowds. We do not care about protocols and dinners."

But she had certainly worked up a crowd. The papers would scream about the people's princess, and people would want to know *all* about her tragedy. Fury rose in him, ruthlessly tamped down.

"You prefer to work in the shadows. Collecting your sheep and your orphans, speaking of your work and your tragedy. You prefer to thwart rules and laws with your *illegal* orphanage. But your preference is no longer material. You are *not* a Russo any longer. You are a Montellero. And you've just crowned yourself the voice of the *people*. That you did all on your own."

"I only wanted to say something…that would comfort me to hear if I were in their shoes. Don't you care about your people at all? Or is it all tradition and protocol?"

"Did it occur to you tradition and protocol is for them as much as us? Did it ever occur to you that this is not all one-sided? We are a symbol. We are leaders. Tradition is *comfort*. It is stability. In a world *full* of tragedy and upset, we offer something to *rely* on, Princess. And now they will rely on you. You wish to disappear, to be thrown in a dungeon. I wish I could arrange it, but instead you've made yourself a point of interest."

"I did not mean…"

Anger was winning. He could feel its claws sinking so deep inside of him he'd never pull them out. He should step away from her. Leave this room. Do damage control.

But he only wanted to step closer. To impress upon her all she'd done. To make it clear to her she was a mistake and he did not tolerate mistakes, even his own.

To put his mouth on hers and devour instead of giving her chaste, public kisses that were only symbols.

"You have compromised everything I set out to do. You have put your king's health in great jeopardy. *You* have failed, and symbol or not, protocol or not, *I* do not accept failure."

"Then I suppose you should end this farce," she shot back.

"There will be no *end*, *tesoro.*" An annulment would be a scandal perhaps bigger than his parents' flouting of Vantonella tradition. No Montellero royal had ever divorced, and he would die before he became the first. "You will atone for your sins, one way or another, *Princess.* You wish for a dungeon, you wish for your little village… Well, you have permanently ruined any chance of having those things you so desire. But consider this marriage prison enough for us both."

She sucked in a breath, a mix of panic and her own brand of anger that poked at his. "My cousin…"

"Your cousin can go to hell for all I care." It was the absolute wrong thing to do, and Frediano knew better than to follow his impulses, but in the moment it was either storm out or pull her into his arms.

He chose to storm.

He had to get control of himself before he faced his grandfather. He walked to his grandfather's office slowly, counting his breaths and steps—that trick he'd given Ilaria not so long ago.

Today, it did not help. He stood outside his grandfather's ornate office door waiting to be granted entrance, and *boiled.*

How had some little mountain girl ruined him so completely? Just because of the color of her eyes and the depth of her reaction to him? It was unconscionable.

The door opened, one of the King's aides gesturing Frediano inside. His grandfather sat at his giant desk and waved him forward as well.

"Come. Sit."

Frediano did as he was told, doing everything to contort his face into the same expression his grandfather wore. Stoic blankness.

King Carlo looked down at a stack of papers on his desk. He was not a man who liked computers, so most things were printed out for him. It was one of the few things Frediano planned to change once he was in that chair.

He studied his grandfather's face for signs of strain and was somewhat relieved to find no new ones.

"I have read your reports and spoken to the aides on the ground," King Carlo said. "I instructed the guards at the border to let Sophia Avida go on her way. We have no use for her now."

"Grandfather—"

King Carlo raised his gaze. Brown, blank eyes stared back at Frediano. How many times had he searched those eyes for some kind of reaction? He'd never found it.

"Frediano, I am surprised at how this all turned out, and yet it seems to be quite a success."

The apologies were on the tip of his tongue before the word *success* penetrated. He blinked. "Sir?"

"My advisors tell me we are viewed as too traditional, too masculine. I thought a sweet, feminine girl like Sophia Avida would be good for that, but… I think your choice might suit better. I liked what she had to say. It will soften us, and the people will like that. Her tragedy will provide much sympathy for her, and in turn you. I'm not sure Sophia could have done such for us, even if her father is in my ministry."

"I…fail to understand."

"You've done well, Frediano."

For a man who twisted the world to suit him, he did not expect his grandfather to somehow twist his own failure into a…success.

"She will be of interest, but not a scandal. Nothing like your parents, spoiled and self-centered." His expression darkened for the briefest moment, before returning to blank. "Her background is interesting." Carlo tapped his fingers on some papers Frediano assumed were the report on Ilaria he'd had sent over this morning. "Everything she's done seems to be quite selfless—whereas a pampered girl from a wealthy family could not have been viewed as *that*. Even if your princcss is not as selfless as she seems, tragedy softens people's hearts more than a good pedigree. It is a great tool, when used correctly. We shall use it correctly, yes?"

Frediano felt almost as unmoored as he had when he'd first stepped out onto the palace terrace as a child. This was not what he expected. This was not what he'd *planned*. But he knew how to roll with the punches, did he not? "Then you'll consider your doctor's advice?"

"Not yet," King Carlo replied, frowning. "You must teach the girl some protocol. Some…obedience. She is of good clay to mold, but she must be molded before I feel comfortable stepping down." He fixed Frediano with a steely stare. "The royal wedding dinner must go well."

"So it will," Frediano vowed.

CHAPTER SIX

ILARIA FELT LIKE she was going to break into a million pieces. Her rooms were large and beautiful, and still the walls felt like they were closing in. Hours passed. She was served dinner in her room. She called Sophia so many times she'd stopped leaving messages because the box was full.

She wanted to cry and wail in her bed, pound the pillows a few times. She wanted to run far, far away. Back home where her world made sense and *she* was in charge of it.

But this was not the first time the world had pulled the rug out from under her. It was simply more difficult this time because there was no one to turn her attention *to*. No one to comfort or care for.

It was just her, alone, in this opulent room.

She'd thought to change, but the wardrobe was full of clothes that were just as over-the-top and fine as the one she wore, and she wasn't sure she'd be able to undo the buttons on the back of this dress without help.

She didn't want help. She wanted to get out of here. Even if only for a few moments. A walk outside, fresh air, some reprieve from this prison would calm her. Soothe her.

You wish for a dungeon, you wish for your little vil-

lage... Well, you have permanently ruined any chance of having those things you so desire.

Those words echoed in her head, in the fierce, furious way Frediano had said them. She supposed it was something. Anger and fury over that icy control, or the utter blankness of his grandfather.

But that didn't truly comfort her, because he was so infuriating, so...arrogant and controlling and *awful*, but he made her feel overpowering *need*. She hated him, and she wanted to touch him. He had *ruined* her life, but he had held her arm and steadied her when she'd wanted to fall apart.

No one had ever given *her* support before. She wished it hadn't been as comforting and steadying as it had been. She shouldn't find comfort from someone ruining her life. Even if he *had* made an effort to help by telling her how to breathe and focus.

Everything he did *for* her was for his own ends. And the powerful attraction between them... She did not know why or how he could make all her thoughts simply vanish. All her wants change into his touch. She had never experienced such a thing.

She was a woman who enjoyed taking care, in helping. She was not a woman who'd ever spent any time considering her own needs or wants.

For a moment, that thought stopped her cold. Was that...wrong?

But of course not. She was a helper. That was a good thing. Better than being selfish and ruining someone's life simply because they could.

She went to the door that led into the hallway. She paused at it. Noemi had tried to keep Ilaria abreast of all the rules and protocols of moving about the palace, but

Ilaria had been too upset to listen. Or maybe she'd simply been in denial.

Now she wasn't quite sure how to proceed. *If you are really stuck being the Princess, you get to proceed however you want.*

She knew that wasn't true, but she decided to hold on to that thought anyway. She pulled the heavy door open and stepped into the hallway.

There was a man right there, dressed in what she was realizing was a kind of palace uniform. Expensive black suits, all perfect and gleaming for the men. The female staff seemed to have more choice in their attire, but it was always black.

"Can I get something for you, Your Highness?"

Never call me that again! She wanted to scream. Instead she smiled at him. She'd decided somewhere along the way to treat them all as she had treated any new orphan or widow when they'd come to the farm in distress. With them she remained calm. Smiled warmly, and never danced around the subject at hand. So she did the same now. "I'd like to get some air. Outside."

The man gave a slight bow. "Allow me to accompany you, Your Highness."

"That won't be necessary, of course." If there was one thing she *had* done before this afternoon's mess, it was familiarize herself with the palace map.

The man looked a little stricken, but he quickly regained his composure. "I'm afraid I must insist."

Ilaria breathed in through her nose, let the breath slowly out of her mouth. She did not allow her fingers to curl into fists. She smiled at the man. "What is your name?"

"Vincenzo, ma'am."

"Vincenzo, are you my jail warden?"

His whole face fell. “N-no, ma’am. Of course not.”

“Then I would like to walk alone.”

“I’m sorry, Your Highness, but I simply can’t allow it.” And he seemed the first in a long line of staff members who apologized to her today that truly meant it. “The paparazzi are everywhere. Your speech caused quite a stir. While the castle is protected, many have found ways of getting glimpses into the outer courtyards where you might walk.”

Her speech. Why hadn’t she read from that paper? Why had she thought she might grab some control in this situation? Frediano was right. She’d ruined *everything*.

She wanted to collapse right there, throw herself on the ground and have a tantrum. As if he sensed her hovering on the edge, Vincenzo quickly stumbled on.

“But I can show you a private path outside you could use. I simply must insist on going with you, though.”

It was something, Ilaria supposed. The cool night air, even with the company of a stranger, was better than staying in that room suffocating. “All right. Thank you, Vincenzo.”

When they stepped outside, it was pitch-black save for the moonlight and a ribbon of dim lights that lined a path out toward the lake and then around.

“See the lights?” Vincenzo asked, pointing down the pathway. “If you truly wish to be alone, you may walk to the end of them and back. I will stand here and watch.” He smiled encouragingly, as if he was giving her a great gift.

She supposed in his way he was. So she offered him a smile. “Thank you, Vincenzo.”

He bowed and she left him there. She’d find an answer in this walk, just like she did in her walks back home when she was sorting through a difficult problem. She loved nothing better than to hike through the mountains, the sheep, feel the wind whip her face and remind her that her problems in this great, wide world were small indeed.

Each step down the path brought her closer to the lake and its soft, calming lapping sounds. She felt hugged by the dark, calmed by the chill in the air. She could take a deep breath again.

No problem was so big she couldn't solve, she decided. Or perhaps tried to decide. Just because Frediano thought she'd ruined everything didn't make it true. Just because the King called her a girl and insisted she needed more work didn't mean she had to *care*.

She hated the King.

It was strange to have seen him up close. To see a flesh and blood man whose indifference had sentenced her father to death. To have seen Frediano's reaction to him, one of warmth and devotion, with so little of it returned. She wondered if anyone knew what the King thought or felt about *anything*. Did Frediano?

It was as if considering the Prince conjured him from the dark. She heard the sounds of water different from lapping, turned, and there he was. Emerging from the water, the silvery light of the moon outlining his wet, exquisite form.

Surely, she was…hallucinating? But he stepped out of the water and walked toward a bench, where a large towel was neatly folded, alongside a few other things she couldn't make out in the shadowy dark.

He was so handsome. Unfairly so. Like in a a fairy tale, tall and dark. Dangerous and compelling. A wolf. A prince. A *villain*. The water dripped from his hair, from his body, and he moved to dry it.

The Prince. *Your husband*.

She blinked at that truth she was still in denial of. But here she could only stand, stare.

Want.

No, she could not, *would not* want him. No matter how her traitorous body throbbed in protest. Her body's reaction was its own, but her thoughts could be controlled.

She wondered if swimming alone could cut *those* muscles into his body, or did he work out in other ways? It really didn't bear thinking about.

Really.

"You should not be alone," he said by way of greeting.

"I'm not," Ilaria said, cursing herself for the squeak in her voice. "Vincenzo is watching me." She pointed back to the man closer to the palace.

Frediano looked, then lifted his hand—a wave, a dismissal. Vincenzo bowed and then disappeared into the castle.

So she was alone. In the dark. *With my husband.*

No, she would not think of him as that word. He was the man she hated. Her jailer. Her *kidnapper.*

"What...are you doing?" she found herself asking, even as her brain instructed her to walk away. Back to the palace. Back to *jail.*

He scrubbed the towel through his hair, regarding her in the shadows. "I swim the lake every evening at this time."

He was back to himself. No more biting anger. Just that controlled detachment, so like King Carlo. Ilaria hated that almost as much as she hated him. "I'm quite certain I saw *two* pools on the palace map."

"A swim in the lake is not the same as a swim in the pools. I much prefer the lake, and at night, even the papparazi with their long scope lenses cannot find me."

Ilaria watched, fascinated as he drew the towel down over his chest. "Is it not cold?" she managed to ask, only sounding slightly breathless.

He stopped drying off and met her gaze in the dim light between them. "That is the point," he said, an edge of darkness to his words that matched the darkness around them.

He pulled a sweatshirt over his head and began to walk toward the palace, and she knew he expected her to follow. So she stayed rooted to the spot. After a few more steps he seemed to realize she had not followed. He turned to face her. The lights of the pathway allowed some sense of him—his outline, his features, but something about the dark made her heart jitter in her chest. Like she was in danger.

Of course you're in danger. This mad man has tricked you into marriage. Into giving up your life. Forever.

She had to return her focus to the reasons she was here. "My cousin—"

"Has been granted her freedom," Frediano interrupted. Causing her to gape at him. He'd said Sophia could go to hell. And now…

"My grandfather was quite impressed with you," Frediano continued, shocking her even farther. "He ensured Sophia was granted access to cross the border with her sailor. You needn't worry about her. She has found what you will not."

Ilaria simply didn't know what to do with this information. That King Carlo had been the one to let Sophia go felt…incongruous. To everything.

"*He* thinks you'll be an asset to the crown," Frediano continued.

The emphasis on *he* brought her back to reality. "But you do not."

"I am not King. Yet. It does not matter what I think. In fact, it does not matter at all. You are my wife. That will not change."

Not just a sentence, but a threat. That there would be no

end to this marriage—there was too much at stake when every year saw more money and autonomy for her farm and orphans. Even if she could give that up, she couldn't simply disappear home, even with an annulment or divorce. Her life was irrevocably changed. She was *known* now, and she did not know how to accept this any more than she knew how to accept this man as her husband.

"Come, Princess. I will walk you back to your room and safety." He offered his arm.

"There is no safety to be found here."

"More than you'll find with scheming journalists and relentless paparazzi," he returned, sending a dismissive wave to the high walls that protected the castle at night.

Her eyebrows drew together as she studied him. There was something that simmered in the way he said those words. "You really hate the press."

"Yes," he replied simply.

His reasons didn't matter, and yet in that way she was drawn to him on a physical level, there was a part of her desperate to understand this confusing man who'd ruined her life. Her father had always encouraged her to find the best in people. The mining accident had changed that for her and her grandfather, but it was still an ingrained habit.

So she asked the simple question. "Why?"

Frediano had not expected the question. He considered not answering. It was, after all, none of her business. But if he was going to fix the mistakes made in the past twenty-four hours, then he had to learn from them as well.

She was not going to take orders—likely too used to giving her own in her little fiefdom she'd created. He was going to have to shape her to his will in some other way. All the reports on her that his men had given him insisted Ilaria was a kind, giving woman who worked hard and told the truth. A rational woman who somehow survived despite all the ways the deck had been stacked against her.

Surely that meant she had a quick mind to be rationalized with. Perhaps if she understood, he could find a way to control this situation completely.

"My parents used the press to suit their whims, mostly in a bid to hurt my grandfather over and over again." He walked as he spoke, being careful to recite facts over the dark, swirling feelings. "They lied, and the press ate those lies up. Got rich and fat on the discord between father and son. Fell for every stupid trick in my mother's book of deceits." *And tried to drive my grandfather to an early grave.*

"You disliked your parents very much," she said softly, finally catching up to walk next to him. Though she never took his arm.

He had the strangest urge to reach out and take her hand in his. He ignored it. "They were hardly parents," he said, looking up at the palace. "They kept me from my grandfather, from my birthright, not because they wanted some better life, or simpler life as they claimed, but because it got them more attention than following tradition and protocol could."

He slid her a glance. She didn't bristle like he'd thought she might at the words *tradition* and *protocol*. Instead, she seemed to consider. When she met his gaze, those green eyes were soft.

"Did it hurt at all when they died?"

Another question he had not expected, but he did not outwardly react. Instead, he considered his answer. He remembered that day, being alone. Of being certain he would follow their fate. For days. Nothing but snow and hunger and certain death.

All because they hadn't wanted to leave him behind

since it did not suit their image. Nannies were seen as a sign of detached parenting practiced by the wealthy, and his parents liked the image that they loved him so much they could not bear to part with him. He wished he could assign some sort of love on their choices, but they had always spoken in front of him as if he did not understand what their words meant.

Even when he hadn't, he'd understood what their actions meant. They cared only for themselves, not *him*, and for how they could get others to fawn all over them.

So he had been certain no one would care that he was frozen and alone at the base of a mountain his parents had fallen from.

Until his grandfather had found him, dug him out with his own two hands and saved him. Not just from that mountain, but from that childhood.

"It was a relief," he returned, though that was too simple a word for all the complicated feelings of that time.

"That must have been difficult," she said softly.

He looked down at her, surprised by the softness in her tone. Moved, more than he wanted to be. "Do you pity me, Princess?"

She jerked her chin up. "Of course not."

"Good."

"I was devastated when my father died. He was my life, my light. And my grandfather's. Our world went dark that day."

"I suppose it did for many in your village."

"You are correct. And do you know why?" She stopped her walking and turned to him. "Because men like your grandfather and my uncle cared more about money than safety. And in the aftermath, when my grandfather was a wreck, and prospectors wanted to buy our farm, and widows and orphans walked through my village like ghosts, *your* grandfather promoted my uncle to his ministry. *Your* hero decided orphans who'd lost everything should be ripped from their homes and sent to the city and their shabby establishments."

Her eyes flashed—not with temper so much as hurt. And though he recoiled against the anger and accusations against his grandfather, what he heard in that diatribe told him many things he could use to mold her into what he wanted.

"And where was *your* grandfather in all this?"

"Mourning," she shot back at him.

"And you, a girl of fourteen, was not?" They stepped into the palace, and the lights were low as it was late. He could hear nothing but the hushed sounds of her harsh, irritated breathing.

"It sounds as though, much like my parents, your grandfather left *you* to the wolves," he continued. To anyone observing them from afar, it would seem husband and wife walking to their rooms. As long as they didn't look closer at the bitter, muttered words. "More destroyed by his grief than grateful for his gifts."

She whirled on him, there in front of her sitting room door. "My grandfather was ten times the man you or your grandfather could ever hope to be. If he had a weakness it was *love*, and that is not a weakness you could ever hope to *imagine* being felled by."

She did not say it, but he felt the words all the same. *If your parents did not love you, who could?*

Love. His grandfather had loved his father, bent over backward to try to keep his son, but all his son had ever done was betray him. His parents had claimed to love each other, but all they'd ever really loved was themselves and the attention they could find from others.

Never him.

All he'd ever seen come from love was *wreckage.*

He could tell she was ready to whirl back around and storm into her rooms, but something possessed him to keep her here. With him. He pressed his palm to the door-frame, blocking her unless she pushed it away or ducked under it.

She did neither. Her shoulders came back. She glared at him. Still in that ridiculous beige dress from this afternoon that did nothing for her and yet he felt a yearning so deep inside him he was convinced she could be dressed in a shroud, and it would not stop this inexorable, impossible *lust.*

But control it, he would.

"I suppose that gives me some insight into you. However, I must warn you. If you ever speak to the press about my grandfather, ever threaten the sanctity of our name, you will *wish* for the dungeon you requested."

"Sanctity," she said, each syllable dripping with disgust. "You wouldn't know the meaning of the word."

He reached out, drew his finger down her cheek, an impulse he would curse himself for later. She shuddered under his touch, even as she glared at him. At least this impossible heat between them was mutual, no matter what *intelligent* feelings they might try to hold on to, chemistry held them in its bonds.

And he found he could not resist poking at it, moth to flame. He leaned closer, so close her eyes widened as their noses were only centimeters apart.

"You hate me, curse me, blame me." He leaned so now their lips were merely a whisper away, giving himself one last moment of torture. "But you want me."

Her breath caught and her cheeks flared a deep, alluring pink. "No," she said, but it was a whisper. More hopeful than truthful. Her breath dancing against his mouth like a promise.

"Would you like me to prove it to you?"

She laughed—or tried, though it came out breathy. "You could never."

"A challenge" he murmured, and in one move she was clearly not expecting, he pulled her to him. He did not wait or hesitate, when he should have until they were somewhere private. But he did not. He simply crushed his mouth to hers.

At last.

He expected her to push him away. To fight. But instead, she melted. She shuddered beneath his hands and leaned into him. Her palms pressed against his abdomen as she moved to her toes to better meet his mouth. His hands moved, though he had not given them permission to travel up her neck, to cup her face, to angle her mouth just so under his.

To take the kiss deeper, darker. To drown in the warmth of her, the innocent openness of the way she kissed him back.

She whimpered against his mouth, her hands smoothing up his chest, and he…detonated.

He had underestimated her. A tactical error that poisoned his blood before he had a chance to correct it. And then there was only the taste of her. Dark and vibrant. Like the shadows of the mountains she came from. His hands streaked down her sides, curling into the fabric, desperate to rid her of this *beige* encumbrance.

He wanted to see where the sun hadn't touched. He wanted to taste every inch of her, this surprising beauty he did not understand.

He wanted…

But that was the problem, and eventually the *want* reminded him of who he was. What he could do.

And what he couldn't.

Rip her dress off in the here and now, where anyone in the palace could walk by and see his loss of control was out of the question, wife or not. A display of passion so out of character, so like his parents, would no doubt get to his grandfather and ruin everything.

Still it was harder than it should have been, to ease his mouth away, to uncurl his fists from her dress. To end the temporary madness that had ruled him, however briefly, and never could again.

She looked up at him, lips swollen, chest rising and falling in a tantalizing seesaw while her eyes were wide and clouded with a lust he wanted to slake here. Now.

Though his blood raged, his body hard and wanting, he stepped back. Away. She was a danger. To everything. And though it was a physical pain to beat back the desperate pulse of desire, pain was simply a reminder that he was doing what was exactly right.

He would have full control over every last urge before he had her in his bed. So that he always knew he could walk away. So that he always knew *he* was in control of everything.

He would take her on a secluded honeymoon and solve all his problems in one fell swoop—tutor her in the ways of etiquette, consummate the marriage as was necessary, perhaps even win her over so that he no longer needed to play such games to keep her in line.

When they returned to the palace in a week's time, she would be a different woman. And he would have everything he wanted. Because once she was perfect, his grandfather would step down, and Frediano would have his control.

"You are my wife. The marriage will be consummated." He smiled at her, enjoying the war he saw on her face—desire and knowledge, want and disgust.

At least he wasn't alone.

"But not until you are ready."

"I will never be ready," she returned, fiercely. With all that fire he denied himself.

"Never is quite the tempt of fate." And then, he left her, his control a tiny thread. But he had held on.

He always would.

CHAPTER SEVEN

ILARIA HAD ALLOWED herself the foolish impulse to cry herself to sleep that night.

Frediano had taken everything away from her—down to the belief she'd get out of this. Even with Sophia free, she could hardly turn her back on the money the Prince offered for her farm, her village. There was no return to her old life.

She had no choices. No options.

So she cried in all the ways she never would've back home, because someone would have heard. Worried.

Here, it didn't matter if she sobbed and wailed or pounded her fists against the wall. *Nothing* mattered.

And amid all of this unfairness was an incomprehensible war of desire and sense. Even alone in her bed, she wanted to relive Frediano's punishing, exciting kiss over and over again. When he spoke of consummating the marriage…she wanted to know what it would be like. Her body felt alive with fire and a reckless restlessness.

No one had ever prepared her for such a confusing war with herself. No matter how she told herself he was the enemy, she wanted him.

But once she was all cried out, she realized this uncharacteristic bout of self-pity felt…cathartic. Her eyes burned and her nose hurt from blowing it. Her temples throbbed, but it was like all that release allowed her to think clearly.

There was no way out, so it was time to accept her fate and make the best of it. It wasn't so different than death. She hadn't wanted to lose anyone she loved, but she had.

She hadn't wanted to lose her life, but she had.

So now she had to find a way to live in this one.

Which meant avoiding being alone with Frediano at all costs. She would never, *ever* willingly go to his bed, give him his heirs. She would never, *ever* let him kiss her as he had last night again.

Or so her brain insisted, while her body relived that moment. His mouth, harsh and demanding, and yet an invitation to some dark pleasure she'd never dreamed of. The way he had touched her. The taste of him, rich and intoxicating. She had never known want at all. So much so that she had been quite sure she would happily live out the rest of her days running her farm and helping her village, with that being all the love and desire she ever needed.

It made no sense, to want nothing to do with a man except feel his body atop hers.

When she finally slept, it was the deep sleep of exhaustion—physical and emotional. She awoke, not to the sounds of people in her room, or to daylight, but to a relentless dark. She looked over at the mobile she'd left on the nightstand.

On a sigh, she grabbed it. If she was to accept her fate, there was one person she still needed to talk to. She dialed Sophia's number, braced for an "Inbox full" message. But to her surprise, Sophia finally answered.

"Ilaria?"

"Sophia. Finally."

"Oh, Ilaria! I'm so sorry I haven't had a chance to call

you back. My phone died and everything has been such a tangle. But it's all right now."

Ilaria stared at the ornate room that was not hers and did not speak her thoughts aloud. *How will this ever be all right*? "So, you are well? And free?"

"Yes. It was scary when the border guards stopped us, but then they let us go. My father has tried to find me, but Tino is so clever, we've mostly managed to go under the radar. And now we're officially married, so it doesn't matter."

"Good."

"And...you've married the Prince," Sophia said, sounding a little uncertain, but forging on nonetheless. "I'm sure you can keep us safe since you're the Princess now."

A spurt of something hot and confusing shot through Ilaria, like a blade. She could not speak for a moment, so consumed by it.

It was anger. She didn't want it. She didn't *like* it. Sophia was soft. Pampered. She needed help and protection. It should give Ilaria yet another cause. A sense of purpose and satisfaction. Her position could continue to help Sophia.

But what about me?

For some reason Frediano's words from last night played back in her head. *It sounds as though, much like my parents, your grandfather left you to the wolves.*

But what Frediano did not understand was that some people were not strong enough to fight the wolves, and so some people were needed to step in and help. In all things, she tended and protected her sheep—be they actual livestock or those she loved. No matter what it cost of herself.

What was done was done, and there was no point in *feeling* anything about it. "It's fine."

"You are the most wonderful cousin in the entire

world," Sophia gushed. "And a princess now! Isn't that amazing?"

Ilaria could not find words. *Sophia* had not wanted to be a princess, so why did she expect Ilaria would want to be one? Why had Sophia not asked if Ilaria was okay? Ilaria had always considered her cousin sweet and in need of protecting, but in this moment she felt nothing but…

Betrayed.

"A million thank-yous will never be enough, Ilaria, but I have to go now. Tino and I are having a bit of a honeymoon breakfast." She laughed, actually laughed, and Ilaria could not find the words to say goodbye. So, when Sophia said them, Ilaria merely clicked End.

She should be thrilled. So happy for her cousin who now had everything she wanted. She should be satisfied her uncle could not get his title now. She should feel so many good things.

Instead she felt empty. And so very much alone.

Not long after the call with Sophia, the staff began to arrive. They got the fire in the hearth going. They set out clothes and makeup and all the things they would poke and prod her with until she was deemed acceptable.

Ilaria sat where she was in the bed and watched the flames flicker and dance. She did not allow herself to think of home. If she did, she might crumble.

And she could not to do that, because the farm still depended on her. It could run without her, as all the messages she'd received with updates told her, but they needed the money Frediano had promised. And they needed the legitimacy she could offer as Princess, should anyone ever get wind of the fact they did not have guardianship over their minor orphans.

"Is everything all right, Your Highness?"

Ilaria forced herself to smile at Noemi. "Of course."

She slid out of the bed and took the robe Aurora handed her. "What is on the schedule for today?"

Noemi's smile was forced, at best. "I believe the Prince would like to inform you of the schedule himself."

Ilaria knew that meant she wouldn't like what was coming, but that was hardly a surprise. Nothing coming would be *good.* So how did she make the best of it? "Noemi… Do you think I will be able to learn enough to prove to the King I can follow protocol before this dinner?"

Noemi seemed to give this some thought, which Ilaria appreciated.

"You seem very determined, Your Highness. I think you can do almost anything you put your mind to."

Though Ilaria had never felt she needed outside reinforcement or assurance, it was nice to hear someone say it. "Thank you, Noemi."

Noemi herded her over to the chair and the hairdresser came over and began to brush while Noemi hovered just out of the way.

"You are very kind, Princess," Noemi continued. "Very warm. I think you will be a great asset to Vantonella. The King and Prince are both honorable and good, but the troubles of their lives have left them…"

"Cold?" Ilaria replied, rather than argue about their *honor.*

"I was going to say reserved, but I can see as how that would come across as cold. Regardless of what it is, you have the warmth to change that. Your speech was so well received. You will be an excellent role model for the young people of Vantonella." Noemi smiled at her in the mirror.

Ilaria managed to smile back. She had no desire to bring warmth to those men. Wasn't sure she believed it possible. But it reminded her that in this little prison she'd somehow gotten herself locked in, there were things to accomplish. The idea she could be a role model…

It was humbling, and an opportunity to help. To be of service.

And by doing so, forget about the loneliness and emptiness that had plagued her after her call with Sophia.

Everything was prepared. Frediano had instructed Ilaria's staff to pack her things, and to get her ready to fly to the most remote royal residence the crown had to offer. It was Frediano's favorite escape, and like it had when he was a boy, the remote and hidden chalet would serve the crown's purposes.

His grandfather had wholeheartedly approved of Frediano's plan—or at least King Carlo's version of *wholehearted.* But approval did not matter, only the result would.

If he could polish Ilaria into the graceful, proper princess he had promised his grandfather, King Carlo would step down and take care of his health after the wedding dinner.

Frediano would have a week to turn Ilaria into the triumph he'd decided she would be.

It would require more than control. It would require balance. Ilaria would not be bested by threats and demands. She had not been raised with the appropriate deference to the crown, or perhaps to anyone, if the picture he was getting of her was correct.

A young woman who was used to being in charge. Taking care of all around her. Good qualities for a queen, he supposed, if she learned her place and used those attributes at the right time.

He would teach her. He would soften her to him. He

would bed her where he could indulge himself in all his wildest wants, and then he would be cured of the distraction of his attraction to her. Perhaps having her wouldn't cure him of *wanting* her, but it would certainly help.

It was always easier to resist the temptation you knew, over the one you did not.

He told himself all these things, and still the sight of her landed like a blow. She was not dressed in yesterday's beige, but in black. The dress was not revealing in any way, but the soft-looking material clung to the shape of her. Her staff had done her makeup so that she looked demure, but those mountain witch eyes could not be contained by soft pastels and an innocent neckline.

She eyed the small plane he stood next to with suspicion. "Where are we going?"

"Our honeymoon, of course."

She turned that skeptical look on him. "I do not think that is necessary or wise."

"It is both, Princess. Away from the palace you will have the space to learn the necessary etiquette without distractions. The chalet will allow a more relaxed atmosphere. Perhaps we can even get to know each other. Put all this nasty business behind us."

She stiffened, her chin coming up, and her eyes flashing as he'd hoped they might. "The nasty business where you forced me into a marriage neither of us want?"

"And yet you've already profited from such a match. Just today I spoke with your woman in charge. Vita, is it?"

"Yes," she replied through gritted teeth.

"She expressed the need for some home repairs and expansion, as your cottages are apparently very cramped. I've instructed my staff to take care of this at once."

"It will be a great improvement for many deserving individuals." She also said this through her clenched jaw, but she did not attempt to hurl any insults or argue with him.

He tilted his head and examined her. "Are you feeling all right, Princess? Perhaps you had trouble sleeping."

Her gaze jerked to his for only a second, before she schooled the shocked guilt back into something more placid.

"Ah, so you did," he murmured. "Interesting."

"I assure you, it is not interesting in the least," she returned. "Should we go?"

He did not move. He was not used to someone aside from his grandfather trying to order him about. "If you did not have trouble sleeping, perhaps it was dreams that plagued you. Maybe you'd like to share them."

She did not look up at him this time. She kept her gaze on the plane. "I dreamt of bloody coups," she returned, then flashed him a sarcastic smile.

It shocked him to his core that he wanted to laugh at that, which was decidedly *not* funny. It was best to get on with this. The sooner he won her over, the better.

He offered his arm. "Come."

She reluctantly placed her hand there, all the while studying the plane they walked toward. She hesitated at the bottom of the stair. When Frediano raised an eyebrow, she shook her head and continued inside. It was small so it was capable of landing on the small, mountain airstrip near the chalet, but no less luxurious than a larger plane.

The seating was plush and comfortable, and he had often worked the short flight as though he were sitting in his office at the palace. He took his usual seat, but she still stood there, awkwardly holding on to a purse.

"I've never been on a plane," she finally said, though he wondered if she knew she'd said it out loud.

"Does the idea of flying frighten you?"

She blinked at the question, then looked out the window, though they hadn't left the ground yet but were only taxiing. "I don't think so. I'd certainly rather try this than speak in front of all those people again."

"You will need to work on that."

Her gaze jerked back to his. She even opened her mouth as if ready for a tart rejoinder, but then she closed her mouth, smoothed out her expression and seemed to consider her seating options.

She settled herself into a chair across from him. She still clutched her purse at her abdomen, but she crossed her legs and he found his gaze drawn to the alluring line of her calf. Would her skin taste like her mouth, crushed wildflowers and wild storms?

He lifted his gaze to meet hers. If she'd noticed his interested perusal, she did not show it. Her mouth was screwed up in a kind of frustrated frown. He did not allow himself to consider the fact that kissing her had not lessened his desire to do so. *Knowing* how she reacted to him did not abate any of the lust coursing through his body.

"Do you honestly intend this farce to go on forever?" she asked abruptly.

The question did not anger him as maybe it should, because she seemed…not exactly lost. She was too self-assured for lost. But perhaps…vulnerable, and it poked at some unknown soft place inside of him he'd rather not acknowledge existed. "I'm afraid it must."

"But why? I realize an annulment or a divorce might cause a bit of gossip, but surely nothing as scandalous as your parents got up to." She flinched a little, as if she expected him to react to what was only the truth.

He had already considered these options, of course. He'd considered them that first night in the cathedral when she'd announced her identity. But it was impossible.

He could not imagine going back then or now for many reasons. The main one, of course, was his grandfather's health. It would take time to find another acceptable bride, time neither of them had. Not to mention his grandfather's reaction to reversing course, and the possibility of the press catching wind.

So it could not be done. "It is out of the question."

She heaved out a sigh. But she did not ask any more questions. She clutched her bag, harder and harder as the plane gained speed and then flung itself into the air.

He enjoyed watching her reactions as they flew. So much that he did not do any of the work he'd been planning. He simply sat and observed as she leaned closer and closer to the window until he finally suggested she move to the window seat.

She hadn't even argued.

There was something so honest about her. None of the artifice he'd grown up with—both his parents and the rich and titled who glittered and gossiped and cared more about that than the good of the country.

Now her nose was practically pressed to the window as they began their descent into the mountains. He heard her breath catch. It was easy to see Ilaria was impressed by a pretty place. Because the Montellero chalet might not have been as big as the palace back in Roletto, but it was a masterpiece of wood and mostly glass nestled into the side of a mountain. Private. Secluded. Perfect for his ends.

And he would remember his own ends above all else.

CHAPTER EIGHT

ILARIA WONDERED IF she'd ever get used to the finery, the sheer beauty of everything in Frediano's world. The chalet was…well, she couldn't use the term *fairy tale* because this was no fairy tale. It was a very opulent prison.

Without escape, apparently.

But as Frediano helped her down from the plane, and then into the car that would take them from airstrip to chalet, it was hard to feel that drumbeat of panic. In some ways, this secluded little hideaway felt like home. The mountains, the blue sky, the cool air. There was only a small staff waiting for them, so that it was almost like they were alone.

The chalet was beautiful and luxurious. The structure seemed to be made almost entirely of glass, with only the necessary wooden beams to hold it together. No doubt inside you could look anywhere and see the beautiful scenery of the Alps around them.

Everything she had decided this morning and on the flight here felt solidified somehow. Noemi saying she could be a role model had started it, but there had been something about looking out the plane window, the world below them like a miniature on display. It had been exhilarating, the closest to a bird she'd ever be. And in that simple joy of flying she'd decided that joy *was* within her power.

Even if little else was.

She would learn the etiquette. Even with as little education as she'd had, she knew that a woman needed to learn the rules in order to break them effectively.

Frediano had been trying to intimidate her earlier when he'd mentioned speaking to Vita and arranging improvements at the farm. He wanted her to feel as though he pulled all the strings. But he'd only given her an idea.

No doubt Roletto orphanages and workhouses needed the same kind of improvements her farm did. No doubt there were trusts and scholarships and whatever else to be created to benefit the orphans of Estraz and other disasters. She would work tirelessly to dedicate her life not to the palace or the King—whether that be Carlo or Frediano. She would dedicate her life to the *people*, just as she'd promised them on that balcony yesterday.

And because thinking of things she could *do* reminded her that she had *some* kind of power now, even if it wasn't the freedom she'd hoped for, she was determined to get everything *she* wanted out of this week.

Frediano craved a biddable, boring wife. Perhaps part of her wanted to rebel at that as a matter of course, but she was smarter than that. Or perhaps she'd just never had the luxury to rebel.

The bottom line was, it did not matter what Frediano wanted. She didn't mind appearing biddable and boring if it suited *her* purposes, because this wasn't about thwarting *him*. He was a prince. Powerful and in line to be the King. There was no sense beating her head against the brick wall of trying to best him. He'd only change the rules and declare himself winner.

But she could focus on making herself happy. On doing

things that would help those *she* cared about. Frediano was simply…an overzealous hound. He would bark at her and herd her into the little path he created, and she—somehow being the sheep in this scenario—would do what she pleased all the same.

"I will show you to your room," Frediano said. "You may rest, then you will change for dinner. We will begin our first lesson then. The staff is limited here, as we have managed to keep the location of this property secret for decades." He led her into a hallway that wasn't glass, but instead cozily constructed of dark woods decorated in various artworks depicting the mountains.

"This is your room," he said, turning the knob and opening the door. But he stood in such a way he blocked her entrance. "I trust you can dress yourself for dinner?" he asked, innocently enough.

There was *nothing* innocent about the comment, she knew full well. Simply from the way her blood heated at the light in his eyes. She reminded herself he was a hound or brick wall—one she would never succumb to—but she couldn't keep all her sarcasm at bay. "I think you know I have survived all these years without help in that department."

His eyes took a long, slow tour of her body, his mouth curving ever so slightly. Giving the strangest appearance of softness when she knew there was no softness to this man. And still she ached for something from him she did not fully understand.

"I would be happy to offer my services to help you undress," he said, and it was something like a purr. The low, resonant tones that had, from the very beginning, affected her in a deep, intimate way.

She knew, despite all her inexperience, just *what* he was suggesting. It should make her angry.

But he held her gaze and she was reminded far too vividly of last night. The feel of his tongue sliding against hers, his hands, the hardness of his body she was crushed to. The heat pulsing at her core.

She should look away, leave, *do* something. She was certain she would. Any minute. Instead of letting all those memories of last night crowd around her. Instead of finding her breath harder and harder to manage. Instead of relishing the waves of sensation battering her as she relived every second of last night.

Not that long ago, she had believed she would be quite happy never experiencing what happened between a man and a woman. She had too much to do around the farm and with the orphans to worry about the needs of a partner.

But these past few days the thought had consumed her. To the point it crowded out the things she had once believed immovable in their weight and importance in her mind.

Frediano had moved out of the way, giving her a clear escape into her room.

She did not take it.

Instead, she stood where she was, certainly flushed and breathing too heavily to hide her reaction to him. He took her hand then, turned it over as if to study her palm. He'd called her hands rough, and though she hadn't done her normal chores in a few days, they were as rough as they had been. Even the palace could not scrape away all her years of labor.

He lifted her hand and held her gaze as he brushed his mouth across her knuckles. "My room is at the end of this hall. Feel free to join me there. Whenever you wish."

There was a moment, such a strange moment, when it seemed like the most sensible course of action. Her body ached for him. He would no doubt show her *some* kind of pleasure, if a simple touch, a simple look could do this much. And then she would know all those things she'd assumed she never would.

But she did not love him, and even if her body understood the need and wants of the act, she had always assumed *love* was part of that. It was supposed to be, she was almost sure of it.

"I will *never* wish it," she said, but it was not the firm statement she'd hoped for. If anything it was breathless, almost whispered, and though she'd said the correct words, she couldn't help but feel as if her *never* sounded a lot like *please.*

He smiled, but he dropped her hand. "*Never* make promises you can't keep, *tesoro.*"

Frediano studied the small dinner table the staff had put together. It was arranged as the royal wedding dinner would be, if on a smaller scale. At this very table, King Carlo had once carefully and patiently taken Frediano through everything he would need to know to be a prince, and so now Frediano would do the same for Ilaria.

My wife.

She had much to learn, and he wasn't convinced she was all that eager to, even with his generous donation to her little farm. He'd thought it would be simple enough to use his money and power—that was what most women in his acquaintance were interested in, after all—to give her what she wanted.

He would need to delve deeper. Learn more about her to better understand her. And once he understood her, it would be easy enough to consummate the marriage and then return to the palace with his obedient bride in tow.

Satisfied with this plan, pushing away all the doubts

that had plagued him as *nothing* with Ilaria had gone according to plan, he waited for her to arrive.

He glanced at his watch, expecting the time to be later than it was. Instead, he was ready early, like some eager schoolboy.

He supposed he was eager. Eager to solve the problem that was Ilaria. She mystified him. He did not know people whose causes weren't themselves, outside of his grandfather, who, like him, lived for Vantonella and upholding the Monetellero name.

Surely Ilaria could not be as good and charitable as she behaved. There had to be some flaw there, and he needed to find it.

He heard her footsteps before she appeared. Normally, he would not turn to look at her. He would have stood still, staring at the window wall and the glorious mountains his parents had thought they could tame, and waited until she was either compelled to speak or make *some* noise.

But this week was not about *him*. It was about getting to the bottom of Ilaria, and if she was not a woman won over by orders and bribes, he would have to attempt something wholly out of character.

Softness. He wasn't sure he knew what that looked like, but he would try. Had to try. He would stop at nothing to get what he needed from her.

So he turned as she entered the room from the hallway. He smiled at her. She was dressed modestly and somewhat casually in dark slacks and a soft red sweater that clung to her generous curves.

She did something to him and Frediano did not know how to stop it. But he would. By the end of this week, he would. If he had to learn her inside and out, glut himself on her until there was nothing left between them. Whatever it took, he would do.

"When you approach a member of the royal family, you are to curtsy," he said, and not as an order but as a *gentle* reminder. He even smiled encouragingly at her.

"Am I not a member of the royal family?" she returned, smiling at him with a kind of bland politeness that crawled under his skin.

He did not falter. "You are, indeed, which means your curtsy must be infallible. Beauty and grace defined in a simple movement."

"A deferential movement," she returned.

"A symbol of respect," he countered. "Just as I bow to my grandfather."

"But I do not respect you, and I respect your grandfather even less." She held his gaze as if what she said didn't border on treason.

He clenched his teeth together. He had promised himself he would not be provoked. If he responded in anger, in frustration, and the biting sarcasm she seemed to drag out of him, he would not accomplish his goals.

"Be that as it may," he said, his tone carefully neutral, each syllable a hard-won battle against his temper. "You will need to curtsy to us both upon your entrance to the wedding dinner. If you wish to be an embarrassment at the royal wedding dinner, I suppose that is your choice," he said. Though he didn't mean it. In the slightest.

But she wanted choice, so he would give her the illusion of such.

She took a deep breath and seemed to shake something within herself. She smiled at him and then preformed a curtsy that was—if not totally beautiful or graceful or natural-looking—very nearly suitable. "I assure you, Your Highness, I am eager to take all the instruction I can get."

She said this with a sweet smile, the picture-perfect version of the wife he'd wanted.

He didn't trust it. Still, he gestured toward the table. Maybe this brief respite from ill will would allow them to cover some ground. "At any meal with the royal family, you will wait to be seated until your husband or king pulls out a chair for you." Frediano moved forward, pulled out a chair and gestured Ilaria toward it.

He watched as she very clearly attempted not to look at him as she took the offered seat, but at the last second her gaze met his. He did not understand the sheer chaos that went on inside of him when she looked at him.

Chaos was not an option, even here in the secluded mountain chalet. So he released her seat and moved stiffly to his, across the table from her.

He gestured for Como to pour the wine, much the same as would be done at their wedding dinner, though with more people on both sides.

"While the wine is poured, we will engage in small talk with those around us. So…how is your cousin?" he asked.

"Married and quite happy," she replied. She muttered something after that clear response. It sounded an awful lot like *no thanks to you.*

"I suppose she thanked you profusely for biting the bullet." That wasn't exactly *small talk*, but he was intrigued by her reaction to her cousin now that Sophia was free. And Ilaria was stuck.

Before, Ilaria had spoken of her cousin brazenly. Like the warrior protecting her village from all who wished to do them harm. There was a moment here before all that zeal returned.

"She did thank me. And hoped I could continue to keep her safe from her father. Because that is the kind of man your grandfather trusts. The kind of men who make their grown daughters terrified."

A dark jolt of old pain landed deep in Frediano's gut. A pain he'd have sworn he'd excised some time ago. But her scenario reminded him of a question that had plagued him in his darkest hours as a teenager trying to earn his grandfather's respect and trust.

How long would he have been a prisoner to his parents' whims if they had not died? Would he have ever been free of the toxic environment they created wherever they went?

A foolish question because it did not matter. They were dead. And he'd chosen to dedicate his life to everything they'd eschewed. No one's whims, selfish wants or desires would threaten him ever again. Even his own.

"No parent should have such a hold on their child, it is true." He said, frustrated his voice was gruff. It made her look up at him with some of that softness he knew was dangerous. Control could not be wielded if he was weak to her softness. He had to have the upper hand. "But these are personal matters I'm sure my grandfather is unaware of."

That softness disappeared. "I would like to make him aware."

"Revenge, Princess?"

"Justice," she returned, clearly having given this some thought. He had the strangest sensation that perhaps she was playing him this evening the same as he was playing her. He did not know what she sought—except perhaps the upper hand.

Maybe he could give her that illusion as well.

He explained the layout of the royal table, how she would be expected to proceed through the dinner. Staff came in with the first course, then the second. Ilaria really did know nothing of etiquette, but he remembered being in the same position. His grandfather had been endlessly patient with him, so Frediano showed the same kind of patience to his wife.

She seemed to be trying, enough that she insisted on resetting her place and then going over the different silverware and glasses once more. It was strange to find himself smiling as she succeeded. To feel proud at how quickly she caught on. He appreciated her tenacity. Her inability to let failure stand.

He studied her as dessert was served. He need not be *impressed* by her, he needed to get to the bottom of her. Revenge on her uncle? He could aid in that. The success of her farm and legitimacy of her orphans without legal guardians? He'd already handled that so long as she met his conditions. But he needed to know her, inside and out, so that she never surprised him. So that his life was in his control alone.

And, of course, present his grandfather with a perfect princess so King Carlo would step down from the throne and take care of his health.

"While all these dinners I'm sure will be beautiful and luxurious, what I'd really like to do is discuss how the palace intends to help those without such luxuries." She met his gaze across the table as she lifted a fork to her lips.

He watched her enjoy the crostata and wondered if she knew her eyes fluttered closed for a moment, and she let out a sigh, just a quiet one, in pleasure.

"You seem to enjoy these luxuries," he said, smiling. He rather enjoyed watching her eat. Watching her forget herself for these small moments.

She did not smile in return. Instead, she put her fork down. "I would happily abstain if I thought it might lead to change. In fact—"

"Your point is taken, Ilaria. You wish your role as princess to be a voice of the people." There was so much that could go wrong there, but there had to be a way to give her the illusion of what she craved, while controlling it all the same. "This is possible, of course. The crown is involved in many charitable efforts."

"Are they?"

"Yes, my grandfather is a patron to many causes. His greatest efforts are in education outreach and historical preservation. Many of our dukes also offer patronages. Military, social services, the arts. Et cetera."

"What about you?" Ilaria asked, studying him.

"Me?"

"Yes, what are you a patron of?"

"It is of no matter." He took a sip of his wine, considering. He had no doubt she would approve of his patronages. But he worried it would allow her too much insight into him. Still, it was public record, and perhaps his personal interests would even soften the philanthropic Ilaria to him.

"It is of *some* matter, as I am interested."

"Very well. I lend my name to many medical organizations. Hospitals, particularly those that cater to children whose families cannot afford or do not care enough to provide treatment for their children."

She frowned, clearly surprised that he might share an interest. "But this is just your name. Signing a check or cutting a ribbon. I don't want to just be a symbol or a voice. I want to *help* people."

He could tell her, of course. That he often volunteered hours, so long as it could be kept away from the press's prying eyes, as he wished for none of the attention his parents had gotten for just what Ilaria had outlined. He could inform her of the long hours he spent working with accounting departments, fundraising efforts, and the like.

But this felt a step too far. So he lifted his wineglass and studied it, before sliding his gaze to her once more.

"Isn't it funny how often helping others leads us directly to our own peril? After all, if you had not stuck your nose into your cousin's problems, you would not have been in the cathedral that night."

There was a moment when he could see he'd clearly caught her off guard, but she recovered swiftly. "While that is a nice fantasy, how could I have been happy knowing my cousin would have been sentenced to a life she didn't want?"

He sipped, set his glass down. "Your cousin seems happy enough with *you* in such a situation."

She paled. As if that thought had not crossed her mind, and perhaps she really was this virtuous. Maybe, despite tragedy, she was so unaccustomed to betrayal she did not recognize it until it was pointed out to her.

"Helping is always the right thing to do," she said, but her voice was small. "One would think the future leader of our country might have more interest in honor." She was trying to regain that strength of purpose, but clearly him pointing out Sophia did not care much for her happiness had taken the wind out of her sails.

"Honor and sacrificing yourself for the needs of others are two very different things, Ilaria."

"Most of us not raised in palaces and with silver spoons shoved in our mouths are taught that *honor* is helping others, being of service to those who *cannot* return the favor."

"At the expense of yourself? What of you, Ilaria? You have suffered tragedy. Don't you deserve some of this help you're always doling out?" He spread his arms to encompass the room. "You are no longer a poor little sheep herder. You are a princess and, yes, you can help all those you wish to help. Easily. In the snap of a finger, really. But what is it *you* want?"

"To help. That is all I need," she said, nodding firmly.

"Noemi said that I can be a good role model. If I cannot be free to return to my life, and I feel that after that ridiculous introduction even if it were possible, it would be different, then I must make the best of the one I have. If I can be a role model, if I can help those who have, as you said, suffered tragedy, then that is what I will do."

"A good monarch can always be a model of some kind." His parents, after all, had taught him what *not* to do. "Service is part of this, of course. But that does not mean you must be a martyr to these causes. That you cannot have your own wants." He gestured at the dessert she'd stopped eating. "And have them be fulfilled."

This was clearly not what she wanted to hear, and he was surprised at how much this angered her. He'd expected her to have something at the ready that he could fulfill. A list of desires as his princess that he would happily give her if it guaranteed her obedience.

Most people in his acquaintance only required a bribe or a threat to behave accordingly. Their wants met, and then they were easily controlled.

Instead, she was silently smoldering. Her eyes turning a deeper shade of green, her cheeks flushing with color. No doubt if he reached over and touched her pulse it would be racing.

He wanted to make it race for completely different reasons. To mold that anger into passion. All this talk of *wants* made it impossible to not think of his own. And in this moment, as he watched her, they all centered on *her*. His wants were dangerous, always, but here, where he could control everything, he could indulge in this one.

"All right, then," she said, leaning forward, temper flashing in her eyes. If he believed in bewitching, he would say that all spells started in their changeable green depths. What would it be like to sink himself into all that magic?

He needed to know. So that once they returned to the palace, he could fight it. He could *control* it.

"If there are some special wants I'm supposed to have for myself, do tell, what is it *you* want, Frediano?"

He rather enjoyed the way she bit out his name. As if it were a curse. He supposed it was perverse of him, but no doubt her passion was like her anger—bright and sharp and dangerous.

He considered his wine, and then her. It would not be tonight, but that didn't mean he couldn't begin the seduction.

"This evening, *tesoro*, the only thing I want is you."

CHAPTER NINE

ILARIA SUCKED IN a breath and cursed herself that she could not be more worldly and handle such direct overtures without reaction. But he spoke those simple words with all that concentrated focus on *her*, and it felt as if her lungs had seized up and no longer worked properly.

Because the terrible truth was, she wanted him, too. It was the only want she could think of, when pinned underneath that dark, intense gaze.

She had to clear her throat to speak. "I do not *like* you. I will certainly never love you." Though it had been hard to hold on to her hate for him when he spoke of his parents. Clearly they had neglected him, and though he had tried to speak of his patronages with some detachment, she knew, the moment he'd spoken of families who did not care enough to afford their children treatment, that the cause was personal to him.

Could it be that under all his hard, domineering, demanding ways, there was kindness? She'd seen flashes of it herself. The way he spoke to his aide as though they were friends, the breathing technique he'd offered in the midst of her panic, and his softness toward his grandfather.

She hated to admit it, but Frediano was not *all* bad.

But he certainly made her feel things she did not know how to navigate.

"Desire does not need to be about like or *love, tesoro,*" he said with a lazy shrug—when she was quite certain he'd never been lazy. "In my experience, few people love anything more than they love themselves."

"Your experience depresses me," she said. She desperately tried *not* to think of the story he'd told her about his parents after his swim, all the anger he held toward them. Because though she'd told him it did not make her pity him…it did. When she didn't harden her heart against it.

Too well she could picture a little boy, the pawn of reckless, selfish people who did not love him and then raised by a cold, detached grandfather who seemed to have only impressed *duty* upon him. If she gave room for those thoughts, for seeing the personal connection beneath his patronages, she understood why he might have become the remote, uncompromising man before her. And she sympathized. It made her see him as more than just the cold, authoritarian enemy.

Her father and grandfather had not been perfect. The more years she lived, the more she understood their flaws, where they'd failed her.

And yet, they had loved her. She never once doubted that. It made all the difference. People could not be perfect, but if they loved… Well, it could be forgiven.

Who loved Frediano?

It does not matter. He is the villain in this story.

"What is love to you, Ilaria?" the Prince demanded. "Someone as inexperienced as yourself, who had never even kissed a man before. Your mother died when you were born, so you did not have your parents' shining example of love and devotion to hold up as an impossible paragon to reach." He spoke with such sarcasm, as if love and devotion were fake and fairy tales. Things to be criticized.

She wanted it to stir her temper once more, but it only made her sadder for him. “My parents loved each other. I may not have seen it, but my father spoke of it. My grandfather and father loved me and each other. Perhaps I have not experienced romantic love, but I know love because I have felt it.”

“And yet you did not marry or have babies. You dedicated your life to saving your cousin from marrying me.”

She looked at him for a moment, truly looked at him—the man behind her abduction and forced wedding, the man behind the facade. She didn’t want to, but when he spoke of important things, all she could see were the wounds underneath his carefully placed masks.

Because clearly he did not understand—could not *fathom* the truth. “Don’t you see? That was love, too.” She had the strangest desire to reach out and put her hand over his. She quelled the urge, but she could not resist the words of truth. “When you love someone, you are willing to sacrifice for them.”

“That sounds even more a tragedy than most of the love stories I have heard.” He pushed back in his chair and stood. He skirted the table and moved next to her, hand outstretched. “Now it is time for your next lesson.”

When she recoiled, he laughed. The sound was dark and deep, and it danced along her skin like a misty morning rain shower in the mountains. She craved more of it, because it was something close to happiness…and nothing about Frediano had ever seemed particularly happy.

It would not do to think about why that was. To allow this feeling of empathy for him to soften her toward him, when there would never be any return tenderness.

"You must learn to dance, Princess. And not a charming country reel. A proper, royal waltz."

His hand remained outstretched, and she supposed because she was so busy feeling sorry for him, wondering about his *happiness*, she didn't think the movement through and slid her hand into his without bracing herself.

So it was a jolt, that no doubt he felt, too. Of all that *want* she kept claiming she didn't have. Because if there was anything she wanted for herself and only herself, it was to discover where all these feelings could lead.

She should be more afraid of that than she was.

He pulled her to her feet and then led her away from the table and into the living room lit by the crackling fire in the hearth and the moon that shone through the glass, and the stars that glittered like jewels.

It felt almost as if they were outside. There was something so familiar about it, like the sky back home.

She should know better than to relax, but the comforting scene conspired against her to ease the tension in her shoulders. He played no music as he slid his hand around her back, his other still holding her hand.

He explained the steps as he moved her through them. She tried to pay attention to memorizing them. She had no interest in dancing, but less interest in looking a fool. So she *tried* to focus on the simple one-two-three rhythm. On moving her feet where they should go.

But her mind kept drifting to the large hand secure at the small of her back. To the slight friction every time their bodies brushed. To the size of his other hand, which held hers.

She didn't dare look anywhere but at her feet—both for fear she'd stumble or step on his, and because if she glanced up… She wasn't sure how she would look away.

How she would dance knowing what his intense gaze did to her.

This was all very dangerous footing, and she had to save herself from all that danger. Somehow.

"You must memorize the steps enough you look at me, Princess. Not your feet."

Ilaria kept her eyes firmly on her shoes. "I think you expect too much of me."

"By all accounts, this is impossible. Your story is one of resilience, intelligence and determination. Surely you can learn a little dance."

She lifted her gaze in surprise because he sounded sincere. She knew he couldn't be if he was complimenting her, but when she looked at his dark eyes there was none of that biting censure, and the cruel line of his mouth was vaguely curved.

As though she…impressed him in some way. As though there could be a softness hidden in this man.

"Let me lead you," he said, and it almost sounded *gentle.* So gentle she found herself obeying without even thinking of it. He took her through the steps again, and she let him move her. Though there was no music around them, she felt some new tune inside of herself and swayed to the beat of it under his steady, dark gaze.

"See what can happen if you trust me?"

It was frightening to feel this way, to feel powerless, when her whole life had been about finding power in all the places she had none. She needed to reclaim some piece of that. "I could never trust you."

"So many *nevers,*" he said, his silky smooth voice sounding wholly unbothered, when she'd expected anger or frustration. He pulled her closer, so that their legs were pressed together and her chest was crushed to his, and between them she could feel the hard, surprisingly large length of him pressed up against her. "A shame, but I shall endeavor to carry on. We cannot always get what we want."

She felt as if he'd pulled the floor out from under her—again. She could rebuild, she always did, but not when he held her. Not when his voice shivered through her. She couldn't find her footing.

"Some people never get what they want," she shot back at him, not sure where the words came from. Surely not from her. Her grandfather had always taught her to be grateful for what they had, no matter how little. Because it could always get worse. And had, so often.

So she was grateful for her health. That her grandfather had been able to live to see her become an adult even if her parents had not. She was even grateful for the chance to save Sophia. She *was*, because it meant she'd done the right thing.

Love was sacrifice, and so she loved. And sacrificed. Over and over again.

Who loves you now that everyone who loved you is dead? Now that you have given Sophia exactly what she wanted? It was a voice that sounded strangely like Frediano's, when he'd uttered no such words. Not that the words he spoke were any more comforting.

"Some people never get what they want?" Frediano asked. "Or *you* never get what you want?"

It felt too close to a truth she didn't want to look at. There would be nothing left if she couldn't hold on to those old beliefs. "I loved my life, until I was tricked into marrying someone."

"Did you?"

"Yes, and I will endeavor to find a way to love this one. To be grateful for it." She tried to pull away from him, but he held her firm. So she stilled and met his gaze with a fierce one of her own. "Because as you once told me, Frediano, the world is cruel and it does not care what becomes of me. But I care. So I will always seek to find the good."

"By always being complacent with the situation in front of you?" His words were calm, but his eyes flashed. "Without ever wanting more than what little you have?"

She did not know why he kept saying things that seemed to twist her heart into knots. That landed like little avalanches. Painful and feeling so sharply true when there was no way it could be true. "I want to help people."

"So you say, but that is not all. Your body wants me, even if your heart does not." He pressed his mouth to the skin just under her jaw and though she tried to strengthen herself against it, she shuddered in response.

"Allow me to give you something you want, Ilaria," he murmured. And there was none of the usual steel in his voice. It was warmth and entreaty. The subtle, drugging use of persuasion. "I promise you, there is no need for love. Pleasure is enough."

Pleasure. It already arced through her like a live wire. It seemed to slither through her body, getting rid of any resolve or intelligence. So that she was only left with that *want* he kept talking about.

As though he'd hypnotized her into thinking of nothing else.

Right and wrong had always been so clear. She had never understood how anyone could be tempted by the devil when he was evil.

But finally she understood. Temptation. The blinding desire to do something you knew could not be smart or good. And how it eradicated that voice inside that chose the right thing, the smart thing.

So there was no voice. There was only the feel of him,

the scent of some expensive cologne, and the flash of his dark eyes. Because he wanted her.

And she wanted him.

Frediano had not planned this, and he knew that following his desires was a mistake. He'd meant to soften her. To arouse her, yes. But to not give in just yet to his own desires.

The taste of her skin was too much. The tremors he could feel as he held her close. The catch of her breath, the *response*.

She did not push him away, she did not tell him no. Perhaps there was a war inside her, but she did not give in to the side that had refused him before. Not yet.

His hands slid under her shirt, to where she was soft and warm. He ran his palms over her ribs, her breasts over the fabric of her bra. There was no longer the pretense of the dance, there was only his hands on her, her body pressed to his of her own free will.

He did not understand her any more than he understood his desire for her. That anyone could truly be so selfless that her own wants were *confronting*. He wished he could believe her a liar, but there was no evidence. She had wrapped herself up in her own sainthood, in her own sacrifices she called love.

He had never seen love sacrifice, but maybe he'd never seen love. His parents had claimed their love was more important than anything. That it was superior to laws, to the demands of royal life, to the responsibilities of being a parent. But maybe it hadn't been love. Maybe, as in all else, it had only been selfishness and wreckage.

But if love was the opposite—sacrifice and nothing more—what would Frediano want with that, either?

It made no earthly sense why he was even contemplating the nature of love. This was about chemistry. Desire and attraction. It was about the practicalities of consummating the marriage and the process of producing heirs.

And nothing to do with *emotions*.

Her head fell back, and he traveled the line of her neck with his mouth, the sound of her ragged breathing erasing everything except this tide of need.

"Ilaria," he said, savoring each syllable of her name. "What do you want?" he whispered before pressing another kiss just under her ear.

She inhaled sharply, and he waited, here on the brink of madness for her to answer his question.

Because he would not give in until she did. No matter how he wanted, no matter how his control strained, *she* would give in. Her innocence meant she did not know all he could show her, and he would make sure she understood how superior *pleasure* could be to *love and sacrifice.*

She did not answer his question in words. She tilted her head so their mouths were just a breath apart, her eyes an ethereal green in the moonlight and starlight around them. Her eyes betrayed nothing but that luminescent desire.

Then, she leaned forward and kissed him, so untested, but not nervous. That was not who she was.

She had already slayed dragons in her life, time and time again. He wondered if she feared anything at this point, and almost envied her for the courage that so impressed everyone she came into contact with. Her orphans, her neighbors, his staff. Even his grandfather had been *impressed.*

She was a triumph. She would be *his* triumph.

She would be his. Only his.

But there could be no mistake. He eased away from

that dangerous mouth, but not to stop this. There was no stopping this.

"Tell me," he ordered. "You will not get to decide I tricked you into this in the morning. This is your choice, *tesoro*. So tell me, what do you want?"

CHAPTER TEN

A CHOICE.

Frediano held her so tightly she was nearly immobile. There was no escape, but the firm grip also didn't allow her to kiss him again. Because she had to choose.

Kissing him had been a choice, but she supposed it had been the coward's choice. Because she hadn't said the words. She'd given in to him.

Giving in to him was not inevitable, no matter how she felt it was, with her body engulfed with a desperate need that had a will of its own.

So she had a choice to make, and whatever it was, she would be the one to live with all the consequences hereafter.

Because she did not love him, and she was under no illusion he loved her, or ever could, considering he did not believe in sacrifice.

But she did not hate him as much as she should. He had revealed too much about what he'd come from for her to *hate* him. How could a cold upbringing create anything other than a cold man? And yes, he'd had far more privileges than she'd ever had, but she knew from experience that a child's financial situation did not change the absence of love. Sophia had not had an easy upbringing simply because her father was alive and rich. Giovanni loved nothing and no one. He had manipulated and emotionally abused his wife and daughter.

Certainly money helped a person, there was no doubt about it, but without love, what did it matter?

Ilaria tried to hold on to the fact that Frediano had forced her into this situation, but if she had decided to make the best of it, how could she hold on to her anger?

All in all, the choice before her now was not a different decision than the one she'd made this morning. That she wouldn't go against him simply to go against him. She would make her own choices, regardless of him. She was supposed to be making the best of her new life. He had introduced the subject of wants. Of getting something *she* wanted. For once.

For once. She looked at his intense, dark eyes, let the heat of him sweep through her. If she let all the outside world go, if she focused only on this and him, there was one clear want.

"I want you," she whispered. It didn't matter that she'd told him *never*, because *this* was what she wanted. To eradicate the distance between them, to have him show her all that dizzying heat they could create.

Maybe it could even be a starting point. Something *good* could come out of it, and if that was the devil whispering what she wanted to hear, well, so be it. For tonight, so be it.

The noise that erupted from him could only be considered a growl. And then *finally* his mouth crashed to hers. Hard and unyielding, fire and need. She threw herself into it. Into him. She melted, yielding softness to demanding hard. His hands molded her body, learning every last inch of her and it did not matter if he touched fabric or flesh, it all burned through her.

He lifted her sweater over her head. Since she had not

picked out any of her clothes, down to her underwear, they still did not feel like hers. And so, him taking them off her somehow felt more right than keeping them on.

Because this was her. Her skin, her freckles, her goose bumps. He unclasped her bra, then spread his fingers wide as he smoothed his hands down her back. His wicked mouth traveled down her neck to her chest, wreaking havoc wherever he kissed, licked, sucked.

"Bellissima," he murmured, his hands cupping her breasts. She had the dim thought she should be embarrassed, to be naked at all, let alone in front of such a man. But her body felt alive, as if for the first time. And she wanted something…something out of reach, which she knew he would give her.

"Let me see how much you desire me." He laid her down on the plush rug, the moonlight dancing over them it its own waltz. He undid the snap of her pants and then drew them down over her legs. Until she was lying completely naked on a rug.

Even though he was still dressed, it somehow seemed exactly right when he looked at her like she was a miracle. Like everything he saw was everything he'd ever wanted.

"Ah, such beauty. Such strength. I promise, this will be no sacrifice. Only your pleasure, my princess." His mouth found hers again, and while one hand leveraged him above her, the other traveled down until he found the center of her aching need.

She did not know anything that would happen beyond the basic mechanics of it all, and yet the unknown only seemed to tangle with the dark twist of needs inside of her so that when he touched her, intimately and expertly, she cried out, so surprised by the bolt of pleasure she reached out for him.

And he was there, his mouth on hers. His broad shoulders sturdy. The strength of him a comfort as this wild and fierce passion swept through her and turned her into something else. As he stroked a finger inside of her. *Her.* When he touched her, where she was slick with need, there was nothing else in the world except him.

She said his name in fevered whispers, in desperate moans, as his finger slid inside of her, and she did not recognize the noises she made, the desperation she felt. It was all so new and intense and different. She arched against him, pulled at him to find some way to be closer. To be one.

And there was no shame in that or him. In *this.*

She only felt as though she had finally found joy.

Ilaria was a curse. Perfect in every way, as if she had been designed for him and his every last desire. She was beautiful and strong and glowing underneath the celestial light shining in through the windows.

Touching the molten core of her was not enough. He needed to be inside of her. To consume her, possess her in every way he could. She had enjoyed no lovers before him, and this made her *his.*

His.

She reached out, her fingers fumbling as she worked to undo the buttons of his shirt while he explored her with his fingers. She rid him of his shirt, then trailed her hands down his chest, her hesitant touch as erotic as anything. Until she stopped at his belt.

He paused, watching her eyes flicker from his pants to him. A hint of uncertainty. He wanted her beyond reason, and yet there was something else here. Something painful and twisting in his chest.

But she did not change her mind as he feared. She did not come to her senses. She held his gaze.

"Show me," she said. "Everything."

Everything. So he kissed her long and deep. And she met every kiss, every nip, every thrust of his hand with one of her own. His courageous princess. Until her fingers were digging into his shoulders as she pressed herself so fully against him.

She was arched in perfect offering for him to take her breast deep into his mouth, teasing nipple with tongue until she was panting. Until she was *begging.*

He knew she did not know what exactly she begged for. There was no practiced seduction here. Only her want and her need and her *desperation.* Her *please* echoing in his ears until there was nothing but that.

It soaked into his bloodstream like a drug. Nothing else mattered except *her*, this center of everything. Giving her everything she deserved to find at the hands of her first lover.

Her only.

He stroked her, finding the bundle of nerves that had her crying out and shuddering in his arms. Her release the sweetest nectar he'd ever encountered.

His own breathing was ragged as though he'd run a marathon, but this was only the beginning. The very beginning.

He dragged his tongue down the elegant curve of her neck. He sampled her skin like the delicacy it was. She was warmth, sunlight after a long, dreary winter. Hope after nothing but disappointment. The taste of something forbidden and irresistible.

And he could not content himself with only this. He needed her. All of her. Now. No more waiting, no more torture. No more long nights haunted by those green eyes. He freed himself and her eyes met his, wild with desire.

He knew she would not refuse him, saw all the ways she wanted him as much as he wanted her. And yet he thought of all her previous refusals and needed to hear her correct them. To take back her *nevers*. That choice he spoke of before.

"Say it," he commanded.

Her eyes widened, but she didn't flinch or pull away. Her eyes dazed with passion, her fingers digging into his shoulders. The color high on her cheeks. There was nothing else in his world except her.

"Yes, Frediano." Her breathing hitched, but she never looked away, never took her hands off his shoulders. "I want you. I want this."

He knew she was not experienced, and though need and lust drove him, wracked him, he was gentle as he entered her. Made her *his*.

Mine. Only mine.

She stiffened, though she did not push him away or make any sound of distress. He kept himself still as he willed her to relax with his palms, his mouth. He sucked her nipple deep into his mouth until she let out a low moan. Slowly the tenseness melted away from her, until it was she who moved against him, their breaths mingling in harsh exhales and shaky inhales.

He let her find her own pleasure for that very first. It was a masterpiece to watch. Until she was shaking, shuddering, coming apart around him. His name on her lips.

But that was not enough. Not nearly enough.

"Again," he growled. And this time he set the pace. To make her as wild and needy as he felt.

"Please," she gasped, meeting his pace with something

fervent and wild herself. The spiky edge of everything that sparked between them, dark and light, good and bad. Until his control cracked, until he was as lost as she. Until she sobbed out his name, and his own release came in a roaring, desperate rush that left him weak.

In the breathless, shuddering aftermath, he knew he would never understand what had come over him. He dropped his forehead to hers, trying to find…some answer. But this had been more powerful and dangerous than simply raw lust. He'd always controlled that before. Ruthlessly. Carefully.

But she was…different somehow, this woman. She was…

His.

He gathered her up, and she held on as he carried her through the chalet and into an ornate bathroom, dominated by a large fireplace that was lit, and kept the room warm and steaming. The bath was large and he carefully lowered her into it.

She sighed as the warm water encased them, her arms still around his neck while he settled into a sitting position. She leaned her head against his shoulder and something overturned inside of him. It felt like a door closing.

Or opening.

"I had never understood why people would do such foolish things for a kiss or a grope in the dark," Ilaria said, sounding far-off and dreamy. "But I did not understand, I suppose, what it could all feel like. I do now."

"Such a compliment," he murmured.

She laughed and the sound warmed him as her body moved against his. He wanted her again with such a surprising bolt of need that his grip on her tightened. If she was uncomfortable with it, she did not express it.

"Did I give you what you wanted, Princess?"

Her misty green eyes met his. There was something searching in her gaze, but he did not know how to give her whatever mysterious thing she searched for. Still, she smiled. "For a start."

CHAPTER ELEVEN

ILARIA HAD SHARED a bed before. When they'd taken in the orphans after the mining disaster, she'd had to share her mattress with two little girls. Those had been long, uncomfortable nights—missing her father and her life before he'd died.

This was very different.

The bed was much larger, for starters. Comfortable, like the mattress back at the palace. Cloudlike and perfect, the sheets smooth and luxurious.

But the main difference had been that during the night, when she'd woken from a dream of Frediano's mouth on hers. She'd needed only to roll over, to touch him. And he had responded in kind. Allowing her to explore him in all the ways she hadn't thought to do the first time around.

He had made her say it—*I want you, Frediano*—again and again and again, until it seemed all she could think was wanting him.

But when she awoke this time, wanting him and reaching for him, he wasn't there. She blinked her eyes open and realized daylight was streaming in the large window on the exterior wall.

Where he stood, looking out said window, fully dressed. "Good morning," he offered, not turning to look at her.

"Good morning," she returned, perhaps a little stiffly as she pulled the sheet up to cover her chest. She hadn't really thought beyond sleep and passion to this moment of just…having to figure out how to navigate this new world they'd created when they'd given themselves to each other.

Worry began to dance in her stomach. Had he not enjoyed it? Was he so fine an actor that she had been tricked somehow? She didn't know the purpose of such a trick, but…

"There is a breakfast tray set up for you," he offered. He turned slowly, something stiff and formal about him. But he went over and grabbed the tray on the table. He carried it over to her and then placed it on the side of the bed where he'd once been.

There were bowls of fruit, a plate of pastries and assorted beverages. It was enough for ten people. She looked up at him, and still he had not returned her gaze. She didn't know what that meant, what any of this meant. She was uncertain as to how to proceed.

She could not regret—not fully. Last night had been… wonderful. It hadn't been about anyone or anything except them, and that was…

When his gaze finally landed on hers, those dark eyes flashed with heat as they had last night and raked over where she held the sheet, because he knew exactly and intimately what she looked like without it.

Her worry evaporated, because she could see his desire for her. If nothing else, he liked the way she looked as much as she liked the way he looked. Their bodies were compatible, and maybe that meant there was hope for the rest of them.

A strange turn of events, but she was determined to be an optimist.

"We have much work to do today," he said, though his

voice was gruffer than it had been. "But I wanted to give you adequate time to rest."

"I feel very well rested," she returned, and took a piece of fruit and nibbled on it. She watched him tear his gaze from her and return it to the window once more. She did not know what to say, naked in his bed, eating a breakfast that should have been feeding an entire banquet hall.

Eventually he turned once more to face her, and his hands were clasped behind his back. He had what she would call his *prince* look on. One of careful detachment and quiet certainty—that whatever he said would be obeyed.

Wariness crept in, because she did not wish to *obey* him. She also did not wish to go back to the way they had been, forever arguing with each other. She wanted… something else. Something more like last night.

"I think it's possible we will make a finc tcam, Ilaria," he said in that careful way of his that reminded her of when he was around his grandfather. "You can help people in all the ways you wish, so long as you fulfill your duties as Princess. I will have a wife our people will love and my grandfather can respect. It need not be a prison sentence for either of us."

It sounded so reasonable, and so much like what she had decided. It would be making the best of the situation. If they could work as a team. If they could be kind to one another.

It did not have to be about love, and she'd never imagined love for herself anyway. Perhaps he was right, and this was not the nightmare it had immediately felt like. She could admit that she quite liked sharing her body with him. He had been right. Love did not have to factor in to the heat that erupted when they touched.

When he made her feel things with her body she did

not know had existed. And perhaps… Perhaps there was room for something pleasant. Care, if not love.

She swallowed, because it felt like a gamble. It would require trusting him in some ways, when she was so sure she never would be able to. But she had already trusted him with her body, and he had delivered. Quite spectacularly. "I suppose…that would be an acceptable outcome."

He smiled, and he was quite handsome when he smiled. She could almost believe that this could…work. That things could be good.

Indeed, they *would* be good. She had only to decide it. And see it through. Like always.

She would miss her old life, but perhaps once they forged a partnership, she would be able to find a way to exist in her new one as well. She was a princess. Surely anything she set her mind to was possible?

So they spent the next few days with protocol lessons in the mornings. If Ilaria had one regret in life—aside from accidentally marrying this prince of course—it was that she had not been able to spend more days in the classroom.

Perhaps she didn't care what fork she chose to eat her dinner with, or what wine went with what course in the evenings when they practiced the royal dinner, but she was endlessly fascinated by history. By the balance of power. What people did with it. And didn't do.

So the lessons on tradition interested her even if the practice meals bored her. She found the line of the Vantonella throne oddly familiar. The history of one family, one place, stretching back a century or more.

"You know, in a very strange way, it is not all that different from the farm," she said as he traced the monarchs he insisted she should have learned in school that she had not.

Frediano raised one of his brows. “You are suggesting your sheep are the same as the citizens of Vantonella?”

She laughed. Because he was clearly offended by the comparison, but she thought it apt. “The farm came from my grandfather’s grandfather’s grandfather. Passed down to the next oldest son and so on and so forth. It is its own tiny kind of kingdom, kept in the family. Ruled by Russos. My parents were the first Russos to have only a daughter. I always thought it rather lucky I did not have to give my birthright to a boy simply because of something I could not control.”

“Your birthright. And yet you have made it sound as if you had no plans to continue your line.”

“I suppose that is the luxury of being a mere peasant. I did not have to think of bloodlines and citizens. It did not matter if it was my own child, or one of our orphans who would take on the farm after me. Only that they loved it as we had.”

She thought of that love. Of what happened next. Vita was running the farm with aplomb. Every report she received said it was functioning like a well-oiled machine. It did not need her. No one there *needed* her.

She studied Frediano. He was so strong, so severe, but when he gave little glimpses into his childhood hurts… Well, maybe *he* could need her. Was that possible? It was a strange thought, but no stranger than bloodlines and the realization she was part of the Montellero bloodline now. That she would be expected to have children, who would then be expected to take on the crown someday.

“There have been so many Montellero sons. What is the law if…” She found it hard to say the words, though the possibility now existed. “…if we should have a daughter?”

The idea filled her with something she did not know

how to untangle just yet. In many ways she'd been a mother figure to some of the orphans at the farm, but she had never given much thought to being a mother herself. It seemed strange and unimaginable, as she remembered nothing of her own mother.

But she…did not dread that outcome. The scary part of it all was, she rather liked the idea of having a child. Their child. Like he had said, they could be a team. And in being a team, they could, hopefully, correct all the mistakes his parents had made, and even a few her own father and grandfather had made.

"When my father married, my grandfather enacted a change in the law," Frediano said, studying the book carefully. "The oldest child shall inherit the crown. If there is more than one, they have the option to pass it down to the next child if they so choose."

Ilaria looked at him, though his gaze stayed firmly on the books they were studying.

"That is a surprise."

"Why?"

"I have seen nothing of your grandfather that speaks to a man who would bend tradition in such a way. Who might even consider that any child could certainly be an heir regardless of gender or birth order."

"You do not know my grandfather at all," he said sharply. "The King you find so offensive yielded and appealed to my father in all the ways he could. He made changes and would have made more, but this was never what my parents wanted. They only wanted attention, so it didn't matter if my grandfather gave them all they asked for, they still weren't satisfied."

He held such bitterness toward his parents. She supposed it was no wonder. He had claimed relief when they'd died, which meant they had hurt him in many ways he'd likely never share with her.

And because she felt sorry for that boy, she let the subject drop. They would never agree.

Or perhaps you've been wrong about King Carlo.

Surely sex had addled her mind if she was considering that? She knew what King Carlo had done. Perhaps he had acted out of ignorance and that detachment, but this did not make it right. A king should care. A king should want to help his citizens always, but especially during tragedy. A smart king would never trust a man like Giovanni.

So they moved from their afternoon lessons to a hike around the mountains. A surprising suggestion from the Prince himself.

Out in the chilly air, Ilaria felt herself relax even more. Here in the mountains, she was safe and free. And Frediano let her bound ahead. Explore. He seemed content to watch her.

She stumbled upon a little alcove of rocks, complete with a sharp cliff wall. A faded outline of a bull's-eye could be seen on the flat surface. She looked back at Frediano.

He stood on a rock, tall and broad, the wind whipping his hair and yet it somehow never seemed out of place. Almost like he was a rock himself.

He nodded to the bull's-eye. "When I was learning to be a prince, my grandfather would give me a few hours in the afternoon to explore. He did not wish me to be afraid of the mountains, nor be cooped up like an animal in a zoo. We would hike, practice archery, do whatever I wished for a few hours. He wanted to give me a taste of freedom, so I would always know how to find it even amid the daily pressures of royal life."

She looked at the bull's-eye, then back at him. "Do you?"

"Do I what?"

"Ever go find that freedom?"

"This is one of my favorite escapes, but lately, no. I do not wish to leave my grandfather alone for long."

She picked her way across the rocky ground to stand below him.

"That's the second time you've made it sound like your grandfather's health suffers."

He stared down at her. She could not read him, but she suspected a million emotions swirled behind that careful mask.

"Come. We must go prepare for dinner."

She could have pushed the issue, but she sensed… It would be like poking her fingers into an exposed wound and she did not want to hurt him.

A very strange turn of events indeed.

"You love your grandfather very much," she said instead.

"He is my grandfather."

"I know. I understand. My grandfather raised me, too. He was always there. I don't know what I would have done without him. Perhaps we are more alike than we've believed up to this point, Frediano."

"Is that so, Princess?"

"No matter the reason, being raised by a grandparent is a different experience. They are older. At some point, younger than perhaps we are prepared for, we become *their* caregiver. Or feel we must repay them in some way."

He stared at her, an expression she'd never seen on his face before. Perhaps because it was an expression with no mask. An arrested kind of ache had settled into his dark eyes. "A debt," he said, so softly she almost didn't hear it over the lashing winds of the mountain around them.

Ilaria nodded, feeling an odd lump form in her throat.

Because at times it had felt, no matter how her grandfather had loved her, that she owed him a debt for being there. Surrounded by so many children who'd been left with no one.

Had she paid that debt? She had nursed him as his health had failed. She had read to him in those long, terrible nights knowing he wouldn't make it. She had tried so very hard not to cry then—not in front of him, or the children. She had been strong, because of that debt.

But he was gone, and all that was left was how much she loved him and missed him. And apparently all those tears she hadn't shed last year when he'd passed.

"Do not cry, *tesoro*," Frediano said, his voice gruff, but not an order. Gently, he reached out and brushed the tears from her cheeks. He pulled her to him and pressed a soft kiss to her temple. An offer of comfort.

And she took it. She leaned into him and let him hold her. She even managed to smile through her tears. Because being comforted…was something new. And wonderful. Deep within Frediano, there had to be a softer heart then he let on if he would offer this.

And more than that, in the memory of how hard she'd held on to her strength in the face of her grandfather's inevitable passing, she understood that hard shell he put on himself. Because there was no one to give *him* comfort.

No one to give him love.

"Perhaps I understand you," she whispered. Because she couldn't quite find the courage to say it as certainly as she wanted to. Or to think too deeply on words like *love*. She couldn't even look at him. She could only keep her cheek pressed to his shoulder.

And feel.

When the tears had stopped, she forced herself to look up at him. She wasn't sure *thank you* was the right response, but she wanted to offer something. He did not cry, and his grandfather was still alive, but there were still hurts inside of him.

She wanted to comfort them, as he had comforted hers.

So she rose on her toes and pressed her mouth to his. Not in the same way she had during their wild, passionate night last night. This was about comfort.

And he did not respond with heat or passion, or even that lazy exploration they had both indulged in last night. No, this was gentler. There was something *soft* about it. Him. The cold mountain wind whipped around them, but he was warm. He was strength. He held her, but his hands did not wander.

When he pulled away, there was a beat of silence where they simply stared at each other.

"We must get back for dinner," was all he eventually said in that gruff voice she was coming to believe meant that deep beneath his masks there were emotions swirling.

He did not look away from her. He seemed almost puzzled, but he simply took her hand and led her back to the chalet in silence.

They engaged in a long, boring dinner about silverware and when she could stand or speak to the people on her right or left. They followed this with another dance practice, which ended the same way as it had last night.

The routine went on for days in the exact same manner, and Ilaria found herself…comfortable. If she thought about it, more than comfortable. She enjoyed this. She was even learning to like her husband. He was a patient teacher, letting her retry things as many times as she wanted without ever acting annoyed. He was a surprisingly astute listener—never forgetting a thing she told him, no matter how minor. If she didn't eat something at a meal because she didn't care for the food, it never appeared again.

"Have you had a report from Vita today?" he asked, as he invariably did. And when she told him of the goings on of the farm, he listened. Asked more questions. As though he might actually *care*. "I do hope the ordered medicine arrived."

"Yes," she responded, watching him carefully as he ate. She had figured he would be bored by tales of sick sheep and leaky roofs, and maybe he was, but he always sought to be part of the solution to the problem.

Again, something she understood. For he might be demanding and cold, but he was not a selfish man. Everything he did was not for himself—but for his grandfather or Vantonella or even now, sometimes, for her.

And it was that realization that had slowly began to change Ilaria's feelings for him, though she could not explain it or fully understand it.

Sometimes she thought their nights together must have altered her brain chemistry in some way. Its own brainwashing. But each night she was so thoroughly pleasured she found she didn't mind it. She'd never had any idea that sex could *mean* something, could become so all-encompassing.

Tonight they lounged, naked and sated, in the gigantic bath. A fire crackled across from them, and outside, the stars shone in a dazzling array that *almost* matched the beauty of her husband.

And he was beautiful. In these nights, she saw the warmth in him. The man behind the self-restraint. He didn't offer much, no matter how she poked and prodded, yet she was beginning to put together the pieces of a man who existed under all that tightly wound control.

She still didn't understand his choices and what drove

them, but she understood the harsh facade and that need to dominate came from a traumatic and cold childhood.

She had asked him about it, over and over again, as they'd studied the history of his family, but he had given her no more than the history books. No reason behind his father's rebellion, no understanding of his grandfather's cool detachment. He was as opaque as the factual tomes meant to preserve Montellero history for the centuries to come.

A history she was part of now. A humbling thought, perhaps made even more humbling by the fact that she and Frediano alone knew that it hadn't meant to be *her*.

"Frediano... You have such a dim view of love and marriage. Why did you seek it out in such a way? You needn't have married *that* night."

If he found her question odd, he did not show it. He considered the dark night outside the windows. And did not look at her when he finally spoke. "I had a plan," he said, opaquely. A nonanswer she knew she would have no luck getting behind. But she was learning to ask different questions, to circle around that which he did not wish to share until she could unearth it by surprise.

"Why did you want to marry Sophia, specifically?"

There was a pause. She'd asked him many questions he'd refused to answer, and she suspected this one to be the same. Maybe she even hoped it, because part of her didn't want to know.

Part of her had come to see him as hers.

He shrugged. "She was simple. She would have known what was expected of her. She likely would have demanded nothing, and your uncle would be forever under my thumb, and I could've made sure his family stayed in line."

She studied the planes of his back as she soaked in

those cold words. So detached. But she was beginning to see the different layers of him. The way he pulled back when he sought control. The way warmth and kindness could pour out of him when he let it go.

She understood he preferred the control. It felt safe to him, because it was what his grandfather clearly prized. What she did not fully understand was his devotion to the man beyond a *debt*.

"And what have I demanded?" she asked.

He turned to her, his eyes tracing the lines of her body until she shivered, knowing what came next after that dark, dangerous stare.

Somehow things were changing, and she had never known how to fight change. It swept in and did its will, and you could only ride out that storm.

She'd long thought Frediano a storm, but all those consequences she'd imagined were not this. Not coming to care for him, wanting to understand him. Not hoping she could find some way to help him open his heart.

To her.

"I thought you wanted nothing, Princess. But to help."

"I do want to help," she said, and this time she did not mean only those less fortunate. She meant him, and that wall he had built around himself to protect a wounded heart.

She slid onto his lap, wrapping her arms around him as she took him inside of her, as had become habit. Habit and joy. Want fulfilled.

He'd asked her what she wanted all through this, and in a million ways he'd shown her just how right she'd been to want to explore the desire between them, but maybe he'd also shown her there was nothing wrong with wanting something for herself. For wanting more than what was on offer.

If she could be a princess who helped people, a woman who enjoyed her lover, a potential mother, why couldn't she be a wife who loved her husband—and have him love her back?

His gaze held hers, but she saw that wariness in him. He desired her, and she thought maybe he'd even come to *like* her, but he didn't have to say that which she already knew.

He would never love. He didn't know how. But he had compassion. He had held her when she'd cried. In some ways, he understood.

So maybe she could show him how to love.

The days were coming to an end, and Frediano found himself dreading a return to the palace. He enjoyed each part of his day here. Waking up to Ilaria, sharing breakfast and history lessons with her. Watching her frustration—that he'd once felt many years ago—over the complex rules of a royal dinner. And most surprising of all, it was not just the nights of pleasure with her he looked forward to. It was their afternoon walks.

They were dangerous, he knew, that first day he'd nearly told her about his grandfather. A secret he could never trust her with until there was no hiding it.

Then she'd cried, over her own grandfather, and he'd felt something shift inside of him—much like their first night together when she'd leaned her head on his shoulder. He did not understand these shifts, the gentleness they seemed to pull out of him. He certainly didn't trust them, and if he was a smarter man, he would not continue with these hikes.

Still he engaged because she...was that freedom he'd spoken of.

He watched her now, climbing gracefully over a boulder before she tilted her head back to the sun. She smiled as the wind teased over her face. She took such joy in so many things.

Back at the palace, she would not be free to tip her face to the sun. They would be under constant scrutiny. There would be no impromptu lovemaking in an open field.

A dark pain twisted inside of him at the thought. He did not wish to take her back to where she might be unhappy. But when had her happiness come to matter? The point of this was not *happiness*. It was understanding her, so he could control all outcomes.

He *had* succeeded in that, but he had let himself become too comfortable in this little fantasy world he'd created to win her over. Part of him insisted he should pull back, but a larger part of him figured they had such little time left he might as well enjoy it.

She made an odd noise, and then he saw her tumble.

He rushed over, but she was laughing, sitting there between rocks, her hair and clothes disheveled. "Just lost my footing," she said cheerfully, her cheeks an alluring pink and her mouth curved in a sweet smile.

But she *could* have hurt herself on these jagged rocks and uneven terrain. Perhaps she was used to it, but he could not stand the thought of her injuring herself out here.

"You must be more careful," he said, scowling at her as he held out his hand to help her up. But she was already getting to her feet on her own, brushing her palms on the pants she wore. She smiled up at him as she noticed his hand, and then took it though she no longer needed the help or the leverage.

She was holding his hand as she moved forward. A casual, intimate gesture of something…far softer than desire.

Something that slithered through his chest and threatened to do…something to him. He did not know what.

Ilaria squinted up at the giant peak in front of them. "Will you tell me about it?" she asked gently.

"About what?"

"What happened when your parents died." She gestured to the peak above them. Not Monte Morte, but certainly similar.

"What happened is of no consequence," he said stiffly, because he could all but see it in his mind's eye. His mother's tumble, the muffled, echoing scream because she'd been too far away to reach, but not far away enough to mistake what had happened.

"I think it is of some consequence," Ilaria continued, using that carefully neutral voice she was learning to employ so well. "And it seems there is more to it than the history books would tell us. Perhaps it would behoove me to know, so I never say the wrong thing about it if asked."

She was smart, his wife. He had noticed over the past few days that she did not plod on headfirst when she did not get the answer she wanted. She watched, she waited, she rephrased, reshaped until she had gotten the information out of him he hadn't meant to give.

"Perhaps I can even use it," she continued. "If I know what happened, I can always present myself to the press in a way that sounds nothing like them."

It was a good reason, it appealed to his fears. She knew what she was doing, and so he should not allow her this win. But…

He wanted to give her what she wanted. In this last day before they had to leave. Maybe this too would anchor the obedience he needed from her.

But that didn't mean he had to give it to her all in her way. "I suppose it is a good conversation to have, as when you produce heirs we will have to be on the same page about their upbringing and how that is portrayed."

She blinked. She did not move forward now, but she did not drop his hand. She stood on a small rock so they were more eye to eye than usual when they were on even ground. "You could say *have children*, Frediano. Not *produce heirs*. We aren't creating them in a science lab."

"No, indeed we are not."

Her cheeks pinkened prettily at that and he wished to change the subject to more pleasant things, but she would not let this line of questioning go, so they might as well finish it.

"As with everything, we will endeavor to appear as different from my parents as possible. They did not like to leave me with nannies. It was bad for the image of being boldly anti-royal and oh-so-common man, you see. But they didn't particularly want me around. They liked to dress me up, teach me funny things to say that might get a laugh from their friends, but they didn't want to have to worry about if I was fed or well."

Her hand tightened around his. A squeeze of comfort. He looked at their joined hands and tried to understand what this woman had done to him.

But understanding did not matter. Only control did.

"We will have nannies, of course, but our children will know us both. They will have a traditional upbringing, so they are ready to take on their duties as they age." He looked around the mountain field where they stood. He could almost picture these phantom children. With her eyes and her smile, enjoying the nature around them as she did.

"And they must know they are loved and never question if they will be taken care of," Ilaria added, making the pain in his heart shove deeper and deeper.

"If you like," he said, and it sounded choked even to his own ears.

"I do. Now, your parents…"

"They liked outdoor pursuits. They were young, athletic people who needed to move, to be involved, to be paid attention to." He looked up at the mountain peak again. "They liked free-climbing. It was dangerous, exciting, and people loved to praise them for it. Exclaim over the danger and ask them about their experiences. Monte Morte was off-limits, of course, and so they simply *had* to do it."

"A foolish risk," Ilaria said. She slid off the rock and surprised him by reaching out to put her hand over his heart. "When they had a son who needed them."

He laughed. Bitterly. "Need them? Everything I was then and am now was in *spite* of them. They sat me at the base of the mountain, then began their preparations. I was to stay where I was until they returned. They had provided me with snacks and blankets. A few books and toys. It was more than they usually thought to remember for my care."

"You were *there*?" Her eyes widened and there was such shock, such horror. He had never spoken of this with anyone. Even his grandfather—because his grandfather had been the one to find him, so he had not needed to speak of it.

But Ilaria's hand on his heart, her soft gaze and the… It wasn't pity, or maybe it was, but whatever it was in her eyes felt tender and warm. It felt like reprieve, and he was powerless not to try and find more of it.

"I saw my mother fall," he said dully. He could see it so clearly, no matter how many years past. Sometimes he woke in the middle of the night, breath clogged in his lungs, that image replaying itself over and over again.

"Frediano." She sounded so anguished for him and he…

He was a grown man. Not a boy. He needed to pull himself together. "I did not see my father, but somehow I knew he had fallen as well. At first I tried to get to them, but I got so turned around and night descended. The snow was unforgiving. I was lost. I was quite certain I would die. Three days I was out there."

Her fingers curled in his shirt. It was so odd. She hadn't known his parents, she barely knew *him* and yet she seemed to care. This information seemed to hurt her somehow, when back at the palace it had only ever been a secret to be carefully guarded.

To be forgotten.

And for good reason.

"But it was my grandfather who found me. Not an aide, not a volunteer mountaineer. My grandfather." He looked at her then, held her gaze. Some part of him needed her to see, to understand. "He dug me out of the snow. He carried me to safety. And when all the stories came out about my parents' tragic and untimely death, he did not use the papers to avenge all they had done to him. He hid the fact I'd been left alone, allowed Vantonella to grieve the tragedy without adding their poor choices to the mix. He allowed me months to recuperate, to prepare outside the spotlight. He gave me time."

Her eyes had filled with tears. For him. He did not know what to do with such emotion.

"He would not be a very honorable man if he used the press to avenge the wrongs done to him by his dead son," she said, her voice cracking with those unshed tears.

"That is the first nice thing you've said about my grandfather."

"Perhaps…" She swallowed. "Perhaps I have misjudged him."

Skepticism at her easy capitulation lowered his brows. “Perhaps you have a fever.”

She laughed, though she still looked sad. “He has still made mistakes, but we all do.” She stepped forward and leaned her head onto his chest next to her hand over his heart. “He has made you feel as though your behavior is a condition of his love. That control is more important than anything else. Perhaps in these circumstances I can even understand you both felt this was the only way to deal with what happened with your parents. I understand your devotion to him now, but there is one thing he did not give you, and there is one thing you need.”

“And what is that, *tesoro*?”

He wished he could keep her here, with the warm sun above them, the mountain air around him. Her leaning into him, as if he mattered to her at all. But her next words froze him from the inside out.

“Love.”

He stiffened. That word. Love would be the end of his control, just as it had once been the end of his grandfather's. And Frediano could not risk it. *Love* would be the end of everything he wished to accomplish in order to ensure his grandfather lived to see another year.

“There will be no love, Ilaria. I have no use for it.”

She lifted her head and stared at him, without saying anything for the longest time. As though if she stared long enough, she would be able to see through him into the depths of his soul.

But hearts and souls were uncontrollable, irresponsible things, and he had no desire to trust his. “Come. We only have one more practice here before the royal wedding dinner on Saturday. And it must go perfectly.”

She nodded, never looking away. Never dropping his

hand. Yet when she spoke, her voice was cool. Detached. "Yes, Your Highness."

It should not hurt. It *did* not hurt.

He wouldn't allow it to.

CHAPTER TWELVE

ILARIA HAD SPENT the remainder of the day feeling battered by the terrible reality of Frediano witnessing his parents' death, nearly dying himself, and the resulting trauma he clearly refused to acknowledge.

He had chipped away at all the defenses and prejudices she'd had against him, until she was nothing but a heart that hurt for him—for what he'd endured as a boy. That was not loss. It wasn't even tragedy. It was neglect and abuse on top of a tragedy.

No wonder he held his grandfather in such high esteem. The King had literally saved his life, and so Ilaria found herself softening to the man as well. Surely he was not all that wrong and bad if he'd done the things Frediano relayed?

But that did not make him right or good. King Carlo had not given that boy what he'd desperately needed, so now as a man he did not know how to accept it or give it.

And somehow she found herself, in all the ways she'd thought she never would, loving this man. A prince. The grandson of the King she had spent the past decade cursing.

But people weren't their families, their crowns. They were the complicated mess of choices they'd made. Because life was always a choice. For princes and peasants alike.

And she understood his. They really weren't all that different. They had both sought to control what they could in their worlds, but she had always had love, someone to turn to, someone to protect or believe in. Even that debt she'd felt to her grandfather had not outshone the love she'd felt for him or received from him.

Frediano had only had duty, and she thought he had the potential to be so much more, have so much more if he learned to trust in love. She wanted to be the one who gave this to him. Needed to believe she could.

And if you can't?

Her chest ached at the thought, but was this not just another storm? She could wait for it to rage, then clean up the mess it left behind. She had to believe she was strong enough to give this to him…because no onc in his life had been.

Being strong for others wasn't just who she was, it was how she expressed her love. Sometimes that was sacrifice—like accepting she would be leaving her farm and life behind and taking on a life completely out of her realm—but sometimes love was simply…believing.

After dinner, she had meant to avoid the dancing lesson. To go to her own room alone, to find the space to figure out what loving Frediano meant, what choice she'd make in lieu of that realization, but instead she found herself dancing with him, following him to bed, and turning to him, again and again, in the night. Wordlessly seeking some answer to the questions that plagued her.

When she woke the next morning, there was no breakfast waiting for her. No husband. Only an outfit carefully laid out on the chair by the window.

She sighed. The honeymoon was over. In more ways

than one. But she had choices. She could yell at him, of course. She could demand this, that and the other.

But Frediano prized control, and so she would use that against him.

She got dressed, found Frediano's aide waiting for her out in the living room surrounded by glass and the mountains.

"Your Highness." Eduardo bowed. "Your things are packed and on the plane. The Prince is waiting for you, whenever you are ready."

"Thank you, Eduardo," she said, smiling warmly at him, though she felt anything but warm.

Frediano was already on the *plane*. It felt like a slap, but she was also growing to understand the man she loved. He wanted control in all things, and clearly at least part of his control was difficult to hold on to when it came to her.

So he had separated himself. Protected himself. She would take this as a win instead of a hurt.

She followed Eduardo to the car, then took the silent drive to the small airstrip, formulating her own plan. Because no doubt Frediano had spent the morning formulating his.

Eduardo led her onto the plane, and Frediano was indeed already there. There was a laptop and a stack of newspapers on the little tray beside him. He was freshly shaven, looking sharp and forbidding. He did not look up from the phone he held in his hand.

"Good morning, Princess," he greeted.

"Good morning, Your Highness," she replied demurely, hoping her lack of reaction might surprise him enough to look at her.

He did not.

So she settled herself into a seat across from him. She entertained herself for a while watching the plane take off. She did enjoy flying. She never would have known, if not for him.

She had determined she would not speak first and was in fact keeping track of how long it took him to speak. It took nearly an hour—so long she'd considered breaking her promise to herself. But he'd eventually broken, though he spoke in that bored, royal tone she didn't like.

"At the royal dinner tomorrow night, I will put you in touch with Signora Costa. She will assist you in whatever patronages you wish to aid. All that you desire to accomplish should be within your reach, so long as your royal duties do not suffer. You can help whomever you wish."

"And if I wish to return home?" she asked, casually.

"All trips must be approved by me and my staff, but you should be able to spend as much time as you wish in Accogliente, within reason."

He did not look at her. He read his phone. Like he had flipped a switch and turned back into the man he'd been before.

But it was a mask. And she had the means to get under it.

"Will you accompany me on these trips home?"

"If it improves our image."

Image. Masks. *Duty.* Things she could not care about when she wanted to get to the heart of *him*. Her next words made her stomach flutter, but she still had to say them. "And if I'm already with child?"

There was a pause, and she was studying him closely enough to see that his fingers tightened ever so carefully on the phone. He shifted, almost infinitesimally. "We have a doctor on staff."

"Important, obviously, but I meant more in terms of what we discussed yesterday. You said you had no use for love, but you will love our child, will you not?"

Still he did not look away from his phone. "No doubt you will be enough for whatever children we have together."

"And that's it?"

"What else would there be?"

"Something more than the robot your grandfather has built himself into." She struggled with her temper now. She could not expect a man to be changed overnight, but she supposed she was selfish enough to wish she was enough to change him. "Being a detached automaton is not something to aspire to. I know you prize control, but—"

"Control is everything, *tesoro.* You would do good to take that lesson on board as we return to the palace. Every aspect of your life will be scrutinized, and you must be above scrutiny if you wish to continue the monetary disbursements to your little farm."

She had forgotten about his bribe, because she had come to care for *him.* So much so that those words hurt. She knew they were meant to and she struggled to keep that from having her reacting. But she did not have the control he did. She didn't *want* it. "You only prize control so much because you never have had any."

He lowered his phone, fixing her with one of those cold stares she remembered from the first days. How had it all changed so much, so quickly? "Do you think you know me, just because I lulled you into a sense of security to teach you the ways of the palace? Do you fool yourself into thinking you understand me? I assure you, you do not."

It took her a moment, longer than it should have really, to fully understand his meaning. He was claiming he'd spent the past week tricking her. She supposed she should have felt some pain. Some betrayal. A terrible kind of shock.

But he'd made a grave error, because she had always been good at reading people. And no amount of his amazing control could stop her from understanding what this was. What he was trying to do.

So she laughed.

Frediano jolted at the noise, looking at her with a startled frown. It occurred to her then that he *believed* the little stories he told himself. She supposed that was why he was so good at control.

Denial.

"Yes, you have fooled me, Frediano," she said, and still she couldn't quite keep the laughter out of her voice. "Acted and lied. And so effectively!"

"Your sarcasm is not lost on me."

She leaned forward. "You can lie to yourself, Frediano, but your body does not lie, and your eyes do not lie. You care for me, against all that well-trained control. Perhaps it is not love, you would have to let go of fear to love me, but it is more than an act."

His gaze remained cool, but there was the flash of *something* before he looked back at his phone. "You may think whatever you wish, Princess."

And he did not speak to her for the rest of the flight, even as they deplaned and were ushered into the palace. Still, he was with her as she walked to her rooms.

He stopped in front of the door, waved the palace staff away. Once they were gone, he looked at her and she thought perhaps he'd say something meaningful. Kiss her.

Or maybe that was wishful thinking, because his body and hers had never been complicated.

"It will not be appropriate for us to share rooms here," he said instead, following the words with a bow. "I will see you at dinner with my grandfather this evening." He turned on his heel and marched away.

She was almost too stunned to speak.

Except to call him a coward as he walked away.

Frediano heard her accusation but chose to ignore it. Like he'd ignored her words in the plane. Her *words* didn't matter any more than her feelings did.

He had no feelings.

All that mattered was his plan.

He took care of some of the business affairs he'd put off while he'd been gone. He double-checked on some of the plans for tomorrow's wedding dinner. He watched the clock as he had an afternoon meeting with his grandfather before dinner.

Frediano had much to do, and absolutely no room to think about Ilaria.

Except as he stood watching the clock, he could not seem to push away the realization that he felt *lonely* without her by his side. Because her presence was warmth. Sunlight. Her passion contagious—not just for what they could find together, but for everything. Helping others. Her farm. Flying. Hiking. She *enjoyed* the world around her.

And he did the same when he was with her.

She had not reacted to his withdrawal as he'd expected. At all. From the many times she'd turned to him in the night, to her careful questions on the plane, to her *laughing* at him. As if she did not believe the honeymoon had been anything more than a carefully executed plan to get what he wanted.

Perhaps he had grown a little distracted, had allowed himself a little too much personal enjoyment, but he'd gotten what he wanted, hadn't he? She'd softened toward him. She'd shared his bed. She'd learned the protocol and even on the plane ride had given the perfect performance of a dutiful princess.

She might even be in love with him, which would allow him a certain amount of sway over her. Always. Just as his grandfather's love for his son had twisted and turned Carlo into changing laws, into bending over backward, into his physical heart giving out because his emotional heart was so burdened.

But the bitter thoughts did not take root as they usually did. Instead, Frediano found himself standing there, thinking of Ilaria climbing those rocks, her laughter on the mountain winds.

This was unacceptable. There would be no more spending time by themselves. He'd gotten what he wanted, and now there would be space. And soon he wouldn't think of her at all.

Frediano assured himself of this, over and over, as he strode through the palace to his grandfather's office. When his grandfather's aide ushered him inside, Frediano was surprised to see his grandfather already sitting. The pale pallor of his face immediately set Frediano on high alert. He looked at the aide, who did not meet his gaze.

"Grandfather, are you well?"

"Merely a little tired." Carlo waved his concern away. "Tell me, how has your wife fared?"

"She will behave impeccably tomorrow night, I can assure you. She wishes to begin charity work almost at once, which will fit into the image she gave at our introduction. I will introduce her to Signora Costa, and Noemi will work with her to make sure the press covers her endeavors in a respectful manner that meets with your approval."

"This sounds quite promising."

Frediano had planned to once again bring up his grandfather's potential stepping down, but there was something about the man that seemed particularly frail today, and something was wrong with Frediano. Because instead of forging ahead and doing what needed to be done, he excused himself.

He motioned for his grandfather's aide to follow. "Has the King seen his doctors?" Frediano asked once they were safely in the hall.

"He was having some pain," the aide said in hushed tones. "We brought the doctor in Wednesday. He urged surgery. The King refused."

"I told you to inform me of any and all changes in his condition," Frediano returned between gritted teeth.

"Your Highness..." The aide cleared his throat, clearly uncomfortable. "My instructions were to inform you of any changes when you called for your check-in. But we had not heard from you since Tuesday, and your grandfather did not wish you to be bothered."

Frediano did not move. He held himself completely still. But inside something had detonated, an odd ringing in his ears as everything inside him crumbled.

His entire adult life had been in service to his grandfather. Had been the repayment of a debt. And it had only taken her a few days to ruin him completely. It didn't even have to be love. Ilaria had swept in and upended every last plan. Every last inch of himself.

And who had suffered? Not Frediano, but everyone around him. Ilaria had lost her home. His grandfather was losing his battle with his health. All because Frediano had let himself be distracted. By his own selfish wants and desires, while his grandfather suffered.

It was unconscionable.

His hands curled into fists, his only reaction to the aide's words. Ilaria had said that love was sacrifice, but all love ever seemed to do when he touched it was sacrifice others. Ruin things, blast in and create wreckage wherever it went. As if there was no escape from his parents' legacy.

Frediano had failed. In all ways.

But his grandfather would not sacrifice for him. Ever again.

CHAPTER THIRTEEN

ILARIA DID NOT see Frediano again. Noemi came that night and told her the King wasn't feeling well and there would be no dinner. Ilaria didn't know how to feel about this. She doubted Frediano would be quite *so* cowardly as to fake an illness for his grandfather, and there had been those times Frediano had mentioned Carlo's health.

Cryptically, in that wounded way of his that had kept her from poking at it. Perhaps something serious with Carlo's health made him stay away from her.

Or perhaps he was just using whatever suited him as a reason. This seemed just as in character.

She considered going to Frediano's rooms despite his clear declaration they would not share one. She had few doubts they would end up in Frediano's bed if she did.

Perhaps that was why she didn't do it. Being intimate would not solve the problems between them. Frediano needed to be ready to discuss what he felt, and that was not something that would happen overnight.

Her team was in her room early the next afternoon, all abuzz about preparing her for the royal wedding dinner. She had requested the jeweled gown from that first day. She knew Frediano liked the way she looked in it, and she planned to use that to her advantage.

She was nervous, she could admit that as she looked

at herself in the mirror. She looked like someone else and would be expected to behave like this someone else. In front of so many strangers.

You've studied and practiced, she reminded herself. And if it was only about not embarrassing herself, she likely would have felt more calm. But she found herself… wanting to make Frediano proud.

Even if that made her a fool.

Once she had been molded and painted into what felt like someone else entirely, she could only stand and stare at her reflection, waiting for Frediano to arrive to escort her to the ballroom.

She breathed, as he had taught her at that first public appearance on the balcony. In, one-two-three, and out. She focused on her breathing to distract herself from her nerves, trying to not think of the audience she would be on display for. And when Frediano finally arrived, dressed in a crisp black tuxedo, she smiled at him. Her handsome husband. So tall, so stern.

He did not meet her gaze, instead looking somewhere just beyond her. "You look lovely," he said. Rotely. He offered his arm.

Ilaria took it. There was little else to do. He said nothing as he led her into the ballroom. Offered no advice or reassurances as the palace staff prepared for their entrance.

Something…had changed yet again. His mood was different. He seemed so withdrawn, so harsh.

"Is everything all right?" she asked.

"What wouldn't be?"

"Your grandfather. Is he feeling better?"

Frediano's mouth flattened, and she hadn't thought that possible. "It is time to enter, Princess." He led her inside the grand room, already full of people.

Ilaria's nerves threatened, as they had when she'd stepped onto that balcony. So many eyes. So many people. But this time she was prepared. And she wanted to impress her husband, so he could see.

She could be everything he needed.

She greeted everyone as they were introduced to her. She curtsied, smiled, and tried to get to know each of her guests. There had been little biographies on all of them that they had studied back at the chalet, and those had been like the history. Far more interesting than correct napkin usage.

She had always liked people and talking to others helped ease her nerves as well. She liked understanding, helping. And people, in turn, had always confided in her. Her grandfather had always told her she had a knack for getting people to spill their guts.

Frediano introduced her to Signora Costa as he'd promised, and the older woman seemed excited to have the Princess's support, so Ilaria enjoyed spending some time with her talking about the charities already in place, and how they could expand the organizations.

"Perhaps you can convince that husband of yours to make his charity work more widely known."

Ilaria stared at the older woman, who seemed to read her surprise and tutted.

"He gives his time and money generously and in equal measure but is always so adamant about keeping it out of the press. But if we could advertise more of his efforts, I'm certain we could convince others to give as well."

Ilaria understood then, on a painful little jab, that in his constant efforts to be the opposite of his parents, he kept even the good he did hidden away. All out of fear.

When he came to her side once more, he behaved like a perfect imitation of King Carlo. Detached. Not seeming fully present. She began to worry about him, but worry for her husband was washed away when her uncle was announced and brought forward, with her aunt on his arm.

For a moment Ilaria forgot everything she'd been taught. Everything she had practiced. A hot, painful wave of rage went through her.

If not for *him*, her father would be alive. If not for *him*, she would be home on her farm. If not for *him*, everything would be different.

"Now is not the time, *tesoro*," Frediano whispered next to her.

She hated that he was right, but she was gratified to see *some* flash of the Frediano who had a beating heart. His hand was firm on her back, and his gaze on Giovanni cool but not fully detached.

Frediano smiled down at the couple. "Giovanni. Mrs. Avida. You grace us with your presence this evening."

"I'm sure you'll have a few moments so we can talk privately," Giovanni said. There was a pleasant enough smile on his face, but when he flicked a glance at her, his eyes were full of hate.

Ilaria's plastered smile became more genuine. She wanted him to hate her as much as she hated him.

"I do not know that I will," Frediano returned smoothly. "This is not a business dinner, Giovanni. It's a celebration of my marriage. To your *niece*. Which is why you received an invitation."

It was a surprising little slap-down. So surprising Ilaria could only stare at Frediano. He gave no indication that he'd done anything special, but she knew that protocol dictated he be slightly more polite than *that*.

"I'm so happy for you, Ilaria," her aunt said. She opened her mouth to say more, but Giovanni's glare had her shutting it and looking down at her feet. They were ushered into the dining room so the next couple could be announced.

Ilaria and Frediano were finally escorted into the dining room. She tried not to grimace when she realized she'd be sitting next to her uncle.

"Sit. Eat. Be merry," the King said from his spot at the head of the table. Ilaria noted he looked a little pale. Perhaps he really had been ill last night. Perhaps there was much more going on than she realized.

Frediano pulled out her chair, and Ilaria sat in it, just as she'd been taught. Then the rest of the gathering took their seats.

She looked at her plate, called back on everything Frediano had taught her. She ate with the right utensils. She smiled and spoke when spoken to and endeavored to make her husband proud. She even ignored the fact her uncle sat next to her.

"King Carlo, you always host the most delicious dinners," Giovanni said, overloud to Ilaria's ears after he'd scraped his plate.

"Thank you, Giovanni," the King returned. Ilaria watched him. Carlo smiled. He spoke with what could only be called friendliness, but there was no warmth behind his words, his eyes. She had always imagined the King and her uncle were great friends, laughing at the lowly commoners they exploited and did not care about.

But Ilaria began to wonder if the King showed that he cared about *anything.* One way or another.

"I suppose you are in the way of family now," the King continued, taking a sip of wine. He made a strange move, almost like a wince. As if he was in pain. Ilaria looked at Frediano to see his expression even more closed off.

"I like to think so," Giovanni returned. He reached over and put his hand on Ilaria's shoulder, bringing her attention back to him. He gave her what she supposed looked like a friendly squeeze.

But it *hurt*.

She looked at Frediano, whose eyes were hot on Giovanni's hand on her shoulder now. He even began to move, as if to remove Giovanni's hand himself. But this would be a disaster, she knew, for so many reasons.

So she stood—Giovanni's hand having to fall off her by her sheer force of movement. "Will you all excuse me for just a moment?" she asked, careful to keep her voice soft and demure and her smile easy and even. "I'll be right back."

She slipped away from the table and then out into the hallway. She'd go to the bathroom. She couldn't put cold water on her face because it would ruin her makeup, but she could take a few moments to breathe in quiet.

She did so, finding the bathroom empty, which allowed her the space and time to try to ground herself. But as she looked at her unfamiliar reflection, she thought of how she missed the chalet, almost as much as she missed her farm. She did not want this glamorous life. She did not want a life of pretend, and yet…

She loved her husband, and if love was sacrifice…

She would sacrifice for him. Because underneath all his issues was a man who wanted to do good. Do the right thing. Like her father and grandfather had been. In her experience, there had been no men in power who had been interested in what was *right*.

But Frediano loved his country and wanted to do right by it. Oh, he had some warped ways of going about it, and he was still controlling in his way. But…

He wanted to *do* good, and if he worked through some of his trauma, perhaps he could even allow himself to believe he *was* good. Good enough to love and be loved.

And with all that love inside of her, she felt strong enough to return. To face the people, and her uncle, and anyone who dared cross her and her husband. She stepped out of the bathroom and into the empty hallway.

"Ilaria."

The sound of her uncle's voice startled her as much as the fact he stood just opposite the bathroom. As if he'd been waiting for her.

His expression was smug, his color high as he'd likely had a little bit too much wine with dinner. He was a short man, no taller than her, but he was wide and had spent a lifetime learning how to intimidate with his size, if not his height. Ilaria struggled not to shrink back.

"You will pay for what you've done to my daughter. One way or another."

"*To* your daughter? Don't you mean *for*?" Ilaria returned, chin raised. She put every effort to sounding as calm and disdainful as her uncle. "I saved her from your schemes. Your unfeeling treatment of her."

"Schemes that would have seen her a princess, wealthy and powerful. Something you have always claimed to be so disdainful of, but you wear that expensive whore's gown. You share the Prince's bed."

It hurt, when it shouldn't. But there was a kernel of truth to his words. She had not *wanted* to be royalty, but she hadn't tried to escape, had she? She'd taken the bribes or blackmail depending on how you looked at it, and she had, in fact, shared the Prince's bed. She stood here in an expensive gown she would have been contemptuous of just days ago. She'd sipped wine and learned etiquette.

She was a hypocrite.

"I did not take you for a scheming slut," he said conversationally, that pleasant smile on his face completely incongruous to the words, but he grabbed her arm and squeezed tight, pulling her closer as he hissed out the next words. "At least you were smart enough to bag a prince, unlike your stupid whore of a mother who would only spread her legs for a *farmer*."

She made a noise. She could not have characterized it—some kind of pained growl or groan of outrage and disgust and *fury*. She wrenched her arm out of his painful grasp and raised her hand. So consumed by hate she didn't fully realize she'd meant to slap him until her uncle smirked and tutted before he jerked his chin to the side.

There Frediano stood, observing, that cold, icy scorn on his face. Her hand hovering there in the air, no way of excusing what she'd been about to do as *anything* other than strike her uncle.

In the palace. During the royal wedding dinner he'd been so adamant go well, with his grandfather's health in a questionable position. With press running about snapping publicity photos and such.

She'd lost her control, and she knew this was something he would not forgive.

Frediano was so consumed by rage that his vision had hazed. He held himself still because if he was within touching distance of Giovanni Avida, he would tear the man from limb to limb.

And they were in public. Though this hallway seemed to be deserted, just beyond those doors was half of Roletto. He needed to somehow, someway, restrain himself.

But the man had put his hands on his wife.

"Princess," Frediano managed without sounding as enraged as he felt. "Perhaps you'd like to drop your hand."

And his wife stood there, hand still raised, staring at Frediano as though *he'd* been the one to hurt her.

So many things rolled through Frediano at once he

could not make sense of any of them, except that he could not stand his wife within reach of her vile uncle.

He moved, barely feeling his body. Barely seeing the world around him. Because his vision was just a replay of Ilaria jerking her arm from Giovanni's angry grasp. Ilaria defending herself, because Frediano had not defended her.

Frediano came to stand next to Ilaria. He put his hand on her back. Her spine was straight, her shoulders back, but there was a slight tremor there, too.

He turned his gaze to the man Ilaria hated so, and Frediano hated him, too. With a boiling, blinding fury that eradicated all good sense. That stripped his composure until there was next to nothing left.

"Giovanni," he said. "If I ever see your hands on my wife again, you will no longer have hands." He delivered this statement as someone might have said, *I prefer chicken to salmon.*

Clearly, it surprised Giovanni, who he stood there, gaping like a fish. "What did you say to me?"

"You heard me. Now I suggest you leave my sight."

"I am your grandfather's Minister of Energy. How dare you—"

"I am Prince Frediano Montellero of Vantonella and twice I have seen you manhandle my wife. Consider this a very gracious response."

"She is *my* niece. You were supposed to marry *my* daughter."

"Perhaps you should have treated your daughter better. Perhaps we both should have. But she is happy now, and I will ensure she remains so. As I will ensure Ilaria has everything she wants. Now, I will give you one last opportunity to leave properly."

"Properly? After you broke promises to me? *I* will ensure the press knows exactly what kind of man you are, Frediano. And as for your *wife*, this lying, Accogliente trash…"

Frediano did not hear the rest. He saw Giovanni's hand begin to reach out—whether to point or grab or do *something* in the general vicinity of Ilaria, it did not matter. Frediano stopped it.

With his fist. Smashing firmly into Giovanni's face. The man stumbled back on a primal scream, and Ilaria made a noise of surprise as well.

But he did not care. He only cared that he had stopped that horrible creature from ever putting hands on his wife again.

Ilaria tugged at his sleeve, and he realized dimly she'd been doing so for some time now. "Frediano…"

But now he heard it. The telltale click of photographs being taken.

And his life being ruined…at his own hands.

CHAPTER FOURTEEN

TIME SEEMED TO speed up. Suddenly there were aides and guards whisking the photographer away, taking Giovanni out of the room while blood spurted from his nose, and Frediano standing in the midst of it all, his hand still curled into a fist. Staring at the spot where Giovanni had once been.

Ilaria was likewise frozen. She did not quite understand everything, but she understood enough that Frediano did not view this as a triumph quite the way she did.

"Your Highness," Eduardo said, his eyes wide as he wrung his hands together. "It is time for the dance."

Frediano finally straightened. When he turned toward her, his gaze was cold. Empty. "Are you all right?"

She blinked at him. She thought…there was some concern there…deep down. But mostly she could not tell. He was a cold ghost of himself. "Yes," she managed.

He held out his arm and she took it, feeling almost as robotic as he acted. All the shock and adrenaline was leaking out of her and she didn't know how else to reclaim this moment.

Now they had to dance in front of everyone. While palace staff scurried about and whispered in corners, Frediano led her to the dance floor.

It was the strangest moment of her life and she didn't

worry about the steps, her uncle, the press. She worried about her husband. He was so stiff. So gray. So *broken.*

He had once claimed princes did not break, but she knew somehow she had brought upon his downfall. He said nothing, but she watched his face. He'd lost control. For her.

She leaned closer and spoke to him in a whisper no one would hear. "Frediano. Surely you can explain the circumstances to the photographer and—"

His words were quiet but flat in return. "The circumstances do not matter. They want a story and I gave them one. Our aides will try to stop it, and they will fail. I have failed."

Her heart broke for him. That even now, in what was a terrible moment, there was no emotion to be found in those words. "Frediano. Look at me."

He did, met her gaze with nothing but King Carlo's practiced distance.

"We can fix this. Together. I promise," she urged. "People make mistakes, and that was… Perhaps it was a mistake, but is it really so awful that you defended me? *Us?*"

"If I had controlled myself, no, it would not be. But I did not. So that incident, like everything else that has involved you, will be wreckage."

This hurt, and she could not excuse that hurt away on his trauma or his obsessive need for control. She swallowed at the lump growing in her throat. "I see. It's all my fault."

"No, it is mine. I made all the mistakes from the start. So now, I must fix them." He swept her around the ballroom until she thought she'd be sick. Until she thought she'd begin crying right here in front of everyone.

"There is only one thing to do," he said, each word grimmer and more detached than the last. "You will go back to Acclogiente. There can be no divorce, but we will live our lives as separately as possible, without the press finding out."

She jerked in his arms. "What?"

But he only continued. "You will stay there and have your life back. Except when absolutely necessary, we will not have any contact."

She could not wrap her mind around this bizarre change. Could not come up with words. The music ended and he dropped her hand. He bowed and she knew she was supposed to curtsy, but she could only stare at him. He gave her a pointed look and finally her knees bobbed in a terrible approximation of a curtsey.

This was the end of the event for them as he led her out of the ballroom. But he immediately dropped her hand and began to stride purposefully away.

"You cannot simply..." She ran after him, scurrying in front of him and standing in his way. "You cannot just... command I go back and that be it."

"But it is it," he replied, sidestepping her. Or trying to, but she merely leaped into his way again.

Finally, *finally* some emotion flashed in the depths of his dark eyes. "You have ruined all my control. And as long as you are near, I will lose it, again and again, until we are all nothing but wreckage, and I will not stand for it. I will not."

She reached out for him, but he moved back so she found only air. "What is between us does not have to be wreckage," she said, and knew she sounded desperate. But if this was not a time for desperation, she did not know what would be.

"Then what would it be, Ilaria? What could it possibly be?"

"It could be love, Frediano," she said, and maybe there

were tears in her eyes or on her cheeks, but all she could really seem to grasp was that he was shaking his head.

"Those are the same things to me. Do you not see what I have done?"

"You have stood up for me. You have cared for me. And in doing so, allowed me to do the same for you. Do you think because your parents did not—could not—love you, or that your grandfather is so bad at showing it, you are not *worthy* of it?"

"I am the Prince of Vantonella, *tesoro*. I am worthy of most things."

She felt a mix of despair and temper and let them both echo in her voice. "That is an evasion and you know it."

"But this is not. My role, my only role, is to keep my grandfather *alive*. Perhaps if you understand that, you can understand why we must handle things *my* way."

It was a dig, but pain and hurt did not well up inside her. Instead, the thought of him losing the one person he seemed to care about had her soft heart hurting for him. "Frediano. What do you mean?"

"My grandfather has several blockages in his heart," he said. His words were calm, sharp, but his eyes were wild. "He can live with them, for now. But all doctors advise he have surgery to remove said blockages. They have told him stress and the demands of his schedule are not tenable. I assured him I would marry acceptably, with no scandal, no shades of my parents' mistakes, so that he could step down and attend to his health. I thought your stunt at the introduction to the public would kill him then and there."

It was a barb, and it hit home. But… "It did not."

"No, it did not. My behavior, in front of all and sundry this evening, did everything you did not. He will see my father's irresponsible behavior stamped on me, and he will not step down, and his life will be cut short. Because I could not control myself."

"It is not your job to control yourself to save him, Frediano."

"You of all people would tell me it is not my job to save someone?"

He had an unfortunate point, but she saw that only as a sign… He understood her, too. Because deep down, under all his fear, he loved her, too. "You can help people, but you cannot make their choices for them. You cannot—"

"In this instance, I make all the choices. You will go home, Princess." Finally, his eyes met hers and there was something almost soft there. Almost…regretful. "Go back to the life you loved."

It was alarming how little she wanted that now. It hurt, beyond telling, that things had changed so irrevocably. Because she didn't want to go home. She wanted to be by his side. "But I love you."

"And I do not love at all," he returned, then turned on a heel and strode away.

Frediano didn't wait to be summoned to his grandfather's office after the dinner. He simply waited.

It was hours—no doubt Carlo was busy doing damage control—but Frediano did not move. He stood outside the hall and stared at the office door and felt nothing.

Nothing but the hollow, echoing failure of ruining everything he'd tried to build. Essentially sentencing his grandfather to death, all for a little personal vengeance.

When his grandfather finally arrived, it was with two aides in tow. One carried a stack of papers.

"Come," was all King Carlo said as his assistant opened the door. Frediano followed his grandfather inside.

The aide spread out the printouts of the online newspaper stories, updated in real time. Frediano was surprised to see a picture that did not feature him and his fists. Instead, it was a picture of Ilaria and Giovanni, Giovanni's hand curled around her arm in an aggressive manner.

Even now, the tide of rage swept through him and he had to hold himself very still not to leave this very office and hunt Giovanni down.

"Frediano." His grandfather's voice sounded exhausted. "You have behaved as your father would have."

Frediano's head jerked up to look at his grandfather, his king. The only person in his life who had ever helped him. It was the cruelest cut his grandfather could have made. Frediano tried to weather it, but his eyes closed against his will.

"I can only apologize for the damage I've caused, Grandfather," Frediano managed to choke out. Because there was no way to fix this. He had behaved as his father would have.

"I would prefer if you take me through the events of this…altercation," Carlo said. He pointed at the paper with the picture of Giovanni and Ilaria. "There are conflicting stories here, and it is best I know the truth so we can decide what to do about it."

Frediano did his best to recite the pertinent facts without emotion. Giovanni's unacceptable behavior towards Ilaria, yes, but he also did not sugarcoat his own mistakes. "Unfortunately, I lost control when he attempted to touch Ilaria again. I punched him. Once."

If the man hadn't fallen backward, he would have likely done it again.

King Carlo was silent, looking at the printouts and tapping his finger against his desk. He sighed. "I suppose you have done the honorable thing, then."

Frediano was sure he'd misheard. "What?"

"Even if he is my Minister of Energy, and her uncle, you could hardly let him treat your wife in such a manner. Perhaps I wish you would have used your words, but I think we should be able to limit the damage." Carlo nodded, then gestured for the assistant to take the papers away.

Frediano was speechless. He kept expecting his grandfather's wrath…only to have Carlo excuse his mistakes. Forgive them, even. Much like the one after the announcement when Ilaria had given her unsanctioned little speech.

His grandfather had not condemned him. There had been no criticism. No recriminations that he had chosen poorly, that Ilaria had done badly. Frediano had expected those things, but instead the King had always twisted the events into a positive.

Frediano thought back to what Ilaria had said. Not that his grandfather didn't love him as his parents hadn't, but that his grandfather was so bad at *showing* love. He did not wish to believe his grandfather bad at anything, but he realized…

Ilaria had been a mistake he'd made from the first, and at every turn his grandfather had tried to make it okay. The one time he could not—this very public disaster—King Carlo was still not blaming him as Frediano had feared. Carlo was disappointed with the situation, yes, but was seeking to solve it.

He had not raged. He had not stripped Frediano of his title. Yes, he had compared him to his father, but then he'd swept the mistake away. As he had always done.

Only Frediano had never realized that in itself was a gift. Maybe even…an expression of his grandfather's *love.*

It shook him, and he tried to deny it, but Ilaria's voice was in his head. And perhaps…he was just as bad. Just as incapable.

But Ilaria had shown him…

"I sent Ilaria away. I thought it best if we maintain as much distance as possible. She much prefers the country."

Carlo looked up at him. "She is your wife."

"Yes." His wife. Who had said she loved him.

Loved him. She'd wanted to stay, and he'd sent her away because… It was a shock to realize all the ways she'd been right. Her love terrified him, so instead of dealing with it or her, or his own feelings, he'd sent her away.

So he could have control. So he could protect himself.

But no matter where she was, the feelings were there. He looked at his grandfather, needing that…guidance. "But I…fear I may love Ilaria. I have let my guard down. I have protected her and forgotten my duties. It is best for the crown if I…if I create the distance that will allow me to…" Frediano had not stumbled over his words this way since he was a boy.

"Love is nothing to be feared," Carlo said, seeming confused. "I quite loved your grandmother," he said, gesturing at the royal portrait behind his desk.

It was something of a shock to hear his grandfather speak of *love*. Of the late Queen at all. "You never speak of her."

"I suppose because…" Carlo studied the portrait, and Frediano saw something strange in his grandfather's gaze. A wistfulness. "I miss her every day. She was my heart. My balance. But I lost her, and then I failed your father in trying to make it up to him. Perhaps I have failed you, too."

"Failed me? You saved me. I have never thanked you for all you have done for me, Grandfather." That debt even Ilaria understood.

Carlo looked at him now, both confusion and that failure he spoke of in his dark gaze. "I tried to love you differently than I loved your father. I hoped to fix my many mistakes of overindulgence and the excuses I made for him. You are so respectful and such a good man, I thought I had succeeded." His grandfather paused, taking a breath that worried Frediano by how labored it sounded. "If you feel the need to thank me, I have failed you. There is no 'thank you' for love. You are my grandson, and you owe me nothing."

Frediano did not know how to take on this information. They had never spoken like this. Never would have…if Ilaria had not introduced the entire notion of love in the first place.

Carlo eased himself into the chair, looking tired and gray. Worry twined with love and confusion and all the mistakes of the past few days. But he saw something in this moment that he had not seen before.

Maybe his grandfather still refused to step down because he saw only duty.

Not love.

"You have never failed me, sir," Frediano said, endeavoring to sound strong. Because the love he had for his grandfather was that strong. "You have given me everything. And the choices I made…" Frediano struggled to deal with all the mistakes he'd made.

He'd made. Because it was not his grandfather's fault that he had seen love as a weakness. Frediano had chosen control, as Ilaria had once accused, because he'd had *none* before coming to the palace.

These were his own failings. And his grandfather had always taught him to own up to his mistakes. To learn, to change. And watching his grandfather clearly struggle with his health in *this* moment, Frediano knew he had to push forward. Even at this worst possible time.

"I think it is time to explain myself more clearly about my wishes for you to step down."

Carlo's face hardened, but Frediano did not let it stop him. If this was about love, not duty or control, then all that mattered was expressing that love. "It is not that I want to see you step down. You are a fine king, and I wish our country could enjoy your leadership for many more years. But personally and selfishly, I do not wish to see you die so soon, when you could spend many more years in my presence, and in my future children's presence. I would like them to know the kind of man their great-grandfather is from experiencc, not my memory."

For the first time in his recollection, Frediano saw true reaction from his grandfather. And it was utter shock. But Carlo did not send him away or mount an argument, so Frediano continued.

"I do not wish to be King for the sake of being King. I wish you to take care of your health. I wish *you* to be all right."

There was silence in the aftermath, as Carlo slowly got a hold of his expression and returned to one of calm detachment.

"I will consider all you've said, Frediano," Carlo said. This would usually be where Carlo dismissed him. Instead, the King stood and crossed to Frediano and put his hand on Frediano's shoulder. "You are a credit to me, Frediano," he said. "And you will be a fine king."

Frediano felt his throat constrict. "Because of you, Your Majesty." And Frediano bowed to the man who had given him love, even though Frediano had not always seen it.

Then, once King Carlo dismissed him, Frediano finally understood what he must do.

CHAPTER FIFTEEN

ILARIA COULD HAVE fought the guard who'd taken her back to Accogliente. But she didn't. She had seen the man she loved broken, and she did not think staying would fix it.

So she arrived home to the farm that was home and now felt strange, hugged everyone tight, and then spent the night in her old room, in her old bed, alone and miserable.

It didn't seem fair in the least. This man she hadn't even known last month had swept into her life and upended it, changed her irrevocably inside and out, and then sent her away.

He had ruined her life in every way possible, and she'd simply let him do it.

No. She sat up in bed, having slept no more than a few small snatches. It was later than she usually got up, the sun streaming in the windows of the cottage. She blew out a frustrated breath. Her eyes were puffy, her head achy, and everything felt *wrong*.

So you must right it.

She *always* righted wrongs. She charged in and solved problems, fixed mistakes, patched up holes. Frediano had been hurt last night. Why hadn't she stayed to mend the hurts? Why hadn't she fought for him when he was at his lowest?

Why should she treat him any differently? Simply because he was a prince?

Well, *she* was a princess now.

She was the one who understood love, so she would have to be the one to fight for it.

She got dressed quickly, then rushed outside. Everyone should be out in the fields at this hour, so she went in search of someone to give her a ride to the train station.

She climbed the mountains of her home and did not feel quite the same old wave of comfort. Oh, she still loved this place, and hoped to bring her future children here for romps among the sheep, but her home had become her husband.

The man she loved and needed to save. When she finally caught the first sign of someone in the distance, she stopped short. This man was tall and broad. His dark hair windswept, and even from the distance she knew.

He was here.

For a moment she only stared. There were a cluster of sheep around him, and he was standing with one of the younger boys, Roberto. But when he straightened, unerringly looked over to her, she felt compelled to move forward.

Before she reached him, he leaned down and said something to Roberto, who scurried off. The boy sent her a jaunty wave as the young sheep bounded after him, but then they were gone.

And it was just her and Frediano. He had begun to walk toward her as well until they met on a patch of grass, separated by a small boulder.

When he finally walked close enough he would be able to hear her over the howling wind, she spoke. She pointed to the two little sheep who found him a curiosity and had followed him.

"They like you."

He gave them both a supercilious stare. "All my dreams have come true," he returned dryly. "Sheep like me."

"Why are you here?" she asked him, because he was so *controlled.* So him. This did not feel like the precursor to anything she wanted.

"You need ask?"

"Yes, I do. You sent me away just last night. Assumed our lives would be lived apart. You told me you could never love. And now you're here."

He reached out, touched his hand to her cheek. "Ah, *tesoro.* I have come for you, because there is *only* you."

Her heart leaped at the words. He moved around the boulder until he stood in front of her, so tall and sure and…

Different, she realized. There was something different in his face, something different in the way he spoke to her. There was…warmth.

"Last night, I spoke with my grandfather. I felt as though I'd failed him, as though I owed him, and he… felt that he had failed me. He informed me that…there is no 'thank you' in love."

She looked up at him, wanting to wrap her arms around him and hold him close, but also needing those words she so desperately wanted to hear. So she held still. "For once I agree with your grandfather."

His mouth curved. A real smile. The kind she thought she'd never see on his face.

"It was your words in my head. Changing the way I saw everything. Him. Myself." He brought his other hand up to hold her face there. "You have taught me to look beyond the walls I erected for myself. To be brave enough to see that…all those feelings I viewed as the enemy, the ones I tried to lock away deep inside are a strength I did not know I possessed. And I always considered myself quite strong."

It surprised a strange little laugh out of her, something almost like a sob. He pulled her closer, into the circle of his arms, and his gaze never left hers. Dark, demanding but…not cold. Not this time.

"I was *afraid* of love. What it looked like, what it meant. I thought it would be wreckage because it wrecked my grandfather, and I thought what I felt was out of control, and perhaps it is, but sometimes control doesn't mean what I thought it did." He looked into her eyes. "I cannot give you all the freedom you deserve. A divorce will simply always be out of the question. But I can give you as much as possible. Whatever you wish. I will sacrifice all I can."

But in his words, in his gesture, she realized… She'd been wrong, too. "Maybe we were both wrong, Frediano. Because I don't want you to sacrifice for me."

"And I do not wish you to sacrifice for me, *tesoro*."

"So maybe…it is balance. Maybe it is giving," she said, touching her palm to his chest. "And receiving," she said lifting his to hers.

"Leaving here would be a sacrifice for you."

"Staying would be as well. Because I love you, Frediano. I love the man you are when you let yourself listen to your heart. I want to build a life with you that exists…in that balance. We will both sacrifice, because we love. And we will both not want the other to sacrifice, for the same."

"I love you, Ilaria," he said, with the hushed reverence those words deserved, even with the mountain wind whipping around them. "I wish never to be apart from you. So we will be together. We must spend most of our time in the capital, but we can summer here. We will raise our children to know this place as well as the palace. We will have a true marriage, and love, and when the time comes, you will make an admirable queen. We will build a life together. And if there is wreckage…"

"We will have to repair it. Together," she said through the lump in her throat. Because it was beautiful.

He reached out and smoothed away the tears that had fallen with the backs of his fingertips. "Oh, Ilaria, my love. I promise to give you everything in my power, and that is quite a lot."

"Yes, it is. But I only want your love, Frediano. That will be enough for me."

He pulled her against him, his mouth a whisper from hers. "It is yours," he vowed, as her arms came around his neck out in the wild mountain winds. As his mouth touched hers under the warmth of a morning sun. "Forever, Princess."

EPILOGUE

LOVE DID INDEED change everything.

King Carlo stepped down to have his surgery and Frediano and Ilaria became the much beloved King and Queen of Vantonella, known for their efforts to aid those in need, particularly children.

They also thrilled their people and the press and the former King by having five children of their own—each more stubborn and strong-willed than the last.

Something Frediano could not deny as his five children stumbled inside after spending the afternoon roaming the mountains of Accogliente with *sheep*. He had insisted on building a house on the farm that would fit all of them so his children could know something of their *Russo* kingdom.

He surveyed his children. They were dirty and disheveled. The knees of Russo's pants were torn, the sleeves of Carlotta's shirt ripped. Pigtails had come undone and young Vinnie even sported a bloody lip.

Frediano looked over at his wife. "Wreckage," he muttered darkly, but he returned the grin she sent him. "I'm not sure you predicted quite *this* much."

"No, but we keep cleaning it up and repairing it all the same."

"That is because we are so good at it."

"Indeed."

And so that was what they did. Cleaned up the children, ate dinner with everyone who worked the farm these days as was tradition in the summers in the mountains. Sometimes, the former King even joined them and could be found some mornings walking the mountain paths with an errant sheep at his heels.

But tonight it was just Frediano and Ilaria as they told bedtime stories, tucked in wiggling children, scolded and offered I-love-yous in equal measure. And when they retired to their own room, Frediano took his queen in his arms.

"Your children will be the death of me, *tesoro*," he said, nuzzling his mouth into her neck until she sighed the way he liked best.

"And you love it," she replied, laughing as he tumbled her onto the bed.

For a moment, he surveyed her, marveling as he often did about the twists of fate that had brought him his heart. He looked down at her, those green eyes as bewitching as they had been all those years ago. "I do. I thank you for showing me that I could."

And then he showed her, as he had many times before and would many times going forward, just how deep his love went.

* * * * *

MILLS & BOON®

Coming next month

THE HOUSEKEEPER'S INVITATION TO ITALY
Cathy Williams

"I'm not following you. Where is he going to move to? London? Leonard has always told me how much he hates London."

"Not that he's actually been there more than a handful of times," Alessio returned drily. "But no. London wasn't what I had in mind."

"Then where?"

"I have a place at Lake Garda in northern Italy. It's close enough to get there on my private jet in a matter of hours so the trip shouldn't be too taxing for him."

"Oh, right. Okay."

"If we plan on leaving in roughly a week's time, it will give me sufficient time to get the ball rolling with the company so that I can install some of my own people to tie up all the loose ends. I'll also have enough time for my PA to source the best crew available to get this job done here and of course, there will have to be time spent packing away anything valuable that needs to be protected. I suggest several of the more robust rooms in the West Wing would be suitable for that."

"Wait, hang on just a minute! We…?"

Continue reading
THE HOUSEKEEPER'S INVITATION TO ITALY
Cathy Williams

Available next month
www.millsandboon.co.uk